A Week in Winter

A Week in Winter

Maeve Binchy

First published in Great Britain in 2012
by Orion Books
an imprint of the Orion Publishing Group Ltd

An Hachette UK company

1 3 5 7 9 10 8 6 4 2

A CIP catalogue record for this book
is available from the British Library.

ISBN 978 1 4091 1399 7

Typeset at The Spartan Press Ltd,
Lymington, Hants

Printed in Canada by Webcom

The Orion Publishing Group's policy is to use papers that
are natural, renewable and recyclable products and
made from wood grown in sustainable forests. The logging
and manufacturing processes are expected to conform to
the environmental regulations of the country of origin.

The Orion Publishing Group Ltd
Orion House
5 Upper St Martin's Lane
London WC2H 9EA

www.orionbooks.co.uk

For dear generous Gordon
who makes life great every single day.

Chicky

Everyone had their own job to do on the Ryans' farm in Stoneybridge. The boys helped their father in the fields, mending fences, bringing the cows back to be milked, digging drills of potatoes; Mary fed the calves, Kathleen baked the bread and Geraldine did the hens.

Not that they ever called her Geraldine, she was *Chicky* as far back as anyone could remember. A serious little girl pouring out meal for the baby chickens or collecting the fresh eggs each day, always saying 'chuck, chuck, chuck' soothingly into the feathers as she worked. Chicky had names for all the hens, and no one could tell her when one had been taken to provide a Sunday lunch. They always pretended it was a Shop Chicken, but Chicky always knew.

Stoneybridge was a West of Ireland paradise for children during the summer, but the summer was short and most of the time it was wet and wild and lonely on the Atlantic coast. Still, there were caves to explore, cliffs to climb, birds' nests to discover and wild sheep with great curly horns to investigate. And then there was Stone House. Chicky loved to play in the huge overgrown garden. Sometimes the Miss Sheedys, three sisters who owned the house, and were ancient, let her play at dressing up in their old clothes.

Chicky watched as Kathleen went off to train to be a nurse in a big hospital in Wales, and then Mary got a job in an insurance office. Neither of those jobs appealed to Chicky at all, but she would have to do something. The land wouldn't support the whole Ryan family. Two of the boys had gone to serve their time in business in big towns in the West. Only Brian would work with his father.

Chicky's mother was always tired and her father always worried. They were relieved when Chicky got a job in the knitting factory. Not as a machinist or home knitter but in the office. She was in charge of sending out the finished garments to customers and keeping the books. It wasn't a *great* job but it did mean that she could stay at home, which was what she wanted. She had plenty of friends around the place, and each summer she fell in love with a different O'Hara boy but nothing ever came of it.

Then one day Walter Starr, a young American, wandered into the knitting factory wanting to buy an Aran sweater. Chicky was instructed to explain to him that it was not a retail outlet, they only made up sweaters for stores or mail order.

'Well you're missing a trick then,' Walter Starr said. 'People come to this wild place and they *need* an Aran sweater, and they need it now, not in a few weeks' time.'

He was very handsome. He reminded her of how Jack and Bobby Kennedy had looked when they were boys, same flashing smile and good teeth. He was suntanned and very different to the boys from round Stoneybridge. She didn't want him to leave the knitting factory and he didn't seem to want to go either.

Chicky remembered a sweater they had in stock which they

had used to be photographed. Perhaps Walter Starr might like to buy that one – it wasn't exactly new but it was nearly new.

He said it would be perfect.

He invited her to go for a walk on the beach and he told her this was one of the most beautiful places on earth.

Imagine! He had been to California *and* Italy and yet he thought Stoneybridge was beautiful.

And he thought Chicky was beautiful too. He said she was just so cute with her dark curly hair and her big blue eyes. They spent every possible moment together. He had only intended to stay a day or two but now he found it hard to go on anywhere else. Unless she would come with him, of course.

Chicky laughed out loud at the idea that she should pack in her job at the knitting factory and tell her mother and father that she was going around Ireland hitchhiking with an American that she had just met! It would have been more acceptable to suggest flying to the moon.

Walter found her horror at the idea touching and almost endearing.

'We only have one life, Chicky. *They* can't live it for us. We have to live it ourselves. Do you think *my* parents want me out here in the wilds of nowhere, having a good time? No, they want me in the Country Club playing tennis with the daughters of nice families, but hey, this is where I want to be. It's as simple as that.'

Walter Starr lived in a world where everything was simple. They loved each other, so what was more natural than to make love? They each knew the other was right so why complicate it by what other people would say or think or do? A kindly God understood love. Father Johnson, who had taken a vow never to fall in love, didn't. They didn't need any stupid contracts or certificates, did they?

3

And after six glorious weeks, when Walter had to think of going back to the States, Chicky was ready to go with him. It involved an immense amount of rows and dramas and enormous upset in the Ryan household. But Walter was unaware of any of this.

Chicky's father was more worried than ever now because everyone would say that he had brought up a tramp who was no better than she should be.

Chicky's mother looked more tired and disappointed than ever, and said only God and his sainted mother knew what she had done wrong in bringing Chicky up to be such a scourge to them all.

Kathleen said that it was just as well she had an engagement ring on her finger because no man would have her if he knew the kind of family she came from.

Mary, who worked in the insurance office and was walking out with one of the O'Haras, said that the days of *her* romance were now numbered, thanks to Chicky. The O'Haras were a very respectable family in the town and they wouldn't think kindly about all this behaviour at all.

Her brother Brian kept his head down and said nothing at all. When Chicky asked him what he thought, Brian said he didn't think. He didn't have time to think.

Chicky's friends, Peggy, who also worked in the knitting factory, and Nuala, who was a maid for the three Miss Sheedys, said it was the most exciting, reckless thing they had ever heard of, and wasn't it great that she had a passport already from that school trip to Lourdes.

Walter Starr said they would stay in New York with friends of his. He was going to drop out of law school, it wasn't really right for him. If we had several lives, well then, yes, maybe, but since we only have one life it wasn't worth spending it studying law.

The night before she left, Chicky tried to make her parents understand this. She was twenty, she had her whole life to live, she wanted to love her family and for them to love her in spite of their disappointment.

Her father's face was tight and hard. She would never be welcome in this house again, she had brought shame on them all.

Her mother was bitter. She said that Chicky was being very, very foolish. It wouldn't last, it couldn't last. It was not love, it was infatuation. If this Walter really loved her then he would wait for her and provide her with a home and his name and a future instead of all this nonsense.

You could cut the atmosphere in the Ryan household with a knife.

Chicky's sisters were no support. But she was adamant. *They* hadn't known real love. She was not going to change her plans. She had her passport. She was going to go to America.

'Wish me well,' she had begged them the night before she left, but they had turned their faces away.

'Don't let me go away with the memory of you being so cold.' Chicky had tears running down her face.

Her mother sighed a great sigh. 'It would be cold if we just said, "Go ahead, enjoy yourself". We are trying to do our best for you. To help you make the best of your life. This is not love, it's only some sort of infatuation. You can't have our blessing. It's just not there for you. There's no use pretending.'

So Chicky left without it.

At Shannon airport there were crowds waving goodbye to their children setting out for a new life in the United States.

5

There was nobody to wave Chicky goodbye, but she and Walter didn't care. They had their whole life ahead of them.

No rules, no doing the right thing to please the neighbours and relations.

They would be free – free to work where they wanted and at what they wanted.

No trying to fulfil other people's hopes – marry a rich farmer in Chicky's case, or become a top lawyer, which was what Walter's family had in mind for him.

Walter's friends were welcoming in the big apartment in Brooklyn. Young people, friendly and easy-going. Some worked in bookshops, some in bars. Others were musicians. They came and went easily. Nobody made any fuss. It was so very different to home. A couple came in from the coast, and a girl from Chicago who wrote poetry. There was a Mexican boy who played the guitar in Latino bars.

Everyone was so relaxed. Chicky found it amazing. Nobody made any demands. They would make a big chilli for supper with everyone helping. There was no pressure.

They sighed a bit about their families not understanding anything but it didn't weigh heavily on anyone. Soon Chicky felt Stoneybridge fade away a little. However, she wrote a letter home every week. She had decided from the outset that *she* would not be the one to keep a feud going.

If one side behaved normally then sooner or later the other side would have to respond and behave normally as well.

She did hear from some of her friends, and had the odd bit of news from them. Peggy and Nuala wrote and told her about life back home; it didn't seem to have changed much in any way at all. So she was able to write to say she was delighted about the plans for Kathleen's wedding to Mikey, and did not mention that she had heard about Mary's romance with Sonny O'Hara having ended.

Her mother wrote brisk little cards, asking whether she had fixed a date for her wedding yet and wondering about whether there were Irish priests in the parish.

She told them nothing about the communal life she lived in the big, crowded apartment, with all the coming and going and guitar playing. They would never have been able to begin to understand.

Instead she wrote about going to art exhibit openings and theatre first nights. She read about these in the papers and sometimes indeed they went to matinees or got cheap seats at previews through friends of friends who wanted to fill a house.

Walter had a job helping to catalogue a library for some old friends of his parents. His family had hoped to woo him back this way to some form of academic life, he said, and it wasn't a bad job. They left him alone and didn't give him any hassle. That's all anyone wanted in life.

Chicky learned that this was definitely all Walter wanted in life. So she didn't nag him about when she would meet his parents, or when they would find a place of their own, or indeed what they would do down the line. They were together in New York. That was enough, wasn't it?

And in many ways it was.

Chicky got herself a job in a diner. The hours suited her. She could get up very early, leave the apartment before anyone else was awake. She helped them open up, did her shift and served breakfasts and was back before the others had struggled into the day. Chicky would bring cold milk and bagels left over from the diner's breakfast stock. They got used to her bringing them supplies.

7

She still heard news from home but it became more and more remote.

Kathleen's wedding to Mikey, and the news that she was pregnant; Mary walking out with JP, a farmer they used to laugh at not long ago as a sad old man. Now it was a serious romance. Brian getting involved with one of the O'Haras, which Chicky's family thought was great but which the O'Haras were a lot less excited about. How Father Johnson had preached a sermon saying that Our Lady wept every time the Irish Divorce referendum was mentioned, and some of the parishioners had protested and said he had gone too far.

Stoneybridge was, after a few short months, becoming a totally unreal world.

As was the life they lived in the apartment, with more people arriving and leaving, and tales of friends who had gone to live in Greece or Italy, and others who played music all night in cellars in Chicago. Reality was, for Chicky, this whole fantasy world that she had invented of a busy, bustling, successful Manhattan lifestyle.

Nobody from Stoneybridge ever came to New York – there was no danger of anyone looking her up or exposing the lies and the pathetic deception. She just couldn't tell them the truth; that Walter had given up the cataloguing of the library. It was so boring because the old couple kept saying he should go home for a weekend and see his parents.

Chicky couldn't see much wrong with that as a plan, but it seemed to spell aggravation for Walter so she nodded sympathetically as he left the job and she took extra hours in the diner to cover their costs in the apartment.

He was so restless these days; the smallest things upset him. He liked her to be always a cheerful, loving Chicky. So that's what she was. Inside, she was tired and anxious Chicky, too, but not showing any of it.

She wrote home week after week and believed in the fairy tale more and more. She started to fill a spiral notebook with details of the life she was meant to be living. She didn't want to slip up on anything.

To console herself, she wrote to them about the wedding. She and Walter had been married in a quiet civil ceremony, she explained. They had a blessing from a Franciscan priest. It had been a wonderful occasion for them and they knew that both families were delighted that they had made this commitment. Chicky said that Walter's parents had been abroad at the time and not able to attend the ceremony but that everyone was very happy about it.

In many ways, she managed to believe this was true. It was easier than believing that Walter was becoming restless and was going to move on.

When the end came for Walter and Chicky it came swiftly, and it seemed to everyone else inevitable. Walter told her gently that it had been great but it was over.

There was another opportunity, yet another friend with a bar where Walter might work. A new scene. A new beginning. A new city. He would be off at the end of the week.

It took ages for it to sink in.

At first she thought it was a joke. Or a test of some sort. There was a hollow, unreal feeling in her chest like a big cavity that was getting even bigger.

It could *not* be over. Not what they had. She begged and pleaded; whatever she was doing wrong she would change it.

Endlessly patient, he had assured her that it was nobody's fault. This is what happened – love bloomed, love died. It was sad, of course, these things always were. But they would stay friends and look back on this time together as a fond memory.

There was nothing she could do except go home, back to Stoneybridge to walk along the wild shores where they had walked together and where they had fallen in love.

But Chicky would never go back.

That was the one thing she knew, the one solid fact in a quicksand world which was changing all around her. She could not stay on in the apartment even though the others were hoping that she would. Outside this life, she had made very few friends. She was too closed; she had no stories, no views to bring to a friendship. What she needed was the company of people who asked no questions and made no assumptions.

What Chicky also needed was a job.

She couldn't stay on at the diner. They would have been happy to keep her, but once Walter was gone she didn't want to be around the neighbourhood any more.

It didn't matter what she did. She didn't really care. She just had to earn a living, something to keep her until she got her head straight.

Chicky could not sleep when Walter left.

She tried, but sleep would not come. So she sat upright in a chair in the room she had shared with Walter Starr for those five glorious months – and those three restless months.

He said it was the longest time he had ever stayed any-where. He said he hadn't wanted to hurt her. He had begged her to go back to Ireland where he had found her.

She just smiled at him through her tears.

It took her four days to find a place to live and work. One

of the workmen on the building next to the diner had a fall and was brought in to the diner to recover.

'I'm not bad enough to go to hospital,' he pleaded. 'Can you call Mrs Cassidy, she'll know what to do.'

'Who is Mrs Cassidy?' Chicky had asked the man with the Irish accent and the fear of losing a day's work.

'She runs Select Accommodation,' he said. 'She's a good person, she keeps herself to herself, she's the one to contact.'

He had been right. Mrs Cassidy took over.

She was a small, busy person with sharp eyes and her hair drawn into a severe knot behind her head. She was someone who wasted no time.

Chicky looked at her with admiration.

Mrs Cassidy arranged for the injured man to be driven back to her guest house. She said she had a next-door neighbour who was a nurse, and if his condition worsened she would get him to hospital.

Next day Chicky called to Cassidy's Select Accommodation.

First she enquired about the workman who had been injured and brought to the diner. Then she asked for a job.

'Why did you come to me?' Mrs Cassidy had asked.

'They say you keep yourself to yourself, you don't go blabbing around.'

'Too busy for that,' Mrs Cassidy had admitted.

'I could clean. I'm strong and I don't get tired.'

'How old are you?' Mrs Cassidy asked.

'I'll be twenty-one tomorrow.'

Years of watching people and saying little had made Mrs Cassidy very decisive.

'Happy Birthday,' she said. 'Get your things and move in today.'

It didn't take long to collect her things, just a small bag to pick up from the big, sprawling apartment where she had lived as Walter Starr's girl with a group of restless young people for those happy months before the circus left town without her.

And so began Chicky's new life. A small, almost monastic bedroom at the top of the boarding house, up in the morning to clean the brasses, scrub the steps and get the breakfast going.

Mrs Cassidy had eight lodgers, all of them Irish. These were not people who had cereal and fruit to start the day. Men who worked in construction or on the subway, men who needed a good bacon and egg to see them through until the lunchtime ham sandwich that Chicky made and wrapped in waxed paper and handed over before they left for work.

Then there were beds to make, windows to polish, the sitting room to clean, and Chicky went shopping with Mrs Cassidy. She learned how to make cheap cuts of meat taste good by marinating them, she knew how to make the simplest of meals look festive. There was always a vase of flowers or a potted plant on the table.

Mrs Cassidy always dressed nicely when she served supper, and somehow the men had followed suit. They all washed and changed their shirts before sitting down at her table. If you expected good manners, you got good manners in return.

Chicky always called her Mrs Cassidy. She didn't know her first name, her life story, whatever had happened to Mr Cassidy, even if there had ever *been* a Mr Cassidy.

And in return, no questions were asked of Chicky.

It was a very restful relationship.

Mrs Cassidy had stressed the importance of getting Chicky her green card, and registering to vote in the city council to make sure that the necessary number of Irish officials got returned to power. She explained how you got a post-office box number so that you could mail without anyone knowing where you lived, or anything about your business.

She had given up trying to persuade the girl to get a social life. She was a young woman in the most exciting city in the world. There were huge opportunities. But Chicky was very definite. She wanted none of it. No pub scene, no Irish clubs, no tales of what a good husband this lodger or that lodger might make. Mrs Cassidy got the message.

She did, however, point Chicky towards adult education classes and training courses. Chicky learned to be a spectacular patisserie chef. She showed no interest in leaving Mrs Cassidy's Select Accommodation, even though a local bakery had offered her full-time work.

Chicky's expenses were few; her savings increased. When she wasn't working with Mrs Cassidy, there were so many other jobs. Chicky cooked for christenings, First Communions, bar mitzvahs and retirement parties.

Each night, she and Mrs Cassidy presided over their table of Select Lodgers.

She still knew nothing about Mrs Cassidy's life history, and had never been asked any details about her own. So it was surprising when Mrs Cassidy said that she thought Chicky should go back to Stoneybridge for a visit.

'Go now, otherwise you'll leave it too late. Then going back would be a big deal. If you go this year just for a flying visit then it makes it much easier.'

And in fact, it was so much easier than she had thought.

She wrote and told them in Stoneybridge that Walter had to go for a week to LA on business, and that he had suggested she use the time to come to Ireland. She would just love to come back home for a short visit and she hoped that would be all right with everyone.

It had been five years since the day her father had said she would never come back into his house again. Everything had changed.

Her father was now a different man. Several heart scares had made him realise that he did not rule the world, or even his own part in it.

Her mother was not as fearful of what people thought as she once had been.

Her sister Kathleen, now the wife of Mikey and the mother of Orla and Rory, had forgotten her harsh words about disgracing the family.

Mary, now married to JP, the mad old farmer on the hill, had mellowed.

Brian, bruised by the rejection from the O'Hara family, had thrown himself into work and barely noticed that his sister had returned.

So the visit was surprisingly painless and thereafter every summer Chicky returned to a warm welcome from her family.

When she was back in Stoneybridge she would walk for miles around and talk to the neighbours, filling them in on her mythical life on the other side of the Atlantic. Few people from these parts ever travelled as far as the States – she was safe in knowing that there would be no unexpected visitors. Her facade would never be brought crashing down by a surprise arrival from Stoneybridge at a non-existent apartment.

Soon she was part of the scenery.

She would meet her friend Peggy, who told her of all the dramas in the knitting factory. Nuala had long ago left to live in Dublin and they never heard from her any more.

'We always know it's July when we see Chicky back walking the beaches,' the three Sheedy sisters would say to her.

And Chicky's face would open up into a big smile embracing them all in its warmth and telling them and anyone else who would listen that there was nowhere on earth as special as Stoneybridge, no matter how many wonderful things she saw in foreign parts.

This pleased people.

It was good to be praised for having the wisdom to stay where you were in Stoneybridge, for having made the right choice.

The family asked about Walter, and seemed pleased to hear of his success and popularity. If they felt ashamed that they had wronged him so much they never said it in so many words.

But then it all changed.

The eldest of her nieces, Orla, was now a teenager. Next year she hoped to go to America with Brigid, one of the tribe of red-haired O'Haras. Could she stay for a little bit with Aunty Chicky and Uncle Walter, she wondered? They would be no trouble at all.

Chicky didn't miss a beat.

Of course Orla and Brigid would come to visit; she was enthusiastic about it. Eager for them to come. There would be no problem, she assured them. Inside she was churning, but no one would have known. She must be calm now. She would work it out later. Now was the time to welcome and anticipate the visit and get excited about it.

Orla wondered what would they do when they got to New York.

'Your uncle Walter will have you met at Kennedy, you'll come home and freshen up and straight away I'll take you on a

Circle Line Tour around Manhattan on a boat so that you'll get your bearings. Then another day we'll go to Ellis Island and to Chinatown. We'll have a *great* time.'

And as Chicky clapped her hands and enthused about it all she could actually imagine the visit happening. And she could see the kind, avuncular figure of Uncle Walter laughing rue-fully and regretfully over the daughters that they never had as he spoiled them rotten. The same Walter who had left her after their short months in New York and headed west across the huge continent of America.

The shock had long gone now, and the real memory of her life with him was becoming vague. She very rarely went back there in her mind anyway. Yet the false life, the fantasy existence was crystal sharp and clear.

It had been what had made her survive. The knowledge that everyone in Stoneybridge had been proved wrong and she, Chicky, at the age of twenty, had known better than any of them. That she had a happy marriage and a busy, successful life in New York. It would be meaningless if they knew he had left her and that she had scrubbed floors, cleaned bathrooms and served meals for Mrs Cassidy, that she had scrimped and saved and taken no holiday except for the week back in Ireland every year.

This made-up life had been her reward.

How was she to recreate it for Orla and her friend Brigid? Would it all be unmasked after years of careful construction? But she would not worry about it now, and let it disturb her holiday. She would think about it later.

No satisfactory thoughts came to her when she was back in her New York life. It was a life nobody in Stoneybridge had dreamed of. Chicky could see no solution to the problem of Orla and her friend Brigid O'Hara. It was too aggravating.

Why couldn't the girl have chosen Australia, like so many other young Irish kids? Why did it have to be New York?

Back at Mrs Cassidy's Select Accommodation, Chicky broke the code that had existed between them for so long.

'I have a problem,' she said simply.

'We will talk problems after supper,' Mrs Cassidy said.

Mrs Cassidy poured them a glass of what she called port wine and Chicky told the story she had never told before. She told it from the very beginning. Whole layers and onion skins of deception were peeled back as she explained that now the game was up: her family who believed in Uncle Walter wanted to come and meet him.

'I think Walter was killed,' Mrs Cassidy said slowly.

'What?'

'I think he was killed on the Long Island highway, in a multiple car wreck, bodies barely identified.'

'It wouldn't work.'

'It happens every day, Chicky.'

And as usual, Mrs Cassidy was right.

It worked.

A terrible tragedy, motorway madness, a life snuffed out. They were so upset for her, back in Stoneybridge. They wanted to come to New York for the funeral but she told them it would be very private. That's the way Walter would have wanted it.

Her mother cried down the phone.

'Chicky, we were so harsh about him. May God forgive us.'

'I'm sure He has, long ago.' Chicky was calm.

'We tried to do what was best,' her father said. 'We thought we were good judges of character, and now it's too late to tell him we were wrong.'

'Believe me, he understood.'

'But can we write to his family?'

'I've already sent your sympathies, Dad.'

'Poor people. They must be heartbroken.'

'They are very positive. He had a good life, that's what they say.'

They wanted to know should they put a notice in the paper. But no. She said her way of coping with grief was to close down her life here as she had known it. The kindest thing they could do for her was to remember Walter with affection and to leave her alone until the wounds healed. She would come home next summer as usual.

She would have to move on.

This was very mysterious to those who read her letters home. Perhaps she had been unhinged by grief. After all, they had been so wrong about Walter Starr in life. Maybe they should respect him in death. Her friends now understood her need for solitude. She hoped that her family would do that also.

Orla and Brigid, who had been planning to come and visit the apartment in Seventh Avenue, were distraught.

Not only would there be no welcoming Uncle Walter coming to meet them at the airport, but there would be no holiday at all. Now there was no possibility of Aunty Chicky to take them on this Circle Line Tour round the island of Manhattan. She was moving on, apparently.

And anyway, their chances of being allowed to go to New York had disappeared. Could anything have been more unfortunately timed, they wondered.

They kept in touch and told her all the local news. The O'Haras had gone mad and were buying up property around Stoneybridge to develop holiday homes. Two of the old Miss

Sheedys had been carried away by pneumonia in the winter. The old person's friend, it was called; it ended life peacefully for those who couldn't catch their breath.

Miss Queenie Sheedy was still there; strange, of course, and living in her own little world. Stone House was practically falling down around her. It was said that she seemed to have barely the money to pay her bills. Everyone had thought she would have to sell the big house on the cliff.

Chicky read all this as if it were news from another planet. Still, the following summer she booked her flight to Ireland. She brought more sombre clothes this time. Not official mourning, as her family might have liked, but less jaunty yellows and reds in her skirts and tops – more greys and dark blues. And the same sensible walking shoes.

She must have walked twenty kilometres a day along the beaches and the cliffs around Stoneybridge, into the woods and past the building sites where the O'Haras were busy with plans for Hispanic-style housing complete with black wrought iron and open sun terraces much more suitable for a warmer, milder climate than for the wild, windswept Atlantic coast around Stoneybridge.

During one of her walks she met Miss Queenie Sheedy, frail and lonely without her two sisters. They sympathised with each other on their loss.

'Will you come back here, now that your life is ended over there, and your poor dear man has gone to Holy God?' Miss Queenie asked.

'I don't think so, Miss Queenie. I wouldn't fit in here any more. I'm too old to live with my parents.'

'I understand, dear, everything turns out differently, doesn't it? I always hoped that you would come and live in this house. That was my dream.'

And then it began.

The whole insane idea of her buying the big house on the cliff. Stone House, where she had played when she was a child in their wild gardens, and had looked up at from the sea when they went swimming, where her friend Nuala had worked for the lovely Sheedy sisters.

It could happen. Walter always said it was up to us what happened.

Mrs Cassidy had always said why not us just as much as anyone else?

Miss Queenie said it was the best idea since fried bread.

'I wouldn't be able to pay you the money that others might give you for the place,' Chicky said.

'What do I need money for at this stage?' Miss Queenie had asked.

'I have been too long away,' Chicky said.

'But you will come back, you love walking all around here, it gives you strength, and there's so much light and the sky looks different every hour here. And you'll be very lonely back in New York without that man who was so good to you for all those years – you don't want to stay there with everything reminding you of him. Come home now, if you like, and I'll move into the downstairs breakfast room. I'm not too good on the old stairs anyway.'

'Don't be ridiculous, Miss Queenie. It's your house. I can't take any of this in. And what would I do with a big house like this all on my own?'

'You'd turn it into a hotel, wouldn't you?' To Miss Queenie, it was obvious. 'Those O'Haras have been wanting to buy the place from me for years. They'd pull it down. I don't want that. I'll help you turn it into a hotel.'

'A hotel? Really? Run a hotel?'

'You'd make it special, a place for people like you.'

'There's no one like me, no one as odd and complicated.'

'You'd be surprised, Chicky. There are lots of them. And I won't be around here for long, anyway; I'm going to join my sisters in the churchyard soon, I'd say. So you should really have to decide to do it now, and then we can plan what we are going to do to make Stone House lovely again.'

Chicky was wordless.

'You see, it would be very nice for me if you *did* come here before I go. I'd just love to be part of the planning,' Queenie pleaded. And they sat down at the kitchen table in Stone House and talked about it seriously.

When Chicky got back to New York, Mrs Cassidy listened to the plans, nodding with approval.

'You really think I can do it?'

'I'll miss you, but you know it's going to be the making of you.'

'Will you come to see me? Come to stay in my hotel?'

'Yes, I'll come for a week one winter. I like the Irish countryside in winter, not when it's full of noise and show and people doing leprechaun duty.'

Mrs Cassidy had never taken a holiday. This was groundbreaking.

'I should go now while Queenie is alive, I suppose.'

'You should have it up and running as soon as possible.' Mrs Cassidy hated to let the grass grow beneath her feet.

'How will I explain it all . . . to everybody?'

'You know, people don't have to explain things nearly as much as you think they do. Just say that you bought it with the money Walter left you. It's only the truth, after all.'

'How can it be the truth?'

'It's because of Walter you came here to New York. And because he left you you went and earned that money and saved it. In a way, he *did* leave it to you. I don't see any lie there.' And Mrs Cassidy put on the face that meant they would never speak of it again.

In the following weeks, Chicky transferred her savings to an Irish bank. There were endless negotiations with banks and lawyers. There were planning applications to be sorted, earth movers to be contacted, hotel regulations to be consulted, tax considerations to be made. She would never have believed how many aspects of it all there were to put in place before the announcement was made. She and Miss Queenie told nobody about their arrangement.

Eventually it all seemed ready.

'I can't put it off much longer,' Chicky said to Mrs Cassidy as they cleared the table after supper.

'It breaks my heart, but you should go tomorrow.'

'Tomorrow?'

'Miss Queenie can't wait much longer, and you have to tell your family some time. Do it before it's leaked out to them. It will be better this way.'

'But to get ready to go in one day? I mean, I have to pack and say my goodbyes . . .'

'You could pack in twenty minutes. You have hardly any possessions. The men in this house aren't great on big flowery goodbye speeches, any more than I am myself.'

'I'm half cracked to do this, Mrs Cassidy.'

'No, Chicky, you'd be half cracked if you didn't do it. You were always great at taking an opportunity.'

'Maybe I'd have been better if I hadn't seized the opportunity of following Walter Starr.' Chicky was rueful.

'Oh yes? You'd have been promoted in the knitting factory.

Married a mad farmer, have six children that you'd be trying to find jobs for. No, I think you make great judgements. You made a decision, contacted me for a job and *that* turned out all right for twenty years, didn't it? You did fine by coming here to New York, and now you're going back home to own the biggest house in the neighbourhood. I don't see much wrong with that career path.'

'I love you, Mrs Cassidy,' Chicky said.

'It's just as well you're going back to the Celtic mists and twilight if you're going to start talking like that,' Mrs Cassidy said, but her face was much softer than usual.

The Ryan family sat open-mouthed as she told them her plans.

Chicky coming home for good? *Buying* the Sheedy place? Setting up a hotel to be open summer and winter? The main reaction was total disbelief.

The only one to show pure delight in the idea was her brother Brian.

'That will soften the O'Haras' cough,' he said with a broad smile. 'They've been sniffing after that place for years. They want to knock it down and build six top-of-the-market homes up there.'

'That was exactly what Miss Queenie didn't want!' Chicky agreed.

'I'd love to be there when they find out,' Brian said. He had never got over the fact that the O'Haras hadn't thought him worthy of their daughter. She had married a man who had managed to lose a great deal of O'Hara money on the horses, Brian often noted with satisfaction.

Her mother couldn't believe that Chicky was going to move in with Miss Queenie the very next day.

'Well, I'll need to be on the premises,' Chicky explained. 'And anyway, it's no harm to have someone there to hand Miss Queenie a cup of tea every now and then.'

'And a bowl of porridge or packet of biscuits wouldn't go amiss either,' Kathleen said. 'Mikey saw her picking blackberries a while ago. She said they were free.'

'Are you *sure* you own the place, Chicky?' Her father was worried, as always. 'You're not just going in there as a maid, like Nuala was, but with a promise that she will leave it to you?'

Chicky patted them down, assured them it was hers.

Little by little they began to realise that it was actually going to happen. Every objection they brought up she had already thought of. Her years in New York had made her into a businesswoman. They had learned from the past not to under-estimate Chicky. They would not make the same mistake a second time.

Her family had arranged for yet another Mass to be said for Walter, as Chicky hadn't been at home for the first one they said. Chicky sat in the little church in Stoneybridge and wondered if there really was a God up there watching and listening.

It didn't seem very likely.

But then everyone here appeared to think it was the case. The whole community joined in prayers for the repose of Walter Starr's soul. Would he have laughed if he could have known this was happening? Would he have been shocked by the superstition of these people in an Irish seaside town where he had once had a holiday romance?

Now she was back here, Chicky knew that she would have to be part of the church again. It would be easier; Mrs Cassidy had gone to Mass every Sunday morning in New York. It was yet one more thing that they had never discussed.

She looked around the church where she was baptised, made her First Communion and her Confirmation, the church where her sisters had been married and where people were praying for the repose of the soul of a man who had never died. It was all very odd.

Still she hoped that the prayers would do someone somewhere some good.

There were a series of minefields that had to be walked very carefully. Chicky must make sure not to annoy those who already ran bed-and-breakfast accommodation around the place, or who rented out summer cottages. She began a ceaseless diplomatic offensive explaining that what she was doing was creating something totally new for the area, not a premises that would take business away from them.

She visited the many public houses dotted around the countryside and told them of her plans. Her guests would want to tour the cliffs and hills around Stoneybridge. She would recommend that they see the real Ireland, take their lunch in all the traditional bars, pubs and inns around. So if they were to serve soup and simple food, she would love to know about it and she would send customers in their direction.

She chose builders from another part of the country, as she wanted to avoid giving preference to the O'Haras or their main rivals in the construction business. It was so much easier than choosing one over the other. It was the same about buying supplies. Offence could easily be taken if she was seen to favour just one place.

Chicky made sure that everyone would get something from the project. She was so good at getting everyone on side.

The main thing was to get the architects in and out and the

workmen on site. She would need a manager, but not yet. She would want someone to live in and help her with the cooking but again, that could wait.

Chicky had her eye on her niece Orla for this job. The girl was quick and bright. She loved Stoneybridge and the life it offered. She was energetic and sporty, into windsurfing and rock climbing. She had done a computer course in Dublin and a diploma in marketing. Chicky could teach her to cook. She was lively and good with people. She would be a natural for Stone House. Irritatingly, the girl seemed to want to stay in London with her new job. No explanations, she just went. Things were so much easier for the young these days than in her time, Chicky thought. Orla didn't have to ask permission or family approval. It was assumed that she was an adult and they had no say in her life.

The plans went on and on. There would be eight guest bedrooms and one big kitchen and dining area where all the guests would eat dinner together. She found a huge old-fashioned table that would have to be scrubbed every day but it was authentic. This was no place for fancy mahogany and place mats or thick Irish linen tablecloths. It must be the real thing.

She got one local craftsman to make her fourteen chairs, and another to restore an old dresser to display the china. With Miss Queenie she drove to auctions and sales around the countryside and found the right glasses, plates, bowls.

They met people who would be able to restore some of the old rugs in the Sheedy home, and who could replace frayed leather on little antique tables.

This was the part that Miss Queenie loved most. She would say over and over what a miracle it was to have all these lovely treasures restored. Her sisters would be so pleased when they saw what was happening. Miss Queenie believed that they knew every detail of what was going on in Stone House, and watched it all approvingly. It was touching that she saw them settled in some happy place waiting for the hotel to open and checking the comings and goings in Stoneybridge.

It was rather more unsettling when Miss Queenie also assumed that Walter Starr would be there in heaven with the two Miss Sheedys, cheering on every development that was being made by his brave, courageous widow.

Chicky made sure to tell her family about her plans each week so that they could be well briefed and ahead of the game. It gave them great status to know in advance that the planning applications had been approved, a walled kitchen garden to grow their own vegetables planned and oil-fired central heating for the whole house installed.

She would probably need a professional designer as well. Even though she and Miss Queenie thought they knew what the place should look like, they *were* pitching for discerning people, they would charge real money and must make the place right. What Chicky thought of as elegant might well be considered tacky.

Even though she had looked at all the hotels and country houses in magazines, she had little practical experience in getting the right look. Mrs Cassidy's Select Accommodation hadn't been a real training ground for style.

There would be a lot of work ahead: she would have to have a website and take bookings online, still a very foreign world to her. This is where young Orla would be her right hand if she were to come back from London. She had telephoned her twice but the girl had been distracted and non-committal.

Chicky's sister Kathleen said that Orla was like a bag of cats and that there was no talking to her on any subject.

'She's more headstrong than you ever were,' Kathleen said ruefully, 'and that's really saying something.'

'Look at how well and sane I turned out in the end,' Chicky laughed.

'The place isn't up and running yet.' Kathleen's voice was full of doom. 'We'll see how well and sane you are when you're open for business.'

Only Mrs Cassidy, over in New York, and Miss Queenie believed it would happen and be a big success. Everyone else was humouring her and hoping it would take off but in the same way that they hoped for a long hot summer and for the Irish soccer team to do well in the World Cup.

Sometimes Chicky would go and walk the cliffs at night and look out over the Atlantic Ocean. Always it gave her strength.

People had had enough courage to get into small, shaky boats and set sail over those choppy waters, not knowing what lay ahead. Surely it couldn't be too hard to set up a guest house? Then she would go back indoors where Miss Queenie would run and make them a mug of hot chocolate and say that she hadn't been so happy since she was a girl, since the days when she and her sisters would go to a hunt ball and hope they might find dashing young men to marry. That had never happened, but this time it would work. Stone House was going to happen.

And Chicky would pat her on the hand and say that they would be the talk of the country. And as she said it, she believed it. All her worries would go. Whether it was because of the walk in the wild winds or the comforting hot chocolate or Miss Queenie's hopeful face or a combination of all three, it meant she slept a long, untroubled sleep every night.

She would wake ready for anything, which was just as well because in the months ahead there was quite a lot she had to be ready for.

Rigger

Rigger never knew his father – he had never been spoken of. His mother Nuala was hard to know properly. She worked so hard for one thing, and she said little of her life in the West of Ireland in a small place called Stoneybridge. Rigger knew she had worked as a maid in a big house for three old ladies called the Miss Sheedys, but she never wanted to talk about it nor her family back home.

He shrugged. It was impossible to understand grown-ups, anyway.

Nuala had never owned anything of her own. She was the youngest of the family so any clothes she got had been well tried out on the others first. There was no money for luxuries, not even a First Communion dress; and when she was fifteen they had found her a job working for the Miss Sheedys in Stone House. Very nice women they were; ladies, all three of them.

It was hard work: stone floors and wooden tables to scrub, old furniture to polish. She had a very small room with a little iron bed. But it was her own, more than she ever had at home. The Miss Sheedys hadn't a penny really between them, so there was a lot of fighting back the damp and the leaks and there was never the money to give the house any proper heating or a good coat of paint – both needed badly. They ate very little but Nuala was used to that. They were like little sparrows at the table.

She looked at them with wonder, as they had to have their table napkins each in its own ring and they sounded a little gong to announce the meal. It was like taking part in a play.

Sometimes Miss Queenie would ask about Nuala's boyfriends, but the other sisters would *tut-tut* as if this wasn't a suitable topic to discuss with the maid.

Not that there was that much to discuss. There were very few boyfriends around Stoneybridge. Any lads her brothers knew had all gone to England or America to find work. And Nuala wouldn't be considered good enough for the O'Haras or some of the big families in the place. She hoped that she would meet one of the summer visitors who would fall in love with her, just like Chicky, and not care that she was in domestic service.

And she *did* meet a summer visitor, called Drew. It was short for Andrew. He was a friend of the O'Haras, and they had all been kicking a ball around the beach. Nuala sat watching the girls in their smart swimsuits. How wonderful it must be to be able to go into town and buy things like that, and lovely coloured baskets and coloured towels.

Drew came over and asked her to join the game. After a week she was in love with him. After two weeks they were lovers. It was all so natural and normal, she couldn't understand why she and the other girls had giggled so much about it at school. Drew said he adored her and that he would write to her every day when he went back to Dublin.

He wrote once and said it had been a magical summer and

that he would never forget her. He gave no address. Nuala wouldn't ask the O'Haras where to find him. Not even when she realised that her period was late and she was most probably pregnant.

When this became more certain to be true, she was at a complete loss about what to do. It would break her mother's heart. Nuala had never felt so alone in her life.

She decided to tell the Miss Sheedys.

She waited until she had cleared and washed up their minimal supper before she began the story. Nuala looked at the stone floor of the kitchen so that she did not have to meet their eyes as she explained what had happened.

The Sheedy sisters were shocked. They had hardly any words to express their horror that this should have happened while Nuala was under their roof.

'What on earth are you going to do?' Miss Queenie asked with tears in her eyes.

Miss Jessica and Miss Beatrice were less sympathetic but equally unable to think of a solution.

What had Nuala hoped they would do? That they might ask her to bring up the baby there? That they would say a child around the house would make them all feel young again?

No, she hadn't hoped for that much but she wanted some reassurance, some pinprick of hope that the world was not going to end for her as a result of all this.

They said they would make enquiries. They had heard of a place where she might be able to stay until the baby was born and given up for adoption.

'Oh, I'm not going to give the baby away,' Nuala said.

'But you can't *keep* the baby, Nuala,' Miss Queenie explained.

'I never had anything of my own before, apart from the room you gave me and my bed here.'

The sisters looked at each other. The girl didn't begin to understand what she was taking on. The responsibility, the fuss, the disgrace.

'It's the 1990s,' Nuala said, 'it's not the Dark Ages.'

'Yes, but Father Johnson is still Father Johnson,' Miss Queenie said.

'Would the young man in question perhaps . . . ?' began Miss Jessica tentatively.

'And if he's a friend of the O'Haras, he would be an honourable person and do his duty . . .' Miss Beatrice agreed.

'No, he wouldn't. He wrote to say goodbye; it had been a magical summer.'

'And I'm sure it was, my dear,' Miss Queenie clucked kindly, not noticing the disapproval from the others.

'I can't tell my parents,' Nuala said.

'So, we'll get you to Dublin as quickly as possible. They'll know what to do up there.' Miss Jessica wanted it off her doorstep soonest.

'I'll make those enquiries.' Miss Beatrice was the sister with contacts.

Nuala's eldest brother Nasey was already living in Dublin. He was the odd one in the family, very quiet, kept himself to himself, they would always say with a sigh. He had a job in a butcher's shop and seemed settled enough.

He was a bachelor with a home of his own, but he wouldn't be anyone she could rely on. He had been too long left home to know her and care about her. She did have his address for an emergency, of course, but she wouldn't contact him.

The Sheedys had found a place for Nuala to stay. It was a hostel where several of the other girls were pregnant also.

A lot of them had jobs in supermarkets or cleaning houses. Nuala was used to hard work, and found it very easy compared to all the pulling and dragging at Stone House. She got jobs by word of mouth. People said to each other that she was very pleasant and that nothing was too much trouble for her. She saved enough to rent a room for herself and the baby when it was born.

She wrote home to her family telling them about Dublin and the people she worked for, but saying nothing of the visits to the maternity hospital. She wrote to the Sheedy ladies telling them the truth, and eventually giving them the news that Richard Anthony had been born weighing six and a half pounds and was a perfect baby in every way. They sent her a five-pound note to help out, and Miss Queenie sent a christening robe.

Richard Anthony wore it at his baptism, which was in a church down by the River Liffey at a christening of sixteen infants.

'What a pity you don't have any family there with you at this time,' Miss Queenie wrote. 'Perhaps your brother would be pleased to see you and meet his new nephew.'

Nuala doubted it. Nasey had always been withdrawn and distant from what she remembered.

'I'll wait until he's a little person before I introduce them,' she said.

Nuala now had to get jobs which would allow her to take the baby with her. Not easy at first, but when they saw the long hours she put in and how little trouble the child was she found plenty of work.

She saw a great deal of life through the households where she worked. The women who fussed about their homes as if they thought life was a permanent examination where they would be found wanting. There were families where husband and wife were barely civil to each other. There were places where the children were spoiled with every possession possible and still were not content.

But also she met good, kind people who were warm to her and her little son and grateful when she went the extra distance and cooked them potato cakes or made old dull brasses shine like new.

When Richard was three it was getting harder to take him to people's houses. He wanted to explore and run around. One of Nuala's favourite ladies was someone they all called Signora, who taught Italian classes. She was a most unusual woman: completely unworldly, wore extraordinary flowing clothes and had long hair with grey and red and dark brown in it all tied back with a ribbon.

She didn't have a cleaner for herself, but paid Nuala to clean two afternoons a week for her mother. Her mother was a difficult, hard-to-please person who hadn't a good word to say for Signora except that she had always been foolish and headstrong and no good would come of it all.

But Signora, if she knew this, took no notice. She told Nuala about a marvellous little playgroup. It was run by a friend of hers.

'Oh, that would be much too expensive for me,' Nuala said sadly.

'I think they'd be very happy to have him there if you could do a few hours' cleaning in exchange.'

'But the other parents mightn't like that. The cleaner's child in with theirs.'

'They won't think like that, and anyway, they won't know.' Signora was very definite. 'You'd like playschool, wouldn't you, Richard?' Signora had a great habit of talking to children as if they were grown-ups. She never put on a baby voice.

'I'm Rigger,' he said. And that's what he was called from then on.

Rigger loved the playschool, and nobody ever knew that he arrived there two hours before the other children while his mother cleaned and polished and got the place ready for the day.

Through Signora, Nuala got several other jobs nearby. She cleaned in a hairdressing salon where they made her feel very much part of it all and even gave her very expensive highlights for nothing. She did a few hours a week in a restaurant on the quays called Ennio's, where again she was involved in the place and they always asked her to try out a bowl of pasta for her lunch. Then she would pick up Rigger and take him with her while she minded other children and took them for walks on St Stephen's Green to feed the ducks.

Nuala's family were entirely unaware of Rigger's existence. It just seemed easier that way.

As happens in many big families, the children who left became dissociated with their old home. Sometimes, at Christmas, she felt lonely for Stoneybridge and for the days when she would decorate the tree for the Miss Sheedys and they would tell her the stories of each ornament. She thought of her mother and father and the goose they would have for Christmas and the prayers they would say for all emigrants – particularly her two sisters in America, her brother in Birmingham and Nasey and Nuala in Dublin. But it was not a lonely life. Who could be lonely with Rigger? They were devoted to each other.

She couldn't think what made her get in touch with her brother Nasey. Possibly it was another letter from Miss Queenie, who always saw things in a very optimistic way. Miss Queenie said that it was probably a lonely life for Nasey in Dublin, and that he might enjoy having company from home.

She could barely remember him. He was the eldest and she the youngest of a big family. He wasn't going to be shocked and appalled that she had a son who was about to go to big school any day.

It was worth a try.

She called to the butcher's shop where Nasey worked, holding Rigger by the hand. She recognised him at once in a white coat and cutting lamb chops expertly with a cleaver.

'I'm Nuala, your sister,' she said simply, 'and this is Rigger.'

Rigger looked up at him fearfully and Nuala looked long and hard at her brother's face. Then she saw a great smile on Nasey's face. He was indeed delighted to see her. What a waste of five years it had been because she was afraid he might not want to recognise her.

'I'm going to be on my break in ten minutes. I can meet you in the café across the road. Mr Malone, this is my sister and her little boy Rigger.'

'Go on now, Nasey. You'll have lots to talk about.' Mr Malone was kindly. And it turned out that they did have lots to talk about.

Nasey was easygoing. He asked nothing about Rigger's father, nor why she had taken so long to contact him. He was interested in the places she worked, and he said that the Malones were looking for someone to help in the house and that they were a really decent family. She could do much worse than go there. He was in touch with another nephew, Dingo, a good lad, full of dreams and nonsense. He made deliveries in his own van. He lived alone, but he always said the people he worked for made up for it, and he loved hearing about their lives. He would be pleased to know he had a new cousin.

Nasey asked about home and she was vague with details.

'They don't really know about Rigger,' she said. She need not even have said it. He understood.

'No point in burdening people with too much information,' he said, nodding soundly.

He said that he had never found anyone suitable for himself but was always hoping that he would meet someone one day. He didn't like picking up girls in pubs, and honestly where else was there? He was too old for kids' dances and clubs.

And from that meeting on, he became part of Nuala and Rigger's lives.

He was the dream uncle who knew a keeper at the zoo, who taught the boy to ride a bike, who took him to his first match. And when Rigger was eleven it was Nasey who told Nuala that the lad was mixing with a very tough crowd at school and that they had been chased out of several stores for shoplifting.

She was appalled, but Rigger was shruggy. Everyone did it; the shops *knew* they did it. It was the system.

Then he was involved in an incident where old people were threatened and forced to hand over their weekly pension. That led to the children's court and a suspended sentence.

And when Rigger was caught in a warehouse stealing television sets, it meant reform school.

Nuala had not known it was possible to cry so much. She was totally shocked. What had happened to her little boy? And when? Nothing had a purpose any more. Her jobs were just that now, jobs.

She barely listened to the chat in Katie's hairdresser's, in Ennio's restaurant or in St Jarlath's Crescent – places where she had once been so happy, so involved.

She decided she would write to him every week but she had no idea what he was interested in.

Football, probably, so she looked up the evening paper to see where the team was playing next and also to know was there any film that Rigger might like. Week after week she wrote. Sometimes he replied, sometimes he didn't, but she continued every week.

She told him how her father had got ill and died and how she had gone back to Stoneybridge for the funeral. She said it was so strange how small it seemed now after so many years away from the place. She hardly knew anyone, and her sisters and brothers seemed like strangers. Her mother looked so small and old. So much had changed, it was like going to a different place.

Rigger wrote back to that letter.

I'm sorry your da died. Why did we never see him, or go back to this place? Fellows here are always talking about their grans and their grandas.

Nuala wrote back.

When you come home I'll take you on the train to Stoneybridge and you'll see it all for yourself. It's such a long story but it's going to be easier to tell you all about it than write it down.

By the time he came back from the reform school, Rigger was sixteen and Nuala's mother had died.

Nasey went on his own to the funeral. Nuala didn't go. She

hadn't been at all easy when she had gone to see her father buried. She fancied that some of the neighbours looked at her oddly and that the sisters in America were annoyed with her for not coming back more regularly. Her brother from Birmingham had given her a very irritating lecture about it being time she settled down and had a family instead of just running around enjoying herself in Dublin.

Nasey told the family that he did see Nuala from time to time but said no more. He kept to his theory that people should not be burdened with too much information. He brought news from home. Two of the Miss Sheedys had died. Now only Miss Queenie remained.

Then came the news that Chicky Starr had come back from America and was going to buy Stone House. Miss Queenie would live there for her lifetime and they were going to make the place into a hotel.

Nuala remembered Chicky well. They had been at school together. Chicky had married an American called Walter Starr and had gone to live in New York. Nuala had written to her there. Her poor husband had been killed in a terrible car crash.

She would have her work cut out for her if she was to make any kind of a fist of that big sprawling house and turn it into a hotel where people would pay to stay.

Rigger didn't talk much about his time at the reform school when he came back. He had learned a bit of this and a bit of that, he said. But he wasn't qualified at anything. They had done a bit of building up in the school: plastering one week, digging another. Nasey said he would try to get Rigger taken on by Mr Malone in the butcher's shop, but times were hard. People were buying more and more of their meat readywrapped in supermarkets.

Signora asked Nuala did she know if Rigger would go back to school. She would give him some lessons to try and help him catch up, but he didn't want that.

He had had enough school, he said.

Nuala had very much hoped that he would have grown away from his old ways, that he could find new friends and a different way of living.

But Rigger was barely home a few weeks when Nuala realised that her son had indeed made contact with those boys he could find from the old days. Some of them were not around any more. Two were in gaol, one on the run – possibly in England – and the others under the fairly constant and watchful eye of the Guards.

Rigger had been warned from every side about the danger of getting a criminal record if he offended again.

He went out early and came home late with no explanation or description of how he spent his time. One night she heard shouting and running and doors banging and she lay shaking in the dark waiting for the arrival of the Guards with their sirens wailing. But nobody came.

Next morning she was drawn and anxious but Rigger had obviously slept well and seemed unconcerned. She was re-lieved when he told her that he was going to look for a job.

Nasey was surprised to see Rigger come into the butcher's shop with two of his friends. Surprised and not altogether pleased.

But Rigger had come to ask was there any casual work going, could they clean up the yard, for example?

Nasey was pleased to see some interest in legitimate work, and he ran to Mr Malone asking if they could have a couple of hours' work. And to give them their due, they did the job well. Nasey reported it all to Nuala with pleasure. The lads had done the job, got a few euro and gone away well satisfied.

Nuala began to breathe properly again. Perhaps she had been overanxious about nothing.

Two nights later, Nasey was taking his late-night walk and passed the butcher's shop. He looked up automatically at the burglar alarm and saw to his astonishment that it was not turned on. Never had he left the premises without switching it to 'Active'. Horrified, he let himself in and heard sounds at the back of the shop from the cold room.

As he went in he saw three men lifting carcasses of beef into a van which was parked in the back yard.

He ran towards them and one of the men dropped a great side of meat and came at him with a crowbar.

'What are you doing?' Nasey cried. As the man was about to hit him, from nowhere a voice shouted, 'Leave him, leave him, for Christ's sake.'

The blow was stopped and Nasey recognised his protector was in fact his nephew Rigger.

'I don't believe it, Rigger.' Nasey was nearly in tears. 'You were paid for your work and you came back to steal their meat.'

'Shut up, Nasey, you big eejit. Just get out of here. You were never here, do you hear me? Just go home and say nothing. No harm done.'

'I can't. I can't let Mr Malone's livelihood be taken like this . . .'

'He's well insured, Nasey. Have some sense, man.'

'You can't do this. What are you going to do with the carcasses?'

'Cut them up. Sell them along the Mountainview Estates.

Everyone round there wants cheap meat. Nasey, get out of here, will you?'

'I'm not going and I'm not going to forget it.'

'Rigger, either you shut him up or I will,' one of the others said.

Nasey felt himself being pushed out the door, and he could feel Rigger's breath hot on his face.

'Jesus, Nasey, have you an ounce of sense? They'd beat the side of your head in. Get *out*. Run. RUN!'

Nasey ran all the way to Nuala's house and told her what had happened. White-faced, the two of them sat drinking mugs of tea.

'Even if I *don't* tell Mr Malone, he'll know anyway. He's not a fool. Who else would have been able to come in and see the lie of the land and suss the place out except those three? And he knows that Rigger is my nephew.'

'I'm so sorry, Nasey,' Nuala wept.

'We have to think what to do with him. He'll go to gaol over this,' Nasey said.

'It's all my fault. I should have been able to control him. I was too busy making money for him. Saving for an education that he'll never have.'

'Stop that. It's not down to you.'

'Well, who else's fault is it but mine?'

'This is no time to be trying to work that out. We have to hide him. The Guards will come looking for him here.'

'Could we send him back to Stoneybridge?' Her face was despairing.

'But who would look after him there? And I thought you didn't want anyone to know about him.'

'I don't want him in gaol either. Who knows about him isn't important any more.'

'None of them would be able to handle him,' Nasey said. 'If there was somewhere he could live in and work . . .'

Nuala strained to think of anywhere.

'Could he work for Chicky at Stone House? Miss Queenie wrote to me not long ago that she was looking for someone to help her.'

'He'd never stick it.' Nasey shook his head.

'He will if he knows it's that or prison.'

'Ring Chicky,' Nasey said.

Nasey didn't hear the phone conversation. He was out on the street waiting for Rigger to come back. He saw the boy running down the street. Rigger was home. His face was white and his hands were shaking. He was willing to blame everyone but himself.

'If I go down, Nasey, it will all be due to you. The other lads just threw me out. They won't let me have any part of what we got. It's so unfair. I set it up. I gave them the way in.'

'Yes, you did,' Nasey said grimly.

'I *told* the others you wouldn't split on us but they don't believe me. They say you'll have gone to the Guards already. Have you?'

'No,' Nasey said.

'Well thank God for that, anyway. Why couldn't you have just backed away?'

'I did. I ran away as you said.'

'And you're not going to tell?' Rigger looked like a child.

'I don't *have* to tell, Rigger. Mr Malone will know.'

'Oh my God, it's *Mister* Malone this, *Mister* Malone that. Would you hear yourself?' Rigger was full of scorn. 'Aren't you big enough and old enough to be your own master instead of yes sir, yes sir, three bags full, to him?'

'They'll find you even if I were struck dumb and never spoke again,' Nasey said.

'Just shut your mouth, Rigger, and listen carefully,' Nuala spoke suddenly.

He looked at her in shock. Her face was hard and unforgiving. He had never known her raise her voice to him like this before.

'We're going to get you out of Dublin tonight. And you're not coming back.'

'What?'

'There's a truck driver taking his lorry back to Stoneybridge tonight. You'll go with him. He will take you to Stone House.'

'What's Stone House? Is it a school?' Rigger was frightened.

'It's where your mother worked when she was young. It's where she left from to have you, all those years ago. With all the pleasure and pride that was to bring her.' Never had Nasey sounded so bitter.

Rigger tried to speak but his uncle wouldn't let him say a word. 'Get your things together, give me your phone, tell nobody where you're going. You'll be in Stoneybridge by the time they open up Malone's in the morning.'

'But you said that the Guards would find me anyway.'

'Not if you're not here, they can't. Not if no one knows where you are.'

'Mam, is that right?'

'Chicky is doing me this one favour. She suggested the driver. She'll keep you for a week to see how it goes. If you get up to any of your old tricks, she'll call the Guards down there and they'll have you back here and behind bars before you know what's happened.'

'Mam!'

'Don't "Mam" me. I was never a proper mother to you. It

45

was only pretending to be a family, that's all it was, and it stops tonight.'

'Nasey?'

'What?'

'Will you get into any trouble?' Rigger asked. It was the first hint that he might care for anyone other than himself.

'I don't know. That remains to be seen. I'll tell Mr Malone that I'm very sorry about it, about getting him to let you all work in the yard. Which I am – very, very sorry indeed.'

'He won't sack you, will he?'

'Who knows? I hope not. Years of work. One mistake.'

'And the other lads . . .'

'As you said, they threw you out, ran off on you. They're not thinking about you. You don't have to think about them.'

'But if they're caught?'

'They will be, but you will be far away, starting a new job.' Nasey was calm and cold.

Things happened quickly then. Rigger's bag was packed in silence. The man with the empty lorry arrived. The wordless driver just indicated the front seat. There would be little conversation on the road across Ireland.

His mother turned away as he tried to say goodbye. Rigger's eyes filled with tears.

'I'm sorry, Mam,' he said.

'Yes,' Nuala said.

And then he was gone. He had no idea a journey could take so long. He also had no idea what lay ahead. He had been given very firm instructions to discuss nothing with his driver. He looked out the window as they passed the small dark fields on either side. How did people *live* in places like this? Sometimes there were dead rabbits and foxes on the road. He would like to have asked why these animals went out into the traffic but conversation seemed to be forbidden so instead, he listened to endless country and western songs all about losers and drunkards and people who had been betrayed.

By the time they got to Stoneybridge, Rigger felt lower than he had ever felt in his life.

The driver left him at the gate of Stone House. His mother had worked here. *Lived* here. No wonder she had never come back. He wondered had she relations around the place? Did his father live here? Married to someone else, maybe?

Rigger asked himself why had he never asked or wanted to know? What on earth was he going to do here until things died down in Dublin, if they ever would?

He went and knocked at the door. A woman with short curly hair answered immediately and placed her finger on her lips.

'Come in quietly and don't wake Miss Queenie,' she said in a low voice with a slight American accent.

Who *were* these people called Chicky and Queenie?

What was he doing in this cold barn of a place? He went into a shabby kitchen with a broken range where a small kitten sat in front, warming itself. It was white with a tiny little triangular black tail and little black ears. Seeing him, it mewed piteously.

Rigger picked it up and stroked its head. 'What's its name?'

'It only arrived today, like yourself. It came in an hour ago.'

'Will it stay?' he asked.

'It depends.' Chicky Starr was giving nothing away.

Rigger looked her in the eye for the first time. 'Depends on what?' he asked.

'If it's willing to work hard, catch mice, if it's no trouble and behaves nicely to Miss Queenie. That sort of thing.'

'I see,' Rigger said. And he did. 'What will I do first?' he asked.

'I think you should have some breakfast,' she said.

And so it began. His new life.

It was a mad notion, turning this house into a hotel. What kind of people did they think would come here, to this place? Still, it was the only game in town.

It was Miss Queenie who had brought the kitten into the household. The last of a litter born in one of the farm cottages down the hill, its survival had been in doubt until Miss Queenie had settled the matter by putting the tiny creature into her pocket and bringing it home. She held it in the palm of her hand and talked to it soothingly as the kitten gazed solemnly at her with its enormous grey-green eyes; she had decided, she told Rigger, to call it Gloria. He realised quickly that Miss Queenie was like something from an old black and white movie; she liked to keep to the traditions of the house as it had been, with a little gong rung to signal mealtimes and proper table settings. She never went out without a smart hat and gloves.

She seemed to think Rigger was a friend, and a very helpful person who had turned up at the right time when they needed him. She told him long, confused tales about people called Beatrice and Jessica and others long dead. She was totally harmless, but possibly not playing with the full deck.

Mindful of Chicky's advice, Rigger realised the importance of being nice to Miss Queenie. He made her a mug of tea every morning and served it in what was called the morning room. At the same time, he fed Gloria.

Miss Queenie knew that you shouldn't give cats saucers of milk, just lots of water and a little pouch of kitten food; certainly Gloria seemed to be thriving on it. She slept most of the day, and for sure was not a kitten of great brains: she seemed to have bouts of huge anxiety because she kept thinking that her tail was another animal following her. Miss Queenie said Gloria wasn't to be blamed for this entirely. After all, her tail *was* a different colour. Miss Queenie had made up a little cat bed in the corner of the kitchen by the range. As Gloria slept, Miss Queenie would watch her happily for hours.

Chicky was less forthcoming. She worked very hard and expected him to do the same. She had little time for small talk.

There was so much to do in the place.

He dug the wild, unkempt gardens of Stone House until his back ached and his face was roughened by the constant sea spray. The soil was hard and stony and the briars and the brambles were enormous. Even though he tried to protect himself he was covered with scratches and cuts. He liked it best when Gloria decided to keep him company, her triangular little black tail held high in the air as she sniffed at the ground where he dug. She pounced on leaves and chewed on twigs and more than once avoided being decapitated only by a whisker as Rigger dug through the brambles. Her curiosity was infinite and insatiable; she explored tirelessly as he worked on. And as he paused, leaning on his spade, she would solemnly roll on to her back and gaze at him upside down.

On the days when the Atlantic storms battered the house and the rain came in horizontally, there were old lofts to be cleared out, furniture to be shifted, woodwork to be painted. The old outhouses were dealt with by a couple of builders who were kept busy hacking out and making good. Rigger worked for them, carrying bricks and stones and wooden planks. He chopped wood for the fires and cleaned the grates out every morning, then poured fresh water and breakfast for Gloria and made tea for Miss Queenie.

She was a nice old thing, away with the fairies, of course, but no harm in her. She was interested in everything and would tell him long stories about the past when her sisters were alive. They would have loved a tennis court, but there was never the money to make one.

'Your mother was wonderful when she was here. We really missed her when she left,' Miss Queenie would say. 'Nobody could make potato cakes like Nuala could.'

This was news to Rigger. He didn't ever remember potato cakes at home.

Rigger had a bedroom behind the kitchen where he slept, exhausted, for seven hours a night. On a Saturday, Chicky gave him his bus fare, the price of a cinema ticket and a burger in the next town.

Nobody ever spoke of why he was there, or the fact that he was in hiding. There was little time to make friends around the place and that was good too, as far as Rigger was concerned. The fewer people who knew about him the better.

And then he heard the news he had been waiting to hear.

Nasey phoned him with the details. Two youths had been arrested for the theft of meat from the butcher's shop. They had been before the court and had been given six-month sentences.

The Guards had watched Nuala's house for several weeks, and when there was no sign of Rigger, and nobody knew where he had gone, the matter was dropped.

'How did they catch them?' Rigger asked in a whisper.

'Someone pointed the Guards in the area of the Mountain-view Estates and there they were, as bold as brass, going from door to door selling the meat.'

Rigger knew that the 'someone' must have been Nasey, but he said nothing. 'And your own job, Nasey?'

'Is still there. Mr Malone sometimes sympathises with me on the fact that you ran away. He even told me that you might be better off out of Dublin.'

'I see.'

'And maybe he's right, Rigger.'

'Thank you again, Nasey. And about my mam?'

'She's still in a bit of shock, you know. She had been so looking forward to you getting back from that school, counting the days, in fact. She had such plans for you, and now it's all over.'

'Ah no, it's not all over. Not for ever, it's not. I can come back now that the others are off the streets, can't I?'

'No, Rigger, those fellows have friends. They're in a gang. I wouldn't advise you coming back here for a good while.'

'But I can't stay here for ever,' Rigger wailed.

'You have to stay for a fair bit more,' Nasey warned.

'I miss my mam writing to me like she did up in the school.'

'I wouldn't say she's up to writing to you. Not yet, anyway. You could always write to her yourself, of course,' Nasey said.

'I could, I suppose . . .'

'Good, good.' Nasey was gone.

Maybe Miss Queenie would help him write to his mother.

She was indeed a great help, telling him things that might interest Nuala: how this garage had been sold, the O'Haras' new houses – which were going to make them millionaires – had now lost all their value and were like white elephants with no buyers. Father Johnson had a new curate who was doing most of the work in the parish.

Rigger didn't know whether his mother found any of this interesting as she never wrote back.

'Why do you think she doesn't write back to me?' he asked Miss Queenie.

The old lady had no idea. Her pale blue eyes were troubled and sad on his behalf as she stroked Gloria on her knee. It was strange, she said, Nuala had been so proud of him and even sent pictures of his christening and his First Communion. Maybe Chicky would know.

Nervously he asked Chicky, who said crisply that he must have an over-sunny view of life if he believed that his mother had got over everything.

'It wasn't easy for her to ring me in the middle of the night. We hadn't seen each other for twenty years, and she had to tell me that I was the only person on earth who could help her. She can't have liked doing that. I would have hated it.'

'Yes, I know, but could you tell her I've changed?' he begged.

'I have told her.'

'And why doesn't she write back to me, then?'

'Because she thinks it's all *her* fault. She doesn't really want to get involved with you again. I'm sorry to be so hard, but you did ask.'

'Yes, I did.' He was very shaken.

By now Rigger had actually become interested in this whole mad plan to turn the old house into a smart guest house. The rough work and clearing of the ground had all been done; it was time for rebuilding. Real contractors would be brought in on the job. He looked on in amazement as the plans for bathrooms and central heating were laid out on the kitchen table as Gloria batted them from one side to the other. He knew there were meetings with bankers and insurance brokers, that designers were planned in the future.

He was unprepared for Chicky to change his terms of employment.

'You've been here six months and you've been a great help, Rigger,' she said one evening when Miss Queenie had gone to bed. He was very pleased with the compliment. There hadn't been many of those coming his way. Rigger waited to hear what would come next.

'When the builders move in properly in a few weeks, I'll need help to get Miss Queenie to and from Dr Dai's and the health clinic. Can you drive?'

'Yes, I can drive,' Rigger said.

'But do you have a licence? Did you do a driving test or anything?'

'I'm afraid not,' Rigger admitted.

'So that's the first thing you must do – get some driving lessons from Dinny in the garage and do the test. Can you grow things?'

'What kind of things?'

'We should have our own produce here: potatoes, vegetables, fruit. We should have hens, too.'

'Are you serious?' Sometimes Rigger thought that Chicky was certifiable.

'Completely serious. We must offer visitors something special; make them feel that this place is providing their food rather than just going into town and buying it all in a supermarket.'

'I see,' said Rigger, who didn't see at all.

'So I was thinking that if I called you my manager and paid you a proper wage you might feel you have more of a stake here. It won't just be a place where you are hiding out. It would be a real job with a real future.'

'Here? In Stoneybridge?' Rigger was astounded that anyone could see *his* future in these parts.

'Yes, here in Stoneybridge indeed. It's not as if you're likely to be able to go back to Dublin at any time in the near future. I hoped you might want to put down some roots here, make something of yourself.'

'I'm grateful to you and everything but—'

'But what, Rigger? But you see a glittering future for yourself in Dublin stealing great sides of beef and beating up decent butchers who try to protect their business?'

'I didn't beat up anyone,' he said indignantly.

'I know that. Why else do you think I took you on? You saved Nasey's life, he says. He was determined you should have a fresh start. I'm trying to give it to you, but it's difficult.'

'Do you like me, Chicky?'

'Yes, I do, actually. I didn't think I would but I do. You're very good to Queenie, you're kind to the kitten, you have a lot of good points. You're very young. I wanted to get you some skills and see that you have a bit of a life. But you just throw it back at me and say that a life here is worth nothing at all. So I'm a bit confused, really.'

'It's just not what I thought my life would be,' he said.

'It's not what I thought *my* life would be either, but somewhere along the line we have to pick things up and run with them.'

'At least your bad luck wasn't your own fault,' Rigger said.

'It probably was in some ways.' She looked away.

'But your husband being killed and all – you weren't to blame for that.'

'No, that's right.'

'I'd be happy to be your manager if you'll still take me,' he said, after a pause.

'We start to dig the vegetable garden tomorrow morning, and your first driving lesson will be with Dinny tomorrow afternoon. You'll start to learn the rules of the road tomorrow night. Miss Queenie will be in charge of that.'

'I'm up for it,' Rigger said.

'And I'll open a post office account for you and put half your wages in each week and give you half in cash. That way you can buy some nice clothes and take a girl to a dance or whatever.'

'Can I tell my mother and Nasey?'

'Oh yes, of course you can. But I wouldn't hold out any hopes about your mother.'

'It will be the first bit of good news she ever had about me,' he said.

'No, she was delighted with you way back when you were born. She wrote and told Miss Queenie all about it. You were six and a half pounds, apparently. But things are different now. Nasey says she needs to see a doctor; it's kind of a depression but she won't hear of it.'

Chicky thought she saw tears in Rigger's eyes but she wasn't sure.

The driving lessons went well. Dinny said that Rigger was fearless but reckless, quick to react but impatient. The rules of the road were a trial, but Miss Queenie loved testing him each evening.

'What does a sign like a circle crossed out mean on the outskirts of a town?' she would ask.

'That you can drive as fast as you like?' Rigger suggested.

'No, *wrong*, it means you can drive at the national speed limit,' Miss Queenie cried triumphantly.

'That's what I meant.'

'You *meant* drive as fast as you like,' Miss Queenie said. 'They would have failed you.'

He passed the test with no problem.

He drove Miss Queenie everywhere: to her appointments with Dr Dai, to the hospital for a check-up, to the vet to have Gloria spayed.

'It seems a pity for her not to have kittens of her own,' Miss Queenie had said as she stroked the little cat on her lap.

'But we'd only have to find homes for them, Miss Queenie. We couldn't have a house full of cats when the visitors come.' He realised that he was beginning to think of himself as part of the whole project.

'Would you like children of your own one day, Rigger?' She always asked strange, direct questions that nobody else did.

'I don't think so, to be honest with you. They seem to be more trouble than they're worth. They'd only end up disappointing you.' He knew he sounded bitter, and tried to laugh and take the harm out of it. Miss Queenie hadn't really noticed.

'We would have loved to have had children, Jessica, Beatrice and myself. We could always see our children playing around Stone House, which was silly really because if we *had* married we wouldn't have been living here any more. It was all a dream, anyway.'

'And was there ever anyone you particularly would have liked to marry, Miss Queenie?' Rigger amazed himself asking her such a thing.

'There was one young man . . . oh, I would have loved to

marry him, but sadly there was TB in his family and so he couldn't marry at all.'

'Why not?'

'Because it was a disease of the lungs and people could catch it and it would pass on to the children. He died in a sanatorium, poor, poor boy. I still have the letters he wrote to me.'

Rigger patted her hand and, embarrassed, he patted Gloria's head as well. They drove on in silence until they arrived at the vet.

'Don't worry, Gloria. You won't feel a thing, pet. And anyway, there's more to life than just sex and kittens,' Miss Queenie said reassuringly as she handed the purring cat over.

The vet and Rigger exchanged glances. This wasn't the normal conversation in the surgery.

While Gloria was being seen to, Rigger and Miss Queenie drove off to do items off Chicky's list. Rigger marvelled at how many people knew him by name in Stoneybridge and the surrounding countryside. Surely his mother would be pleased to know that he was so accepted in this place where she had grown up.

But still there was no word from her.

He had written to Nuala telling her about the day-old chicks they had bought and had to protect from Gloria, who wanted to practise her hunting skills; and how hard it was to dig potato drills. He told her about how the builder was going to charge a fortune to make a walled garden, so Rigger had built it himself, stone upon stone, and raised growing beds. How every time he dug a hole to plant something, Gloria arrived and sat in it, gazing at him seriously. Despite that, now there were shrubs and plants grown up against the wall, which was called espalier. They had runner beans and courgettes and whole rakes of salads and herbs.

He did not tell his mother about the lovely girl called Carmel Hickey, who was studying hard for her Leaving Certificate but could be persuaded to go out to the cinema or for a drive down the coast with Rigger.

Some of the neighbours, and indeed her own family, worried that Rigger lived in Stone House with the two women.

Chicky laughed. People said that it looked odd, that was all. But she dismissed it and life went on easily for the three of them, working long hours and coping with people who didn't turn up on time or at all. She taught Rigger to make the kind of meals that Miss Queenie liked: little scones and omelettes. He mastered it quickly. It was just another thing to learn.

Rigger sometimes asked Chicky's advice about what girls liked. He wanted to give Carmel a treat. What would she suggest.

Chicky thought that Carmel might like to go to the fairground that came every year to a nearby town. There would be fireworks and bumper cars, a big wheel and a lot of fun.

And apparently Carmel liked it a lot.

It was touching to see Rigger getting dressed up to take his girl out in the old van. Chicky sighed as she saw them heading off by the cliffs. Rigger didn't drink so she never worried about there being any danger ahead. She could not have foreseen the conversation a few short months later.

Carmel was pregnant.

Carmel Hickey, aged seventeen and about to sit her Leaving Certificate, was going to have the child of Rigger, who was eighteen. They loved each other, so were going to run away to England and get married. Rigger was very sorry to let Chicky down and leave her like this, but he said it was the only thing to do. There was no question of a termination and Carmel's parents would kill them both. There would be no tolerance in the Hickey family.

Chicky was unnaturally calm about it all.

First thing she said was they must tell nobody. Nobody at all.

Carmel was to do her exams as if nothing was wrong. Then, in three weeks' time when the exams were over, they could get married here, in Stoneybridge, and take it from there.

Rigger looked at her as if she was mad.

'Chicky, you have no idea what they'll be like. They'll skin me alive. They have such hopes for her: a career, a life and eventually a great catch as a husband. They don't want her married to a dead end like me. They'd never stand for it, not in a million years. We *have* to run away.'

'There's been far too much running away,' Chicky said. 'Your mother ran away from here. I ran away. You ran away. It has to stop sometime. Let it stop now.'

'But what can I offer Carmel?'

'You have a job here – a good job – you have savings already in the post office. I'll let you have that cottage beside the walled garden. You can make a home there. You will be providing all the produce for Stone House and for anyone else you can sell it to. You're a genuine businessman, for God's sake. These days they'd be hard put to find anyone so ready and able to make a home for their daughter.'

'No, Chicky. You don't know what they're like.'

'I *do* know what they are like. I've known the Hickeys all my life. I'm not saying they'll be pleased, but it beats the hell out of getting the Guards to find you in England or asking the Salvation Army to trace you.'

'Married? Here in Stoneybridge?'

'If that's what you want then yes. I think you're both too young. You could get married much later, but if you want it now then leave Father Johnson to me.'

'It won't work.'

'It will if you say absolutely nothing and just get that house done. You have to have it ready to show to the Hickeys the day you tell them that Carmel is pregnant.'

'Chicky, be reasonable. If it were going to work, we can't do all this in three weeks or a month.'

'If I tell the builders that Stone Cottage is the priority then we can. And you can take some of the furniture we have stored here.'

He looked at her with some hope in his eyes. 'Do you really think . . . ?'

'We haven't a minute to waste, and don't tell your mother either. Not yet.'

'Oh God, she's going to go mad too. More bad news.'

'Not when she hears it as a package. Not when she hears that you have a house, a proper job and a bride. Where's the bad news there? Aren't these the things she always hoped for, for you?'

Carmel Hickey proved to be amazingly practical. She swore she would focus entirely on her exams while saying that she wanted to learn bookkeeping and commercial studies as a career. She insisted that Rigger spend every waking hour getting Stone Cottage up and running. She seemed vastly relieved that they were not going to catch the emigrant ship and live on nothing in England.

Carmel had every confidence in Chicky, even to the point of keeping Father Johnson on side.

And Carmel was right to be confident. By the time the Leaving Certificate exams were over, Father Johnson had been convinced that a good Christian marriage to be solemnised between two admittedly very young and very slightly pregnant people was a good thing rather than a bad thing.

And when the Hickeys began to wail and protest, Father Johnson was reproving and reminding them not to stand in God's way.

The Hickeys were somewhat mollified after their first tour of Stone Cottage, and the evidence that Rigger appeared to be his own boss rather than just Chicky's handyman. They had to admit that the place was very comfortable and what they called 'well appointed'.

Gloria had decided to come and dress the set. She sat washing herself by the small range, giving the place an air of domesticity. Old lamps that the Miss Sheedys had once loved had been taken out and polished, rugs had been made by cutting out the better bits of old carpets and everything was brightly painted.

The wedding would be small and quiet. They didn't want any show.

Nuala wrote one short letter and made one brief telephone call to wish them well but to say that she wouldn't be able to come to the wedding.

'Ah Mam, I'd love you to be here to meet Carmel and to see our home.' Rigger hadn't believed that she would refuse to come.

'I'm not able to, Rigger. It wouldn't work. I send you both my good wishes and my hopes for the future. I'm sure I will come one day and visit you another time.'

'But I'll only have one wedding day, Mam.'

'That's one more than I had,' Nuala said.

'But why are you still against me, Mam? I did what you and Nasey said I should do. I made a life here. I worked hard. I gave up all that stupid way of going on. *Why* won't you come and see us getting married?'

'I failed you, Rigger. I gave you no upbringing. I couldn't look after you or guide you. I let you make a mess of your life. I have no part of what you have become. You did all that without me.'

'Don't talk like that. I'd be *nothing* if it weren't for you. I was the eejit who wouldn't listen. Please come, Mam.'

'Not this time, Rigger. But maybe one day.'

'And about the baby . . . if it's a girl, we were going to call her Nuala.'

'*Don't!* Please don't do that. I know you think it would please me but truly I don't want it.'

'Why, Mam? Why do you say that?'

'Because I'm not worth it. When did I ever do anything properly for you, Rigger? Anything that worked? I ask myself that over and over and I can't find an answer.'

She sent a wedding gift of an expensive glass vase with a card saying she was so sorry not to be able to be there in person.

Carmel understood.

'We should let her wait until she's ready. When the baby is born she'll be here like a flash and then we'll show her what a good job she made of you.'

The wedding day itself went better than they might have hoped. Nasey came from Dublin with Rigger's cousin Dingo.

Nasey smoothed things over with the Hickeys. Rigger's mother would definitely have been here if she could, but sadly she had not felt strong enough to travel. She sent everyone her good wishes.

Privately he told Chicky that his sister was retreating further and further.

No need to upset the boy by telling him this, but she seemed to have disengaged with her son entirely.

Miss Queenie was totally resplendent at the wedding in a dark pink brocade dress that she had last worn thirty-five years ago, and with a matching hat with flowers round the brim. Chicky bought herself an elegant navy silk dress and jacket. She got a plain straw hat and put navy and white silk flowers on the brim. The Hickeys were going to get a run for their money at this wedding.

Chicky served a delicious roast lamb for lunch in Stone Cottage, and they had made a wedding cake that was the equal to anything the Hickeys might have seen in a five-star hotel, if they had ever been to one. There was no honeymoon; the young couple were hard at work fixing up the hen runs and the new milking shed. Three cows had already been bought at the cattle market and were grazing in the fields. Stone Cottage would supply its own milk for the guests as well as yogurt and even organic butter. There was a great deal to be done.

Carmel helped Chicky to go through colour schemes for the bedrooms. She had a good eye and discovered where to source materials. She was deeply cynical about the expensive advice and taste of some of the interior designers they met along the way.

'Honestly, Chicky, they don't know any more than we do. Less, in fact, because you remember this house as it used to be. They're just trying to stamp their own image on the place.'

But Chicky said that they were spending so much already, the cost of an interior designer wouldn't make that huge a difference. At least they would know if they were going in the right direction.

Chicky's niece Orla wasn't sure but agreed. Give the designers a crack at it. Orla had come back from London after talking to Chicky again. She had committed to be on Chicky's team a few weeks ago.

'I couldn't come back to Stoneybridge now,' Orla had said, 'not after London, and my mother is driving me mad. Chicky, can I stay here with you in Stone House? There's plenty of room.'

'No, I've done enough to annoy the family in the past. I'm not going to be accused of hijacking you now. Just go home and sleep at your mother's house.'

'I can't do it. She's on my case all the time: why didn't I get engaged to a banker like Brigid O'Hara did? What was I *doing* in London that I didn't meet some thick-as-a-plank rich boy like Brigid did?'

'I don't want Kathleen on *my* case, either. Stick it out, Orla. And if you *do* decide to come and work with me, we'll find you a place of your own. There's a lot of falling-down cottages here. We can do one up.'

'That would mean saying I'm going to stay in Stoneybridge for ever.'

'No it wouldn't. We can always rent it or sell it afterwards. I'd give you great training. You'll cook like a dream when I'm finished with you. But don't stay here in this house. You need to be able to shake a place off at the end of the working day.'

'You're a miracle, that's what you are.'

'No, I'm just very experienced,' Chicky had said and the decision had been made.

*

Rigger and Carmel, determined to prove themselves in front of everyone, worked all their waking hours to turn their plans into reality. Rigger wanted to do deliveries to faraway farms up near Rocky Ridge, but Carmel warned that her cousins who ran the local grocery shops would resent this and claim that Rigger and Carmel were taking the bread from their mouths. So instead they made marmalades and jams and found attractive little jars for them with Stone Cottage painted on each one.

Like Chicky had done already, they had to look for business without alienating the shopkeepers who made their living around the area. They must try to provide a new service rather than replace existing ones.

Soon the hotels and tourist shops were buying from them and asking for more.

Carmel found some old cookbooks and learned to make chutneys, pickles and a particularly good carrageen moss made from the local red-brown seaweed that washed up on their shores. Chicky remembered that back when she was young people *had* made it as a dull milky pudding but Carmel's was a different dish altogether. With eggs and lemon and sugar it was as light as a feather, and she served it with a whipped cream laced with Irish whiskey.

Miss Queenie was very interested in the new baby, and she was the first to hear when Carmel and Rigger came back stunned from the hospital where they had learned that it was not going to be one baby but twins.

Dr Dai Morgan, a Welshman who had been taken on as a locum in Stoneybridge nearly thirty years before, was delighted for them.

'Twice the pleasure and half the effort,' he said to the two youngsters, who were still unable to take it on board.

'How wonderful! A ready-made family all in one go, and they'll be great company for each other.' Miss Queenie clapped her hands.

It was exactly what Rigger and Carmel needed to hear after their own reaction: that one baby was going to be hard enough to manage, two would be impossible.

It was difficult to make Carmel take things more easily. But between them they managed to get her to realise that this was a priority.

And slowly the weeks went by. Carmel had her suitcase packed and ready. Rigger jumped a foot in the air if she even took a deep breath.

It happened in the middle of the night. Rigger kept calm. He phoned Dr Morgan, who said to wake Chicky at once and tell her to get things ready. It sounded too late for the hospital. He would be there in ten minutes, and he was in the door of Stone Cottage before they had time to take in what was happening.

Chicky was there too with towels and a sense of control that calmed them down. The baby girl and boy were born and in Carmel's arms well before dawn.

When Miss Queenie came to breakfast, she found Chicky and Dr Dai having a brandy with their coffee.

'I missed it all,' she said, disappointed.

'You can go over and see them in half an hour. The nurse is there at the moment. They're all fine,' the doctor said.

'Thanks be to the good Lord. Now I think I should have a tiny brandy too, to wet the babies' heads.'

All day they went in and out to see the new babies.

Miss Queenie could see family resemblances already, even though they were only a few hours old. The little boy was the image of Rigger; the girl had Carmel's eyes. She was dying to know what they would call them.

Chicky was about to say that the parents probably needed time but no, they had the names ready. The boy would be Macken after Carmel's father, and the girl would be Rosemary. Or maybe Rosie.

'Where did you get that name?' Chicky asked.

'It's Miss Queenie's name. She was baptised Rosemary,' Rigger said.

Chicky smiled at him through her tears. Imagine, Rigger, the sulky, mutinous boy who had arrived on her doorstep, knowing that and having the kindness to think of honouring the old lady. She felt a wave of sadness that Nuala couldn't share this excitement. It was as if she herself had taken over Nuala's role as a second grandmother for the babies. Nuala should be here, wresting the power from Granny Hickey instead of living in some mad guilty fog in Dublin and working herself to death for nothing.

But it was such a pleasure to look at Miss Queenie. Nobody had ever taken to child-minding like she had.

'Well I *never* thought this would happen!' Miss Queenie would say in wonder. 'You see, our own children didn't materialise and I never had any nieces so there would have been nobody to be called after me, and now there is.'

There was a lot of nose-blowing and clearing of throats and then Miss Queenie asked suddenly, 'Is Nuala just delighted that the babies are here?'

Nuala.

Nobody had actually told her yet.

'If you'd like me to . . . ?' Chicky began.

'No, I'll call her myself,' Rigger said. He went away from the group and dialled his mother's number.

'Oh, Rigger?' She sounded tired, but then she probably *was* tired. Who knew how many cleaning jobs she had taken on these days.

'I thought you'd want to know. The babies are here: a boy and a girl.'

'That's good news. Is Carmel all right?'

'Yes, she's fine. It all happened very quickly and the children are perfect. Perfect. They weighed four and a half pounds each. They're beautiful, Mam.'

'I'm sure they are.' Her voice still flat rather than excited.

'Mam, when I was being born, was it quick or did it take a long time?'

'It took a long time.'

'And were you all on your own in a hospital?'

'Well, there were nurses around and other mothers having babies.'

'But there was nobody of your own with you?'

'No. What does it matter now? It's long ago.'

'It must have been terrible for you.'

There was a silence.

'We are going to call them Rosie and Macken,' he said.

'That will be nice.'

'You *did* say you didn't want us to call her Nuala.'

'Yes I did, Rigger, and I meant it. Stop apologising. Rosie is fine.'

'She's going to run the world, Mam. Her and her brother.'

'Yes, of course.'

And then she was gone.

What kind of woman could care so little about the birth of grandchildren? It wasn't normal. But then, since that night after the episode in Malone's butcher's shop, Mam had not been normal. Had he in fact driven her mad?

Rigger would not allow it to get him down. This was the best day of his life.

It would *not* be ruined.

There was no shortage of people to help with the twins, and the babies grew to feel equally at home in their own house and in the big house. They would sleep in their pram while Chicky and Carmel went through catalogues and fabric samples at the kitchen table. Or if everyone was out, Miss Queenie sat there staring into the two little faces. And occasionally picking Gloria up on to her lap in case the cat felt jealous.

Nasey announced that he was going to get married in Dublin to a really wonderful woman called Irene. He hoped that Rigger and Carmel would come to his wedding.

They discussed it. They didn't want to leave home, and yet they wanted to be there to support Nasey as he had them. They were also dying to see this Irene. They had thought Nasey was well beyond romance. It would be the ideal way for them to meet Nuala on neutral ground.

'She'll be bowled over when she sees the children,' Rigger said.

'We can't take Rosie and Macken.'

'We can't leave them.'

'Yes we can. For one night. Chicky and Miss Queenie will look after them. My mother will. There's a dozen people who will.'

'But I want her to meet them.' Rigger sounded like a six-year-old.

'Yes, when she is ready she'll meet them. She's not ready yet. Anyway, it would be making us centre stage at the wedding with our twin babies. It's Nasey and Irene's day.'

He saw it was sensible but his heart was heavy at the mother who couldn't reach out in such a little way. He knew that Carmel was right. Not this time: it was enough that he would see his mother again. Things must be done in stages.

When Rigger saw his mother, he hardly recognised her. She seemed to have aged greatly. There were lines in her face that he never remembered and she walked with a stoop.

Could all this have happened in such a short time?

Nuala was perfectly polite to Carmel but there was a distance about her that was almost frightening. During the party in the pub, Rigger pulled his cousin Dingo aside.

'Tell me what's wrong with my mam? She's not herself.'

'She's been that way for a good bit,' Dingo said.

'What way? Like only half listening?'

'Sort of not there. Nasey says it was all the shock of . . . Well, whatever it was back then.'

Dingo didn't want to rake up bad memories.

'But she must be over that now,' Rigger cried. 'Things are different now.'

'She felt she made a total bags of raising you. That's what Nasey says. He can't persuade her that it's nonsense.'

'What can I do to tell her?'

'It's got to do with the way she feels inside. You know, like those people who think they're fat and starve themselves to death. They have no image of themselves. She probably needs a shrink,' Dingo said.

'God Almighty, isn't that desperate.' Rigger was appalled.

'Here, I don't want you getting all down about it. It's Nasey and Irene's day. Stick a smile on your face, will you.'

So Rigger stuck a smile on his face and even managed to sing 'The Ballad of Joe Hill', which went down very well.

And when Nasey was making his speech he put an arm

around Rigger and Dingo's shoulders and said that he had the two finest nephews in the western world.

Rigger looked over at his mother. Her face was empty.

Carmel noticed everything and understood most things without having them explained to her. It didn't take her long to get the picture here. She had talked to her mother-in-law about subjects far removed from Rigger and the family. One by one, however, the topics she raised seemed to run into the ground. No use asking about television programmes – Nuala didn't own a television set. She rarely went to the cinema. There wasn't time to read. She admitted that it was harder to get decent jobs because of the recession. Nobody paid you more than the minimum wage. Women didn't give you their clothes like they used to, they sold them online nowadays.

She answered questions as if it was an interview in a Garda station. There was none of the normal to and fro of a conversation. Apart from hoping that all was well back at Stoneybridge, she asked nothing about her grandson and granddaughter.

'Do you take a drink at all, Nuala?' Carmel asked.

'No, no, I never got in the habit of it.'

'Rigger doesn't drink either, which makes him fairly un-usual in our part of the world, but I do love the occasional glass of wine. Can I get you one?'

'If you'd like to, yes,' said Nuala.

Carmel brought two glasses of white wine back to their little table.

'Good luck to the bride and groom,' she said.

'Indeed.' Nuala raised her glass mechanically.

'I'm taking a big risk here but I'm just going to tell you something. I *love* Rigger with all my heart. He is the perfect husband and the perfect father. You won't know this because you haven't seen him in that role. He works all the hours God sends. There is one thing he is not – he is not a son. He is nobody's son. As a father himself now he would love to know something about his own father, but he wouldn't ask you any questions about him, not in a million years. But much more important than anything, he wants his mother back. He wants so much to share this good life he has now with you.'

Nuala looked at her, astonished.

'I haven't gone away,' she said.

'Please, let me finish then I promise that I will never mention this again. He's just not complete. You are the one piece of the jigsaw that's missing. He never thinks that you were a bad mother. Every single thing he says about you is high praise. I would die happy if I thought my son Macken would talk so well of me. You don't *have* to do anything at all, Nuala. You can forget I said any of this. I won't tell him. He wanted to bring the children up to meet you but I asked him not to. I said that one day they would meet their grandmother Nuala, but not until she was ready. You say you feel guilty about letting him run wild. He now feels guilty that he has made you unbalanced and ruined your life.'

'Unbalanced?'

'Well, that's what it is, isn't it? You've got the balance wrong. You need someone to help you to mend the scales. Like as if you had a broken leg. It wouldn't heal without someone to set it.'

'I don't need a doctor.'

'We all need a doctor some time along the way. Why don't you try it? If it's no use then it's no use, but at least you gave it a try.'

Nuala said nothing.

So Carmel decided to finish. 'We will always be ready. And

he needs to be a son again. That's all I wanted to say, really.' She hardly dared to look Nuala in the eye. She had gone too far.

The woman was not well. She lived in a world of her own. All Carmel had done was to annoy her and upset her further.

But she thought that the lined, strained face had changed slightly. Nuala still said nothing but she definitely looked less tense, her hands didn't grip the edge of the table so hard.

Was this fanciful, or was it real?

Carmel knew she had already said more than enough. She would not speak any more. She sat very still for what seemed a very long time but was probably only a minute or two. Around them, the wedding party was singing 'Stand By Your Man'.

Rigger came towards them.

'They'll be going in a few minutes, do you want some confetti to throw?' he asked.

Now Carmel realised that Nuala's face had changed. She was definitely looking at the eager, happy face of her son with different eyes. It was as if she could see that this was not someone she had destroyed but a proud, happy man secure in himself and steady as a rock.

'Sit down for a minute, Rigger, knowing Nasey it will be hours before they get going.'

'Sure.' He was surprised and pleased.

'I was just wondering who was looking after Rosie and Macken tonight?' she asked.

'Chicky and Miss Queenie. They have our mobile number. Chicky rang an hour ago to say they were all asleep except herself – Miss Queenie, the twins, Gloria . . .'

'Gloria?'

'The cat. She's a heavy sleeper.'

'The cat wouldn't sleep in the pram?' Nuala looked anxious.

'No, Gloria's much too lazy to get up to that height. Anyway, they're watched all the time.'

'Good, good.'

'Chicky wanted to know how it was all going,' Rigger said.

'And what did you tell her?' His mother was actually asking a question, looking for information.

'I said it was a great wedding,' Rigger reported.

'Will you be talking to her again tonight?' Nuala wondered.

'Oh, you can be sure we will. This is the first night we've ever left them,' Carmel said.

'Could you say to her that she's to keep a sharp eye on them, and to tell them that I'll be coming to see them myself before too long? I've just got a few medical things to sort out but then I'll be there.'

Rigger struggled for the words. He was determined not to break the mood. This was not a time for hugs and tears.

'And won't they be so pleased to hear that, Mam,' he said. 'So very pleased.'

Just then there was a rush to the door. The bride and groom really *were* leaving.

Carmel looked at Nuala. She wanted to tell her that with those words she had made her son feel complete.

But there was no need. Nuala knew.

Orla

When Orla was ten they got a new teacher in St Anthony's Convent. She was Miss Daly, she had long red hair and she wasn't remotely afraid of the nuns or Father Johnson or the parents, who were demanding that the girls get first-class honours and scholarships to university. She taught them English and history and she made everything interesting. The girls were all mad about her and wanted to be just like her when they grew up.

Miss Daly had a racing bicycle and could be seen flying across cliff roads pedalling madly. They *must* all take exercise, she told them, otherwise they would end up as little wizened old ladies crawling around. If they were fitter they would have more fun. Suddenly the girls of St Anthony's became fitness freaks. Miss Daly had an early-morning dance exercise class and they all turned up eager for new routines.

Miss Daly told them that they were very foolish to resist the computer skills classes, this was the future, this would be their passport out of a dreary life. And even the noisy, troublesome pupils like Orla and her friend Brigid O'Hara listened and thought it made sense. They became part of the fundraising drive to get more computers for the school.

Their parents had mixed feelings about Miss Daly. They were glad, and indeed astounded, that she had such an effect on the children and was able to control them like no other teacher had even begun to do. On the other hand, Miss Daly wore very short shorts on her racing bike; she was almost *too* healthy, with wet hair and a just-out-of-the-sea look in all seasons. She drank pints in the local pubs, which women didn't usually do.

It was reported that one elderly bar owner had hesitated before pulling a pint for her, saying that ladies didn't normally get served in this manner. Miss Daly is meant to have said politely that he would pour the pint or deal with a complaint to the Equality Commission, whichever he preferred, and he poured the pint.

Miss Daly was not seen regularly at Sunday Mass but she put in more hours at that school than any other staff member had ever done. She was there half an hour before lessons began with her dance exercise class, and after the bell went at four o'clock she was there in the computer room helping and encouraging. A generation of girls in St Anthony's became confident with Miss Daly as their role model. She told them there was nothing they couldn't do and they believed her utterly.

When Orla was in her last year, Miss Daly announced that she was leaving St Anthony's, leaving Stoneybridge. She told everyone, including the nuns, that she had met a fabulous young man called Shane from Kerry. He was twenty-one and trying to set up a garden centre. He was quite gorgeous, twelve years younger than her and besotted with her. She thought she'd help Shane put his garden centre on the map.

The nuns were very startled by this and sorry to see her go.

The Reverend Mother made the mistake of hinting that marriage to a much younger man might have its pitfalls. Miss Daly reassured her that marriage was the last thing on her mind and that confidentially marriage was really outdated.

Reverend Mother was shocked, but Miss Daly was unrepentant.

'But didn't you realise that yourself, Reverend Mother? I mean, you were ahead of your time deciding to give the whole thing a miss . . .'

The girls organised a goodbye picnic for Miss Daly – a bonfire on the beach one night. She showed them pictures of Shane, the young man in Kerry and she begged them all to travel and see the world. She told them to read a poem every day and think about it, and whenever they went to a new place, to find out about its history and what had made it the place it had become.

She said they should learn all sorts of things while they were still young, like how to play bridge, how to change a wheel on a car and how to blow-dry their own hair properly. These things weren't hugely important in themselves but they stopped you wasting time and money later on.

She gave them her email address and said she would expect to hear from them about three or four times a year for ever. She expected them to do great things. They cried and begged her not to go, but she told them to look at the picture of Shane again and ask themselves seriously would any sane person let him slip through their fingers.

Orla did write to Miss Daly, and told her about the course in Dublin she had done, how she had won the medal at the end of the year. She told Miss Daly that she found her mother totally unbearable, full of small-town attitudes, and when Orla came back from Dublin it was usually only three days before she and her mother had a blistering row about something totally unimportant like Orla's clothes or the time she came home at night. Her father just begged her not to cause trouble. Anything for an easy life. Her aunt Chicky, who came home from America, was so different; a real free spirit, and Orla was hoping to go out on a holiday with Brigid to New York to see her. Orla always asked about Shane and the garden centre but got no response to that. Miss Daly was only interested in her pupils' lives, not in telling them tales of her own.

Then Orla wrote and said that the whole trip to New York had been cancelled because Uncle Walter had been killed in a horrific crash on a motorway. Miss Daly reminded her that her life was in her own hands. She must make her own decisions.

Why not get a job away from home and come back for short bursts? It was a big world out there; there were even further horizons than just going to Dublin.

So Orla reported that she and Brigid were going to London.

Brigid got a job in a public relations agency which handled publicity for a rugby club, among other clients. They would meet an amazing amount of fellows. Orla got work with a company that organised exhibitions and trade fairs. It was full of variety; at any moment they might be dealing with health foods or vintage cars. James and Simon, the two men who ran the company, were both workaholics and taught Orla to be tough and to work under pressure. After a month there she found herself able to talk firmly and with great authority to people who would normally have terrified her.

To her surprise, both James and Simon found Orla very attractive and each of them made a move on her. She almost laughed in their faces — two more unlikely suitors she could not imagine. Married men who scarcely saw their families and whose main interest was beating their rival companies. All they wanted was some on-the-spot entertainment.

They took the rejection cheerfully. Orla dismissed it all as a childish mistake and went on to learn more and more.

She wrote to her teacher saying that Miss Daly should be proud of her. This job was a whole education in itself, and she was rapidly becoming expert in the world of taxation, websites and networking, as well as setting up exhibitions.

Orla and Brigid shared a flat in Hammersmith. It was all so gloriously free compared to home. And there was *so* much to do. She and Brigid went to tap-dancing classes in Covent Garden on Tuesday nights. Orla also went to a lunchtime calligraphy class every Monday.

James and Simon protested in the beginning about this. She was not fully committed to the job if she insisted on being free to learn fancy handwriting. Orla took no notice of them whatsoever. If she had to earn her living in their busy, dreary, business-obsessed world, she said it was completely necessary that she have some safety valve of a little artistic input to start the week. They didn't dare say a word against it after that.

And at night they went to the theatre or to receptions that Orla organised or to various functions at the exhibition halls. They were young, lively and unimpressed and people loved them. So far, there was nobody special for either of them but neither Brigid nor Orla were in any hurry to settle down.

Until Foxy Farrell turned up.

Foxy was the kind of man they both hated. Loud, confident, big car, big sheepskin jacket, big job in a merchant bank, big opinion of himself. But he was completely besotted with Brigid. And, oddly, Brigid started to find this less hilarious and embarrassing than it had seemed at the start.

'He's basically decent, Orla,' she said defensively.

'I know he is,' Orla spoke without thinking. 'But could you *bear* it? I mean, imagine waking up beside him in the morning.'

'I have,' Brigid said, simply.

'You never have! When?'

'Last weekend, when I was in Harrogate. He drove all the way up to see me.'

'So you made it worth his while.' Orla was still reeling from this news.

'He's very nice, really. That old showing-off thing is just the way they go on in his set.'

'I'm sure he is when you get to know him properly . . .' Orla began the backtracking, which she hoped was not too late.

'Yeah, well, I'm going to get to know him improperly next weekend. We're going to Paris,' Brigid said, with a giggle.

'We're going home to Stoneybridge for the long weekend,' Orla protested.

'I know we were *meant* to. You'll have to cover for me.'

'Couldn't you go to Paris another weekend with Foxy?'

'No, this is special.'

'So I have to cover for you and explain? What *do* I explain, actually?' Orla was annoyed. They went home together dutifully three or four times a year. This was the price they paid for their freedom. Just a long weekend.

'Oh, as little as possible at the moment.' Brigid was airy and casual about it. 'I don't want to be getting their hopes up.'

'Their hopes *up*? About Foxy?' Orla had an unflattering amount of disbelief in her voice.

'Sure,' Brigid said. 'He's absolutely loaded. I'd never hear the end of it if I let Foxy slip through my fingers.'

So Orla went back to Stoneybridge on her own with vague reports of Brigid being tied up at work.

Nothing ever changed much in Stoneybridge except that Orla had always forgotten how beautiful it was and would catch her breath as she walked along the cliff paths and looked at the sandy beaches and dark jagged rock face.

Her aunt Chicky was up to her eyes doing up the Stone House, with old Miss Queenie hovering around and chattering and clapping her hands with pleasure at it all. Rigger, who helped Chicky in the place, had become much less surly. He had learned to drive and would even stop to give Orla a lift if he saw her on the road. He asked her if she remembered his mother, but Orla didn't. She had heard of this Nuala but she had gone to Dublin before Orla was born.

'Chicky would know all about her,' Orla suggested.

'I don't ask Chicky about things,' Rigger said. 'She doesn't ask me about things either, it's good that way.'

Orla took this on board. She was on the point of asking Rigger about himself. This had warned her off in good time.

So instead they talked about the renovations at Stone House, the new walled garden, the plans. He seemed to think it was going to be a huge success and was excited to be in at the start.

Orla's mother, however, had been pouring a lot of cold water on the enterprise. Chicky was always the same, getting carried away by lunatic ideas, like the time she ran off to America without a by-your-leave.

'Well *that* worked out all right, didn't it?' Orla was defensive about the aunt who had always treated her as a grown-up. 'She had a great marriage and he left her enough money to buy Stone House.'

'It's odd he never came back here himself though, isn't it?' Kathleen was never totally at ease with any situation.

'Aw, Mam, will you stop it. Something's always wrong with everything.'

'It mainly is,' Kathleen agreed with her. 'And another thing: there's a lot of talk about Chicky living with just that young lad and the old woman above in the house. It isn't fitting, it's just not the way things should be.'

'*Mam!*' Orla was pealing with laughter, 'what a fantastic world you live in. Do you think Rigger is pleasuring Aunty Chicky in the walled garden? Maybe they have a threesome going with Miss Queenie as well!'

Her mother's face flushed dark red with annoyance. 'Don't be so crude Orla, please. I'm only saying what's being said all around the place, that's all.'

'Who's saying that all round the place?'

'The O'Haras, for one.'

'That's only because they're furious that Miss Sheedy didn't sell it to *them*.'

'You're as bad as your uncle Brian – always attacking them! Isn't Brigid your own best friend?'

'She is, but that's her uncles being greedy speculators. She knows that too.'

'Where *is* she, by the way, that she couldn't be bothered to come home to her family?'

'She's working hard for a living, Mam. As am I, which is why *you* are so much luckier than the O'Haras because I put you first always, don't I?'

And her mother really had no answer to that.

Orla spent as much time as she could with Chicky. Despite all the activity and people coming and going in Stone House, Chicky was very calm. She never asked whether Orla had boyfriends in London, and if she intended to live there permanently. She never said that people would think it odd if Orla wore short skirts or long skirts or torn jeans or whatever she was wearing at the time. Chicky wasn't even remotely aware what people were saying or thinking or wondering. Chicky never told her what she really should be doing with her life.

So it was surprising when this time Chicky asked her was she a good cook.

'Reasonable, I suppose. Brigid and I cook from recipes two or three times a week. She does great things with fish. It's different over there, not full of bones and tasting like cod liver oil like it does here.'

Chicky laughed. 'Not any more, it doesn't. Do you make pastry?'

'No, it's too hard, too much trouble.'

'I could teach you to be a great cook,' Chicky offered.

'Are *you* a great cook, Chicky?'

'I am, as it happens. It was the last thing I ever expected to be, but I do enjoy it.'

'Did Uncle Walter cook also?'

'No, he mainly left it to me. He was always so busy, you see.'

'I know.' Orla didn't know but she could recognise when Chicky was closing down a conversation. 'Why would you teach me to cook?' she asked.

'In the hope that one day, not now, but one day, you might come back home here and help me run this place.'

'I don't think I could ever come back to Stoneybridge,' Orla said.

'I know.' Chicky seemed to think that was reasonable. 'I never wanted to come back either but here I am.' That day she showed Orla how to make a really easy brown bread and a parsnip and apple soup. It seemed completely effortless and they had it for their lunch. Miss Queenie said that she had never eaten such lovely food in her life until Chicky had come to the place.

'Imagine, Orla, we grew those parsnips here in our own garden and the apples are from the old orchard, and Chicky made them all taste like that!'

'I know, isn't she a genius!' Orla said with a smile.

'She is indeed. Weren't we lucky that she came back to us and didn't stay over there in the United States? And tell me, are you having a wonderful time over in London?'

'Not bad at all, Miss Queenie, busy of course and tiring, but great.'

'I wish I had travelled more,' Miss Queenie said. 'But even if I had, I think I would always have come back here.'

'What do you like particularly about here, Miss Queenie?'

'The sea, the peace, the memories. It all seems so right here, somehow. We went to Paris once, and to Oxford. Very, very beautiful, both places. Jessica and Beatrice and I often talked about it afterwards. It was great but it wasn't real, if you know what I mean. It was as if we were acting a part in a play. Here you don't do that.'

'Oh, I know what you mean, Miss Queenie.' She saw Chicky flash her a grateful look. Orla had no idea what poor Miss Queenie had meant but she was glad she had given the right response.

Back in London, she made brown bread and parsnip soup to welcome Brigid back from Paris.

'God, you've become domesticated,' Brigid said.

'And you've got something to tell me,' Orla said.

84

'I'm going to marry him,' Brigid said.

'Fantastic! When?'

'In the summer. Only, of course, if you'll be my brides-maid.'

'Only, of course, if I don't have to wear plum taffeta or lime-green chiffon.'

'Are you pleased for me?'

'Come on, will you look at yourself, you are *so* happy. I'm thrilled for you.' Orla hoped she was putting enough enthusiasm in her voice.

'You don't think he's just foolish old Foxy?'

'What do you *mean*? Of course I don't think that. I think he's lucky Foxy. Tell me where and when did he propose?'

'I *do* love him, you know,' said Brigid.

'I know you do,' Orla lied, looking into the face of her friend Brigid who, for some reason that would never be explained, was going to settle for Foxy Farrell.

Things moved swiftly after that.

Brigid left her job and spent a lot of time with Foxy's family in Berkshire. The wedding would be in Stoneybridge.

'What a pity that Chicky's place won't be up and running in time. It would be great if the Farrells could take it over for the wedding. They'll be appalled by Stoneybridge,' Brigid said.

'I was half thinking of going back there,' Orla said, suddenly.

'You're never serious?' Brigid was shocked. 'Look at how hard it was to get out of there in the first place.'

'I don't know . . . it's only a thought.'

'Well, banish that thought.' Brigid was very definite. 'You'd only be back twenty minutes before you were on all fours trying to get out of it again. And where would you work, for God's sake? The knitting factory?'

'No, I might go in with Chicky.'

'But that place is doomed, I tell you. It won't last for two seasons. Then she'll have to sell it and lose a packet. Everyone knows that.'

'Chicky doesn't know that. I don't know that. It's only your uncles who say that because they wanted to buy it themselves.'

'I'm not going to fight with my bridesmaid,' Brigid said.

'Swear you aren't thinking of mauve taffeta,' Orla begged, and they were fine again. Apart from Orla's disbelief that anyone could want to marry Foxy Farrell.

As she often did at times of change, Orla wrote to Miss Daly for advice.

'Am I going mad, sort of wanting to go back to Stoneybridge? Is it just a knee-jerk reaction to Brigid deciding to marry this eejit? Were you bored rigid when you were there?'

Miss Daly wrote back.

I loved the work. You were great kids in that school. I adored the place. I still look back on it with pleasure. I'm in the mountains here. It's lovely, and I can drive to the sea but it's not the same as Stoneybridge, where the sea was there at your feet. Why don't you try it out for a year? Tell your aunt that you don't want to sign up for life. Thank you for not asking about Shane. He's having a little time out with something marginally more interesting than me, but he'll be back. And I'll take him back. It's a funny old world. Once you realise that, you're halfway there.

In Orla's office, James and Simon were very tight-lipped these days. Business was not good. The economy was sluggish, it didn't matter what politicians said. They knew. People weren't booking stands at exhibitions like they used to. Trade fairs were smaller than last year. The prospects were dire. They were placing all their hopes on Marty Green, who was very big in the conference business. They were having drinks in the office to impress him.

'Ask that sexy redhead friend of yours to come and help us dress the set,' James suggested.

'Brigid's just got engaged. She won't want to be a party-party girl these days.'

'Well, tell her to bring her fiancé. Is he presentable and everything?'

'You're worse than my mother and her mother put together. Very presentable, richer than God,' Orla said.

Brigid and Foxy thought it would be a laugh and turned up in high good form. Marty Green was delighted with them all and seemed to be taking the sales pitch on board. He was also very interested in Orla, who had dressed to kill in a scarlet silk dress she had found in a charity shop and really expensive red and black shiny high heels. She passed around the white wine and the tray of canapés.

'These are very good,' Marty Green said appreciatively, 'who's your caterer?'

'Oh, I did these myself,' Orla smiled at him.

'Really? Not just a pretty face, then?' He was definitely impressed, which was what this reception was all about. But Orla felt he was rather too impressed with her and not enough with the company.

'That's very nice of you, Mr Green, but I wasn't hired here to make canapés and smile. We all work very hard, and as James and Simon were saying, this has paid off. We know the market and the situation very well. It's good to get a chance to tell you about it personally.'

'And very pleasant it is to hear about it personally.' His eyes never left her face.

Orla moved away but knew he was watching her all the time. Even when James was giving statistics, when Simon was talking about trends, when Foxy was braying about great new restaurants and Brigid was asking if Mr Green was interested in rugby, as she could get him tickets.

Marty Green wondered if Orla would like to have dinner with him.

She saw James and Simon smiling at each other in relief and suddenly felt hugely resentful. She was being offered to Marty Green. It was as simple as that. She had dressed up, spent her lunchtime making finicky, awkward little savouries, rolling asparagus spears in pastry and serving them with a dipping sauce, arranging little quails' eggs artistically with celery salt on lettuce leaves, and now they wanted to send her out like a sacrificial lamb to be pawed by Marty Green.

'Thank you so much but sadly I have plans of my own tonight, Mr Green,' she said.

He was suave; she would give him that much. 'I'm sure you must indeed have plans. Another time, perhaps?'

And they all smiled different smiles: Orla's was nailed to her face, James and Simon's were like a horror mask. Brigid's smile hid her shock that Orla would pass up on a date with such a wealthy and charming man as Marty Green. Foxy's smile was vague and foolish, as always.

Marty Green left saying that he would be in touch. Orla poured herself a large drink.

'Why did you have to be so very rude to him?' Simon asked.

'I wasn't at all rude. I thanked him and told him that I had my own plans.'

'That's what I mean. You don't *have* any plans.'

'Oh, yes I do. I plan *not* to go out with some businessman as if I were an escort or a hooker.'

'Come on now, that wasn't remotely what was suggested,' James said.

'It was spelled out in capital letters.' Orla was furious now. 'Take the nice man out, bill and coo at him, get his name on a contract.'

'We are all in this together. We assumed that—'

'Why didn't you bring a pole in here and put it up in the office and I could have taken off my clothes and danced around it? That would have helped too, wouldn't it?'

'It was only dinner,' Simon said.

'Yes, and at the end of an expensive dinner I'd be able to get up and say goodbye and thank you Mr Green? What world do you live in? If I'd gone out to a meal with him and then not gone back to his hotel, I would have been a tease. I would have led him on. He'd have been more annoyed still. This way we all save face. Well, most of us do.'

'Hey, Orla, you're being a bit heavy about this,' Foxy said.

Brigid glared at him but he didn't see.

'I mean, that's what tonight was all about.'

'You never said a truer word, Foxy,' Orla said.

Next day James and Simon were prepared to be generous. They had discussed it, they *could* have given the wrong impression. The last thing they wanted to do was . . . well, what Orla had suggested they were doing.

Orla listened politely until they had finished. Then she spoke very carefully.

'This isn't just a hissy fit. I've been thinking of leaving for quite a while. My aunt is setting up a hotel in the West of Ireland. I just needed something to focus my mind, and this is it. *Please* don't take this as a sulk or as part of a campaign to make you grovel. It's far from that. It's just a month's notice, with great gratitude for all I've learned here.'

Nothing they said made any difference. Eventually they had to agree to let her go.

Orla had told Chicky it would only be for a year, just to get the place up and running.

'Maybe it's hardly worth your while teaching me to cook like a dream.'

'It's always worthwhile teaching people to cook.'

'You might run a cookery school for real people,' Orla suggested.

'The main thing we have to offer here is the scenery. They could learn to cook anywhere,' Chicky said. 'Anyway, we should keep the magic to ourselves.'

'How will I manage not to take an axe to my mother when I get back?' Orla wondered.

'Don't live at home,' Chicky advised.

'Can I live with you?'

'No. That would cause bad feeling. We'll find you somewhere to live. Rigger will do it up. Your own little place. Leave it to me. When will you be arriving?'

'Any time now. They don't need me to work my notice out. They're only going to hire someone part-time to replace me, anyway. Am I stone mad to be doing this, Chicky?'

'As you said, it's only a year. You won't notice it slipping by.'

*

By the time she arrived, Rigger was busy doing up an old cottage beside the walled garden for himself and Carmel Hickey. He said that there was an old gardener's cottage and the roof was sound, so it hadn't ever got damp. It hadn't taken much more than a good clean-out to make it habitable.

Orla's new home was ready for her.

'I hope you're not going to have the morals of Miss Daly and be the talk of the town,' Orla's mother said on her first night home.

'Oh, Mam, I do hope not,' Orla agreed fervently. She could see Chicky hiding a smile.

'Your father and I don't know what you have to go and get yourself an old, damp cottage like that for anyway. You've a perfectly good home here. People will think it's very strange.'

'You know, Mam, they won't. They won't even notice,' Orla spoke automatically.

How very wise Miss Daly and Chicky had been about being independent. Now she hoped her instinct about coming back had been right and not a foolish notion.

There was little time to wonder about it. They were plunged into work straight away. Orla began to look back on the busy days in the office with James and Simon as if it had been one long holiday. She had not believed it possible that there would be so much to organise.

Chicky's financial system left a lot to be desired. It was honest and thorough and the books were kept . . . in a fashion. But it was not computerised. Chicky had never used accounting software and instead worked on a system of ledgers and cardboard files. It was like something from fifty years ago. So the first thing Orla did was to choose a room as an office. Somewhere she and Chicky could store the computer, printer and all the reference books, drawings and filing cabinets they needed.

Chicky suggested one of the several large pantries that opened off the kitchen. Orla managed to get Rigger to leave aside a few hours from doing up his own house to impress Carmel Hickey's family in order to get the office shelved and painted.

'It'll be worth it in the end,' she insisted. 'Then we will be out of everyone's hair instead of spreading everything over the kitchen table and gathering it all up again.' She found them a computer and set up the programs she needed. Then she insisted Chicky come in and learn it from the start.

'No, no, that's your department,' Chicky protested.

'Excuse *me*. I spent two hours last night learning how to make choux pastry. I didn't say it was *your* department. Today you're going to learn to deal with the bookkeeping software. It should take forty-five minutes if you concentrate.'

Chicky concentrated.

'That wasn't too bad,' Orla approved. 'So tomorrow we'll set up a bookings system, and then the next day you'll learn how to buy and sell.'

'Are you sure that we need me to . . .' Chicky was fearful at spending too much time in the office instead of out dealing with the daily problems.

'Totally sure. Suppose you wanted to buy a piece of kitchen equipment? This will save you all the time making phone calls and going shopping.'

'I suppose,' Chicky agreed, doubtfully.

But she did agree that it was great to have everything at their fingertips, and when Orla would give her a little test like asking her how would she find someone who had made a reservation for next month and wanted to extend by another week, Chicky was soon able to summon up the bookings system on the screen. And at the same time, Orla learned how to make sauces that complemented meat dishes and ways of cleaning, filleting and serving fish straight from the sea in a way that an experienced fishmonger would envy.

One by one they beat down the obstacles.

There was the pathetic attempt of the O'Hara uncles to oppose planning permission. Chicky managed to sort it without falling out with anyone, a miracle in itself. They coped with the environmentalists' lobby, who worried lest the new hotel would disturb the habitat of birds and other wildlife. Tea and scones were served to the concerned enquirers before they were taken on walks to show how nature was being protected in every way.

They all left satisfied.

The builders were encouraged in their efforts by the thought of a home-cooked meal every day; Chicky put it on the kitchen table at one o'clock and had everyone back to work at one-thirty. Most of the men, used to bringing their own sandwiches, regarded this big lunch as the high spot of the day. They went home and told their wives that the Irish stew or bacon and cabbage was very different over at Mrs Starr's place than it was at home, and it caused a lot of resentment.

The landscaping was beginning to show results, and old Miss Queenie said the house looked like it had when she was a girl – before the money had got so short.

And away from Stone House, they could see Stone Cottage taking shape. They all enjoyed furnishing it for Rigger. Orla knew he was very nervous about dealing with the Hickeys when the plan was announced but she learned from Chicky that these things were just not discussed.

It was all so different from living with Brigid, where everything was talked about and analysed down to the bone. That was, of course, the old days. Brigid wasn't the same any more. She was obsessed by this wedding, by guest lists and wedding lists and seating plans, and she expected Orla to be some kind of wedding planner since she was on the spot in Stoneybridge.

Could Orla check the church and see what kind of bouquets they could hang on the end of each pew near the aisle? In vain did Orla say that nobody had ever seen these in Stoneybridge. Brigid was in 'Mad Bride' mode and could not be stopped.

In despair, Orla asked Chicky's advice; Chicky gave it some thought.

'Tell her that her own family want to be involved and that *they* should be doing all this sort of thing.'

'But she doesn't trust them, she thinks they're country hicks.'

'She's probably quite right, but stress that her family are very hostile to anything to do with Stone House and that it would be awkward if you were involved. That will get you out of it.'

'You're wasted here. You should be in the United Nations,' Orla said, admiringly.

Brigid visited twice before the wedding, stressed and anxious.

'Can I stay in your cottage?' she begged Orla. 'My mother will be the deceased mother of the bride if I stay at home.'

Orla was reluctant to have Brigid in the house. It would indeed cause bad feeling with her family, and also it would mean that Orla would get sucked into the lunatic preparations.

'I can't have you, Brigid. Miss Daly is coming to stay.'

'Miss *Daly*? *Our* Miss Daly? From school?'

'Yes, it's all arranged.'

'Lord, you've been behaving very oddly since you got back to Stoneybridge.'

'I know. It's all that sea air.'

'Since when were you such pals with Miss Daly?'

'I always have been.'

'I think that working with Miss Queenie is bad for you, Orla. You've become a total eccentric.'

'But not quite mad enough to wear canary yellow. Have you decided the colour of my bridesmaid's dress yet?'

'Oh, wear what you like. You will anyway.'

'Good. I have the very thing: dark gold with some cream lace. Restrained but smart.'

'Is it long?'

'Yes, of course it is.'

'Well, where is it? Will we go to see it when I'm over there?'

'I have it.'

'You bought it *already*?' Brigid was outraged.

'I don't have to wear it at the wedding. Just have a look at it.'

'But what will you do with it if it's not suitable? Can you give it back?'

'It will always come in useful.'

'Useful? Washing pots in a guest house? God Almighty, Orla, what's to become of you?'

'God knows,' Orla agreed.

Her main focus was to get Brigid to see the dress without knowing that it had belonged to Miss Queenie. Sixty years ago Miss Queenie had worn it to a hunt ball where she had been a great success. It fitted Orla as if it had been designed especially for her.

*

Miss Daly looked exactly the same as she had always looked. She had brought two suitcases and her bicycle.

'You're very good to come at such short notice.' Orla was grateful that her teacher had responded to the emergency call.

'It suited me very well. Shane's passing fancy turned out to be more permanent than we had thought.'

'I'm sorry,' Orla said.

'I'm not, really. It had run its course. I needed a short sharp shock.'

'And you got one?'

'Yes, a very pregnant eighteen-year-old, and the whole we-are-delighted-about-the-baby routine. It was just the right time to have a few days out to reconsider.'

'Is that what you're going to do while you're here?'

'Yes, it's a good place to think. Out by that ocean you feel smaller, less important somehow, it puts things into proportion.'

'Wish it would work for Brigid,' Orla sighed.

'You feel you've lost her, don't you?' Miss Daly was sympathetic.

'Yes, to be honest. We've been best pals since we were ten. It's all as if it were some kind of phase. You know, like when she and I were into tap-dancing for a bit and we wore leotards and did shuffle-hop-step, tap-ball-change, over and over. But this is for life. And with Foxy!'

'Maybe she loves him.'

'No. If she loved him she wouldn't be going insane trying to impress his family.'

'Or she could just need security.'

'Brigid? She's *so* well able to look after herself.'

'And have you ever loved anyone, Orla?'

'No, not *loved*. Fancied, yes.'

'Well at least you know the difference, which is more than some of us. Let me give you a hand planting some stuff that will survive up in Stone House. Half those things you put in will die in the winter.'

Miss Daly cycled around and had a pint in several of the local pubs to mark her territory. And when Brigid came home, she asked all the questions that Orla didn't dare to. Like what would Brigid *do* all day after the honeymoon if she wasn't going to work? Did they plan a family immediately? Would she be seeing a lot of the Farrell in-laws?

The answers were deeply unsatisfactory and seemed to centre around going to a lot of race meetings and popping down to Foxy's sister's place in Spain. But there were some small mercies. Brigid just loved Miss Queenie's dress, describing it with approval as *vintage*. Foxy's sister was going to be wearing a vintage dress also. It would be very suitable.

The wedding was just as awful as Orla had feared. It was totally over the top, with a giant marquee and conspicuous wealth on display everywhere.

The O'Haras had pushed the boat out and even done up a few of the townhouses which they had bought during the property boom but had been standing idle since the recession. They had been given a quick paint job and refurbished for the Farrell family to stay in, which met with much approval.

Foxy's best man, Conor, another clown who had left behind his Irish roots with his Irish accent, made a speech of profound vulgarity where he said that one of the perks of being best man was that you got to shag the bridesmaid, and that this wouldn't be too great an ordeal tonight. Foxy laughed uproariously. Orla stared ahead stonily and tried not to meet Chicky's eye.

Chicky whispered to her brother Brian that he was well out of that lot. But Brian, who still smarted at his rejection by the O'Hara family, had lingering regrets about Sheila O'Hara – now separated from her gambling husband – who had once been thought to be such a good catch.

After the bride and groom had left for Shannon airport, Conor approached Orla.

'I hear you have your own place,' he said.

'Don't you have a wonderful way about you,' she said admiringly, 'I bet all the girls love you.'

'We're not talking about all the girls, we're talking about you, tonight. How about it?' he said, taking her remarks at face value.

Orla looked at him, astounded. He hadn't realised she was sending him up. If Conor and Foxy were bankers, it was no wonder the Western economy was in the state it was.

'If I were to die wondering what sex was about I wouldn't go within an ass's roar of you, Conor,' she said, smiling at him pleasantly.

'Lesbian,' he spat at her.

'That must be it all right.' Orla was cheerful.

'OK, be a ball-breaker then. I was only asking because it was expected.'

'Of course you were, Conor.' Orla's voice was soothing.

Miss Daly had been on a great trek across the mountains to avoid going to the wedding. She had met two French dentists who were on holiday there. They were heading up to Donegal tomorrow. Miss Daly was going to go with them. They had a car with a roof rack – perfect for her bicycle.

Orla sat and gaped at her.

'I know, Orla, the world is divided into people like me and people like Brigid. Aren't you lucky to walk a middle road.'

She had little time to think about it. Rigger's wedding was upcoming. This was going to be a much more normal affair.

Chicky was going to serve roast lamb in Stone Cottage, and they made a magnificent cake for Rigger and Carmel. Compared to the nonsense in the marquee and the posturing of the Farrell and O'Hara factions, this was very relaxed and full of charm.

Chicky, Orla and Miss Queenie sat and congratulated each other when it was over and the Hickeys had gone home happy.

The major building work was almost completed now on Stone House; there only remained the design and decor to be agreed. Chicky still wanted to hire professionals, and Orla insisted that nobody be paid any money until they proved they could do the job. Orla thought Chicky would be well able to do it herself. She had the original source material, after all. Miss Queenie could tell them what the place looked like in the old days.

Chicky understood comfort and style, yet she was hesitant and holding back about her own ideas.

'We are charging serious money for people to come and stay here. We don't want to have them saying that the place is phoney or tatty or anything.'

'I met a lot of these designers in London,' Orla said. 'Some of them were brilliant, I agree, but a lot of them were cowboys. Real emperor's new clothes. You'd want to watch them like a hawk.'

They settled on a couple called Howard and Barbara. They came well recommended by Brigid, who had met them with Foxy Farrell at a party in Dublin.

Orla hated them on sight. They were in their early forties, with affected accents and made lots of use of the words 'darling' and 'so', usually when dismissing something.

'Darling, you mustn't even *think* about having that grandfather clock in the hall. It will be *so* disturbing and unsettling for sleep rhythms.'

'There was always a grandfather clock in the hall,' poor Miss Queenie said, mildly.

'Hallo, we *are* talking about making this place acceptable, aren't we? That's what we're here for, darling.'

They gave Howard and Barbara one of the best bedrooms with the big windows and balcony looking out to sea. They sniffed as they looked around the room. They exchanged glances as they came downstairs. They shuddered slightly at things they didn't like, like the stone floor in the kitchen. It should be ripped out and replaced by a very good solid-wood floor. Orla said that the stone floor was authentic and had been there since the house was built in the 1820s.

'I rest my case,' said Howard. 'It's time for it to go.' But Orla won that battle. The stone floor was not negotiable.

Barbara and Howard didn't want the morning room called the Miss Sheedy Room. They said it was rather *twee*, and, darling, if there was one thing that could let a place down it was to have an element of tweeness about it. They left their own room in a great mess, with wet towels thrown on the bathroom floor and an amazing amount of dirty coffee cups, glasses and ashtrays despite the no-smoking policy that had been mentioned several times.

They didn't rate the walled garden, saying it was very amateur; the guests would be used to much bigger and more manicured landscaping. They frowned darkly at Gloria and said it was unhygienic to have a cat anywhere near food. In vain did Miss Queenie, Chicky and Orla try to convince them that Gloria was a cat with impeccable manners who would never approach a dining table when a meal was in progress. Admittedly, Gloria did mistake Howard's leg for a scratching post and, when alarmed by his screeching, tried to climb up inside his trouser leg. Barbara shouted and waved her arms at the poor cat who ran behind the sofa and hid, trembling, until rescued by Miss Queenie. By now, Orla was not the only one who hated Howard and Barbara.

Defeated by the pro-Gloria lobby, they turned their hostility towards the fact that Carmel was so obviously pregnant. They hoped that she would be kept well out of the equation when the baby was born. The last thing guests wanted, darling, was the sound of a screeching infant. It would be *so* full of bad vibes.

They never praised the delicious food that Chicky and Orla served them; instead they suggested that Stone House should have a proper wine cellar, and asked for large brandies after dinner.

Orla became very firm. After breakfast on the second day, she said that she hoped they were ready to give practical advice about the decor, materials and colours that they would suggest, together with recommendations on where they should source everything.

Barbara and Howard were slightly startled by this. They had envisaged several days soaking up the feel of the place, they said. This is what Orla had suspected. She brought a coffee percolator into the office after breakfast and sat down expectantly beside the computer.

'It's a very late Georgian house, of course,' Orla said confidently. 'I've been online to research images of this kind of house at the time, and printed some of them out for discussion. I was wondering what references *you* were going to offer us so we could compare.'

They looked at her, alarmed. 'Well, of course we all know the classic Georgian great houses . . .' Barbara began. Orla could spot somebody blustering at twenty miles distance.

'Yes, but of course this isn't a great house. It's a small gentleman's residence and almost Victorian, really, rather than what was distinctively Georgian. We wondered what colour schemes you had come up with.'

'It all depends very much on where we are coming from, darling, doesn't it? It's *so* like saying how long is a piece of string. Just asking for colours,' Howard began sonorously.

'And where do you think we should source fabrics?' Orla was shuffling a heap of further printouts. She saw Howard and Barbara exchanging glances.

Chicky joined in.

'We have our own ideas, of course, but we were anxious to have real professionals to guide us. You will have so much more experience and so many more contacts than we do.'

'I didn't realise you were so computer-savvy,' Barbara said to Orla, coldly.

'You're talking about my generation,' Orla smiled. 'I was wondering, by the way, why you don't have a website.'

'Never needed one,' Barbara said smugly.

'So how do people find you, then?' Orla's look was innocent.

'Personal recommendation.'

'Yes, that's how they find your *names*, but how do they know what you've actually *done*?'

Again, the face was innocent but the challenge was there.

By the time the meeting was over, it was clear that the parting of the ways had come.

Barbara mentioned a payment for their time and input so far. Chicky and Orla looked at each other, bewildered. Howard suggested they part as friends, no harm had been done. They wished the enterprise success. They spoke in tones of regret and disbelief that Stone House would remain open for longer than a week, *if* it ever opened at all.

Rigger drove them to the station.

He reported afterwards that they sat in complete silence for the journey. When he asked would they be coming back to supervise the decorating, they had said that it wasn't on the cards.

'Well, I hope you enjoyed your visit,' Rigger had said.

'Enjoy would be *so* too strong a word, darling,' they had said as he lifted their luggage on to the train.

Chicky, Carmel and Orla chose their colours and fabrics that night and got the show on the road the next day. It had been a lesson to them. There might well have been superb designers out there, but they had not found them. There was no time to try again. They would have to trust themselves.

Little by little the place took shape.

Their website was up and running, with pictures of the views from Stone House as well as full descriptions of what they could offer. They got many enquiries but as yet no definite bookings.

Orla set up a press release which she sent to every newspaper, magazine and radio programme. She offered a Winter Week at Stone House as a prize in several competitions, on the grounds that it would bring them publicity. She bought a big scrapbook and asked Miss Queenie to keep any cuttings that might result. She contacted airports and tourist offices, book clubs, birdwatching groups and sporting clubs; she set up a Facebook page and a Twitter account.

Chicky loved being able to access such a world from their little office in Stone House. They had perfected their menus and posted them online; now they had their daily routine, with the suppliers and deliveries worked out and timed to run smoothly. Gradually the definite bookings came in, and they were within sight of receiving their first visitors when Carmel gave birth to twins.

Miss Queenie told Orla that she had never been happier. There was so much happening in Stone House these days, and she was here at the centre of it all. The morning room was now officially called the Miss Sheedy Room. There were restored photographs from their childhood showing Beatrice and Jessica and Miss Queenie as girls. She knew everybody in Stoneybridge nowadays instead of only a very few. She had delicious meals and a warm house. Who could have guessed that life would get so much better as she grew older?

'I worry about Chicky, though, she works so hard,' Miss Queenie confided in Orla, shaking her head. 'She's still a young woman, well, to me she is, anyway. She gets a lot of admiring glances but she never thinks of looking at anyone as a possible husband.'

'And what about *me*, Miss Queenie? Don't you worry about me too?'

'No, Orla, not even a little bit. You will work here with Chicky as you promised until your year is up then you'll go off and conquer the world. It's written all over you.'

Instead of being pleased with such a vote of confidence, Orla suddenly felt lonely. She didn't *want* to go off and conquer the world. She wanted to stay here and see it through.

'I'm in no hurry to go off from here, Miss Queenie,' Orla heard herself say.

'It's dangerous to stay too long in Stoneybridge. We can't marry the seagulls or the gannets, you know,' Miss Queenie said.

'But didn't you say yourself that you were never happier than you are now?'

'I made the best of things, and I was lucky. Very lucky,' Miss Queenie said.

Next morning when Orla brought the old lady her tea, she knew from one glance at the bed that Miss Queenie had died in her sleep. Her hands were folded. Her face was calm. She looked twenty years younger, as if her arthritis and aches had gone away.

Orla had never seen anyone dead before. It wasn't very frightening.

She carried the cup of tea to Chicky's room.

Chicky was already awake. When she saw Orla she knew at once what had happened.

'There *can't* be a God. He wouldn't let Queenie die before the place opened. It's so unfair,' Chicky wept.

'You know, in a way it might be for the best,' Orla said.

'What *can* you mean, Orla? She was dying to be part of it.'

'No. She was nervous. She asked me more than once whether she would sit down to dinner with the guests or not.'

'But of course she would have.'

'She was afraid she might be too old and feathery . . . Her words, not mine.'

'How can you be so calm? Poor Queenie. Poor, dear Queenie. She had no life.'

Orla stretched out her hand. 'Come in and see her, Chicky.

Just look at her face. You'll know she had a life, and you gave it to her.'

They walked into the room where Miss Queenie had slept for over eighty years. From back in the 1930s when Ireland was only ten years old as a state.

Gloria the cat came in too. She didn't get up on the bed but looked respectfully from the door as if she knew that all was not well. They stood and looked at Miss Queenie's face. Chicky leaned over and touched Miss Queenie's cold hand.

'We'll make you proud, Queenie,' she said, and they closed the door behind them and went to tell Rigger and Carmel and to call Dr Dai.

Stoneybridge said a big goodbye to Miss Queenie Sheedy. A great crowd gathered outside Stone House to walk behind the hearse as it drove her slowly to the church.

Father Johnson said that next Sunday would be the first time there would not be a Sheedy in this church for many decades. He said that Miss Sheedy had called in to him last week and asked if they could sing 'Lord of the Dance' at her funeral, whenever that was to be. Father Johnson had said that we would all have long gone to our heavenly reward by the time Miss Queenie herself was ready to go, but the Lord was mysterious and now she had gone to join her beloved sisters, leaving behind her a memory of a life well lived.

The congregation all sang 'Lord of the Dance'. They blew their noses and wiped away a tear at the thought of Miss Queenie peering good-naturedly at them and their children for years, back as far as they could remember.

Rigger was one of the four who carried the small coffin to the graveyard. His face was grim as he remembered how the old lady had welcomed him to her home and been so excited about everything, from the walled garden to Stone Cottage to the drives around in his van and then the arrival of the twins.

He was sorry that Rosie and Macken would not have such a lovely old granny figure in their lives. They would tell them all about her. One day, when he was being carried to this grave-yard they would tell their own children about the great Miss Queenie, a good relic of an often stormy past in Ireland.

There were no Sheedy relatives, and Rigger was asked to put the first spadeful of clay on the grave. He was followed by Chicky and Orla. And the great crowd stood in silence until Dr Dai, who had a powerful Welsh baritone, suddenly sang 'Abide With Me' and they all filed back down the hill.

Tea and sandwiches were served in Stone House.

Gloria had hunted high and low for Miss Queenie and sat confused outside the front door, washing furiously.

As soon as Orla was busy passing the food around she recovered enough to realise how many people had attended. Brigid and Foxy had come over from London. Miss Daly had heard from somebody and she turned up with one of the French dentists who had now become a close friend. All the O'Haras were there, their previous animosity forgotten; all the builders, the suppliers, the local farmers, the staff of the knitting factory and Aidan, a solicitor from a nearby town, who was said to fancy Chicky.

Miss Queenie would have clapped her hands and said, 'Imagine them all turning up for me! How very kind!'

Aidan drew Orla aside to tell her that Miss Queenie had made her will last week. She had left everything she owned to Chicky apart from two tiny legacies, one to Rigger and one to Orla.

He also asked Orla whether she thought Chicky might go out with him to dinner if he asked her nicely.

Orla said that maybe he should wait until Stone House had opened to the public. Chicky was very centred on that at the moment, but she reassured Aidan that there was nobody else on the scene.

'I'd be no trouble,' he told her.

'God, isn't that a great recommendation,' Orla said, fervently looking at some uncles and the woeful Foxy.

'Must say, Barbara and Howard did a great job on this place,' Foxy said approvingly.

'Didn't they just?' Chicky agreed.

Rigger was about to open his mouth and say how unhelpful they had been but Orla frowned. Life was short. Chicky had decided to play it this way. Let it go.

Only a few days to go and the first guests would arrive. They were nearly full. Only one room remained unoccupied. Orla and Chicky sat down every evening going over the list of people. They were coming from Sweden, England and Dublin. Some by car, some by train. Rigger had been alerted to everyone's arrival times.

They went over the menus again and again checking that they had every ingredient. They tried to envisage all these people sitting around their table at night and assembling for breakfast each morning. They had left a selection of magazines and novels in the Miss Sheedy Room; they had maps and bird books and guide books at the ready. Wellington boots, umbrellas and mackintoshes were all available in the boot room.

Gloria had gradually got over her short period of mourning for Miss Queenie and returned to sit by the fire with a purr that would soothe the most troubled heart.

'You have your running-away money now, Orla,' Chicky said on the last evening.

'I *always* had my running-away money,' Orla said.

'It's just that I won't hold you back. You've delivered everything you promised and more.'

'Why is everyone trying to get rid of me?' Orla asked. 'Queenie was the same. The night before she died she said I couldn't marry the seagulls and the gannets in Stoneybridge.'

'And she was right,' Chicky agreed.

'But what about *you*? Aidan was asking after you.'

'Oh, give over, Orla!'

'I bet Walter would have liked you to marry again.'

'Yes, indeed.'

'So?'

'So what? Grab Dr Dai from his wife? Take Father Johnson out of the priesthood? Go online offering "rich widow with own business"?' Chicky laughed. 'It's *you* we are talking about. You've only one life, Orla.'

'So what's wrong with living it here for a while?' Orla asked. 'It would be more than a human could bear to go before we had the first year of running the place over us.'

Chicky sank back in her chair. Gloria stretched approvingly.

The grandfather clock in the hall struck midnight.

This was the day that Stone House would open its doors to the public. They wouldn't sit alone in this kitchen for many a night to come.

They raised their glasses to each other, and outside the waves crashed on the shore and the wind whipped through the trees.

Winnie

Of course Winnie would like to have married. Or to have had a long-term partner. Who wouldn't?

To have someone there out for your good. Someone you could share with and eventually have children with. It was obvious that was what she wanted. But not at any price.

She would never have married the drunk that one friend had — a man who got so abusive at the wedding party that the ripples were still felt years later.

She would not have married the control freak, or the miser. But a lot of the men her friends had married were good, warm, happy people who had made their lives very complete.

If only there was someone like that out there.

And if there was, how could Winnie find him? She had tried internet dating, speed dating and going to clubs. None of it had worked.

When she was in her early thirties, Winnie had more or less given up on it all. She had a busy life: a nurse doing agency work, one day here, one night there, in the Dublin hospitals.

She went to the theatre, met friends, went to cookery classes and read a lot.

She couldn't say life was sad and lonely. It was far from that, but she would love to have been able to meet someone and know that this was the right one. Just know.

Winnie was an optimist. On the wards they always said she was a great nurse to work with because she always saw something to be pleased about. The patients liked her a lot – she always made time to reassure them and tell them how well they were doing and how much modern medicine had improved. She wasted no time moaning in hospital canteens that the men of Ireland were a sorry lot. She just got on with it.

She was still vaguely hopeful that there was love out there somewhere – just a little less sure that she might actually find it.

It was on her thirty-fourth birthday that she met Teddy.

She had gone with three girlfriends – all of them married, all of them nurses – to have dinner at Ennio's restaurant down on the quays by the Liffey. Winnie wore her new silver and black jacket. She had been persuaded by the hairdresser to get a very expensive conditioning treatment for her hair. The girls said she looked great, but then they always told her that. It just hadn't seemed to work in terms of attracting a life partner.

It was a lovely evening, with the staff all coming to the table and singing 'Happy Birthday', a drink of some Italian liqueur, on the house. At the next table two men watched them admiringly. They sang 'Happy Birthday' so lustily that the restaurant included them in the complimentary drink. They were polite and anxious not to impose.

Peter said he was a hotelier from Rossmore and that his friend was Teddy Hennessy who made cheese down in that part of the world. They came to Dublin every week because Peter's wife and Teddy's mother liked to go to a show. The men preferred to try out a new restaurant each time. This was their first visit to Ennio's.

'And does your wife not come to Dublin too?' Fiona asked Teddy, quite pointedly.

Winnie felt herself flush. Fiona was testing the ground, seeing was Teddy available. Teddy didn't seem to notice.

'No, I don't have a wife. Too busy making cheese, everyone says. No, I'm fancy-free.' He was boyish and eager; he had soft fair hair falling into his eyes.

Winnie thought she felt him looking at her.

But she must not become foolish and over-optimistic. Maybe he could see that, of the four women, she was the only one without a wedding ring. Maybe it was pure imagination.

The conversation was easy. Peter told them about his hotel. Fiona had tales of the heart clinic where she worked. Barbara described some of the disasters her husband David had faced setting up his pottery works. Ania, the Polish girl, who had trained late as a nurse, showed them pictures of her toddler.

Teddy and Winnie said little, but they looked at each other appreciatively, learning little about each other except that they were comfortable to be there. Then it was time for the men to go and pick up the ladies from the theatre. The drive to Rossmore would take two hours.

'I hope we meet again,' Teddy said to Winnie.

The three other women busied themselves saying heavy goodbyes to Peter.

'I hope so,' Winnie said. Neither of them made any move to give a phone number or address.

Peter did it for them in the end.

'Can I give you ladies my business card, and if you know of any other good restaurants like this you could pass them on to us?' he said.

'That's great, Peter. Oh, Winnie, do you have a card there?' Fiona said meaningfully.

Winnie wrote her email address and phone number on the back of a card advertising Ennio's Good Value Wine. And then the men were gone.

'Really, Fiona, you might as well have put a neon sign over my head saying *Desperate Spinster*,' Winnie protested.

Fiona shrugged. 'He was nice. What was I to do, let him escape?'

'Cheesemaking!' Barbara reflected. 'Very restful, I'd say.'

'Mrs Hennessy . . . That has a nice sound to it,' said Ania with a smile.

Winnie sighed. He was nice, certainly, but she was way beyond having her hopes raised by chance encounters.

Teddy rang Winnie the next day. He was going to be in Dublin again at the weekend. Would Winnie like to meet him for a coffee or something?

They talked all afternoon in a big sunny café. There was so much to say and to hear. She told him about her family – three sisters and two brothers, scattered all over the world. She said it was a series of goodbyes at the airport and tears and promising to come out to visit, but Winnie had never wanted to go to Australia or America. She was a real home bird.

Teddy nodded in agreement. He was exactly the same. He never wanted to go too far from Rossmore.

When Winnie was twelve her mother had died and the light had gone out of the house. Five years later her father had married again; a pleasant, distant woman called Olive who made jewellery and sold it at markets and fairs around the country. It was hard to say whether she *liked* Olive or not. Olive was remote and seemed to live in another world.

Teddy was an only child and his mother was a widow. His father had been killed in an accident on the farm many years ago. His mother had gone out to work in the local creamery to earn the money to send him to a really good school. He had enjoyed it there but his mother was very disappointed that he had not become a doctor or a lawyer. That would have been a reward for the long, hard hours she had worked.

He loved making cheese. He had won several prizes and it was a good, steady little business. He met a lot of good people and was even able to give employment in Rossmore to workers who might have had to go away and find jobs abroad. His mother, who had turned out to be a superb businesswoman after her years in the creamery, did the accounts for him and was very involved in the business.

Winnie told of her life as a nurse, and explained what it meant to be registered with an agency. You literally didn't know where you were going to work tomorrow. It might be one of the big shiny new private hospitals; it could be a busy inner-city hospital, a maternity wing or a home for the elderly. In many ways it was great because there was huge variety, but in other ways it meant that you didn't get to know your patients very well – there wasn't as much continuity or in-volvement in their care.

They had both been to Turkey on holiday, they liked reading thrillers and they had both been the victims of well-meaning friends trying to fix them up on dates and marry them off. Either it would happen or it wouldn't, they told each other companionably. But they knew they would meet again very soon.

'I *have* enjoyed today,' he said.

'Maybe I could cook you a meal next time?'

His face lit up.

And after that he was part of her life. Not a huge part, but there maybe twice a week.

For several visits to her flat he left before midnight and drove the long road back to Rossmore. Then one evening he asked if she might agree that, perhaps, he could stay the night. Winnie said that would be very agreeable indeed.

Once or twice, they even went away for a weekend together but it had to be a short weekend. She soon learned that nothing could or would change his mother's plans. Teddy could never be free on a Friday because that was the evening that he took his mother to dinner in Peter's hotel.

Yes, every single Friday, he said regretfully. It was such a small thing, and Mam did love it so much. And when you thought about all she had given up for him over the years . . .

Winnie pondered about this to herself. He didn't *seem* like a mummy's boy, but she felt that he was nervous of introducing her to his mother. As if she might not pass some test. But this was fanciful. He was a grown man. She wouldn't rush it.

Instead, she concentrated on the idea of their taking a little holiday together.

Winnie had heard about this place that was opening in the West called Stone House. The picture on the brochure had looked very attractive. It showed a big table where all the guests would get together in the evening, a cute little black and white cat sitting beside a roaring fire; it promised excellent, home-cooked food, and comfort, with walks and birdwatching and the chance to explore the spectacular coastline.

Wouldn't that be a great place for her to go with Teddy? If

only she could prise him away and break the hold of those precious Friday nights with his mother.

His mother!

She had better get the meeting over and done with before she suggested whisking the dotey boy off to the West of Ireland! But on the other hand, this place looked as if it might be really popular. Teddy would just love the idea when it was presented to him, and if it didn't suit him she could always cancel the reservation . . .

And then it *was* time to meet her – this mother who had sacrificed so much for her boy, the mother whose Friday evenings could never be disturbed. She had asked Teddy to bring his friend Winnie from Dublin to have Friday dinner in the hotel and to join them for a lunch the following day.

Winnie took great care of what to dress in, what she thought Mrs Hennessy would like.

This old lady rarely moved from Rossmore. She would be suspicious of anything flashy.

Winnie's silver and black jacket might be too dressy. She wore a sensible navy trouser suit instead.

'I'm quite nervous of meeting her,' she confided to Teddy.

'Nonsense. You'll get on so well together they'll have to call the fire brigade,' he said.

She would take the train to Rossmore with her overnight bag. Peter and his wife Gretta had invited her to stay in their hotel as their guest. Mrs Hennessy would not be told about their sleeping arrangements, so this seemed the sensible option.

'We'll give you our best room. You'll need every creature comfort after meeting the dragon lady,' Peter had said.

'But I thought you liked her!' Winnie was startled.

'She's a great dame, certainly, and the best of company, but you never saw a mama animal in the wild as protective of its young as Lillian is. She scares them away, one by one,' Peter laughed at it all.

Winnie pretended not to hear him. Battle lines were not going to be drawn over Teddy. He was an adult, a man who could and would make his own decisions.

Teddy was at the railway station to meet her. 'Mam has made up a great guest list for lunch tomorrow as well,' he said with delight. 'She says we must make it worth your while coming all this way.'

'That's very generous of her,' Winnie murmured. 'And I get to see your home, too.' She was very pleased that she had already packed a small gift for Mrs Hennessy. This was all going to be fine.

At the hotel, Peter and Gretta were in a state of high excitement. 'Do you want to see your room now, and change for dinner?' Gretta asked.

'No, not at all. I'm fine going straight in just as I am,' Winnie said. She knew what a stickler for punctuality Mrs Hennessy was and how she hated to be kept waiting.

'Whatever you think,' Gretta said, doubtfully.

Winnie moved purposefully into the bar and dining room of the Rossmore Hotel. She would reassure the old lady and win her over. It was all a matter of letting her know that Winnie was no threat, no rival. They were all in this together.

She could see no elderly figure sitting in the big armchairs. Perhaps Mrs Hennessy's legendary timekeeping had been exaggerated. Then she saw Teddy hailing a most glamorous woman sitting at the bar.

'There you are, Mam! Beaten us to it, as usual! Mam, this is my friend Winnie.'

Winnie stared in disbelief. This was no clinging, frail old woman. This was someone in her early fifties, groomed and made-up and dressed to kill. She wore a gold brocade jacket over a wine-coloured silk dress. She must have come straight from the hairdresser's. Her handbag and shoes were made of soft expensive leather. She wore very classy-looking jewellery.

There had to be some mistake.

Winnie's mouth opened and closed. Never at a loss for something to say, she now found herself totally wordless.

Mrs Hennessy, however, was able to cope with her own sense of surprise with much more dignity.

'Winnie, what a pleasure to meet you! Teddy told me all about you.' Her eyes took Winnie in from head to toe and up again.

Winnie felt very conscious of her big, comfortable shoes. And *why* had she worn this dreary navy trouser suit? She looked like someone who had come in to move the furniture in the hotel, not to have a dressed-up dinner with this style icon.

Teddy beamed from one to the other, seeing what he had always wanted: a good meeting between his mother and his girl. And he remained delighted all through the meal while his mother patronised Winnie, dismissed her and almost laughed in her face. Teddy Hennessy saw none of this. He only saw the three of them establishing themselves as a family group.

Mrs Hennessy said that *of course* Winnie must call her Lillian, after all, they were friends now. 'You are so very different to what I expected,' she said admiringly.

'Oh, really?' Poor Winnie wondered had she ever been so gauche and awkward.

'Yes, indeed. When Teddy told me he had met this little nurse in Dublin I suppose I thought of someone much younger, sillier somehow. It's marvellous to meet someone so mature and sensible.'

'Oh, is that what I seem?' She recognised the words for what they were: *mature* and *sensible* meant *big, dull, ordinary* and *old*. She could hear the sigh of relief that Lillian Hennessy was allowing to hiss out from her perfectly made-up lips. This Winnie was no threat. Her golden son, Teddy, couldn't possibly fancy a woman as unattractive as this.

'And it's so *good* for Teddy to have proper people to meet when he's in Dublin,' Lillian went on in a voice that was almost but not quite a gush. 'Someone who will keep him out of harm's way and from making unsuitable attachments.'

'Indeed, I'm great at that,' Winnie said.

'You are?' Lillian's eyes were hard.

Teddy looked bewildered for a moment.

'Well, I'm thirty-four and I kept myself out of making any unsuitable attachments so far,' Winnie said.

Lillian screamed with delight. 'Aren't you just wonderful! Well, of course Teddy is only thirty-two, so we have to keep an eye on him,' she tinkled.

Lillian knew everyone in the dining room and nodded or waved at them all. Sometimes she even introduced Winnie as 'an old, *old* friend of ours from Dublin'. She chose the wine, complained that the Hennessy cheeses were not properly displayed on the cheese plate and eventually called the evening to an end by talking about her invitation to lunch the following day.

'I had been in such a tizz wondering who to invite with you, but now that I've met you I see you'd be perfectly at ease with anyone. So you'll meet a lot of the old buffers around here. All very parochial, I'm afraid, compared to Dublin, but I'm sure you'll find a few likely souls.' Then she was out in the foyer tapping her elegantly shod toe until Teddy walked Winnie to the lift.

'I *knew* it would be wonderful,' he said. And with a quick kiss on the cheek he was gone to drive his mother home.

In the Rossmore Hotel, Winnie cried until she had no more tears. She saw her stained face in the mirror. An old, flat face; the face that could be introduced to old buffers. Somebody no one would get into a tizz over. *Where* did the woman get these phrases?

She wept over Teddy. Was he a man at all to leave her at the lift doors and run after his overdressed, power-crazed mother? Or was he a puppet who had no intention of having a proper relationship with her?

She would *not* go to this awful lunch tomorrow. She would make her excuses and take the train back to Dublin. Let them all work it out as they wanted to. The last few months had been a fool's paradise. Winnie should have known better at her age.

And talking about age, Lillian had said Teddy was thirty-two, making him sound as if he were still a child. He would be thirty-three in two weeks' time. He was only fourteen months younger than Winnie. She and Teddy had already laughed at the age difference. To them it had been immaterial. How had Lillian managed to change it all and make her seem like some kind of cougar stalking the young, defenceless Teddy?

Well, never mind. This was the last she would see of either of them.

She fell into a troubled sleep and woke with a headache.

Gretta was standing beside her bed with a breakfast tray.

'What? I didn't order . . .'

'God, Winnie, you've had dinner with Lillian. You probably need a blood transfusion or shock treatment but I brought you coffee, croissants and a Bloody Mary to get you on your feet.'

'She's not important. I'm going back to Dublin on the next

train. I'm not letting her get to me. Believe me, I know when to leave the stage.'

'Drink the Bloody Mary first. Go *on*, Winnie, drink it. It's full of good things like lemon juice and celery salt and Tabasco.'

'And vodka,' Winnie said.

'Desperate needs, desperate remedies.' Gretta held out the glass and Winnie drank it.

'Why does she hate me?' Winnie was begging to know.

'She doesn't hate you. She's just so afraid of losing Teddy. She grows claws whenever anyone looks as if they might take him away. This side of her comes out when she's in a panic. But she's not getting away with it this time.'

During the coffee, Gretta explained that there was a wedding in the hotel that day and that a hairdresser was on hand. She would come to the room and do a quick job on Winnie and then so would the make-up artist.

'It's too late for all this makeover stuff,' Winnie wailed. 'She saw me the way I was. I deliberately didn't bring any smart clothes because I didn't want to dazzle her. *Me* dazzle *her*? I must have been mad.'

'I have a gorgeous top I'm going to lend you. She's never seen it. It's the real deal – a Missoni. Truly top drawer. I got it from one of those outlet places. You'll knock her eyes out.'

'I don't want to knock her eyes out. I don't care about her or her son.'

'None of us cares about her, but we all love Teddy. You're the only one who can save him. Go on, Winnie, one lunch. You can do it. Believe it or not, underneath she's a very decent person.'

And somehow Winnie found herself in the shower and then with a hairdresser and having her eyebrows plucked and a blusher applied to her cheekbones. Eyeshadow to match the beautiful lilac and aquamarine colours of the Italian designer blouse.

'Even if you are leaving the stage, then leave it fighting,' Gretta warned as she admired the results.

'Get back and deal with the wedding, Gretta. This is your bread and butter. Your livelihood.'

'I don't care about the wedding. I care about getting Teddy out from under that woman's thumb. Look, Winnie, she *is* our friend, but Teddy *must* be allowed to live his own life, and you are the one who will do it. I don't know how but it will come to you.'

'I'm not going to issue any ultimatums. Either Teddy wants to be with me or he doesn't.'

'Oh, Winnie, if only life was as easy. You don't do weddings every week like we do all year long; you don't know the rocky roads to the altar.'

'I'd prefer a road with no rocks, a pleasant, easy road and to walk it alone,' Winnie said.

'You can do this. Go for it, Winnie,' Gretta begged.

Lillian had gathered over a dozen people for lunch. Fresh salmon was served with new potatoes and minted peas. There were very elegant salads with asparagus and avocado, walnuts and blue cheese.

Winnie looked around her. This was a very comfortable, charming house: there were wooden floors with rugs; big chintz-covered sofas and chairs were dotted around, framed family photographs covered the little side table.

A conservatory, where a table of summer drinks was laid out, opened into a well-kept garden. This was Lillian's domain.

Winnie was impressed but she would not fawn and admire

and praise. Instead, she concentrated on the other guests. Despite herself, she found she liked Lillian's friends.

She was seated next to the local lawyer, who talked about how Ireland had become very litigious with people looking everywhere for compensation, and told her marvellously funny stories about cases he had heard about. On her other side were Hannah and Chester Kovac who had founded and ran a local health centre, and they talked about the problems in the health service. Opposite, there was a gentleman called Neddy, who ran an old people's home and his wife Clare, who was the headmistress of the local school; their friends, Judy and Sebastian, told her they had started with a small newsagent's shop in the town centre but now had a large store in the main street of Rossmore. There had been a big fuss about the bypass when people thought that it would take trade away from the town, but it turned out there had been great business in selling Dubliners second homes in the Whitethorn Woods area.

These were normal, warm-hearted people, and they seemed perfectly at ease with Lillian Hennessy. The woman must have a lot more going for her than she was showing to Winnie.

She noticed Lillian glancing at her from time to time with an air of some speculation. It was as if she realised that Winnie had changed in more than her appearance since last night. What Winnie did not notice, however, was the way the lawyer kept refilling her glass with what he said was an excellent Chablis. By the time the strawberries were served, Winnie was not thinking as clearly as she would have liked.

She found herself looking over at Teddy's face and thinking how genuinely good-natured and warm he was. She admired his courtesy with his mother's friends, and his eagerness that everyone should have a good time. He looked across at her a

123

lot and always smiled, as if the dream of his life had been realised and that she had come home.

Lillian was a good hostess. Winnie had to give her that much.

She managed to make her guests move around so that they talked to other people. Winnie had watched the little dance, and was determined to get up and go to the bathroom to avoid being closeted with Lillian.

But she hadn't moved in time.

'What a lovely Missoni top,' Lillian said to her admiringly.

'Thank you,' Winnie said.

'Could I ask where you got it?'

'It was a gift.' Winnie closed down the line of enquiry.

'I hope you haven't been bored here. I'm sure you think it's a real country-bumpkin outing.' Lillian in her cream linen dress and jacket looked as if she were dressed for a smart society wedding.

'I've loved it, Lillian. What wonderful friends you have.'

'I'm sure you have a lot of good friends in Dublin, too.'

'Well, yes, I do. Like you, I enjoy people, so I suppose I do have a lot of friends.' Winnie felt her voice sounded tinny and faraway. She might indeed be a little drunk. She must be very careful.

Lillian's eyes seemed to narrow but the piercing look was still there. With a shock Winnie realised that Lillian quite possibly hated her. It was as strong as that. This was territorial. Winnie would not get her hands on the golden son. His mother would fight for him. She was almost too tired to fight back. The night of weeping, the exhaustion of all the morning preparations, the breakfast Bloody Mary and all this unaccustomed lunchtime wine had taken their toll. Why take on a battle she could never win?

Then she saw Teddy smiling at her proudly across the table. He did love her. He didn't think she was old and dull. He was far too good to give up without some struggle.

'Your home is very elegant, Lillian. Teddy was lucky to grow up in such a lovely place.'

'Thank you.' Lillian's eyes were as hard as they had been last night. Now there was no attempt to conceal the hostility.

'I can see why you don't want to go away on holidays. You have everything here.' Winnie hoped the smile was fixed securely to her face.

'Oh, but I do like to travel, of course, and see things, visit places. Don't you, Winnie? I mean, what are your holiday plans this year?'

Teddy had moved over to join them. He was smiling from one to the other. Things were going better than he had even dreamed. Suddenly, Winnie found herself describing Stone House to them both.

Lillian was interested. 'It does sound good, like a retreat almost. And who do you think you would go with? I'm sure you can find someone, if it's as good as you say. It's the sort of place I'd love to go to myself, and I'd have thought it would appeal to a more sophisticated clientele. Do you know anyone who would like it? One of your nursing friends? Or are they all sun-lovers?' She was not letting it go.

'Yes indeed, you're right there, but not everyone wants to escape to the sun when it gets cold here,' Winnie floundered. 'I actually *like* the wind and rain when the place is beautiful, and there's going to be a nice hot bath and a good dinner at the end of the day. I'm sure a lot of people feel the same.'

'You're bound to find someone.' Lillian was patronising.

'I was thinking that perhaps Teddy would come with me,' she said, emboldened by drink and brave as a lion.

'Teddy!' Lillian seemed as alarmed as if the name of an international war criminal had been suggested.

'What a wonderful idea!' Teddy said, delighted. 'That part of the country is very unspoiled, and winter would be much more attractive than going with the crowds in summer. Will we be able to get a booking, do you think?'

'It won't be any problem,' Winnie said.

Teddy looked as if all his birthdays had come at once.

'Why don't we *all* go?' he said. 'It sounds so wonderful, and now that you've got to know each other, wouldn't it be great if the three of us went?' He looked from his mother to his girlfriend, enchanted with the way things had fallen out.

How could he have been unaware of the stunned silence that greeted his remark? But it seemed to have passed him by.

'I can't think of anything I would like more,' he said, looking again from one face to the other.

It was Lillian who first found the breath to speak. 'Of course, as you just said it might in fact be difficult to get a booking,' she began tentatively.

It was now up to Winnie. Any intelligent response deserted her. She found herself only able to speak the truth. 'I sort of provisionally booked a week already.' Winnie looked at the ground.

'Well isn't that just *great*?' Teddy was overjoyed. 'Now it's settled. What date is that?'

Winnie stumbled out the date. This could not be happening. He could not want to bring his mother on their holiday? If they ever did marry, would he invite her on the honeymoon as well? Please God make the date impossible.

She saw Teddy's face had clouded over.

'Oh *no*! That's the week of the cheesemakers' conference. That's the only week in the year I can't make,' he said.

Winnie thanked God from the bottom of her heart, and said she would pay much more attention to Him in future.

'Oh well, it was silly of me to make a booking without checking but it was only a vague arrangement. I'll call them and tell them . . .' Winnie was apologetic, and hoped that her relief didn't show.

'And it might have been very cold – damp, even,' Lillian chimed in quickly.

But Teddy was having none of it. 'The two of *you* must go together.'

Lillian coughed, but appeared to give the matter some thought. 'No, darling, we'll wait and set it up another time.'

'It would be a bit like *Hamlet* without the Prince,' Winnie said with a terrible forced smile that she felt must look like a death's head.

'There are other weekends, other places,' Lillian pleaded.

'Let's not even think of going without you.' Winnie practically tore Lillian's good linen table napkin into shreds.

'But what would I like better when I am away than to think of the two of you having a holiday together? Getting to know each other properly. The two people I love.' He was clearly sincere, and both women were trapped.

'Well, of course we will get to know each other, Teddy, it's just that we don't want *you* to lose out on a holiday,' Lillian began.

'Your mother could come to Dublin, and I would take her on a day out while you are away.' Winnie felt a whimper in her voice.

'This place sounds so right for you both, and it's booked. You must go,' he said.

'It might be the wrong age group for us. There could just be a house full of young people.' Lillian was grasping at straws. 'It's not a holiday that would attract young people, of course,' she said eventually.

'Yes, we might be out of place.' Winnie nodded so fervently she feared her poor, tired, muddled head might fall off.

But these were just the dying gasps of beached fish. They looked at each other. They both knew that to refuse would be to lose him. And neither of them was willing to take that step. They began to backtrack.

Lillian caved in first.

'But if it's what you really want . . . Yes, all in all, it has a lot going for it. Certainly, I'd be very happy to go with you, Winnie.'

'What?' Winnie felt as if she had been shot.

'Teddy is right. We *do* need to get to know each other. I could easily go with you then. And, do you know, I think I'd enjoy it.'

Winnie felt the room tilt around her.

She must speak this very moment, or else she had agreed to go on a week's holiday with this hateful woman. But her throat was dry and she could not find her voice. She felt herself nodding dumbly. She was like a drowning woman with the waters closing overhead but she could not stop it happening. She realised that if she did *not* speak, she would end up going to the West with Lillian Hennessy.

Lillian's small, spiteful face was very near hers. She was planning this week in the West as her way to destroy whatever Teddy and Winnie might claim to have.

Winnie straightened herself up.

In her mind she said, *All right, bring it on, then let's see who wins*, but aloud she said, 'It's a great idea, Lillian. I'm sure we'll have a wonderful time. I'll confirm the booking for the two of us.'

Somehow the meal came to an end and it was time for Teddy to drive her to the station.

'We'll be in touch before we go,' Lillian called from the hall door.

'What did I tell you?' Teddy asked. 'I *knew* you two would get on together.'

'Yes, she was very kind, very welcoming.'

'And you are both going off on a holiday together – isn't that magical?'

'Yes, she said she liked the sound of this place over in Stoneybridge.'

'Mam doesn't go on holidays with anyone, you know. She is very choosy. So she must have taken to you immediately.'

'Yes, isn't it great . . .' Winnie said. She felt flat and defeated and as if her hangover was about to kick in. It was a warning to her to go easy on wine at lunchtime for the rest of her life. A warning that had come way too late.

Winnie stared out the window as the train hurtled through rural Ireland. What kind of people worked moving cattle around these small green fields, or digging those crops into hard earth? They were people who would never have had too much wine at lunchtime, or any time. They would never have agreed to go on a week's holiday with the most hateful woman in Ireland. She tried to sleep but just as the rhythm of the train was beginning to lull her into some kind of rest, she got a text message on her phone.

It was from Teddy.

I miss you so much. You lit up the whole party at lunchtime. They were all mad about you. And so am I. But you'll never know just how wonderful you were to my mother. She has talked of nothing else but her holiday with you. You are brilliant, and I love you.

It didn't cheer her. It made her feel even worse about herself. She was a grown woman. She wasn't a schoolgirl. She had messed everything up. In ten weeks' time she would go to Stone House with Lillian Hennessy. It was like the Mad Hatter's Tea Party. It was like one of those terrible dreams that are both silly and frightening at the same time.

Winnie's friends noticed a change in her. She just shrugged when they asked her about her visit to Rossmore. They hardly dared to enquire whether Teddy was still visiting. Winnie refused the idea of going on any holidays with them.

Fiona and Declan had begged her to come and stay in the holiday home they had rented in Wexford. There would be plenty of room and they would love to have her. But Winnie didn't even consider it. Nor the suggestion that she go on a bus tour of Italy with Barbara and David, who were heading that way. And Ania's pictures of the boat they were renting on the Shannon River didn't raise a flicker of interest.

'You have to have *some* holiday,' Fiona said in desperation.

'Oh, I will. I'm going for a winter week to the West. It will be great.' She managed to make it sound as if it were going to be root-canal work.

'And is Teddy going with you?' Barbara could be brave sometimes.

'Teddy? No, it's the same week as the thing he goes to every year. The cheesemakers' thing.'

'Couldn't you have chosen another week?' Fiona wondered.

Winnie seemed not to have heard.

Teddy did come to visit, and stayed over in Winnie's little flat once or twice a week. He was as cheerful and happy as ever, and seemed to take it for granted that the planned holiday was the natural result of an instant friendship between the two women. Something he had always thought likely but couldn't believe had been so spectacular. He was so endearing, and in every other way he was the perfect friend, lover and life mate. He was already talking about a wedding. Winnie had tried to keep things light.

'Ah, that's way down the road,' she would laugh.

'I've it all worked out. We need an office for the cheese in Dublin anyway, and we could live half in Rossmore and half here.'

'No rush, Teddy.'

'But there is. I'd love us to have a huge wedding in Rossmore and show you off.'

Winnie said nothing.

'Or, of course, if you prefer, we could have it here in Dublin with all your friends. It's your day. It's your choice, Winnie.'

'Aren't we fine as we are?'

Winnie knew that there might well be no future to consider by the time she and his mother got back from this ill-starred holiday at Stone House.

There were several letters, texts and phone calls with Lillian. It took every ounce of skill and self-control for Winnie not to scream down the phone that it had all been a terrible mistake.

Then Teddy set off for the cheese gathering, and the following morning Winnie drove west from Dublin and Lillian Hennessy drove north-west from Rossmore.

They met at Stone House. They arrived, by chance, at almost the same time and parked their cars. Winnie's was a very old and beaten-up banger that she had bought from one of the porters in a hospital where she worked. Lillian drove a new Mercedes-Benz.

Winnie's luggage was one big canvas bag which she carried. Lillian had two matching suitcases, which she left beside the car.

Mrs Starr was waiting at the front door. She was a small woman, possibly in her mid forties. She had short curly hair, a big smile and a slightly American accent. Her welcome was very warm. She ran out to pick up Lillian's suitcases and led them into a big warm kitchen. On the table were warm scones, butter and jam. A big log fire blazed at one end, a solid-fuel cooker stood at the other. It looked just like the brochure.

They were ushered in and seated immediately.

'You are my very first guests,' Mrs Starr said. 'The others will be here in the next hour or so. Would you like tea or coffee?'

In no time at all, Mrs Starr had discovered more about Lillian and Winnie than either woman had ever known. Lillian talked about her husband being killed when her son was only a small child, and the terrible day when she had been given the news. Winnie explained that her father was married to a perfectly pleasant woman who made jewellery and all her brothers and sisters were overseas.

If Mrs Starr thought that the two women were unlikely friends and companions for a holiday, she didn't give any hint of it.

Winnie had insisted that Lillian be given the bedroom with the sea view. It was a tranquil, warm room with a big bay window. There were several soothing shades of green, no television but a small shower room. This place had been very beautifully refurbished. Winnie's room was similar but smaller, and it looked out on to the car park.

Winnie realised how tired she was. The drive had been long, the weather wet and the roads, as she got near Stoneybridge, had been narrow and hard to negotiate. She would indeed lie down and have a rest. The room contained one large bed and one smaller one. If they had been the friends that Lillian had managed to imply they were, they could have easily shared this room. Even made each other further tea from the tray already set with a little kettle and barrel of biscuits, looked together at the books, maps and brochures about the area that lay on the dressing table.

But Winnie was past caring what anyone thought. Mrs Starr was a hotelier, a landlady and a businesswoman. She had little time to speculate about the odd couple who had arrived as her first guests.

Winnie felt herself drifting off to sleep. She heard the murmur of conversation downstairs as further guests were being welcomed. It was reassuring, somehow. Safe, like home used to be. Years and years ago, when Winnie's mother was alive and the place was full of brothers and sisters coming and going.

Mrs Starr had said she would sound the Sheedy gong twenty minutes before dinner. Apparently, the three Sheedy sisters, who had lived in genteel poverty in this house for many years, always rang the gong every evening. The ladies often had sardines or baked beans on toast for their evening meal but the gong always rang through the house. It was what their mama and papa would have liked.

Winnie woke to the mellow sound of the gong. God! Now she had to put in an evening of Lillian patronising everyone

133

and six more nights in this wild, faraway place. She must have been insane to allow things to go this distance. That was the only explanation.

Before she left the room, a text came in.

Have a lovely evening. I so wish I were there with you both rather than here. I used to enjoy these gatherings, but now I feel lonely and miss you both. Tell me what the place is like. Love you deeply, Teddy.

The other guests were gathering. Mrs Starr had asked them to introduce themselves to each other as she wanted to concentrate on the food. She had a young niece called Orla who helped her serve.

Winnie saw Lillian, dressed to kill as might have been expected, slipping into gear and beginning to charm people. She was explaining to a young Swedish man how she and Winnie were old, *old* friends, and they hadn't seen each other for a long while and were so looking forward to walking for miles and catching up.

She talked to a retired teacher whose name was Nell. This visit had been a gift from the staff in her school. They had said they thought it would suit her. Nell wasn't at all certain. Lillian lowered her voice and said that she also had her doubts in the beginning, but her old, *old* friend Winnie had insisted she come. So far Lillian had to admit that it all seemed very pleasant.

Winnie spoke to Henry and Nicola, a doctor and his wife from England. They had found the place online when they were looking for somewhere very peaceful. Winnie thought they might have had a bereavement. They looked pale and a bit shaken, but then she could have been imagining it.

Another couple looked vaguely dissatisfied and didn't say much. There were other people further down the table. Winnie would meet them later.

They ate smoked trout with horseradish cream and home-made brown soda bread to start, then a roast lamb expertly carved by Mrs Starr. There were vegetarian dishes as well, and a huge apple pie. Wine was poured from old cut-crystal decanters. The Sheedy sisters used to pour their orange squash and lemonade from these very decanters. They were beautiful antiques and felt like part of the house.

Winnie couldn't help but admire the way that it was all working out. The guests seemed to be talking easily. Mrs Starr had been quite right not to fuss around introducing them to each other. Everything had been cleared seamlessly and young Orla had stacked a big dishwasher and gone home. Mrs Starr joined them for coffee.

She explained that breakfast would be a continuous buffet but if people wanted a cooked meal they must assemble at nine. A packed lunch would be supplied for anyone who needed one, or else they could have a list of pubs in the area that served light lunches. There were bicycles outside if anyone would like to use them, and there were binoculars, umbrellas and even a selection of wellington boots. She told them about the various walking routes they might try and the local points of interest. There were a number of pretty creeks and inlets which were great to explore when the weather was calm. There were cliff-top walks though the paths down to the sea needed great care. There were caves that were worth exploring, but they must check the tides first. Majella's Cave was a good one. That had been a great place for lovers in the summertime, she had explained. It was easily cut off by the tide, so the boy and girl who wandered there had to stay for much longer than they had expected to until the seas had drawn back and let them go free . . .

After dinner, Winnie texted Teddy to tell him the place was charming and very different and that they had been made very welcome. She added that she loved him deeply also. But she wondered was this actually true.

Perhaps she was living in some never-never land. Acting a role, playing a part, cast now and possibly for ever as the old, *old* friend of her future mother-in-law. She fell into a deep sleep and didn't wake until there was a knock at the door.

Lillian, fully dressed, made-up and ready to roll.

'Thought you wouldn't want to miss the cooked breakfast,' she said. 'At our age we need a good start to the day.'

Winnie felt an overpowering rage. Did Lillian seriously think they were the same age?

'I'll be down in ten minutes,' she said, rubbing her eyes.

'Oh dear, you don't have an ocean view,' Lillian said.

'I have lovely mountains, though, and I just *love* mountains,' Winnie said through gritted teeth.

'Right. Great thing about you, Winnie, is that you are easily pleased. See you downstairs then.'

Winnie stood in the shower. The week ahead seemed endless, and she had no one to blame but herself . . .

The young Swede had gone off with the small intense woman called Freda. Henry, the English doctor, and his wife were ordering grilled mackerel. Other guests looked at the map Mrs Starr had provided and talked enthusiastically about the places they might go. There was an American man called John who was suffering from jet lag and looked very tired.

The weather was bright – no need for the umbrellas or wellington boots. Packed lunches were prepared already and in waxed paper for those who wanted them. Others had the names of pubs listed.

By ten o'clock, all the guests had left Stone House and Mrs Starr's niece Orla had arrived to do the bedrooms. A routine had been established. It was as if this holiday had been up and running for years rather than taking its first faltering steps.

Winnie and Lillian had chosen the cliff walk. Four miles with spectacular views, then you would arrive in West Harbour. There they would go to Brady's Bar. And after lunch, they would catch the bus that left every hour for Stoneybridge.

Winnie looked back longingly at Stone House.

How good it would be to go back and sit with Mrs Starr at the table having further tea and fresh soda bread and talk about the world. Instead, she had hours of competitive banter with Lillian Hennessy. But by the time they got to Brady's Bar, Winnie felt her shoulder muscles had relaxed. The views had been as spectacular as had been promised. Lillian had been mercifully untalkative.

Now, however, she was back to her opinionated self.

'It was a pleasant walk, certainly, but not really challenging,' she pronounced.

'Beautiful scenery. I could look at that big sky for ever,' Winnie said.

'Oh, indeed, but we should go the other way tomorrow, take the route south. There's much more to see, Mrs Starr said. All those little creeks, inlets; we can look in the caves.'

'It looked like a trickier route. Let's see if any of the others have done it first.' Winnie was cautious.

'Oh, they're all sheep. They won't take on anything adventurous. That's what we came for, isn't it, Winnie? One last gesture to fight the elements before we settle into middle age.'

'You aren't settling anywhere,' Winnie said.

'No, but you are showing dangerous signs of becoming very middle-aged. Where's your spirit, Winnie? Tomorrow we'll take a packed lunch and hit the south face of Stoneybridge.'

Winnie smiled as if in agreement. She hadn't a notion of putting herself at risk because Lillian was playing games. But that could all be dealt with tomorrow morning. In the meantime, she would just put in the time being charming and pleasant and unruffled. The prize was Teddy.

Please, dear, kind God, may he be worth it all.

They went back to Stone House on the bus and the guests were coming back from their excursions. The log fire blazed in the hearth. Everyone was drinking tea and eating scones. It was as if they had always lived this life.

At dinner, Winnie sat across from Freda, who said she was an assistant librarian. Winnie explained that she was a nurse.

'Do you have an attachment?' Freda asked.

'No, I work through an agency; a different hospital every day, really.'

'I actually meant a love attachment.'

Lillian was listening. 'We are all a bit past love interests at our age,' she tinkled.

'I don't know . . .' Freda was thoughtful. 'I'm not.'

'Very odd woman, that,' Lillian said later, in a whisper.

'I thought she was good fun, I must say,' Winnie said.

'As I've said before, Winnie, you are totally undemanding. It's amazing how little you ask from life!'

Winnie's lips stretched into a smile. 'That's me,' she simpered. 'As you said, easily pleased.'

All the others were talking about tomorrow's weather. Storms coming in from the south, Mrs Starr said, great care needed. These creeks and inlets filled up very rapidly; even local people had been fooled by the strength of the winds and tides. Winnie sighed with relief. At least Lillian's daft plan of behaving like an explorer would be cancelled.

But when they took their packed lunch next morning, Lillian headed straight in the direction that they had been warned against. Winnie paused for an instant. She could refuse to go. But then Lillian was possibly right. Mrs Starr was being overcautious to cover herself.

Winnie could do it. She was thirty-four years of age, for God's sake. Lillian was fifty-three, at the very least. She had put up with so much already, invested so much time and patience – she wouldn't check out now.

And at first, it was exhilarating. The spray was salty and the rocks large, dark and menacing. The cries of the wild birds and the pounding of the sea made talking impossible. They strode on together, pausing to look out over the Atlantic and realise that the next land was three thousand miles away in the United States.

Then they found the entrance to Majella's Cave that Mrs Starr had told them about. It was sheltered there and the wind wasn't cutting them in half. They sat on a rocky ledge to open the bread and cheese and flask of soup that had been packed for them. Their eyes were stinging, their cheeks were red and whipped by the wind and sea air. They both felt fit and alive and very hungry.

'I'm glad we battled on and came here,' Winnie said, 'it was well worth it.'

'You didn't want to really,' Lillian was triumphant. 'You thought I was being foolhardy.'

'Well if I did, I was wrong. It's good to push yourself a bit.' As she spoke, Winnie felt a great slosh of water across her face

– a wave had come deep into the cave. Oddly, it was not withdrawing out to sea again as they thought it would; rather it was followed by several more waves coming in and splashing around their feet. The two women moved backwards speedily. But still they came, the dark, cold waters, hardly giving any time for the previous wave to recede. Wordlessly, they climbed to an even higher ledge. They would be fine here, well above the water level.

The waves kept coming, and in an attempt to scramble even higher, Lillian kicked the two canvas bags that had held their picnic, their mobile phones and the warm dry socks. They watched as the waves carried the bags out to sea.

'How long does it take for the tide to change?' Lillian asked.

'Six hours, I think,' Winnie was crisp.

'They'll come for us then,' Lillian said.

'They don't know where we are,' Winnie said.

They didn't speak any more then. Only the sound of the wind and waves filled Majella's Cave.

'I wonder who Majella was?' Winnie said after a long time.

'There was a Saint Gerard Majella,' Lillian said doubtfully. It was the first time that she had ever spoken without a sense of certainty.

'Very probably,' Winnie agreed. 'Let's hope he had a good record in getting people out of situations, whoever he was.'

'You agreed to come. You *said* you were happy we had battled on.'

'I was. At the time.'

'Do you pray?' Lillian asked.

'No, not much. Do you?'

'I used to once. Not now.'

There didn't seem to be anything more to say, so they sat in silence listening to the crashing of the waves and the howling of the wind. There was only one higher ledge, which they might have to climb up on if things got worse.

They were cold and wet and frightened.

And they were of no help to each other.

Winnie wondered would they die here. She thought about Teddy, and how Mrs Starr would have to break the news to him. He would never know that her last hours had been filled with a cold hatred of his mother and with a sense of huge regret that she had allowed herself to be sucked into this idiotic game of pretence which could only end badly. But, truly, who could have known how badly?

She couldn't see Lillian's face, but she sensed her shoulders shivering and the chattering of her teeth. She must be frightened too. But it was *her* bloody fault. Still, however they got there, they were both in it together now.

After an age, she said, 'It doesn't really matter one way or another, but why are we here together? In Stoneybridge, I mean. You hated me on sight. But we both love Teddy, that should be a bond, shouldn't it?' This was the first time that love for Teddy had ever been mentioned. Here in Majella's Cave, as they faced death by drowning or hypothermia. Up to now, Winnie had been treated as some menopausal old fool who was keeping an eye on Teddy for them both.

'I love Teddy,' Winnie said loudly. 'And he loves you, so I tried to get to know you and like you. That's all.'

'It hasn't worked though, has it?' said Lillian grimly. 'We got here by accident. I didn't want to be here with you any more than you wanted to be with me. You found the place, Stone House, you went along with coming here today. And now look at us.'

141

A silence.

'Say something, ask something,' Lillian begged.

'How old are you, Lillian?'

'Fifty-five.'

'You look a lot less.'

'Thank you.'

'Why do you pretend that you and I are the same age? You were twenty-one when I was born.'

'Because I wanted you to go away, to leave Teddy as he was, with me.'

Another silence.

Eventually Winnie spoke. 'Well, in the end neither of us got him.'

'Do you think we're going to get out of here?' The voice had aged greatly. This was not Lillian of the Certainties.

Some small amount of compassion seeped through to Winnie's subconscious. She tried to beat it back but it was there.

'They say you have to be positive and keep active,' she said, shifting around on the ledge.

'Active? Here? What can we do to be positive here?'

'I know that. We can't move. I suppose we could sing.'

'*Sing*, Winnie? Have you lost your marbles?'

'You *did* ask.'

'OK, start then.'

Winnie paused to think. Her mother's favourite song had been 'Carrickfergus'.

> I wish I had you in Carrickfergus,
> Only three miles on from Ballygrand.
> I would swim over the deepest ocean
> Thinking of days there in Ballygrand . . .

She paused. To her astonishment, Lillian joined in.

> But the seas are deep and I can't swim over,
> And neither more have I wings to fly.
> I wish I could find me a handy boatman,
> Would ferry over my love and I.

Then they both stopped to think about the words they had just sung.

'There might have been a more inappropriate song if I could have thought of it,' Winnie apologised.

For the first time, she heard a genuine laugh from Lillian. This was not a tinkle, a put-down or a sneer. She actually found it funny.

'You could have picked "Cool Clear Water", I suppose,' she said eventually.

'Your call,' Winnie said.

Lillian sang 'The Way You Look Tonight'. Teddy's father had sung it to her the night before he was killed on the combine harvester, she said.

Winnie sang 'Only The Lonely'. She had found the record shortly after her father had married the strange, distant stepmother who made jewellery. Then Lillian sang 'True Love', and said that she had always hoped to meet someone again after Teddy's father had died but never did. She had worked long hours and tried too hard to make them people of importance in Rossmore. There had been no time for love.

Winnie sang 'St Louis Blues'. She had once won a talent competition by singing it in a pub and the prize had been a leg of lamb.

'Are we wasting our voices in case we need to call for help?'

Lillian wondered. She asked as if she really wanted to hear what Winnie would say.

'I don't think anyone would hear us anyway. Our best hope is to keep positive,' Winnie suggested. 'Do you know any Beatles songs?' So they sang 'Hey Jude'.

Lillian said that she remembered her mother had said the Beatles were depraved because they had long hair. Winnie said that her stepmother had never known who they were and that even her father was vague about them. It was so hard to have a real conversation with them about anything.

'Do they know you're here?' Lillian asked.

'Nobody knows we're here. That's the problem,' Winnie sighed.

'No, I mean in the West of Ireland. Do they know about Teddy?'

'No. They hardly know any of my friends.'

'Maybe you should take him to meet them. He said he hadn't met your folks yet.'

'Well, you know . . .' Winnie shrugged as if to make little of it all.

'He took you to meet me.'

'Yes, didn't he?' The memory of that meeting was still bitter, and Winnie cursed her foolishness trying to take on this mother-in-law from hell, locking horns with her and pretending friendship to win the son. Look where it had ended up. In this cave, waiting for at the worst a slow death by drowning or at the very best rheumatic fever.

'I wasn't entirely overjoyed at first,' Lillian admitted after a pause. 'Neither were you, but it was you who suggested coming on this holiday.'

'I did *not* suggest you come on the holiday. I told you about

Stone House and that I wanted to come here with Teddy, that was all. You invited yourself.'

'He invited me. You went along with it.'

'It doesn't matter now,' Winnie said. There was defeat in her tone.

'Don't get all down about it, please. I'm frightened. I liked it better when you were strong. Can you think of any other songs?'

'No.' Winnie was mulish.

'You *must* know some more songs.'

'What about "By The Rivers Of Babylon"?' Winnie offered.

It turned out that Lillian had been at a wedding in St Augustine's church in Rossmore where the bride and groom had chosen this as one of their wedding hymns, and the Polish priest had thought it must be an old Irish tradition and sang along with it.

Winnie said that one year, when she was working the Christmas shift in a hospital, they had all made a conga line and danced through the wards singing this song to cheer the patients up, and even the sour ward sister had agreed that it worked.

Then Lillian said there was nothing to beat 'Heartbreak Hotel', so they sang that. Winnie said she actually preferred Elvis doing 'Suspicious Minds', but they only knew one line of that, which was something about being caught in a trap. Still, they sang it over and over until it began to sound hollow.

During an attempt at Otis Redding's 'Sitting On The Dock Of The Bay', they both noticed that the level of the water had gone down. They hardly dared to say it in case yet another huge wave would crash in. But when it was clear that the tide had turned, and their throats were raw from singing and the salt spray, they reached out their hands to each other. Cold, wet and trembling, they just held on for a few seconds. Words would have destroyed the fragile hope and shaky peace they had managed to reach.

Now it was a matter of waiting.

Mrs Starr called Rigger when it was obvious that two of her guests had gone missing. He rounded up a search party, including Chicky's brothers-in-law.

'I warned them against the south cliffs, so you can be sure that's where they went,' she said in a clipped voice. Rigger asked her if there were any specific places she had told them about and when Chicky thought about it, it was clear what had happened. She had seen the challenge in Lillian Hennessy's face as she had dismissed the weather warnings the previous night. And she had noticed how Lillian left without any hint of her direction that morning.

The men said they would go towards Majella's Cave and phone her as soon as they had any news.

Before she heard from them, however, there was a call from Teddy Hennessy, who said he was Lillian's son and phoning from England. He apologised for interrupting her but said he couldn't reach his mother or Winnie by mobile phone. They must have switched them off.

Chicky Starr was professional and guarded. No point in alerting him to any possible danger until she had proof that there was a real need to be worried. She took his number carefully.

'They've gone walking over the cliff paths and should be back soon, Mr Hennessy.'

'And they're having a good time?' He sounded anxious to hear it was all going well.

'Yes; I'm sorry they're not here to tell you themselves. They'll be upset to have missed you.'

'I got a text from Winnie last night. She said the place was wonderful.'

'I'm pleased they are satisfied with it all.' Mrs Starr felt a lump in her throat. 'It's good to see old friends enjoy themselves . . .' Please God may she not have to talk to this man in an entirely different way in a few hours' time.

'Lillian's my mother, as I said. This holiday was their way to get to know each other properly, you see. It's great to know it's working so well.'

He sounded hopeful and enthusiastic. How could she tell him that his hard, brittle mother had not been getting on at all well with Winnie, who turned out to be his girlfriend? The relationship had not even been acknowledged. How would history have to be rewritten if the worst had happened?

She stood with her hand at her throat until Orla tugged at her sleeve asking whether the meal should be served now or not. She pulled herself together and got the guests seated. They were all anxious to hear news of the missing women and an unsettled air hung over the table.

'They're all right, you know,' said Freda suddenly, 'they're fine. You mustn't worry. They'll be cold and hungry, but they'll be all right.' She said it with great confidence, but it seemed like everything was in slow motion until the telephone rang.

They were safe. The search party were bringing them first to Dr Dai's house but there seemed to be nothing worse than cold and shock. Without giving any hint of her relief, Chicky Starr told the other guests that Winnie and Lillian had been caught by the tide and would need hot baths but that everyone was to start dinner without them.

When they came in the door, white-faced and wrapped in rugs and blankets, everyone cheered.

Lillian made very light of it all.

'Now you've all seen me without my make-up, I'll never recover from this!' she laughed.

'Were you trapped by the tide?' Freda was anxious to know what had happened.

'Yes, but we knew the tide would have to go out again,' Winnie said. She was trembling but there was going to be no drama.

'Weren't you very frightened?' The English doctor and his wife were concerned.

'No, not really. Winnie was great. She sang all the time to keep our spirits up. She does a very mean "St Louis Blues", by the way. She might give us a recital one night.'

'Only if *you* do "Heartbreak Hotel",' Winnie said.

Mrs Starr interrupted. 'Your son rang, Lillian, from England. I said you'd call him when you got back.'

'Let's have a bath first,' Lillian said.

'Did you actually tell him that—' Winnie began.

'I told him you'd been delayed, that's all.'

They looked at her gratefully.

Lillian looked thoughtful. 'Winnie, why don't *you* call him? He's your fellow. It's *you* that he wanted to talk to anyway. Tell him I'll talk another time.' And she headed towards her bath.

Only Chicky Starr and Freda O'Donovan saw any significance in that remark. They both realised that some great shift had taken place during the long hours waiting for a high Atlantic tide to change. It wouldn't all be sunshine or an easy road ahead, but it wasn't only the weather that looked a lot calmer and less troubled than it had that morning.

John

John had to remember that they were talking to him when they called out his name. It had been so long since anyone had called him John, which was in fact his real name, or at least the name he had been given in the orphanage all those years ago.

Everyone else knew him as Corry.

There was a character called Corry in a children's book which the nuns used to read at bedtime. A little cherub of a toddler that everyone loved. So John thought this was a good name, and the nuns humoured him.

There was a gardener in the orphanage; an old man who came from a place called Salinas. He was always telling them that this was a great part of the world and one day, when he had enough money, he would go back there and buy himself a little place.

Corry used to say the name Salinas over and over. He liked it.

He had no name. This would be his name.

He was Corry Salinas and when he was sixteen he got his first job working in a sandwich bar.

They had a contract to do lunches for film crews, and Corry soon caught everyone's eye. It wasn't just his dark eyes above the aquiline nose, his hair which curled slightly at the temples, his intelligent eyes which always seemed to smile conspiratorially – it was the way he remembered who liked peanut butter and who liked low-fat cheese. Nothing was too much trouble; even the most tiresome and self-obsessed starlets, who changed their minds and said that he had delivered the wrong sandwich, were impressed.

'I don't know where you get your patience.' Monica, who worked with him, had a shorter fuse.

'There are other sandwich bars. We want them to choose ours so it needs a bit of extra effort at the start.' Corry was cheerful. He was not afraid of hard work. He lived in a room over a laundromat and cleaned the place each morning instead of paying rent.

He didn't have to spend any money on food since there was always something to eat in a sandwich business. His savings account grew, and every cent was earmarked for acting lessons. No way could you live in Los Angeles and not want to be a part of the industry.

He and Monica were now an item.

Corry's good looks meant that being an extra would have been easy. But that wasn't really an option. It would mean hanging around all day for what was considerably less money than he earned through the lunch trade. He would hold out until he got a speaking part, and maybe an agent.

It was all part of the dream.

Monica's dream was different. She thought they should move into a place of their own and set up their own fast-food business. Why work all the hours God sent just to make the employer even more wealthy?

But Corry was firm. His dream was to be an actor. He could not commit full-time to a catering business.

Monica was upset by this. She had seen too many people waste a lifetime chasing after a Hollywood dream. Her own father was one of them. But Corry was the love of her life, this handsome boy with the mobile face and the confidence that he would make it in the movies. She didn't want to push him and risk losing him.

And then Monica was pregnant. She didn't know how to tell Corry. She feared so much that he would say he couldn't get involved. Contraception had been her responsibility. And Monica had not deliberately forgotten to take the pill. She spent days wondering how to tell him in the way that would least upset him. In the end she didn't have to; he guessed.

'Why didn't you tell me sooner?' he seemed full of love.

'I didn't want to destroy your dream.'

'Now I have two dreams: a family *and* a movie career,' he said.

They were married three weeks later, and Monica moved in over the laundromat. They found even more work to keep up their funds. Acting lessons cost a lot of money, and people told them that having a baby didn't come cheap either.

By the time that Maria Rosa was born, Corry Salinas had an agent and had been cast as one of three singing waiters in a big musical comedy. Not a great role, his agent had explained, but it would get him on the ladder. It was a vehicle for an ageing and difficult actress who was going to make life hell for everyone during the shoot. And if they liked him, who knew what could follow?

Corry made sure they liked him. He was attentive and endlessly patient for long, long days of work. He treated the First Assistant Director as if he were God. He made special fresh juices for the difficult movie star. She told everyone that he was cute.

The other two singing waiters might let their irritation show, but Corry never did. His ready smile and willingness to please paid off. By the time the shoot was over he had been offered a part in another movie.

Maria Rosa was the most beautiful baby in the world.

Monica's family did a great deal to help as they waited hopefully for Monica's husband to get a serious job that paid properly. Corry had no family to help them out but he often wheeled the baby up to the orphanage where he had been raised, and got a great welcome. He always asked if they could tell him anything at all about his own natural parents, and always they said no. He had been left at the gates of the orphanage aged about three weeks with a letter in Italian begging them to look after him and give him a good life.

'And you *did* give me a good life,' Corry always told them. The nuns loved him in the orphanage. So many of their charges had left bitter and saddened, resentful that they had spent their youth in an institution. Times had changed now, and nuns could go out to movies and theatres. They promised Corry they would go to everything he appeared in and even start a fan club for him.

Monica said it was going to be very hard getting the baby buggy up and down the stairs over the laundromat, but Corry said they couldn't move yet. Acting was a perilous career. They would indeed have a lovely home for the baby, but not at the moment.

The second movie, where Corry played a troubled teenager and the ageing, difficult actress played his stepmother, was written off as a movie too far for the diva. Her time was over, the reviewer said, her day was done. The boy, however! Now here was a talent! And so the offers started coming in.

Corry bought the house that Monica had longed for. But by the time Maria Rosa was three, everything had begun to fall apart. He spent more and more time in the bachelor apartment the studio had provided for him. He had to be seen at receptions and night clubs and at benefit nights.

Monica read that his name was coupled with Heidi, his co-star in the latest film. The next weekend when he had come home for a whole two days, she asked him directly was there any truth in what the gossip columns were saying.

Corry tried to explain that the publicity people demanded this kind of circus.

'But is there anything in it?' Monica asked.

'Well, I'm sleeping with her, yes, but it's not important, not compared to you and Maria Rosa,' he said.

The divorce was swift, and he could see Maria Rosa every Saturday and for a ten-day vacation each year.

Corry Salinas did not marry Heidi, as had been confidently predicted in the gossip columns. Heidi behaved badly about it. She got a lot of publicity as the victim of a love rat.

Monica remained silent and gave no interviews. She was never in the house when Corry arrived to pick up Maria Rosa for his Saturday visit; either her father or mother would hand over the child with few words, a look of resentment and disappointment.

Sometimes Corry was lonely and tried to ask Monica to review the situation. The answer was always the same.

'I bear you no ill will, but please contact me only through the lawyers.'

The parts were getting better; the years rolled by.

He married Sylvia when he was twenty-eight. A very

153

different wedding day to his first one. Sylvia was from a very wealthy family that had made several fortunes in the hotel business. She was a beautiful and much-indulged daughter who had been denied nothing, and when she had insisted on a giant society wedding as her twenty-first birthday present, she got that as well.

Corry was stunned that this dazzling girl wanted him so much. He went along with all the arrangements that Sylvia's family suggested. One request, that his own ten-year-old daughter, Maria Rosa, be one of the flower girls was refused point-blank. So firmly that he did not mention it again.

Sylvia's lawyers arranged a series of prenup agreements with Corry's lawyers. The publicity for the wedding was intense and the photographic rights hotly fought over.

The day itself passed in a blur. If Corry remembered, a little wistfully, the small wedding party when he and Monica were eighteen and full of hope, then he put the thought far from his mind. That was then, this was now.

Now did not last long. Corry was needed for long hours at the studio, for costume fittings, for publicity tours, for foreign movie festivals. Sylvia was bored. She played a lot of tennis and raised money for charities.

For Corry's thirtieth birthday Sylvia planned another lavish event. It came at a time when he was very much in the public eye with his latest film, where he played a troubled doctor with a difficult moral choice to make. Posters were everywhere showing Corry's sensitive face pondering what he was to do. Women longed to meet him and take the tortured look from his eyes.

He went through the invitation list. The great of Hollywood and the hotel industry were well represented. His daughter's name was not there.

This time he did insist.

'She's twelve years of age. She'll read about it. She *has* to be there.'

'It's *my* party and I don't want her there. She's part of your past, not your present, or indeed your future. Anyway, I was thinking it's time for us to have our own child.' Sylvia was very insistent. She had only agreed to meet her stepdaughter, Maria Rosa, half a dozen times since the wedding, saying she wasn't good with young girls – they were all so silly and giggled over nothing.

There was something so dismissive about the way she spoke, something that sent out the message that Sylvia would always get what *she* wanted. The rosebud smile he had once thought so entrancing looked more like a pout now.

He tested the water to ask if he could include some of the people from the orphanage where he was raised.

'But darling Corry, they would be *so* out of place. Surely you can see that?'

'They will never be out of place in my life. They raised me, made me who I am.'

'Well, send them money, sweetheart, help them in fundraising – that's worth twice as much as some gesture of inviting them to a glitzy do where they will be fish out of water.'

Corry did already send money to his orphanage. He was on the board of a fundraising committee, but this was not the point. Three of those gentle plain-clothes nuns, as he called them, would so enjoy being guests at a huge catered event. How could these women, who had looked after him since he was found on their doorstep, be out of place anywhere?

He felt a vein in his forehead; a throbbing sensation. He

even felt slightly dizzy. He could hear his own voice as if it were far away. It didn't seem to come from inside.

'I don't want a party if I can't have my daughter and the people who educated me, fed and clothed me.'

'You're overtired, Corry. You work too hard,' Sylvia said.

'That's true, I do work too hard. But I am serious. I have never been more serious in my life.'

Sylvia said they should leave the matter for now.

'If you send out those invitations, *then* we can leave the matter.'

'I will not be bullied or blackmailed into doing something I don't want to do.'

'Fine,' Corry said, and the marriage ended.

It was fairly painless, all things considered. Corry's lawyers dealt with Sylvia's lawyers. Settlements were agreed. But afterwards Sylvia found that a social life without Corry Salinas on her arm was not nearly as bright as it had been. She was tempted to give interviews about their tempestuous marriage.

Corry read them in disbelief. It hadn't been at all like this.

He tried to tell his daughter, Maria Rosa, that life with Sylvia had been a series of staged events, all set in a goldfish bowl to encourage the admiration and envy of others. There had been none of these violent arguments. Corry had always given in to her. The truth was that he and Sylvia barely knew each other.

'Why did you marry her then, Dad?' Maria Rosa asked.

'I guess I was flattered,' he said simply.

Maria Rosa was wise beyond her years and, because she had heard the same explanation from her mother, she believed him.

*

During the next two decades, Corry Salinas became a household name, not only in the United States but all over the world. He could raise the money for any movie he was involved in. He was seen with elegant women in and out of high-profile occasions, film premieres, Broadway first nights, art openings and on the grandest, most expensive yachts in the Mediterranean. The gossip columnists were always marrying him off to film stars, heiresses and even minor royalty, but nothing transpired.

Maria Rosa was dark-eyed and romantic-looking like Corry, practical and even-tempered like Monica. She had inherited their work ethic, trained as a teacher and did voluntary service overseas. Her father's A-list celebrity lifestyle didn't attract her remotely. When she was growing up it had been the enemy of any kind of family life.

She had spent too much of her youth fleeing from paparazzi, refusing to talk to people in case she was misquoted in the press. Any door would have been open to her as the daughter of Corry Salinas, but she never wanted to walk through them.

She was never hostile or resentful about her father. She always called him whenever she came back to LA to suggest a pizza or a Mexican dinner in a neighbourhood restaurant, where they could sit quietly in a booth without all the attendant publicity that Corry Salinas trailed wherever he went.

He heard from his daughter that Monica had married again, a gentle guy called Harvey who ran a flower shop. Her mother had never been happier, Maria Rosa explained; the only cloud in the sky was that there was no sign of *her* upcoming wedding and maybe grandchildren. But, Maria Rosa sighed, she just hadn't met anyone, and Lord wasn't this town an awful warning about how marriage could go horribly wrong.

People often said that it was unfair how men looked better as they aged; Corry could still play passionate leading roles when women in their fifties were struggling to get character parts. But he knew this could not go on for ever.

When Corry was in his late fifties, he knew that what he needed was one utterly unforgettable part to play. Something with gravitas and sensitivity. A part that would for ever be associated with him. Yet it didn't seem to come his way.

His agent, who was called Trevor the Tireless, had been trying to direct him towards a television series, but Corry would have none of it. When he had been starting out they always thought that only old, failed actors went into television. The real arena was the movie theatre; nothing else counted.

Trevor sighed.

Corry was way behind the times, he said. They were in a golden age of television, he said. There were fabulous writers doing their best work for television. There was a part on offer which had all the gravitas he was looking for – he was going to play a President of the United States! Corry could write his own ticket. The real rule for success was to be adaptable, he kept saying. But Corry would not listen.

It wasn't a matter of changing agents. Not at this stage. Trevor was indeed tireless in his efforts to find the perfect part for his most famous client. And Corry knew the old saying that changing agents was like changing deckchairs on the *Titanic*.

Corry had always been relaxed and easy-going. Suddenly he had become stubborn, utterly certain that he knew better than agents, the studios and the whole industry.

Corry hadn't listened to the kind nuns who had wanted him to be a priest, or to the man who ran the first sandwich bar who had offered Corry a permanent position. He had turned a deaf ear to those who said his acting lessons were an expense he could not afford. He had always been his own man.

Soon he would be sixty. Trevor wanted to be able to announce something great to coincide with this anniversary, but all he came up with was yet another television offer.

'It's a peach of a part,' Trevor begged. 'You play an Italian who thinks he has a fatal illness and goes back to Italy to find his roots before he dies. Then he meets this woman. They're lining up to play her if you are going to be the lead, you wouldn't believe the names we have.'

'Not television,' Corry said.

'It's all changed, believe me. Look at the awards! They're all going to television stars now.'

'No, Trevor.'

And that's how things stood for weeks.

Corry told Maria Rosa about it all.

'Why don't you do it, Father? None of my friends has time to go out to movie theatres. They all watch TV or download things on to their computers. It's all changed. Everything has.'

She was more right than either of them knew.

Corry's business manager, who had always advised him well, had been badly stung by the recession. Investments had not paid off, so even more hasty and unwise investments were made. It all blew up the day that the manager was killed in a car wreck.

He had driven straight into a wall, leaving behind him a financial confusion that would take years to unravel.

Now, for the first time in decades, Corry had to make

a career decision based entirely on the need to make money. Most of his property had to be sold off piece by piece.

Trevor was his usual tireless self in keeping Corry Salinas's financial woes out of the papers. But he did clear his throat several times about the television series. And this time Corry had to listen.

The money people were meeting in Frankfurt. They wanted Corry to be there to say that he was interested. This would help them raise the financing. It was going to be huge, Trevor said; Corry would get his property back.

'I only want to make sure my daughter is left well provided for,' Corry said glumly as he packed his bag for Germany.

They always boarded Corry discreetly, seconds before the plane took off. He slipped into his seat in first class with the minimum of fuss. If other passengers recognised him, they gave no sign. He had the treatment and sample scripts for the new television series on his lap and opened them reluctantly. His heart was just not in the project which, according to Tireless Trevor, would turn his financial life around and make him even more of a household name than he already was. When he got to Frankfurt he would shower, change and settle himself in the hotel and only then would he make up his mind about what to do. He was tired, and after a few minutes in his comfortable seat he drifted off to sleep.

He woke to realise that the plane had not yet taken off. The cabin steward was offering him some fresh orange juice. There had been a delay, he was told, an instrument check, but all was fine and the captain said they would be taking off shortly.

Corry checked his watch; there was an announcement. This plane was going nowhere. The flight was cancelled. Arrangements were being put in place to get everyone on to the next day's flight. Anyone who didn't want to wait would be transferred to another airline, but the flight would not be direct. The next day would be too late; he'd miss the meeting entirely. So much for settling down in his hotel beforehand. Trevor would never believe it. He'd never forgive him.

At the airport, all hell was breaking loose as everyone was trying to move to different airlines; in the end it was only flying by way of Shannon airport in Ireland that he had any chance of getting to Frankfurt at all. He just had time to call Trevor who, to save time, would now pick him up. He'd arrange for the media to photograph him coming through the airport. He'd make a story about the delayed flight, a few interviews and then he'd take him straight to the meeting. Whatever happened, he had to be there. Everyone was counting on him.

Everyone was counting on him, were they? Oh well. So, he'd be late, but he just might make it. He knew he would not speed the plane or shorten the journey by worrying about it, so he slept as the plane went eastwards through the night and then they were landing in Ireland.

He looked down at the small patchwork green fields far below. He could see the coastline. Maria Rosa had been to Ireland once with a student group some years back. She said she had enjoyed it. Everyone she met had some kind of story to tell. He thought fancifully about what it would be like to go on a vacation with his daughter. She was now in her early forties – a handsome woman absorbed in her teaching, equally at ease in the flower shop with her mother and Harvey, or having drinks with her father in the top Hollywood hotels.

Still no sign of a romance in her life, but she laughed it away and so Corry stopped enquiring. She might even *enjoy* a holiday with him. As soon as he got home, he'd call her and suggest it.

He looked at his watch again. This was going to be very close. He would have to run to catch his connection to Germany.

It was, in fact, too close. Corry stood and watched the flight to Frankfurt leave without him.

Tireless Trevor would be waiting at the airport, the publicity machine would meet a plane on which he was not travelling. He called Trevor's cell phone and held his own phone away from his ear as his agent fumed, protested and raged about the news. Eventually, he ran out of adjectives and abuse and just sounded weary.

'So what *are* you going to do?' he asked.

Corry said, 'I'm tired. Very tired.'

'*You* are tired?' Trevor's voice had risen again dangerously. '*You* have nothing to be tired about. It's the rest of us that have things that are making us tired, like trying to explain what can never be explained.'

'It was the airline . . .' Corry began.

'Don't give me the airline. If you had wanted to be here, you'd have been here.'

'Can they not have the meeting tonight or tomorrow?'

'Of course they can't. Who do you think these people are? They've all flown in specially. They got on planes that didn't sit on their butts on the tarmac,' Trevor raged.

'Then I'm staying here for a week. If it's too late for the meeting, then to hell with it. I'm getting out for a while.'

'Hey, this is no time . . . I've set everything up.'

'And I tried to get there, but the airline let me down. Goodbye, Trevor, talk to you in a week's time.'

'But where are you going? What are you doing? You can't go wandering off like this!'

'I'm a grown man. An *old* man, as you never tire of hinting. I can have a week's vacation here or a month, if I like. See you back in LA.' Corry closed his phone and turned it on to message.

He went to get himself another coffee. This kind of freedom was new to him. He had escaped the meeting he had been dreading. He could now do what he wanted to without consulting any handler, manager or agent. He was actually free.

The airline had done him a favour.

But where would he go? Perhaps he should buy a tourist guide book or find a travel agent. On the tables around there were various brochures offering suggestions of what to do in the region. There was a medieval banquet in a castle. There was a tour to some spectacular cliff face called Moher, which was meant to be one of the Wonders of the World. There were golf packages. None of them appealed to Corry.

But one little sheet advertised A Week in Winter and promised a warm, welcoming house and miles of sand and cliffs and wild birds. He called the number to know if there was a vacancy.

A pleasant-sounding woman said there was indeed room for him, told him to rent a car and drive north. He should call again when he arrived in Stoneybridge for directions to the house.

'About payment?' Corry began; he didn't want to give his name, and there was a possibility that he might even go unrecognised, which would be a real treat.

'We'll sort all that out when you get here,' Mrs Starr was brisk. 'And your name is . . . ?'

'John,' Corry said, without pausing.

'Right, John, take your time, and be very careful of Irish drivers, they are inclined to pull out suddenly without indicating. Assume they are going to do that and you'll be fine.'

His shoulders felt less tense. He was an ordinary tourist going on an ordinary holiday. There was no press reception, no junket of showbiz writers following him.

It was a cold, bright morning. Corry Salinas put his bag into the back of the rented car and drove north obediently.

He must remember he was called John from now on.

The other guests seemed to have settled in. The house looked just as it had done in the brochure. John turned his collar up to shield his face partially.

He was so used to people doing a double take when they met him and shouts of, 'Oh my God, you're Corry Salinas!' But at Stone House, nobody recognised him. Perhaps Tireless Trevor had been right when he said that Corry Salinas was in grave danger of being a forgotten brand.

He told them, when asked, that he was a businessman from Los Angeles taking a well-deserved week off. And then he began to feel that there was no need to turn up his collar any more. If they recognised him, they were not going to say anything. But it was much more likely that they hadn't a clue who he was.

The food was good, the conversation was easy, but he felt very weary. He was used to putting on an act, giving a performance. It wasn't demanded here, which was a relief, but on the other hand he felt somewhat at a loss. What *was* his role?

He was the first to go to bed. He asked them to forgive him

and to believe that he hadn't invented the International Date Line. They laughed and told him to sleep well.

And indeed John did sleep well, immediately, in his comfortable bed, but jet lag meant he did not sleep long. Still on California time, he woke at three a.m., alert and ready to face the day.

He made himself tea and looked out the window at the waves crashing on the shore below. He wanted to call Maria Rosa. It was eight or nine hours earlier back home. Perhaps she would have come back to her apartment after a long day's teaching.

He picked up his mobile phone but before he dialled her number, he paused. Would she really be interested to know that he had booked into this bizarre vacation? She was always polite but distant, as if anything her father did happened in an unreal, childlike maze of ratings and reviews and column inches of publicity. To Maria Rosa it had little to do with the real world.

Then he told himself to stop analysing it.

He dialled the number.

'Maria Rosa? It's Dad.'

'Hey, Dad. How are things?'

'Just fine. I'm stuck in Ireland, of all places. I missed the connection when I was heading for Germany.'

'Ireland's OK, Dad, you could be in worse places.'

'I know. It's fine. Very wild where I am, right on the Atlantic.'

'And cold, I guess?'

'Yes, but it's a warm hotel. I'm going to stay here for a week.'

'That's good, Dad.'

Was she interested? Was she bored? It was so hard to know

from six thousand miles away. 'I just thought I'd call to say hi.'

'It's good to hear from you.'

There was a pause. Was she ending the conversation?

'And you.' He was loath to let her go. 'Can you hear the waves crashing outside? They're really big. They're like a sort of drum roll.'

'What time is it there?' she asked.

'Just after three a.m.,' he said.

'Hey, Dad, you need to sleep,' his only daughter said.

Corry said goodnight, and felt more lonely and lost than he had ever felt in his life.

He dozed fitfully after that, and felt sluggish and groggy as he went down to breakfast. Several people were already at the table and they commiserated with him over his jet lag. A young woman called Winnie, who was a nurse, gave him sound, practical advice and although he promised he'd follow it, he allowed himself to be persuaded to try a full Irish breakfast as an alternative remedy. Mrs Starr placed a cafetière of coffee in front of him and told him to help himself.

After breakfast, he lingered over a last cup as Orla cleared the table and Mrs Starr busied herself with maps and binoculars and packed lunches for the guests setting out on walks. As the last of them left, he saw her shoulders relax and he realised how much anxiety lay under the surface.

She caught his eye as she turned round and saw that he had been watching her.

'This is our first week,' she explained.

'But you're no stranger to the business, I can tell,' he said.

'You're right,' she said, 'but that wasn't my own business. I worked for someone else. Now I'm where the buck stops. So listen, John, what would you like to do today? Would you like another cup of coffee, and I'll tell you what's around?'

They chatted companionably over another pot of coffee; and so, refreshed, John set out in blustery sunshine for his first day's walk.

Following Chicky's advice, he chose to go inland. He walked over a lonely road, saw big sheep with black faces and twisted horns. Or were they wild goats? There had been little time to study nature when he was growing up. There were huge gaps in his understanding of so many things.

He found a small pub and went from the bright, cold sunshine into the dark interior where a turf fire burned in a small grate and half a dozen men looked up from pints, interested to see a stranger come in.

John greeted them all pleasantly. He was an American, he explained unnecessarily, staying at Stone House. Mrs Starr had suggested this pub would be a good place to visit.

'Decent woman, Chicky Starr.' The landlord was pleased with the praise, and he polished the glasses with greater vigour than ever.

'She spent most of her life in America. Did you know her from there?' an old man asked him.

'No, indeed. I just saw an advertisement yesterday in Shannon airport, and here I am!'

Was it only yesterday? He already felt completely disconnected from any other life.

A large man wearing a big cap looked at John keenly. He had a broad red face and small curious eyes.

'You know, you're sort of familiar-looking. Are you sure you were never this way before?'

'Never. This is my first visit. You people sure live in a wonderful part of the world.'

That satisfied them. John had perfected the easy transferring of the attention away from himself, coupled with praise for their having lucked out in where they found themselves living.

'Chicky Starr was married to a Yank, you know. He was killed in a terrible car crash, the poor devil,' the red-faced man said.

'The Lord have mercy on him,' said the others in unison.

'That's terrible,' John said.

'Yes, she was very cut up. But she's got great guts altogether. She came back here to her own people and bought the old Sheedy place. She took ages doing it up. You wouldn't believe all the work that went into that house.'

'It's certainly a very comfortable place to stay,' John said.

'When you get back home, will you tell your friends in America to go there?'

'Sure I will.' John wondered did he know anyone in Los Angeles who would come to an outpost like this.

They left him to his soup and his pint of Guinness. He felt oddly at ease in their company, and listened while they talked about old Frank Hanratty who had painted his old van bright pink so that he could find it without any difficulty. Frank was still driving round the place peering through his glasses, seeing nothing ahead of him or behind. He had never been in any accident. *Yet*.

Frank had never married, apparently, but had a better social life than any of them; he called here, there and everywhere and was welcome wherever he went. He was mad keen on the cinema and would drive the pink van thirty miles every week and see at least two films in the big town . . .

Their conversation drifted around John. He had an image of this peaceful, undemanding life the man Hanratty lived, happy with the way the cards had been dealt. He wondered if he should buy everyone a drink. That's what would happen in a movie. But life wasn't a movie. These men might be affronted. He gave them his big, enveloping smile and promised he would come back again.

'Great soup that, lumps of chicken in it,' he said.

He couldn't have said anything that pleased the landlord more.

'That chicken was running around the back yard yesterday morning,' he said proudly.

The day's walking did wonders for his jet lag, and he slept soundly that night. He woke at six but found himself happy to lie in bed listening to the sounds of the wind and the sea. It was louder today, he felt sure. The wind seemed to have changed direction and was battering against the windows; when eventually he got up, there was a dark and angry look to the waves.

Sure enough, Mrs Starr was issuing weather warnings to everyone over breakfast. He had thought he might try the walk down to the shoreline with the little rocky inlets, but thought better of it, given her advice. Not sure what alternative route to take, he found himself lingering over a last cup of coffee, the other guests bustling around the doorway; as the last of them left, he smiled at Chicky Starr and, raising an eyebrow, invited her to join him.

'I hear you were in New York for a while,' he said.

He started to look forward to their chats. There was something restful about being able to have a normal conversation with people who had no preconceived notions about him, no idea about his other life and no expectations. The following morning, once again, John stayed back and was the last to leave after breakfast. He watched as Orla cleared away the plates.

'You are lucky to have family to help you here,' John said.

'Yes. Orla had different plans but they didn't work out, so I think she's happy to be here, for a while anyway.' Mrs Starr never usually seemed in a hurry but this particular morning, she seemed slightly preoccupied.

'Am I keeping you from anything, Mrs Starr?'

'I'm so sorry, John, I am indeed a little distracted. My car has died on me and Dinny from the garage will be up to fix it but not until this evening. Rigger, that's our manager, has to go to the doctor with his babies – they're having inoculations. We need to go shopping, Orla and I. I'm just working out how we can . . .'

'Why don't I drive you?' he suggested immediately.

'No, that would never do. This is *your* holiday.'

Orla was at the table, listening in. 'Oh, go on, Chicky, John doesn't mind. And it's only fifteen minutes down the road. I'll go with him and get myself a lift back.'

It was settled.

They drove companionably to the town. Orla was a handsome girl with easy conversation.

'It's unfair to ask you to do this on your holidays but it's Chicky's first week ever. She has enough to think about. I thought you wouldn't mind.'

'No, I'm very pleased to help. And by the way, I'll come with you. I actually like going to the stores,' John offered. He was indeed captivated by Orla's conversations with the butcher, the cheesemaker and all the feeling and prodding of vegetables in the greengrocer's. Soon it was all packed and paid for.

Orla was very grateful. 'Thank you so much. I'll ask one of the O'Haras for a lift back now, so off you go and enjoy your day.'

'I was going to have yet another coffee,' John admitted. 'I see a place over there. Why don't you put the shopping in the car and we'll go to the café for ten minutes.'

They chatted easily. Orla told him how she had nearly gone to New York to see Uncle Walter and Chicky, but then of course there had been the accident. Poor Uncle Walter had been killed.

Orla said she had done a course in Dublin and then she and her friend Brigid had gone to London to work. It had been good fun for a while but then her friend had got engaged to and married a madman and anyway, she had been feeling restless and longed for the seas and cliffs of Stoneybridge. There would have been no work for her without Chicky. There was something healing about this place. It helped to take the ache out of her heart.

'I think I see what you mean about this place being healing,' John said. 'I've only been here a short time, and I can feel it getting to me.'

'It must be very different from the life you're used to,' she was sympathetic.

'Very,' he said, without elaborating on the life he was used to.

'I suppose you couldn't sit and have a cup of coffee in a place like this out where you live . . .'

He looked at her sharply. 'What do you mean?' he asked eventually.

'John, of course we know that you are Corry Salinas. We knew the moment we saw you, Chicky and I.'

'But you didn't say.' He was stunned.

'You came here as John. You wanted to be a private person. Why should we say anything?'

'And the others, the guests? Do *they* know?'

'Yes. The Swedish guy copped you the first night, and the English couple, Henry and Nicola, asked Chicky discreetly if you were here incognito.'

'It's true what I said. I *was* on my way to a business meeting in Germany, and I *did* come here on the spur of the moment.'

'Sure. And call yourself whatever you want to, John, it's your life, your holiday.'

'But if everyone knows . . . ?' he said doubtfully.

'Honestly, they'll respect your wanting to be an ordinary person. They're mainly concentrating on their own lives anyway.'

'It would make life easier, certainly, if they know already. It's just that I was hoping to leave that world behind, at least for a while, just spend some time without all that baggage.'

'It must be desperate having to explain everything and be asked if you know Tom Cruise or Brad Pitt.'

'It's not that so much as they have such high expectations of me. They think I actually *am* the guys I play in the movies. I always feel I disappoint them.'

'Oh, I doubt that. Everyone here thinks you're full of charm. Me too. I've sort of gone off men myself personally, but you'd put a spark back into the eye.'

'You mock me. I'm an old, old man,' he laughed.

'Oh, I do *not* mock you, believe me. But I suppose I wish you got more fun out of it: being world famous, successful, everyone loving you. If I had done all you've done, I'd be delighted with myself and go round beaming at everyone.'

'It's only role-playing,' he said. 'That's my day job. I don't want to have to do it in real life as well.'

Orla considered this seriously. 'But you can be yourself with family, can't you?' she asked.

'I don't *have* any family, apart from one daughter. I called her in California the other night.'

'Did you tell her about Stone House? Will she come and bring her family here one day?'

'She doesn't have a family. She's a teacher.'

'I'm sure she's very proud of you. Do you go to her school and talk to the kids?'

'No. Lord, no. I'd never do that.'

'Wouldn't they love to meet a film star?' Orla said, surprised.

'Oh, Maria Rosa wouldn't want that,' he said.

'I bet she would. Did you ask her?'

'No. I don't want to push myself and my kind of life on her.'

'Lord, aren't you the most marvellous father. *Why* didn't I get parents like you?'

Corry was back in listening mode, where he was always at ease.

'Are they difficult?' he asked, full of sympathy.

'Well yes, to be honest. They want me to be different, I suppose. They think it's a bit fast to have my own place to live. They think I'm wasting myself washing dishes for Chicky – that's how they put it. They want me to marry one of the God-awful O'Haras and have a big vulgar house with pillars in front of it and three bathrooms.'

'Is that what they say?'

'They don't need to say it, it's there in the air like a great mushroom cloud.'

'Maybe they just wish the best for you and don't know how to put it.'

'Oh no, my mother always knows how to put it, usually in four different ways all saying the same thing – which is that I am wasting my life.'

'And leaving what you call the God-awful O'Haras aside, do you have anybody you *do* like?' He was gentle, not intrusive; interested.

'No. As I told you, I've sort of closed down a bit on men.'

'That's a pity. Some of them are very good people.' He had a wonderful smile, slightly ironic, full of conspiratorial fun.

'I don't want to take the risk. I'm sure you know that yourself.'

'I do know. I've been married twice and involved with a lot more women. I don't really understand them but I didn't ever give up on them!'

'It's different for you, John, you have the whole world to choose from.'

'You look to me like a girl who would have a fairly wide choice, Orla.'

'No. I can't get my head around it. At best it's a kind of compromise. At worst it's a nightmare.'

'Were you never in love?'

'Truthfully, no. Were you?'

'With Monica, my first wife, yes, I am sure I was. Maybe it was because we were young and it was all so new and exciting and we had Maria Rosa. But I think it was love . . .'

'Then you had more than I had.'

'Do you set out to avoid it, the love thing?'

'No, but I do set out not to be made a fool of and not to compromise. I've seen too much of that. My mother and father have very little to talk about, supposing they ever had . . . My aunt Mary is married to a man who is about a hundred because he owns a big property, but he really doesn't know what day it is. Chicky *did* marry for love, but then her fellow was wiped off the face of the earth in a car crash. Not much of a recommendation for love, any of this!'

'Maybe you have a suit of armour up before they get a chance to know you,' he suggested.

'Maybe. I don't *want* to be a ball-breaker or anything. That's just the way it seems to turn out.'

'No, I didn't mean to suggest that . . .'

'And I suppose the *real* irritation is my parents. They are much *too* interested in my life. It's getting harder and harder not to show them how annoying it is.'

'Oh, parents always get it wrong, Orla. It goes with the territory.' John sounded rueful.

'You seem to have it sorted though with your daughter.'

'No way. I want so much for her. I want her to have the best but I *know* I'm not delivering it. I get it so wrong.'

'And what kind of parents did *you* have?'

'None. I have no idea who my father was, and my mother never came back to find me.'

'Oh, I'm so sorry.' Orla reached out and laid her hand on his. 'I'm such a clown. I didn't know. Forgive me.'

'No, it doesn't matter. I'm just telling you why I'm so hung up and holding on to family,' John said. 'I never knew any one thing about my mother except that she spoke Italian and left me wrapped up at the door of an orphanage nearly sixty years ago. The hours, weeks and years I've wondered about her, and hoped she was all right and tried to work out why she gave me away.' Orla's hand was still on his. She squeezed it from solidarity.

'I bet she was thinking of you all the time, too. I *bet* she was. And look what you did with your life! She would have been so proud.'

'Would she? OK, I got to be famous but, as you say, I don't get enough joy from it, enough fun. She might have liked me to have a good time and been happier, less restless.'

'Let's do a deal,' Orla suggested. 'I will have more of an open mind about men. I won't assume they are all screaming bores. I'll do that American thing of assuming that strangers are just friends you haven't met yet!'

'I don't think it's just American,' John said defensively.

'Possibly not. Anyway, I won't vomit at the thought of going out with one of Brigid O'Hara's awful brothers or uncles. I'll give them a chance. Does that sound reasonable?'

'Very much so.' He smiled at her intensity.

'*You*, on the other hand, are going to enjoy being who you are. People *love* to meet a celebrity, John. It does them good. We live dull lives. It's just great to meet a movie star. Be generous enough to understand that.'

'I promise I will. I didn't think of it like that.'

'Oh, and about your daughter; maybe you should tell her the kind of things you've told me about love. I'd love a father who could speak like that.'

'I never have before,' he said.

'No, but you could start now and maybe tell her that you would love to see her and meet her friends, if it wouldn't embarrass her or them. I bet she'd be pleased.'

'I guess I'm afraid she'll reject me.'

'I'm going to face men who might reject me. This is meant to be a deal, isn't it?'

'Right. And will you cut your parents some slack too? They may be driving you nuts but they *do* want what's best for you.'

'Yes, I'll try. I will probably be canonised in my own

lifetime, but I'll try!' she laughed. They shook hands on the deal and began to drive back to Stone House.

On the way they passed Stoneybridge Golf Club. A few hardy golfer souls were out on the course. Outside the door was parked a violent pink van.

'Oh Lord, Frank's at the hot whiskeys already,' Orla sighed. John braked suddenly.

'I'd love a hot whiskey myself,' he said.

'You can't, you're not a member of the Club. Anyway, you've only just had your breakfast.'

But John had parked the car and was striding to the main door.

Alarmed now, Orla ran after him.

Alone at the bar, on a high stool, peering at a newspaper with a magnifying glass, sat a tousled old man. He looked up when the door opened with a crash. A total stranger came through, a man in his fifties in an expensive leather jacket.

'Well, if it isn't Frank Hanratty, as I live and breathe,' the stranger said.

'Um . . . Yes?' Frank was rarely approached by people who did know him, and scarcely ever by people who didn't.

'Well, how are you keeping, Frank, my old friend?'

Frank peered at him. 'You're Corry Salinas,' he said eventually in disbelief.

'Of course I am. Who else would I be?'

'But how do you know *me?*'

'We were only talking about you in the pub yesterday. I know you are a great film buff, and now today I find you in here.'

'But how did you know I was in here?' Poor Frank was bewildered.

'Isn't that your van outside?' John said, as if it was as simple as that.

Frank nodded thoughtfully. It made sense, sure enough. 'And will you have a hot whiskey, er, Corry?' Frank offered.

'I'm no good at morning drinking. I'd love a cup of coffee, however. And do you know my friend Orla?'

They sat and talked about movies, and the boy who served them brought their coffees to a table.

'I can't believe you came in here to see me.' Frank was happier than he had ever been.

John and Orla exchanged glances.

The bargain had been made.

Henry and Nicola

When Henry had qualified as a doctor his parents had hoped that he would go on and specialise, perhaps in surgery. His mother and father, both doctors, regretted that they hadn't studied further. Look at the worlds it could have opened up, they would say wistfully.

But Henry was adamant. He was going to be a GP.

There wasn't any room for him in his parents' practice but he would find a small community where he and Nicola would soon know everyone. They would have children and be part of the place.

Henry had met Nicola during the first week at medical school. Although they were so very young, they both knew in a matter of weeks that this was it. The two sets of parents begged them to wait, let the romance run a bit before getting married. Four years later, they said they would wait no longer.

It was a small, cheerful wedding in Nicola's home town. The guests all said that in a complicated world full of confusion and misunderstandings, Henry and Nicola stood out like two rocks in a stormy sea.

They prepared themselves well for careers in general

179

practice with six-month postings in a maternity hospital, a heart clinic and a children's facility. Soon they felt ready to hang up their names outside a door, and while they were looking for the perfect place to settle, they also decided to try for a child. It was time.

It was hard to find the perfect place to live, but even harder to conceive a child. They couldn't understand it. They were doctors, after all; they knew about timing and fertility chances. A medical examination showed no apparent problem. They were encouraged to keep trying, which they were certainly doing anyway. After a year they tried IVF, and that didn't work either.

They endured the well-meaning and irritating comments of their parents who were hoping to be grandparents, and of friends offering babysitting services.

It would happen or it would not happen. Henry and Nicola could weather anything. They even survived a tragedy which unfolded in front of them during a stint in an A&E department. A crazed young man high on drugs brought in his battered girlfriend and, in full view of everyone, shot her dead and then killed himself.

On the surface, they coped very well: Henry and Nicola were much praised for the way they handled the situation and protected the other patients from trauma. But inside it had been a very serious shock, and there remained a memory of the morning when, at a distance of five feet, they had watched two lives end. They were trained to deal with life and death but this was too raw, too cruel, too insane. It took its toll. They slowed down in their efforts to find the perfect place to live and to practise. Compared to the violence they had seen close up, it didn't seem so important any more.

One day, Nicola saw an advertisement for a ship's doctor

with a cruise company that sailed the Mediterranean. They laughed at it together. What a life: deck tennis, cocktails with the Captain and dealing with a little indigestion or sunburn, which would be the most likely problems. What a picnic it would be. And something seemed to click with both of them. They had worked hard always; there was never time for foreign holidays. Maybe this was what they needed.

A little sun, a rest, a change. Anything that might blot out the memory of that day and their pointless sense of regret that they had not been able to second-guess a drug addict and his intentions.

They applied and went to the interview.

The shipping line said it could only employ one doctor but that they could travel together, if the other one would be able to busy herself or himself doing something else on board.

Nicola offered to teach bridge and run the ship's library.

'Or you could be the doctor,' Henry said, 'and I will do something else.'

'They would only want you to dance with the old ladies. I think you're safer in a white coat in a surgery,' Nicola laughed.

And they signed up.

They were a very popular couple on the ship, and they took to the life easily. Cruise passengers were mainly eager and innocent; their health problems were mostly connected with old age. They needed reassurance and encouragement. Henry was very good in both areas.

Nicola went from strength to strength in her little world. She even started classes in technology, teaching passengers how to work their mobile phones, Skype and basic computing skills.

They saw places they would never have visited otherwise. What other way would they have been able to visit the souks and marketplaces in Tangiers, the casinos in Monte Carlo, the ruins of Pompeii and Ephesus? They stood by the Wailing Wall in Jerusalem and swam in the blue seas around Crete.

It was only intended to be a six-month posting but when the company offered to renew the contract, it was very hard to say no. This was the first time they had ever been totally relaxed; they had time to talk to each other, to share experiences. There was a lightness of spirit they hadn't known before. The terrible events of the shooting in the A&E department were beginning to become less sharp.

And the winter-cruise schedule they were offered would be in the Caribbean. How else would they ever see places this far away? What an opportunity! They signed on again.

As they walked through the old plantations in Jamaica, or sat among the exotic flowers in Barbados, they congratulated themselves on the good fortune they had happened upon. Sometimes they talked about going back to 'real' medicine and the business of having a family by adoption. But this was not a regular conversation. They were just so lucky to have this time out.

And it wasn't as if it was all leisure. They did what they were asked to do. They looked after the people on board. Henry saved a boy's life by spotting a burst appendix and having him airlifted to a hospital. Nicola did a Heimlich manoeuvre and saved an elderly woman from choking. Henry confirmed that a sixteen-year-old girl was pregnant and helped her break the news to her parents. Nicola sat for hour after hour with a depressed woman who had considered coming on this cruise to end her life. The woman wrote to the chairman of the shipping line saying that she had never had such caring attention in her life and that she felt much better now.

So Henry and Nicola were offered a Scandinavian cruise the following spring.

Nicola had a new idea, which she ran past the Cruise Director. Why not get a hairdresser to give the men lessons in how to dry their wives' hair?

He looked at her in puzzlement.

But she persisted. Women would like the involvement and care of a partner who knew the basics. Men would buy the idea because it would save them money.

'What about the beauty-salon business?' the Cruise Director had asked.

'They have to have one cut and style in your salon first. Believe me, they will love it. It will all even out.'

And she had been right: the blow-drying sessions were among the most popular of the ship's activities.

They both loved the coastline of Norway from Bergen up to Tromsø. They stood side by side watching the sights at the ship's railings and pointed out the fjords to each other. The light was spectacular. The passengers were the usual mix of experienced cruise folk and first-timers overawed by the amount of entertainment, food and drink on offer.

It was on the third day out that Beata, one of the stewardesses, came to see Henry. An attractive blonde, Polish girl, she said that this was a very awkward matter, very awkward indeed.

Henry told her to take her time and explain the problem. He hoped she was not going to tell him there was something seriously wrong with her but Beata, twisting her hands and looking away, told him a different tale.

It was about Helen Morris, a woman in Cabin 5347. She was there with her mother and father. Beata paused.

Henry shook his head. 'Well, those are the family state-rooms, aren't they? What is the problem, exactly?'

'The parents,' Beata said. 'Her father is blind and her mother has dementia.'

'No, that can't be possible,' Henry said. 'They have to declare any pre-existing conditions before they come on board. They have to sign a document. It's for the insurance.'

'She locks the mother in the cabin and takes her father for a walk around the deck to get some fresh air, then she locks him in and takes her mother for a walk. They never go ashore for excursions. They have all their meals in the cabin.'

'And why are you telling me this? Should you not tell the Captain, or the Cruise Director?' Henry was puzzled.

'Because she would be put ashore at the next port. They wouldn't risk having those people on board.' Beata shook her head.

'But what can I do?' Henry was genuinely at a loss.

'You *know* now, that's all. I just couldn't keep it a secret. You and your wife are very kind. You'll find a way out of it.'

'This woman, Helen Morris, how old is she?'

'About forty, I think.'

'And is *she* a normal person, a *balanced* person, Beata?'

'Yes, she is a very good person. I go to their cabin and take the meals in for her. She trusts me. She said this was the only way to give them a holiday. You will know what to do.'

Henry and Nicola talked about it that night. They knew what they *should* do. They should report that a passenger had lied about the health and incapacity of her relatives. They knew that the hefty insurance payments the company paid would not cover this deception.

But what a call to make!

'Why don't you see her, talk to her?' Nicola suggested.

'I don't want to be dragged into colluding with her.'

'No, you will do what you have to do, but don't let her be a name; a statistic. Talk to her, Henry. Please.'

He looked them up on the manifest. There was no mention of impairment or disability in either parent. Helen's address was in west London, where she lived with both of them.

He knocked at the door of Cabin 5347. She was a pale woman with long straight hair and big anxious eyes.

'Oh, Doctor?' she said with some alarm.

Henry held a clipboard. 'Just a routine call. I'm visiting all passengers aged over eighty, just to see that everyone's in good health.' He felt his voice must sound brittle and over-bright.

'They're fine, thank you, Doctor.'

'So perhaps I could meet your parents, just to—'

'My mother is asleep. My father is listening to music,' Helen said.

'Please?' he asked.

'Why are you really here?' Her face was crumpling.

'Because they haven't come to meals, and so I was afraid they might be seasick.'

'Nobody told you anything?' Her voice was fearful.

'No, no.' Henry was very definite. 'Just routine. Part of my job.' He smiled at her and prepared to be invited in.

Helen looked at him for thirty seconds, her eyes raking his face. Eventually she made her decision.

'Come in, Doctor,' she said, and opened the cabin door wide.

Henry saw an old man in an armchair listening on headphones and tapping his foot to whatever he heard. His sightless eyes faced across the cabin. Outside, spectacular scenery of the Norwegian fjords passed by slowly, unseen. His wife sat on the bed holding a doll in her arms. 'Little Helen, little Helen,' she said over and over, and rocked the doll to sleep.

Henry swallowed. He had no idea that it was going to be like this. 'Just routine, as I said.' He cleared his throat.

'Do you have to tell?' Her eyes were red-rimmed and beseeching.

'Yes, I do,' he said simply.

'But why, Doctor? I've managed fine for four days. There are only nine days left.'

'It's not as simple as that. You see, there's a very clear policy.'

'There's no policy that's going to help me to give them a holiday, some fresh air, a change from the flat in Hammersmith with flights of stairs up and down . . . it was my only chance, Doctor.'

'But you didn't tell us the full story.'

'I *couldn't* tell you the whole story. You wouldn't have let us come.'

He was silent.

'Listen, Doctor. I am sure you've had a happy life with nothing going wrong, and I'm glad for you, but not everyone gets that deal. I am an only child. My parents have nobody else. They were so good to me. They got me educated as a teacher. I can't abandon them now.' She paused as if to collect herself. Then she spoke again. 'I work from home correcting and marking papers from a correspondence course. It's endless and back-breaking but at least I can look after them. And they ask so little . . . So is it really some sort of a crime to take them on a little holiday? And have a rest myself, and see such lovely places?'

Henry felt humbled.

Helen was twisting her hands in her lap. Her father smiled,

listening to his music; her mother cradled the baby doll in her arms, cooing and chuckling and calling it Helen.

'I do understand, really I do,' he said, feeling useless.

'But you still must tell, and then they'll put us off the ship?'

'They won't want to take the risk . . .' he began.

'But could *you* take the risk, Doctor? You, who have had all the good luck in the world, a great education, a lovely wife. I've seen you together. You have a dream job where it's all a holiday. You haven't known anything like this. Your life has been easy. Could you find the kindness somewhere to take a risk for us? I'll be so careful, believe me, I will.'

Henry contemplated telling her that his life had not been easy. They had failed to have the children they both wanted. They had seen at close quarters two violent deaths, which they still felt that, if they had been more quick-witted, they might have prevented. They were vaguely unsettled and slightly guilty about the lifestyle on board ship. But what was this compared to the life of the woman in front of him?

'How were you able to afford . . . ?' he began.

'Dad's brother died. He left him ten thousand pounds. It seemed like an opportunity that might never come again, so I ran with it.'

'I see.'

'And up to now it's been great. Just great. Better than I even dreamed.' She was full of hope.

'It won't be easy,' he said.

Her smile was his reward. He wondered if there was anyone at all in her life able to share the burden of care and the sheer determination that kept her going.

'I'll ask Nicola to join us,' Henry said, and the deal was done.

In the end, it was not too arduous. Nicola would sit in the cabin each day while Helen took her father for a walk and even a swim. Then Henry would take his paperwork and sit with the old man while Helen and her mother took the doll for a walk on deck.

Helen was adept at managing to avoid chatting to other passengers. She was looking stronger and more relaxed every day.

Henry said nothing to Beata about the arrangement but he knew she was aware of it, and that it was appreciated.

There were a few near misses. At the daily cruise conference, the Cruise Director mentioned that someone had reported an elderly man who stumbled on deck. Was Dr Henry aware of him? Was there any problem there?

Henry lied smoothly. Yes, the old chap was a bit frail but his daughter seemed very much in control.

One day when Nicola was looking after the old lady, there was a spot check by the Cabin Supervisor. She arrived at the door unexpectedly with Beata in tow.

Nicola swallowed. She had to keep her nerve. 'I'm just doing a one-to-one computer lesson,' she explained with a big smile. Mercifully Helen's mother did not choose that moment to sing a lullaby to the doll. The Supervisor moved on to the next cabin, saying that a one-to-one computer lesson was what everyone over forty needed.

'Well, come to my office and make an appointment,' Nicola begged. 'I'll fit you in to tie in with your time off.'

Then there was the Captain's cocktail party, where they noticed that there was nobody from Cabin 5347.

'They're having an early supper,' Nicola explained.

'They like to be left on their own,' Henry added.

They got to know Helen over the nine days. She said how she missed teaching; she had loved the classroom, and the joy of making children understand something in the end. She thanked them from the bottom of her heart and said they were good people who deserved all their happiness. Henry and Nicola probed her gently about what things would be like when she returned home.

'Same as before,' she said glumly, 'but at least we will have all this to look back on. It was money well spent.'

'Any more legacies likely?' Henry tried to lighten it a little.

'No, but I still have a thousand pounds. That will buy a few treats.' Again that sad smile.

They docked at Southampton. Nicola and Henry began to breathe more easily.

Helen had hired a car to drive them to London. They would take a taxi from the disembarkation point to bring them to the car-rental place.

They exchanged addresses.

'Send me a postcard from your next cruise,' Helen said, as if they were casual shipboard acquaintances rather than accomplices for nine days and nights.

'Yes, and you tell us how things are going,' Nicola said. Her voice was hollow.

It would be, as Helen had foreseen, the same as before.

The officers and crew stood on deck to bid farewell to the passengers. Nicola and Henry embraced Helen as she left, supporting a parent on each arm. They saw her walk down the gangway, her stocky little figure steady and her head held high.

The cleaners were already at work on the ship when Nicola and Henry began to disembark. They would drive home and spend ten days catching up with their parents and friends until the next cruise, this time to Madeira and the Canary Islands.

They were just saying goodbye to the Cruise Director when they heard the news. There had been a terrible accident just outside Southampton, a car crash, three fatalities – all of them passengers just disembarked from this cruise. Henry and Nicola looked at each other, stricken. Before the Cruise Director spoke, they knew.

'It appears to be suicide, can you believe it? She got into her hired car and drove them all into a wall. A total wreck, they were all killed instantly. They found the labels for the cruise ship, so they contacted us. It must have been that woman Helen Morris and her parents from Cabin 5347, apparently . . .'

'It must have been an accident.' Henry could barely speak.

'Don't think so. Witnesses say she stopped the car and reversed a distance and then drove straight at the wall. God, why did she do that?'

'We don't *know* that she did . . .' Nicola began.

'We *do*, Nicola. The law is here, they are making enquiries. We have to talk to the police, make statements.'

The Cruise Director was crisp and to the point.

'We *are* covered, aren't we, Henry? You didn't spot any-thing, did you?'

It seemed to Henry like an age before he answered but it was probably only four seconds.

'No, she seemed fine. Very positive.' The Cruise Director was relieved but still worried.

'And the old folk? Were they OK?'

'They were frail but she was well able to look after them,' he said, and set in train a series of lies that he and Nicola managed for the next twenty-four hours.

Before they left the ship, Henry sought out Beata. Had she

heard the news? Yes, everyone had heard. Beata looked at Henry with a very steady, level glance.

'It is so sad for the poor lady and her family, but how good that they had a happy holiday at the end of their lives.' She was begging him to say nothing. She too would be in trouble for keeping the secret.

He kissed her goodbye on the cheek.

'Perhaps we will meet on another cruise, Dr Henry.'

'I don't think so,' Henry said. He felt his days as a ship's doctor were over. From now on he would do what he had set out to do: heal people, make their quality of life better, not bend rules for sentiment's sake and end up with the deaths of three people on his hands.

'She would have done it anyway,' Nicola pleaded as they drove back to Esher.

He stared ahead without answering.

'She would have done it in Bergen or Tromsø or wher-ever . . .'

Still silence.

'You know, you just gave her nine extra days of a holiday. That's all you did. All *we* did.'

'I broke the rules. I played God. There's no escaping that.'

'I love you, Henry.'

'And I love you, but that doesn't change what has happened.'

They told nobody about it. They gave no explanation to anyone about why they were giving up what sounded like the very best job on earth. They offered themselves as volunteers in programmes researching suicide prevention and coping with depression. They withdrew from friends and family. They took short-term locum positions. The dream of a small country practice had slipped away. They didn't feel they would be up to it. They had been tested and were found wanting.

Eventually, Henry's parents decided to speak their minds. It was after yet another silent, depressed Sunday lunch in their home.

'You've changed very much since you came back from that cruise ship,' his father began.

'I thought you didn't approve of it. You suggested that it wasn't *real* medicine,' Henry said huffily.

'I did say, and I'll always say that you should have specialised. You could be a consultant by now, all the chances you had open to you.'

'We just want you to be happy. That's all, dear,' his mother explained.

'Nobody is happy,' Henry said, and he went out to their garden to throw sticks for the old dog.

So Henry's parents decided to speak their minds to Nicola. They caught her in the kitchen as she was sipping a cup of tea and looking into the middle distance.

'We don't want to interfere, Nicola dear,' Henry's mother began.

'I know, you never do, you're really great,' Nicola said admiringly, wondering whether she could evade the 'but' that was approaching.

'It's just that we worry . . .' Henry's father didn't want to let the discussion end before it had begun.

But Nicola had a bright, empty face. 'Of *course* you worry,' she agreed, 'that's what parents do.'

'You've been moping around for over two years, settling to nothing. Look, I know it's not really our business but we do care.' Henry's father was begging to be heard.

Nicola turned and faced him.

'What do you want us to do? Just tell me straight out. Perhaps we just might do it.'

There was something in her face that frightened him. He had never seen her so angry. He immediately tried to row back.

'All I was saying . . . what I was going to say was that . . . that . . . you should have a holiday, a break of some sort . . .' His voice trailed away.

'Oh, a *holiday*!' Nicola sounded hysterically delighted with the idea. A holiday she could just cope with. Just. 'It's funny you should say that because we *were* talking about having a holiday. I'll talk to Henry, and we'll let you know our plans.' And she fled from their kitchen before they could say any more.

She mentioned the holiday to Henry as they drove home that evening.

'I don't think I have the energy for a holiday,' he said.

'Neither do I, but I had to say something to get them off our backs.'

'I'm sorry. Your folks don't go on nagging at us like that.'

'Yes they do, but not in front of you. They're a little afraid of their son-in-law, you know!'

'Would you *like* a holiday, Nicola?'

'I would like a week somewhere before the winter settles in but I don't really know where we would go,' she said.

'Well, neither of us wants to go to the Canaries for winter sun, that's for certain,' Henry said.

'And I don't want winter snow, either. I'd hate skiing,' Nicola said.

'And I'm not crazy about a bus tour,' Henry offered.

'Or Paris. It would be too cold and wet.'

'We've become very crotchety and difficult to please, and

we're not even forty,' Henry said suddenly. 'Lord knows what we'll be like when we really *are* old.'

She looked at him affectionately. 'Maybe we've got to get through this elderly phase first, and then eventually we might become normal.' She spoke lightly but there was general wistfulness in her voice.

'I know what we'll do,' Henry said. 'We'll go on a walking holiday.'

'Walking?'

'Yes, somewhere we've never been before; the Scottish Highlands, or the Yorkshire moors.'

'Or Wales, even?'

'Yes; we'll look up a few places when we get back home.'

'We don't have to stay in youth hostels, do we?' Nicola pleaded.

'No! I think we should find a warm hotel with lots of hot water and good food.'

Nicola sat back in the passenger seat and sighed.

For the first time in two years she believed they might really have turned a corner. A week's holiday in winter would not solve all their worries and end all their woes but it might just be the beginning of some journey back.

Later that evening, when they got back to their house in Esher, it was very cold. Henry lit a fire in the small grate, the first time he had done this for two years. He saw the surprise in Nicola's face.

'Well, if we're going to take the huge decision of choosing a holiday, let's break every other tradition as well,' he said in explanation.

Nicola brought them hot chocolate. Another first. Normally when they came back from visiting either set of parents they felt exhausted, but tonight they seemed to have more energy. They brought the laptop to a small table near the fireplace and began to search for a holiday.

There were some extraordinary places on offer. A farmhouse in Wales, miles from anywhere. But too remote. They didn't want to be quite so isolated. Log cabins in the New Forest where wild ponies might come up to your windows? Yes, maybe. But would they tire of wild ponies after a day or two? An old coaching inn near Hadrian's Wall? Certainly a possibility, but they weren't instantly convinced.

Then they saw a picture of a house in the West of Ireland. A big stone place on a cliff looking down over the Atlantic Ocean. It offered walks and wild birds and peace and good cooking. There was something about it that seemed to draw them.

'It could be just a bit overwritten . . . it might not be like that at all, of course.' Nicola was almost afraid to be enthusiastic.

'Yes, but they couldn't fake those pictures – the waves and the big empty beaches . . . all those birds.'

'Should we call them? What's her name again . . . ? Oh, Mrs Starr.'

The voice that answered had a slight American accent. 'Stone House, can I help you?'

Nicola explained that they were in their thirties, they had been working very hard and needed a holiday and a change. Could she tell them a little more about the place.

And Chicky Starr told them that it was all very simple but in her own opinion, a very restful and healing place. She used to work in New York and came back here every year for a holiday. She walked and walked, and stared out at the ocean and when she got back to America, she always felt able to cope with anything.

She hoped that her guests would feel the same way.

It was beginning to sound too good to be true.

'Will it be all sing-songs and, you know, like an Irish pub?' Henry asked diffidently.

'I very much hope not,' Chicky laughed. 'There will be wine served with dinner, of course, but if people want a more lively nightlife they can go out to the local pubs, which have music.'

'And do we all eat together?'

Chicky seemed to understand the implications of the question.

'There will be about eleven or twelve of us around the table each evening, but it won't be an endurance test. I worked in a boarding house all my life before I set up this place. I'll make sure that no one is forced into being over-jolly. Believe me.'

They believed her, and made the booking straight away.

Henry's parents were pleased.

'Nicola *did* tell us you had plans,' his mother said. 'I was afraid I had been intrusive but she said it hadn't been firmed up.'

'No, Mother. No question of you being intrusive,' he lied.

Nicola's parents were astonished.

'Ireland?' they gasped. 'What's wrong with Britain? There are thousands of places here you haven't seen.'

'It's Henry's decision,' Nicola lied. That sorted it out. They were indeed slightly in awe of their son-in-law.

They flew to Dublin and took a train to the West. They looked out of the windows at the small fields, the wet cattle and the towns with unfamiliar names written in two languages. It felt quite foreign, even though everyone spoke English.

The bus to Stoneybridge did indeed meet the train as

Chicky Starr had promised them that it would. She said she would collect them in her car.

'How will we know you?' Henry had asked anxiously.

'I'll know you,' said Mrs Starr, and so she did.

She was a small woman who waved at them immediately and chatted easily as they drove to Stone House.

The place looked exactly like the photograph on the website. The house stood four-square on a gravelled pathway; the light was already going from the day and the windows glowed with soft light. A black and white cat sat in one of the windows, curled up in an impossibly small ball of fur and paws and ears.

Behind them the creamy, frothy foam on the waves rolled in towards the shore and crashed against the stark cliffs, which were somehow both majestic and containable at the same time.

Chicky gave them tea and scones and showed them to their room, which had a little balcony looking right out to sea.

She was calming, and asked them nothing about their lives or the reasons they had chosen her hotel. She reassured them that the other guests, some of whom had already arrived, all seemed delightful people. They lay down in their big bed and drifted off to sleep. A siesta at five o'clock in the afternoon! For Henry and Nicola it was another first.

Only the sound of the gong woke them, otherwise they might have slept all night. Cautiously they came down to the big kitchen and met the others.

Already gathered was an American man called John, who looked very familiar though they couldn't at first place him. He said he had come here on an impulse because he'd missed a flight at Shannon. Then there was a cheerful nurse called

197

Winnie, who was travelling with her friend, an older woman called Lillian. They were both Irish and seemed an odd couple though each was entertaining company. There was Nell, a silent, watchful, older woman who seemed a bit reserved, and a Swede whose name they didn't catch.

The food was excellent; the advice about touring the area very thorough. Nobody arrived with a fiddle or an accordion and a medley of Irish songs. As Mrs Starr's niece Orla cleared the table, the group all drifted off to bed easily without speeches or explanations. Back in their room, Nicola and Henry hardly dared tell each other that it looked like being a success. Over the past two years they had been through so many false starts.

A kind of superstitious magic made them tread carefully but they slept again deeply, and the sound of the waves crashing below the cliff was comforting rather than alarming.

The next morning, they woke to scudding clouds and blustery winds and felt that this was indeed going to be the place that let the fresh air in. Their acquaintance with the other guests was close enough to be familiar but not so much as to be intrusive. When Winnie and Lillian went missing the following night, Henry offered to join the search party in case medical assistance was needed; Mrs Starr said she would rather he and Nicola stood by at the house in case the two missing women made it back by themselves. The local doctor, Dai Morgan, had been alerted and was waiting in his surgery.

'Dai Morgan? That doesn't sound very Irish,' Henry said.

'No, indeed, he came here from Wales as a locum thirty years ago when old Dr Barry was sick. Then poor Dr Barry died and Dai stayed. Just as simple as that.'

'Why did he stay?' Nicola asked.

'Because everyone loved him. They still do. Dai and Annie settled in very well here. They had a little girl, Bethan, and she loved it all here. She's a doctor too, now. Imagine!'

The next day, Dai Morgan called round to Stone House to check that the two ladies had no ill effects from their time in the cave. Chicky gave him coffee at the big kitchen table and left him there with Henry and Nicola, who were in between walks.

He was a big square man in his mid-sixties with an easy, reassuring manner and a broad smile.

'Chicky tells me the pair of you are in the same trade as myself,' he said.

Immediately they were guarded. They really didn't feel like answering questions about what they had been doing and how their careers had developed. Still, they couldn't be rude to the man.

'That's true,' Nicola said.

'For our sins,' Henry added.

'Well, I suppose there are worse than us out there,' Dai Morgan said.

They smiled politely.

'I'll miss this place,' he said suddenly.

'You're leaving?' This was a surprise. Chicky Starr had mentioned nothing about that.

'Yes. I only decided this week. My wife, Annie, has had a bad diagnosis. She would like to go back to Swansea. All her sisters live there and her mother, fit as a flea, aged eighty.'

'I'm very sorry,' Nicola said.

'Is it as bad as you think?' Henry asked.

'Yes, a matter of months. We've had second and third opinions, I'm afraid.'

'And she has accepted it?'

'Oh, Annie is a diamond. She knows what it's all about. No fuss, no drama, just wants to be with family.'

'But afterwards . . . ?' Henry asked.

'I wouldn't have the heart to come back here. Stoneybridge was the two of us. It wouldn't be the same on my own.'

'They love you here. They say you made a difference to people,' Nicola said.

'I loved it here too, but not alone.'

'So when will you go?'

'Before Christmas,' he said simply.

They talked about him later as they sat in a mountain pub where black-faced sheep came and looked in the door. Strange thing for a man and his wife to have come so far away from their roots, stay so long and then go back in the end.

They still spoke of the Welsh doctor when they were walking over a long, empty beach and were the only people there. What could have persuaded him to stay in a small, lonely place like this where he knew nothing of the patients and their backgrounds?

They talked about him at night in their room with the waves crashing beneath the cliffs.

'You know what we are really talking about?' Henry said.

'Yes, we're talking about *us*, not him. Would we find peace in a place like this, just as he did?'

'It worked for him. It mightn't work for everybody.' Henry was anxious not to get swept away.

'But there might be somewhere, some place where we could be part of things, *doing* something rather than trying to get round a system.' Her eyes were bright with hope.

Henry leaned over to her and put both his hands around

her face. 'I *do* love you, Nicola. Helen was right. I am a lucky person to have a happy life, and that's because you are the centre of it.'

They found themselves more and more drawn to talk to Dai Morgan. He seemed to like their company. They didn't give him any false comfort about his wife. They were less buttoned up, less watchful than when he had met them first, and slowly they told him of their hopes of finding a place, a community where they could make a difference; something, in fact, like he had done.

'Oh, I've left a lot undone here,' Dai Morgan sighed. 'If I had my time over I'd do some things very differently.'

'Like what?' Henry didn't sound intrusive. He sounded as if he wanted to learn.

'Like a big bully from the new townhouses over there. I was called to the place twice. His wife Deirdre had some kind of vertigo, he said. She had fallen from a ladder once and from the car another time. Broken bones and bruises. It looked to me as if he could have beaten her. I didn't like him but what could I do? The wife swore that she fell. Then the third time I knew. But it was too late. She didn't recover.'

'Oh, God . . .' Nicola said.

'Oh God, indeed. Where was my God, or her God, when that bastard came at her the last time? I didn't speak before because I only had intuition and a gut feeling. Because I didn't trust that feeling, Deirdre died.'

'And did you speak then?' Nicola's eyes were full of tears.

'I tried to but they shut me up. Her own family, brothers and sisters, said that her name mustn't be tarnished in this way. She must be buried as a loved wife and happy mother, otherwise it wouldn't make sense of her life. I couldn't understand it. I still don't understand it. But if I had it all over again I would have spoken the first time.'

'What happened to him? The husband?'

'He lived on here, a few crocodile tears, a few references to My Poor Wife Deirdre. But then he met another woman, a very different kind of person entirely, and the first day he hit her she was straight into the Guards. He was done for assault. He served six months and left in disgrace. Deirdre's family put it all down to his great grief over his wife's death. In a way, I suppose, it was a result.' He looked grim at the recollection of it all.

'And do you think about it a lot?' Nicola asked.

'I used to, all the time. Every day I pass the graveyard where Deirdre is buried. Every time I saw their house, I remembered her face as she swore to me that she fell from a ladder. But then Annie said it was tearing me apart and I would be no use to anyone else in the place unless I got over it. So I suppose I got over it, in a way.'

Dai watched them nod in such genuine sympathy and understanding that he realised they really did understand; perhaps something similar had happened to them too.

He spoke carefully. 'Annie said that in a way I was putting myself centre stage, making it all *my* problem, *my* involvement, or lack of it. There were other factors to consider: he was always going to be a cruel bastard, handy with his fists; she was always going to be a victim. Did I think I was some kind of avenging angel sent down to sort out the world? And it made sense.'

'You forgave yourself?' Henry asked.

'Something else happened just then. I was in my surgery when one of the young O'Hara children was brought in. His mother said he'd got some stomach bug and he was vomiting.

She said he was very sleepy and had a temperature. Something about it didn't seem right to me, and I gave him a thorough examination. I thought he had meningitis and gave the hospital a call. They said he needed to come in straight away for tests. It would have taken too long to get an ambulance out here, so I just picked him up and ran outside and put him and his mother on the back seat. I drove like a demon to the hospital and they were ready with the tests and the antibiotics, and we saved him. He's a great big lout of a fellow now, could drink for the county. Nice lad, though. He's very good with the youngest boy, Shay. Takes care of him a bit. Every time I pass by he says, "That's the great man who saved my life", and I ask him to tell me one good reason why I should be pleased about this. But I know I did, and that for once I made a difference.'

'I'm sure it wasn't just for once,' Nicola said.

'Maybe not, but it was a kind of redemption and badly needed at the time, I tell you.'

Henry and Nicola talked about it all as they sat in their room at Stone House waiting for the dinner gong.

'Redemption . . . that's what we have been looking for,' Nicola said.

'Maybe the Tooth Fairy might find some for us.' Henry was not dismissive or cynical; he was actually smiling, and held her hand.

They were the first in for dinner.

Chicky and her niece Orla were preparing a tray of drinks for the guests. They were talking seriously about something.

'What can they *do*, Chicky? Chain his leg to the bed?'

'No, but they can't let him wander out on his own at night.'

'Try stopping him. He's going to go out anyway . . .'

When they saw Nicola and Henry they immediately broke off. Chicky was very professional. Domestic matters were never discussed in front of guests. The place ran smoothly, almost effortlessly, though it was all down to careful preparation. They enquired about what Nicola and Henry had done during the day. They took out the bird books to identify a goose that the couple had seen strutting across the marshy fields near the lake. It had pink legs and a big orange beak.

'That's a greylag goose, I'd say.' Chicky turned the pages of *Ireland's Birds*. 'Is this it, do you think?'

They thought it was.

'They come from Iceland every year. Imagine!' Chicky paused in wonder at it all.

'It would be lovely to know all about birds, like you do.' Nicola was envious of the way Chicky could lose herself in the thought of a goose flying from Iceland.

'Oh, I'm only a real amateur. We had hoped to have a real birdwatcher for you here. There's a local boy, Shay O'Hara. He knows every feather of every bird that flies the skies. But it didn't work out.'

'It would have been the making of him,' Orla shook her head sadly.

Chicky felt this needed some explanation. 'Shay's not himself these days. He's depressed. Nobody can reach him. We're all hoping it's just a phase.'

'Depression in young men is very serious,' Henry said.

'Oh, I know it is, and Dr Dai is on the case but Shay won't take medication or go for counselling or listen to anyone,' Chicky sighed.

The others had begun to arrive in the kitchen so the matter was dropped.

*

Nicola sat beside the handsome American who was still calling himself John, and who had found a new friend in a local man called Frank Hanratty. Frank had driven him miles over mountain roads in a pink van to meet an old film director who had retired to this part of the world years back. A very pleasant and contented gentleman who had given them nettle soup.

'Did he recognise you?' Nicola asked, unguardedly.

Up to now they had never acknowledged out loud that John was in fact a film actor, a celebrity.

John took it all casually. 'Yes, he was kind enough to say he knew my work. But he was fascinating. He has hens, you know, and beehives and a goat. He has a house full of books – he's as happy as anyone I ever met.'

'Extraordinary,' Nicola was wistful. 'It must be wonderful to be happy.'

John looked at her sharply but said no more.

Before they went to bed, they went outside to breathe in the cold sea air. Orla was just wheeling out her bicycle and on her way home.

'Do you ever get tired of this view?' Henry asked her.

'No, I missed it so much when I lived in London. Some people find it sad. I don't.'

'What about the poor birdwatcher you were telling us about? Does he find it sad?'

'Shay finds everything sad,' Orla said, and cycled home.

It was at three o'clock in the morning that Henry and Nicola were wakened by the sound of birds crying out to each other. It wasn't nearly time for the dawn chorus or the early-morning gathering of the gulls. Possibly it was a bird in distress out on their little balcony.

They got up to investigate.

Silhouetted against the moonlit sea was the thin figure of a teenage boy in a thin jumper, holding his arms around himself, his head back and weeping.

This must be Shay. Shay, who found everything sad.

Without even consulting each other, they put on their coats and shoes and went downstairs. They let themselves out into the cold night air.

The boy's eyes were closed, his face contorted. They couldn't make out the words that he was still crying aloud. He was shaking, and his thin shoulders were hunched in despair. He was dangerously near the edge of the cliff.

They moved towards him steadily, talking to each other so that he would not be startled at their approach.

He opened his eyes and saw them. 'You're not going to change my mind,' he said.

'No, that's true,' Henry said.

'What do you mean?'

'You're right. I'm not going to change your mind. If you don't do it now, you'll do it later tonight or next week. I know *that*.'

'So why are you trying to stop me?'

'Stop you? We're not trying to stop you, are we, Nicola?'

'No. Lord, no. People do what they want to do.'

'So what *are* you doing then?' His eyes were huge and filled with terror and his thin body was shaking.

'We wanted to ask you about the greylag goose. We saw one today. I gather it flew in from Iceland.'

'There's nothing odd about seeing a greylag goose. Sure, the place is coming down with them. Now if you'd seen a snow goose, *that* would be something to talk about,' said Shay.

'A snow goose? Do they come from Iceland too?' Nicola

was moving round behind him but almost nonchalantly, and looking vaguely out to sea as if hoping to catch a snow goose in the light of the moon.

'No, they're from Arctic Canada, Greenland. You'd see them over in Wexford on the east coast. They don't come here much.'

'Have you seen them yourself?' Henry wondered.

'Oh yes, often, but as I say, not round here. I saw a bean goose last year. That's fairly rare.'

'A *bean* goose!' Henry tried to put awe and admiration into his voice.

The boy smiled.

'Could you come in and show us the bean goose in the bird book?' Nicola asked, as if the thought had just come to her.

'Ah, no. I'd only have Chicky going on and on about my going to the doctor. I hate doctors.'

'Oh, I know.' Nicola rolled her eyes to heaven as if sharing his view.

'Anyway, you could look it up yourself. She has all the books in there.'

'It's not the same. You could explain . . .'

'No, I wouldn't feel easy about it.' He was about to back away. Nicola was right behind him.

She put her hand gently on his arm. 'Please come in with us. Henry can't sleep, you see, and it would be such a help to us.'

'All right, so. Just for a bit,' he said, and came with them into the kitchen of Stone House.

They found him a big tartan jacket while his thin sweater was drying on the radiator. Nicola made them tea and they had some bread and cheese. He was still there explaining how you would tell a barnacle goose from a brent goose when the O'Haras arrived, calling out his name.

They had read the note he had left on their table; the note saying he was sorry but this was the only way out. They had been praying as they ran across the cliffs that they would be in time.

Shay's father sat down at Chicky's table and cried like a baby.

They phoned Shay's mother, who had been so deeply in shock that she couldn't come with them in the search. Chicky had come downstairs and was coping with everything as if this was to be expected in a day's work.

'We need a doctor,' Shay's sister said.

Shay looked up, annoyed at the idea.

Chicky was about to explain that there were already two doctors in the kitchen. Henry shook his head.

'I'm sure Dr Dai would come,' he said.

'He'll know what to do,' Nicola agreed.

Chicky understood.

Next morning at breakfast they didn't talk about it. Orla already knew. The whole of Stoneybridge had heard how the two English visitors had talked the boy out of the death he had planned. She looked at them gratefully as she served the food.

Some of the guests had thought they heard shouting in the night. A thing of nothing, Chicky explained, and they moved on to talk about plans for the day.

They called on Dai Morgan later in the morning.

'There's a human being alive today because of you,' he said.

'But for how long?' Henry asked. 'He'll do it again, won't he?'

'Maybe not. He has agreed to go into hospital for

observation. He says he will take his medication and he might talk to a counsellor. That's a long way further down the road than before.'

Henry and Nicola looked at each other.

Dai went on talking. 'I'm anxious to get my own move started as soon as possible. I'll start telling people today. I was wondering . . . it's a bit far out, but I was wondering . . .'

They knew what he was going to say.

'I'll need a locum for a couple of months. Would you think of it?'

'They wouldn't trust us. We're outsiders.'

'I was an outsider.'

'But that's different. They don't know anything at all about us.'

'They know you saved Shay O'Hara's life. That's as good a calling card as any,' said Dai Morgan.

And then there was a lot to talk about, as plans were made.

'It doesn't have to be for thirty years, like me,' Dai told them.

He watched them as they stood together in the winter sunshine, relaxed now as they had never been before.

'Or then again, of course, you might even stay longer,' he added.

Anders

When Anders was at school and they asked him what would he be when he grew up, he always said that he would be an accountant like his father and grandfather. He would go to work in the big family firm with its impressive office in Stockholm. Almkvist's was one of the oldest companies in Sweden, he would tell you proudly.

Anders was a very happy child with blond, floppy hair in his eyes. He loved music from an early age and could play the piano creditably at the age of five. He wanted a guitar when he was older, and learned to play without any instruction. You could hear him playing in his room night after night after he'd finished his homework; then their housekeeper, Fru Karlsson, introduced him to the *nyckelharpa*, the traditional Swedish keyed fiddle. It had belonged to her grandfather, and as she had learned how to play from him so she now showed Anders. She taught him some traditional Swedish songs to play on it, and he fell in love with its ethereal sound.

He lived with his parents, Patrik and Gunilla Almkvist, Fru Karlsson and their dog, Riva, in a beautiful apartment overlooking Djurgårdskanalen. He told people that his was the best school in Sweden, and that Riva was the best dog in the world. To praise Papa's office was only just another part of the contented world he lived in. Two of his cousins, Klara and Mats, had gone to work in the family firm already, gaining office experience as they did their accountancy studies. Mats was a bit self-important but Klara was very down to earth and already knew the business inside out. They knew that Anders, as the heir and successor, would leave his piano and his *nyckelharpa* behind and go away to university to be groomed for the job that would one day be his. Meanwhile, they would take him out for coffee and tell him stories of the clients they met.

All kinds of well-known personalities from big business, sports and entertainment filed through the big arched doors of the office. There were meetings in the boardroom, there were discreet lunches in the private dining rooms of restaurants. Everyone in the office dressed very well; Mats wore designer suits and immaculate shirts, while Klara always managed to look elegant. Although she wore understated, sober office clothes she always looked as though she was ready to step on to a catwalk. Efficiency, style and discretion were the watch-words at Almkvist's. Mats and Klara looked and sounded the part. Anders wondered whether he would ever feel comfortable in this world.

It was the style aspect Anders found the most challenging. He hardly noticed what other people wore, and always liked to dress comfortably himself. He could not begin to understand the importance of handmade shoes, precision Swiss watches and pure silk ties, and they certainly didn't figure in the world of folk music to which he was most drawn.

His mother laughed at him affectionately.

'Well-cut clothes make you look much more handsome, Anders. The girls will admire you if you dress well.'

'They won't notice clothes. Either they will like me or they won't like me.' He was fifteen, awkward, unsure.

'So wrong, so very wrong. They'll love you but first they have to look at you. It's the first impression that counts. Believe me, I know.' Gunilla Almkvist always looked elegant. She worked for a TV station where they set a high value on style. She never left the house before she was properly prepared for what the day would bring. She walked the two kilometres to work wearing her trainers; her elegant high-heeled shoes were kept in her office on the bottom shelf – seven pairs of them.

She made every effort to interest Anders in dressing more smartly, trying to build an enthusiasm where none existed. By the time he was eighteen she had stopped cajoling.

'It's not a joke any more, Anders. If you were in the army you'd have to wear a uniform. If you were going to be in the Diplomatic Service there would be rules about what to wear. You are going to work in Almkvist and Almkvist Accountants. There are rules. There are expectations.'

'I'm going to study accountancy, isn't that what it's about?'

'It's what *some* of it is about. But it's also about respecting the family traditions, about fitting in.' There was something different, something odd in her tone this time.

He looked up. 'None of that's important, surely? It's not what life is about.'

'If you remember nothing else I've ever told you, just remember this. I agree that in the great scheme of things it is *not* important, but it is one small thing you can do to make life easier. That's all. Just remember I told you that.'

Why was she sounding so strange?

'You're *always* going on about clothes and style. I don't have to remember it, you keep telling me.' He smiled at her, willing everything to be normal.

Everything was not normal.

'I won't be here to tell you,' she said, her voice sounding as though her throat was constricted. 'That's why it's important you listen now. I am going away. I am leaving your father. You will be going to university this autumn. This is the time for change.'

'Does he know you are going?' Anders' voice was a whisper.

'Yes. He knew that I would wait until you had finished school. I am going to London. I have a job there, and that's where I will set up home.'

'But won't you be lonely there?'

'No, Anders. I have been very lonely *here*. Your father and I have grown apart over a long time. He is married to the company. He will hardly miss me.'

'But . . . *I* will miss you! This can't be true! How did I not see anything or know about all this?'

'Because we were all discreet. There was no need for you to know anything until now.'

'And do you have somebody else in London?' He knew he sounded like a seven-year-old.

'Yes, I have a warm, kind, funny man called William. We laugh a lot together. I hope as the years go on you will get to know him and to like him. But for your father's sake, just remember what I said about smartening yourself up. It will make your whole life much simpler.'

He turned his head away so that she would not see his distress. His mother was going off to London with a man called William who made her laugh. And what was she talking about as she left? Clothes. Bloody *clothes*. He felt his world had turned sideways and everything had slipped out of focus.

His mother and father hadn't grown apart. They had had a dinner party last Friday. Papa had raised a glass to her across the table. 'To my beautiful wife,' he had said. And all the time he knew she was going to leave with this William.

It couldn't be true, could it?

His mother stood there, afraid to touch him in case he shrugged her off, shook her away. 'I love you, Anders. You may find that hard to believe, but I do. And your father does too. Very much. He doesn't show it but it's there; great pride and great love.'

'They are different things, pride and love,' Anders said. 'Was he proud of you too, or did he love you?' Anders looked at her properly for the first time.

'He was proud that I kept my side of the bargain. I ran the house well; I was a satisfactory escort to him at all those interminable dinners; I was a good hostess. I gave him a son. I think he was pleased with me, yes.'

'But love?'

'I don't know, Anders. I don't think he ever loved anything except his firm and you.'

'He never sounds as if he loves me. He is always so distant.'

'That's his way. He will always be like that. But I have been there for all of your life and he does love you. He just can't express it.'

'If he had expressed it for you, would you have stayed?'

'That's not a real question. It's like wishing that a square was a circle,' she said. And because he believed her, Anders held his hands out to her and she sobbed in his arms for a long time.

It all moved very swiftly after that.

Gunilla Almkvist packed her clothes, as Fru Karlsson sniffed in disapproval, but left all her jewellery behind. A cover story was devised. She had been offered this post in London working for a satellite broadcasting station. It would be criminal to let the opportunity pass. Anders was going off to university; her husband was fully supportive of the move. That way there would be no accusations about a runaway wife, a failed marriage. None of the oxygen of gossip, which would be so relished and yet so out of place at Almkvist's.

Patrik Almkvist seemed courteous and grateful. He never discussed the matter with his only child. He looked pleased that Anders had had his hair properly cut and that he'd been measured for a good suit.

He spent more and more time at the office.

The night before Anders' mother left, the three of them went out to dinner together. Patrik raised his glass to his wife. 'May you find all you are looking for in London,' he said.

Anders stared at them in disbelief. Twenty years of life together, two decades of hope and dreams ending, and his parents were still acting out a role. Was this what everyone did? He had a feeling at that moment that he would never fall in love. It was all for the poets and the love songs and the dreamers. It wasn't what people did in real life.

Next day, he set off for Gothenburg and university. His new life had begun.

He had only been there a week when he met Erika, a textile and design student. She came straight over to him at a party and asked him to dance.

Later, he asked her why she had approached him that night.

'You looked smart, that's all. Not scruffy,' she said.

Anders was very disappointed. 'Does that sort of thing matter?' he asked.

'It matters that you care enough about yourself and about the people you meet to present yourself well. That's all. I'm tired of scruffy people,' she said.

They were an item from then on, it seemed. Erika loved to cook but only when she wanted to and what she wanted to. But she loved to have people to her apartment, and when she found out that Anders could play the *nyckelharpa* she was appalled that he hadn't brought it with him to university. So the very next time he went home she insisted that he bring it back with him. And then she set about organising jam sessions at her place, and she would make the most delicious suppers.

Erika was small and funny and thought that women's rights and fashion were not incompatible. She loved to dress up for any occasion, and astonished Anders when she was the most attractive and stylish woman in the room. They made each other laugh, and quite soon became inseparable.

It was just before Easter time that she told him she would never marry him because she thought marriage was a kind of enslavement, but she would love him all of her life. She said she needed to explain this to him at once lest there be any grey areas.

Anders was startled. He hadn't *asked* her to marry him. But it all looked good, so he went along with it.

Erika asked him home to meet her parents.

Her father ran a tiny restaurant; her mother was a taxi driver. They welcomed Anders warmly, and he envied the kind of family life they all had. Her sister and brother, twins aged twelve, joined in everything and argued cheerfully with their parents about every subject from pocket money to breast implants, from God to the royal family – subjects that had never been discussed in the Almkvist household. The twins asked Erika when would she be going to meet Anders' family. Before he could answer, Erika said quickly that there was no hurry. She was an acquired taste, she explained. It would take longer for people to welcome her in.

'What's an acquired taste?' her brother asked.

'Look it up,' Erika teased.

Later, Anders said, 'I would be happy for you to come and stay at my father's house.'

'No way. I don't want to give the man a heart attack. But I might go with you and stay at your mother's in London, though.'

'I'm not sure if that would be a good idea . . .'

'You just don't want to meet William and think of him sleeping with your mother, that's all.'

'Not true,' he said and then, because he couldn't keep up the lie, 'Well, I suppose it's a little true.'

'Let's see if we can get to London. I'll try and find a project, and we can improve our English *and* see London *and* check out your new stepfather at the same time.'

It was April when they finally made the visit to London. The daffodils were out in all the parks and gardens and everything seemed alive and sparkling. Gunilla and William were living in an elegant house in a beautiful square quite close to the Imperial War Museum; from there, it was only a few minutes' walk to the River Thames and all the history and pageantry London was famous for. It was the first time they had seen the city and all the richness and bustle. The crowds and the noise were daunting at first, but they dived in with enthusiasm, determined to make the most of every moment.

Gunilla was relaxed and delighted to see them. If she had any doubts about Erika's suitability as the partner of the next head of Almkvist's, she did not even hint at them. William was very welcoming and took three days off work from his television production company to show the young visitors the real London. The first stop was the London Eye, from where they could see for miles in every direction. He had looked up a few of the folk-music clubs in the city so they could take off on their own for an evening if they wanted to. To Anders' delight, William had even found out that there would be *nyckelharpa* playing at a Scandi session in a pub not far away in Bermondsey.

Anders found that it was easier to talk to his mother than it had ever been. No longer was she complaining about how he looked. In fact, she was full of admiration.

'Erika is just delightful,' she told Anders. 'Have you taken her to meet your father yet?'

'Not yet. You know . . .'

If his mother *did* know, she didn't say so.

'Don't leave it too long. Take Erika to meet him soon. She's lovely.'

'But you know how snobby he is, how much he cares about what people do, and are. You've forgotten what he's like. She stands up for herself. She hates big business. She can't bear the kind of people he deals with all day.'

'She will be much too polite to let any of that show.'

Anders wished he could believe her.

Gunilla wanted to know about the office. Did Anders go in there much when he went home?

'I haven't been home much really,' he admitted.

'You should go and keep an eye on your territory, your inheritance,' she said. 'Your father would like that.'

'He never asks me or suggests it.'

'You never offer, you never visit,' she answered.

When they got back to Sweden, Anders telephoned his father. The conversation was formal: it was as if Patrik Almkvist was talking to a casual acquaintance. In as far as Anders could understand, his father sounded pleased that he was coming home for the summer and hoped to work in the office.

'Somewhere that I can't do too much damage,' Anders suggested.

'Everyone will go out of their way to help you,' his father promised.

And so it was. Anders noticed, with some embarrassment, that people in the firm *did* go out of their way to help and encourage him. They spoke to him with a respect that was quite disproportionate for a student. He was definitely the young prince-in-waiting. No one wanted to cross him. He was the future.

Even his two cousins, Mats and Klara, were anxious to show him how much they were pulling their weight. They kept giving him an update on all they had done so far and how well they were handling their own areas. They tried hard to understand what interested young Anders. He didn't seem to want expensive meals in top restaurants; he wasn't concerned with business gossip; he didn't even want to know of rivals' failures.

He was a mystery.

His father, too, seemed to have problems working out where Anders' interests lay. He asked courteous questions about life at university. Whether the teachers had business experience as well as academic records.

He asked nothing about whether Anders had other interests or a love life, whether he still loved music, still played the *nyckelharpa* or even who his friends were. In the evenings, they sat in the apartment in Östermalm and talked about the office and the various clients that had been seen during the day. They ate at Patrik's favourite restaurant some evenings; otherwise they had supper at home sitting at the dining table and eating cold meats and cheese laid out by the silent and disapproving Fru Karlsson. The more his father talked, the less Anders knew about him. The man had no life apart from the one that was lived in the Almkvist office.

Anders had promised his mother that he would make an effort to break his father's reserve but it was proving even harder than he had thought. He tried to speak about Erika.

'I have this girlfriend, Father. She's a fellow student.'

'That's good,' his father nodded vaguely and approvingly as if Anders had said that he had updated his laptop.

'I've been to stay with her family. I thought I might invite Erika here for a few days.'

'Here?' His father was astounded.

'Well, yes.'

'But what would she do all day?'

'I suppose she could tour the city and we could meet for lunch, and I could take a few days off to show her around.'

'Yes, certainly, if you'd like to . . . Of course.'

'She came to London with me when I went to see Mother.'

'Oh yes?'

'It all worked very well. She found plenty to do there.'

'I imagine everyone would find something to do in

220

London. It would be rather different here.' His father was glacial.

'I'm very fond of her, Papa.'

'Good, good.' It was as if he was trying to stem any emotion that might be coming his way.

'In fact, we are going to move in together.' Now he had said it.

'I don't know how you expect to be able to pay for that.'

'Well, I thought it might be something we could discuss while I'm here. Now, may I invite Erika for next week?'

'If you like, yes. Make all the arrangements with Fru Karlsson. She will need to prepare a bedroom for your friend.'

'We will be *living* together, Father. I thought she could share my room here.'

'I don't like to impose your morality and standards on Fru Karlsson.'

'Father, it's not *my* morality, it's the twenty-first century!'

'I know, but even with your mother's shallow grasp on reality she realised the importance of being discreet and keeping one's personal life just that. Fru Karlsson will prepare a bedroom for your friend. Your sleeping arrangements you can make for yourselves.'

'Have I annoyed you?'

'Not at all. In fact I admire your directness, but I am sure you see my point of view also.' He spoke as he would in the office, his voice never raised, his sureness that he was right never wavering.

Erika arrived by train the first week in July. She was full of stories about her fellow passengers. She wore jeans and a scarlet jacket and had a huge backpack of work with her. She said she was going to study in the mornings and then meet him for lunch each day.

'My father will insist on taking us out to some smart places,' he began nervously.

'Then it's just as well you got yourself some smart clothes,' she said.

'I didn't mean me, I meant . . .'

'Don't worry, Anders. I have the shoes, I have the dress,' she said.

And she did. Erika looked splendid in her little black dress with the shocking-pink shawl and smart high heels when they went to his father's favourite restaurant. She listened and asked intelligent questions, and she spoke cheerfully about her own family – her demon twin brother and sister, her mother's adventures in the taxi trade, her father's restaurant which served thirty-seven different kinds of pickled herring. She talked easily about the trip to London and how Anders' mother had been a marvellous hostess. She even talked openly about William.

'You probably don't know him, Mr Almkvist, because of the circumstances and everything, but he was quite amazing. He'd found a pub in Bermondsey where they were playing the *nyckelharpa* – Anders loved it – and then we went to dinner in a restaurant with the most amazing gold mosaic ceiling. He owns a television production company, did you know? Totally capitalist, of course, and against any kind of social welfare, which he called a handout. But generous and helpful as well. Proves that people can't be put in pigeonholes.'

Anders watched his father anxiously. People didn't usually talk to the head of Almkvist's in this manner. They normally skirted away from topics like inequality and privilege. But his father was able to cope with the conversation perfectly well. It was as if he was talking to a casual acquaintance. He asked nothing about Erika's studies, or her hopes and plans for the future.

Anders wondered, had he ever shown any enthusiasm or eagerness for anything except the firm he had worked for all his life?

Erika had no such worries. 'He's just blinkered,' she said. 'Lots of people are. It's that generation. My father doesn't care about anything except the taxes on alcohol and customers going off on a ferry to Denmark to buy cheap booze. My mother is fixated on the need to have women-only taxis. Your father is all hung up on tax shelters and asset management and trusts and things. It's what they *do* in his world. Stop being dramatic about it.'

'But it's not a normal way to live,' Anders insisted.

Erika shrugged. 'For him it is. Always has been and always will be. It's what *you* want that's important.'

'Well I don't want to end up like that, with no interests apart from the office. Blinkered, as you say.'

'So you de-blinker yourself. Why don't we go out and look for some good music tonight?'

Erika was totally practical about everything. She saw nothing wrong with pretending to Fru Karlsson that she slept in the guest bedroom. It was a matter of respect, she said.

Too soon the week was over, and Anders and his father sat again in the empty house speaking only of audits, new business and mergers that had been the order of the day at work. Anders found he enjoyed the business conversations and relished the debates, but he longed to be back at university and moving into his new apartment with Erika. He sensed his cousins were relieved that he would be leaving the office again. His father seemed indifferent, shaking his hand formally and hoping that he would study well and bring all today's thinking and economic theory back to Almkvist's.

Once he was back at university, the voice of his father seemed to Anders like something from a different planet.

The months flew by. He did as he had promised his mother and kept in touch with his father. He made a phone call every ten days or so; a stilted conversation where they ended up talking about personnel at Almkvist's, or new business that had come in their direction. Sometimes he told his father of a business development or an element of tax law he had come across, or the long weekend when he had gone to Majorca with Erika's parents. But he was always relieved when the call was over and felt that his father thought exactly the same.

When it came to the summer holiday the following year, Anders wrote saying that he and Erika were going to spend two months in Greece. If his father was startled that the months would not be spent in the office learning the ropes, he said nothing. Anders felt rather than heard the disapproval.

'I've worked very hard. I need a break, Father.'

'Indeed,' his father had said in a chilly voice.

They had a magical summer in the Greek islands, swimming, laughing, drinking retsina and dancing at night to bouzouki music in the tavernas.

Erika told him of her plans. When she graduated, she was going to be part of a new venture conserving ancient textiles; the funding had been put in place. It was very exciting. And where would it be based? Well, right here in Gothenburg, of course. It was going to be attached to the World Culture Museum.

Anders was silent. He had always hoped she would eventually find work in Stockholm. That they would get a little apartment on one of the islands in the city centre.

They would not marry because Erika still considered it a form of slavery but they would live together when he ran Almkvist's, and have two children.

This did not seem to chime in with Erika's plans. But he would say nothing until he had thought it out.

'You're very silent. I thought you'd be so pleased for me.'

'I am, of course.'

'But?'

'But I suppose I hoped that we would be together. Is that selfish?'

'Of course it's not, but we were waiting until we knew what we wanted to do. You haven't decided yet, so I came up with my plan first to see if you could work round it.' She looked anxious that he should understand.

'But we *know* what I'm going to do. I'm going back to run the family firm.'

Erika looked at him oddly. 'Not seriously?' she said.

'Well of course, seriously. You know that. You've been there. You've seen the set-up. I have to do that. There's never been anything else.'

'But you don't want to do it!' she gasped.

'Not like the way it is, but you told me to de-blinker myself and I did, or I am trying to, anyway. I'm not going to live for the place like my father does.'

'But you were breaking free. Isn't that why we were able to come to Greece instead of you working there all summer?' She was totally bewildered.

'But we know I have to go back, Erika.'

'No, we don't know that you have to go back. You have only one life, and you don't want to spend it there, in that little world with cousins and colleagues.'

'There's no alternative. He only had one son. If I had

brothers who could have taken it over . . .' his voice trailed away.

'Or sisters,' Erika corrected automatically. 'It's only fair to tell him now rather than waste his time, their time, *your* time.'

'I can't do that. Not until I've tried it, anyway. It would be an insult. You're very strong on the respect thing. I owe him that much respect.' In the warm evening air as they sat in the little taverna beside the sea, they heard other people laughing in the distance. Happy people on holiday. Musicians were beginning to tune up.

Anders and Erika sat there, aware of a huge gap opening up between them.

It was now out of their control. The future that had looked so great half an hour ago was about to disappear entirely.

They tried to salvage the rest of the holiday but it was no use. It hung over them: Anders' belief that he would spend his life at Almkvist's and Erika's belief that he had yet to find what he would do were too far apart to gloss over. By the time they got back to Sweden, they knew that there was nothing ahead for the two of them.

They divided up their records and books amicably. Anders took a room in a student block. He told his father that he and Erika were no longer together.

His father's reaction was about the same as it might have been if he had said that a train was running late. A mild and distant murmur that these things happen in life. Then on to the next subject.

He studied hard, determined to get a good degree. Sometimes on the way to and from the library he would see Erika within a laughing group and feel a great pang of regret. They always greeted each other cordially; sometimes he even joined them for a beer in the student cafés.

Their friends were mystified by it all. They had always got on so well. Nothing had changed on the outside; they just were not together any more.

His mother had emailed to say she was sorry to hear they had separated. Erika must have told her. Gunilla said she and William had thought that Erika was a delightful girl, and that Anders must remember that when doors closed they could often be opened up again. She also advised him to do something with his music, or to learn to play tennis or bridge or golf, *something* that would give him a world outside Almkvist's. Perhaps he might even go back to playing the piano. He had even stopped playing the *nyckelharpa* since he and Erika broke up.

Anders was touched, but there would be little time to spend inventing hobbies. He had his final exams to concentrate on; he couldn't take up his place at Almkvist's unless he came away with a good degree. It was time to knuckle down and just get on with it.

He went home every month and worked for a few days in the office, keeping his hand in. He learned how to express his views and how to make decisions. He had a good business head, and people had begun to take him seriously. He was no longer the son and heir of the senior Almkvist: he was a person in his own right. He found himself able to talk to his cousin Mats about his drinking, which had become a matter of some concern; as Mats was family, the problem had so far not been addressed. Anders had been firm but fair. He showed little condemnation, but gave a very clear warning at the same time. Mats pulled himself together sharply and the situation was sorted.

If his father knew of it, he said nothing. But he tended to leave more and more to Anders. Anders, in turn, leaned on

Klara. She was willing to share her experience with him, which was a great help as his final exams were now only weeks away.

On a sunny day in June, Patrik Almkvist sat next to his wife Gunilla for their son's graduation. William had stayed at home because of business commitments, he said. Privately, Anders thought that might just have been a diplomatic retreat. It might have been a miserable ordeal. Instead, Anders was pleased to see, it wasn't just good manners that kept them all smiling throughout the afternoon and into the evening. He realised that now his parents no longer lived together, they could relax. To his astonishment, a kind of friendship had emerged and they were both able to enjoy their son's achievements.

The conversation over dinner was filled with talk of the future: for a long time, it had been planned that after his graduation Anders would spend a year in a big American firm of accountants, a place with a distinguished name where he would learn a great deal in a short time. It had all been arranged with the senior partners, and Anders was hugely looking forward to it. Klara had been very helpful with her Boston contacts and had arranged everything. Gunilla had contacts there too, it emerged, and he would have a marvellous time in the city. As they strolled through the streets of Gothenburg, Anders felt that everything was falling into place.

The following morning, Patrik Almkvist collapsed in the hotel lobby.

It was a heart attack.

It was not major, the hospital told them; Mr Almkvist was not in any danger but still he had to rest. Anders and Gunilla sat by his bedside for two days and then, as his mother flew back to London, Anders took his father back home to Stockholm.

Fru Karlsson took charge immediately, and Anders knew his father would be in good hands. He was making arrangements with her for home nursing and support but his father cut straight across.

'There's no way you can go to Boston now. You have to go in at the deep end, Anders. I need you in there as my eyes and ears. It's your time now.'

It couldn't be his time yet. He was much too young. He hadn't even begun to live properly.

Boston was cancelled. Soon it seemed as if Anders had always been in charge; he welcomed the challenges, yet he knew he would not have been able to cope without Klara's expertise and loyalty. She briefed him before every meeting, gave him background information on every client. He did make time to swim at lunchtime each day rather than go to eat the heavy meals in dark, panelled dining rooms that the previous regime had favoured. Once a week he went to listen to some live music but every other evening he sat with his father as Fru Karlsson cleared away their supper, and he spoke about what had gone on at the firm that day.

Little by little, Mr Almkvist's strength returned. But never to the level it had been. When he came back to work it was for short days and mainly involved meetings in the boardroom, where his presence managed to give weight and importance to the occasion.

The weeks turned into months.

Sometimes Anders felt a bit crushed by it all; other times he felt that out there somewhere was a real world with people doing what they really wanted to do or what mattered, or both. But he realised that he was privileged to have inherited such a prestigious position. In a world of uncertainty and anxiety about employment and the economy, he was amazingly lucky to be where he was, doing a job that presented new challenges every day. Privilege brought duties with it; he had always known this. This was where his duty lay.

It was his father who suggested the holiday to him.

He said that the boy was working too hard and must go to recharge his batteries. Anders was at a loss to know where to go. His friend Johan from the folk club said that Ireland was good. You could just go there and point yourself in some direction and there was always something good to see or to join in with.

He booked a ticket to Dublin and set out with no plans. Unheard-of behaviour from anyone at Almkvist's, who normally researched everything forensically before setting out anywhere. He missed Erika desperately at the airport. They had set out from here to London, to Spain, to Greece. Now he was on his own.

Had he been mad to let her slip away?

But there had been no other decision he could have made. Anders could not have stayed for ever with Erika in Gothenburg, where she had found the perfect career. And she would not have come to live in the shadow of Almkvist's and be a complaisant company wife like his mother had done.

He had hoped that he would forget her, and it was easy to find companions for dinner or dancing. As the heir to Almkvist's he was considered a very eligible catch, but no woman ever held his interest for long. He went to all the social occasions but never cared about anyone enough to seek out their company, and he had been pleased to learn that Erika had not formed any other attachment. Now, at the airport, he wanted so much to speak to her and tell her he was going to Ireland. She answered her phone immediately and was genuinely glad to hear from him. She seemed interested in everything he had to say, but then Erika was always interested in everything and everyone. It didn't make him special.

'Are you going with friends?' she asked.

'I don't want to go with friends,' he said ruefully. 'I want to go with you.'

'No, you don't get the sympathy vote by saying something like that. You have all the friends you need. You have the life you chose.' Her tone was light but she meant it. He *had* made his choice. 'You'll make lots of new friends in Ireland. I go to an Irish bar here. They have great music. They're easy people to get to know.'

'Well, I'll send you a postcard if I find an Irish bar when I get there.'

'I believe it will be hard *not* to find one. But do that anyway.'

Did she sound as if she really would like to hear from him, or was she just being Erika – easy, relaxed and yet focused at the same time?

He walked glumly to the plane.

Erika would have loved the Dublin hotel, which managed to be both chaotic and charming at the same time. They advised him to take a city bus tour to orientate himself and to go to a traditional Irish evening in a nearby pub that night. Then, at breakfast the next morning, he met a group of Irish Americans who were discussing renting a boat on the River Shannon. It was proving to be more expensive than they had hoped. They really needed another person to share the cost. Would he like to make up the numbers?

Why not, he thought? The brochure looked attractive — lovely lakes and a wide river, little ports to visit. Before he realised it he was en route to Athlone in the middle of Ireland, going aboard a motor cruiser for a lesson in navigation. Soon they were cruising past reeds and riverbanks and old castles, and places with small harbours and long names. The sun shone and the world slowed down.

His fellow passengers were five easy-going men and women from an insurance company in Chicago. They were meant to be looking for ancestors and relatives, but this sat lightly on them. They were more interested in finding good Irish music and drinking a lot of Irish beer. Anders joined in enthusiastically.

He bought three postcards at a tiny post office and sent them to his father, his mother and Erika.

He puzzled for a long time before he wrote the few lines to his father. There was literally nothing to say that would interest the old man. Eventually, he decided to say that the economy of the country had taken a serious hit because of the recession. That at least was something his father would understand.

When the river cruise was over, the Irish Americans had gone off on a five-day golfing tour. They invited him to come with them but Anders said no. Bad as he was at manoeuvring a boat on the Shannon, he didn't want to upset real golfers by going out on the course with them.

Instead he found a coach tour of the West of Ireland.

John Paul, the cheerful, red-faced bus driver, claimed that he knew all the best music pubs on the coast, and every night they found another great session. John Paul knew all the musicians by name and told the coach party their history and repertoire before they got to the venue each evening.

'Ask Micky Moore to sing *"Mo Ghile Mear"* for you, it'll make the hairs rise on the back of your neck,' he would say. Or else he knew when some old piper was going to come in from retirement and do a turn. Anders was interested in it all.

It turned out that John Paul played the pipes himself. Not bagpipes. No, indeed, bagpipes were Scottish. Real pipes were the uilleann pipes. You didn't have to blow into them like the Scots did; instead there was a kind of a bellows under your arm which you pressed with your elbow. *Uilleann* was actually the Irish word for elbow.

The music was haunting, and Anders was mesmerised by it all.

John Paul said that if ever he got some money together he would open his own place and welcome all kinds of musicians there.

'Here, in the West?' Anders wondered.

'Maybe, but then I don't want to take the bread and butter away from the people who are already here. They are my friends,' he said.

John Paul and Anders talked about God and fate and evil and imagination. He asked John Paul how old he was. The man looked at him, surprised.

'You speak such good English, I forget you're not from round here. I was born in 1980, nine months after Pope John Paul visited Ireland. Nearly every lad who was born that year was called John Paul.'

'And will you go on driving the bus all your life?' Anders wondered.

'No, I'll have to go home to the old man sometime. The others have all gone far and wide, done well for themselves. I'm only John Paul the eejit, and my da is not really able to manage the place on his own. One of these days I'll have to face it and go back to Stoneybridge and take over.'

'That's hard.' Anders was sympathetic.

'Ah, go on out of that! Haven't I bricks and mortar and beasts in the field and a little farm waiting for me? Half of Ireland would give their eye teeth for that. It's just not what I want. I'm no good at going out looking for sheep that have got stuck on their back with their legs in the air and turning them the right way up. I hate having to deal with milk quotas, and what Europe wants you to plant or to ignore. It's life-blood for some people; it's drudgery for me, but it's a living. A good living, even.'

'But your own place with the musicians?'

'I'll wait until I'm reincarnated, Anders. I'll do it next time round.' His big, round, weather-beaten face was totally resigned to it.

On the last night of the coach tour, the passengers all clubbed together to take John Paul out for a meal. And as a thank you, he played them some airs on the uilleann pipes. He got a group photograph taken and everyone wrote their names and email addresses on the back.

Anders had a cup of coffee with John Paul on the last morning.

'I'll miss your company,' Anders said. 'Nobody to discuss the world and its ways like you.'

'You're making a mock of me! Isn't Sweden full of thinkers and musicians like ourselves?'

Anders felt absurdly flattered to be thought of as a musician and a thinker.

'It probably is. I just don't meet them, that's all.'

'Well they're out there,' John Paul was very definite. 'I've

234

met great Swedes travelling here. They can play the spoons, they can all sing "Bunch Of Thyme". And wasn't Joe Hill himself from Sweden?'

'Maybe you're right. I'll let you know when I find them.'

'You keep in touch, Anders. You're one of the good guys,' John Paul said.

Anders wondered if he really was one of the good guys when he went back to work at Almkvist's. He learned within an hour of his return that his cousin Mats, who had had the problem with alcohol, had apparently revisited that part of his life in spectacular fashion. Moreover, one of Almkvist's most prestigious clients had absconded with a very young woman and a great deal of assets weeks before a major audit.

His father looked more grey-faced and concerned than ever. Only a few hours after he was back, Anders felt the benefits of his holiday in Ireland slipping away from him. He played some of the music he had brought home with him. The lonely laments played on the uilleann pipes, the rousing choruses where everyone had joined in, reminded him of the carefree days and the easy company, but he knew it was only temporary. It was like a child wanting a birthday party to last for ever.

His father showed no interest in any stories of his trip, no matter how he tried to tell them.

'Why don't you let me show you some of the photographs I took?' he suggested. 'Would you like to listen to some of the music with me? We were listening to some marvellous traditional Irish music . . .'

'Yes, yes, very interesting but it was just a holiday, Anders. You're like Fru Karlsson who wants to tell you what she dreamed about last night. It's not relevant to anything.'

He decided at that moment that he would move out of his

father's apartment. Get himself a small place of his own, break this never-ending cycle of discussing work from morning to night.

He hoped he would have the energy to make the move. Everyone was going to resist it. Why leave a perfectly comfortable, elegant place which would be his one day anyway? Why disrupt Fru Karlsson and her ways? Why leave his father alone instead of being his companion in these latter years?

Anders thought of John Paul going to look after *his* father, setting sheep back on their four legs again and abandoning his dream of a musicians' haven in order to do his duty. But even John Paul would have some time off to himself. Maybe he could go and play his pipes of an evening. He didn't have to discuss farming with his father as the moon rose in the sky.

If Anders ever had a son of his own he would tell the boy from the outset that he must follow his heart, that he would not be expected to play his role in Almkvist's. But it didn't seem likely that he would have a son. He could never see himself settling with anyone but Erika. And he had thrown that away.

Nevertheless, he telephoned to tell her about his trip to Ireland.

Erika was interested in everything and knew a lot about Irish music already. She had bought a tin whistle and was teaching herself to play.

'Come and stay for a weekend and I'll take you to The Galway. You'd love it,' she suggested.

A weekend away from Almkvist's; away from dramas about his cousin's rehab, the client who had absconded with funds and girlfriend, his father's anxiety, the general downturn in business . . . it was just what he needed.

As he drove towards Gothenburg, where he had been so

236

happy as a university student, Anders wondered if he would stay at Erika's apartment. Nothing had been said. She might have booked him into a hotel. If he *did* stay at the flat, then would they share a room? It would be so artificial if she made up a mattress for him on the floor. And after all, Erika didn't have any partner or companion these days – nor did he, so there would be no question of cheating on anyone.

But then he couldn't expect things to return to the way they had once been. He sighed, and knew that he would have to wait and see.

Erika looked wonderful, her eyes dancing and her words tumbling over each other as she told him about how successful the conservation project was; they had got serious recognition and an important grant. She cooked supper for him, the Swedish meatballs which had always been their celebration meal. The apartment hadn't changed much – new curtains, more bookshelves.

After supper they went to The Galway, the bar where Erika was greeted as a regular. She introduced Anders to people on both sides of the bar, and then they settled in for a music session. Suddenly he was back in the West of Ireland, with the waves beating on the shore and a new set of faces bent over fiddles, pipes and accordions every night. The music swept him away.

Later, he talked to the people who had played. Particularly to a man called Kevin, the piper.

'Do you know the theme from *The Brendan Voyage*?' he asked.

'Indeed I do, but I don't usually play it because whenever I played it in the London pubs it made people cry.'

'It made me cry too,' Anders said.

Erika looked up, surprised. 'You never cry,' she said.

'I did in Ireland,' he said wistfully.

'We have a habit of upsetting people,' Kevin said ruefully. 'Come in tomorrow night and I'll play it for you, then we can have a bawl over it together, and a pint.'

'That's a date,' Anders agreed readily.

Later, back in Erika's flat, they drank beer and picked at some of the leftover food. She lit candles on the coffee table and they sat opposite, suddenly acutely aware of each other. She gazed at him seriously.

'You've changed,' she said.

'I haven't changed about being very fond of you,' he said.

'Me neither, but you are still sleeping in the spare room,' she laughed.

'It seems a pity.' He smiled.

'Yes, but I'm not going to spend yet more weeks and months regretting what might have been.'

'*Did* you spend weeks and months regretting it?'

'You know I did, Anders.'

'But you still wouldn't consider coming to live with me and just putting up with Almkvist's.'

'And *you* wouldn't consider giving up Almkvist's and coming to live with me. Listen, we've been through all this before. It's well-trodden ground.'

'You know I had responsibilities. Still do.'

'You don't like it, Anders my friend. You're not happy. You have told me not one word about your life there in the office. That's my one complaint. If I had thought that it was what you wanted then I might have considered it.'

'You call me your friend . . . !' he said.

'You are. You will always be my friend, when you and I are long married to other people.'

'It won't happen, Erika. I've looked around. There's no one out there.'

'Well, then we will have to look harder. Tell me more about Ireland.'

He told her about the Irish Americans on the Shannon, and about John Paul who had to go back to look after his father. And then he went to bed in the brightly painted guest room. He stayed awake for a long time.

At The Galway next day, Anders and Erika sat and listened while Kevin played the pipes. As he listened, Anders again heard the waves breaking on the wild Atlantic shore and he felt a surge of misery overwhelm him. He suddenly saw his life stretching in front of him in an unending straight line: getting up in the morning, putting on a suit, going to work at the office, coming home to a lonely apartment, going to bed, getting up the following morning . . . Responsibility. Loyalty. Duty. Rules. Expectations. Family tradition. And when the musicians took a break, Anders tried to explain to Erika why he had to stay with his father, but the words weren't there. He found his sentences trailing away.

'It's just that . . .' he began, then faltered. 'It's the family tradition. I mean, if I don't . . . There are these expectations . . . It's who I am. And I can do it. I *am* doing it. I am the next Almkvist. They're all waiting for me. All my life . . . And in any case, if I'm not that, who am I?'

'Anders, stop, please. Look, it isn't that you are in your father's business that I don't like. It's that you hate it and always will. But you won't do anything else. It's your decision, not theirs. It's your life, not theirs. You can do anything with your life. At least think what else you might do. When you find what the something else is, then you will consider leaving.'

She leaned over and stroked his hand. 'Leave it for now,' she suggested.

'Which means leave it for ever,' he said sadly.

'No, you've gone as far as you can down the road and you always reach the same fork. Maybe something will happen. Something that you will want more than that office. Then when that day comes, you can think about it again.'

He ached to say that he wanted Erika more than he wanted the office, but it was not strictly true. He could not walk away, and they both knew this. They hugged each other before he set out on the long drive home.

His heart was heavy as he played his music in the car. It was only a dream, a holiday memory. It was childish to think it might be another life for him.

The weeks went by, and his father was cold and distant about Anders moving into his own apartment. Fru Karlsson was bristling with resentment. She tried to exact a promise that he would turn up at his father's every night.

Often he ate alone in his flat, putting a ready meal into the microwave and opening a beer. Back in the big apartment, his father would also be dining alone.

Once a week Anders turned up for dinner, already armed to cope with the resentment and the pressures which would be there to greet him. Either his father or Fru Karlsson would remind him that his room was there and ready should he wish to stay the night. There was heavy sighing about the size and emptiness of the family apartment. His father said how hard it was to know what was going on in the office these days since he himself only went in for three hours a day, and Anders was off enjoying himself every evening and not there to discuss the day's events.

He often wondered how John Paul was faring in the

months since he had seen him. Had life on the farm turned out better than he had feared, or was it worse? Had the sacrifice been worthwhile? John Paul might have regretted the intimate revelations of his reluctance to go and look after his father. He might not relish having it all brought up again.

One evening Anders looked up Stoneybridge, the place where John Paul was going home to live. On his laptop he saw that it was a small, attractive, seaside town that clearly only came to life for the summer months and would be fairly desolate in these winter days. Yet he read that a new venture had begun there; a large place on a cliff called Stone House, offering a winter week on the Atlantic coast with spectacular scenery, good food, walking and wild birds. There would be music in the pubs if guests cared to seek it out. It was a ludicrous idea and he knew it was, but still he went online and booked a week there.

He told his father little about the trip – just a winter week's holiday. His father, of course, asked nothing, only registered vague disapproval of his sudden decision to go.

And Anders did not tell Erika about the trip. Their last meeting had been a kind of watershed. There was no point in telling her he was going to Ireland again; she wouldn't come with him. She would just go on about him wasting his life. She couldn't understand that he simply had no choice in the matter. He didn't want to have that conversation again.

He flew to Dublin and caught a train to the West.

Chicky Starr met him at the station. She seemed to see nothing odd about a young Swedish accountant flying over to spend time in this deserted place. She complimented him on his excellent English. She said that Scandinavians were wonderful at learning languages. When she had lived in New

York, she had been astounded at how new arrivals from Denmark, Sweden and Norway adapted so quickly.

He was relaxed and comfortable long before they arrived at the wonderful old house and he met his fellow guests. The American man was the absolute image of Corry Salinas the actor, even spoke like him too. Anders found himself wondering what on earth Corry Salinas would be doing here. He found himself exchanging glances with the English doctor, who had also spotted the actor. But so what? If the man wanted a rest, a change, he'd be no different from all the other people who had gathered there. No one would bother anyone else.

Over dinner, he found himself in conversation with a nice woman called Freda, who seemed surprised to hear of his interest in music. He'd come to the right place, she said; music was in the very air they breathed in this part of Ireland. She'd be keen to hear some good music herself.

'You play an instrument yourself,' she said. It was a statement rather than a question. Anders found he was telling her about the *nyckelharpa* and about his love of music.

'And what do you do for a living?' she asked.

'I'm just a boring accountant,' he said with a wry smile.

'Accountants are no more boring than anyone else,' she replied, 'but if your heart is elsewhere, would you not want to follow your destiny?' As she spoke, her eyes looked into the distance.

'Ah, no,' he said wistfully, 'I know perfectly well where my destiny lies. I will take over from my father very soon and run the business which was his life's work. And once or twice a week I will go to a tiny club and play music to half a dozen people. And that will be my life.' And then, as if to take the bleakness out of his words, he smiled and added, 'But this is my holiday, and I'm going to find the best sessions in the county. Care to join me?'

It was agreed. The very next day they would meet after breakfast and go off in search of the best music to be found.

It was all totally undemanding and he was glad that he had come. When he went to bed and looked out on the crashing waves in the moonlight, he knew he would sleep properly. He would not wake twice, three times during the night, restless and unsure. That alone made it worth coming to this place.

The following morning, Anders asked Chicky Starr about music venues.

She knew of two pubs, both of them known locally for their sessions. One of them did terrific seafood at lunchtimes, if he was interested in sampling the local food.

As they were talking, Freda joined them, ready and eager for the day. The weather looked set fair and, with high spirits, the two set out in the direction of the town, Anders carrying his small rucksack on his back with his maps and guides inside. They passed whitewashed cottages, farmhouses and out-buildings. For a while, the road followed the coastline, and high as they were on the clifftop, the wind and spray stung their faces. Even the trees were bent double and stunted by the Atlantic gales. Then the road took them inland so that the sea was out of sight. As they got nearer to the town, the fields disappeared, ploughed up and replaced with new housing, row after row looking eerily empty.

The main street in Stoneybridge was lined with two- and three-storey houses, each one painted a different colour. The pubs were easy to identify, but the two explorers made the little café their first stop. They talked easily, comparing notes on their first impressions of their fellow guests at Stone House.

Freda, Anders noticed, gave little away about her own reasons for coming to Stone House but she had observed everyone else quite closely. The doctor and his wife, she said, shaking her head a little, were very sad – there had been a recent death, she could tell. Quite how she could tell she didn't say. And that nice nurse – what was her name? Winnie, was it? – was having a dreadful time with her friend Lillian, but it would all be worth it in the end.

They went for lunch into the larger of the pubs: great bowls of steaming, succulent mussels and fresh crusty bread. And then, as if in response to some silent cue, a small, red-faced man sitting in the corner produced a fiddle and started to play. The session had started . . .

At first, musicians outnumbered audience but gradually more people arrived. Most would arrive in the evening, it was explained, but some liked to play in the afternoons and everyone was welcome to join in. The music, at first gentle and haunting, grew faster and faster. At one side of the room, a couple started dancing and Anders himself borrowed a guitar and played a couple of Swedish songs. He taught everyone the words of the songs and they joined in the choruses with great gusto.

He had, he admitted rather shyly, brought a traditional Swedish instrument with him on his holiday and he could bring it in the following day. Only if they'd like him to, of course . . .

Freda looked at him oddly as he returned to their table. 'Once or twice a week, to an audience of six people?' she said, so quietly he could hardly hear her over the cheering. 'No, I don't think so.'

244

Anders began to feel as if he had lived nowhere else. The American man actually *was* Corry Salinas, obviously here in hiding and calling himself John. The two women, Winnie and Lillian, were nearly drowned on their second day there and had to be rescued from a cave: Anders had missed all the excitement as he had stayed on in the town for the evening sessions. This time he had taken his *nyckelharpa* with him and had found himself called upon time and time again to play and sing along. Of John Paul there was no sign, although Anders did move between both pubs.

Eventually, on one of his visits, he asked a craggy-faced man who played the tin whistle did he know a piper from the area called John Paul?

Of course he did. Everyone knew him, very decent lad. Immediately, four other musicians joined in the conversation. They all knew poor John Paul. Stuck up there in Rocky Ridge with his old divil of a father whom no one could please. A discontented man who wished he had taken the emigrant's ship years back and blamed everyone but himself that he hadn't.

'And does John Paul play the uilleann pipes anywhere round here?'

'He hasn't been in here in months now,' one of the men said, shaking his head sadly. 'A group of us went up for him in a van one day but he said he couldn't leave the old fellow.'

The following morning, Anders asked Chicky how to get to Rocky Ridge and she packed a lunch for him.

'I'm sure John Paul would make a meal for you, but just in case he's not there you'd want to be prepared,' she said.

It was a longer walk than he had expected, and he was weary when he arrived at the big, untidy farmyard. There seemed to be nobody around. As Anders approached the door some hens ran out clucking, annoyed to be disturbed.

An old man sat at the table trying to read a newspaper with a magnifying glass. A big sheepdog lay at his feet. It looked more like a rug than a dog.

'I was looking for John Paul . . .' Anders began.

'You and half the country are looking for him. He went out of here God knows how many hours ago and no sign of him. I'm his father Matty, by the way, and I haven't even had my dinner and it's gone three o'clock.'

'Well, I'm Anders and I brought a picnic with me, so we might as well have that,' Anders said, and opened the waxed paper in the little bag that Chicky had packed.

He got two plates and divided the cold chicken, cheese and chutney. He made a pot of tea and they sat and ate it as normally as if it was quite commonplace for John Paul's father to be served a meal by a passing Swedish tourist.

They talked about farming and how it had changed over the years, about the recession and how all the townhouses that the uppity O'Haras had built were standing empty like a ghost estate because people had been greedy and thought that the Celtic Tiger would last for ever. He spoke about his other children, who had done well for themselves abroad. He said that Shep the dog was blind now and useless but would always have a home.

He wanted to know about farming in Sweden, and Anders answered as best he could but said that he wished he could tell him more. He was really a city boy at heart.

'And what brings you to this place, if you are a city boy?' Matty wanted to know.

Anders explained how he had met John Paul on the bus tour.

'He loved that old bus, dead-end job, in and out of shebeens the whole time, happy as a bird on a bush. Even thought of setting up his own shebeen, but he thought better of it and decided to row in here to try to get the last few shillings out of this place,' he said, shaking his head in disapproval.

Anders felt his gorge rising in anger. This was the thanks that the old man was giving for his son's sacrifice. Could life be any more unfair?

In a reasoned way he tried to explain that perhaps John Paul had wanted to help his father.

'You don't want to buy the place here, by any chance?' Matty peered at him through half-closed eyes.

'No, indeed, are you selling?'

'Oh, if only we could. I'd be out of it by this evening.'

'And where would you go, Matty?'

'I'd go into St Joseph's. It's a sort of a home in the town. I'd have people calling in to see me there, and company. I wouldn't be stuck up here on Rocky Ridge with John Paul working all the hours God sends, and for what? For next to nothing.'

'Did you tell him this?'

'I can't. He thinks there's a living in the place. He did nothing for himself in life but he's got a good heart, and he deserves a crack at making the place work. I couldn't go and sell it over his head.'

Anders sat there silently for a while. Matty was a man who was used to silences. Shep snored on. Maybe life was full of these misunderstandings.

John Paul was out there on mountain tops dealing with things he hated, his father was yearning to live in a nice warm, safe place where people could call in to him and his dinner would be served at one o'clock every day. They each thought the other was desperate to keep the farm going.

Could it be the same situation in Sweden?

Did Anders' father wish that he could hand the firm over to others, release his son from a life which he did not enjoy? Was this only wishful thinking? A false parallel?

Problems don't solve themselves neatly like that, due to a set of coincidences. Problems are solved by making decisions. Erika had always said that, and he had thought she was being doctrinaire. But it was true. Deciding not to change anything was a decision in itself. He hadn't fully understood this before.

The light went from the sky and Shep stirred in his dreams. Anders made more tea and found them some biscuits. Matty told him about Chicky marrying this man who was killed in a car crash in New York, and how he had left her money to come home and buy the Sheedy place. Matty said Chicky was a real survivor; she didn't expect anyone to fight her battles for her. Many a man had shown an interest in her, but she was fair and square with all of them. She was her own woman, she told them.

But you never knew what the Lord had planned for you. Maybe some nice American man might come for a holiday and sweep her off her feet again. Was there anyone among the guests that looked suitable?

Anders thought not. There *was* a pleasant American there, all right, but he hadn't seen any sign of a romance.

'Oh, is that Corry Salinas? I heard he was staying there,' Matty said.

'You did?'

'Yes, he was trying to keep it a secret but everyone here recognised him. Frank Hanratty was only telling some daft story that he came into the golf club to buy Frank a drink because he saw his pink van outside the door. Frank had better take a hold of himself.'

Just then they heard the van arrive and John Paul ran into the house.

'Da, the cattle had got through a fence up in the top field. They were wandering all over the road. Dr Dai was trying to get them back into the field through the gap with one of his golf clubs. He was worse than myself. And by the time we got someone to fix the fence—' He broke off when he saw Anders. His big face lit up with pleasure.

'Anders Almkvist! You came to see us!' he said, delighted. 'Da, this is my friend . . .'

'Don't I know all about him. We've had a long chat waiting for you to get back, and I know all about why the Swedes are better off with their krone than the euro,' Matty said.

John Paul looked on, open-mouthed.

'*And* he brought me my dinner as well,' his father pronounced. The final accolade. Anders got another mug and poured out tea for John Paul.

There was no rush. There would be plenty of time to explain everything.

139 -78 57

John Paul drove Anders back to Stone House. 'Imagine you coming back here and up to Rocky Ridge to see me!' he said.

'I was hoping to hear you playing in one of the local pubs, but they say you work too hard. You're too tired.'

'I was hoping that *you* had come to tell me that you'd left that office of yours,' John Paul said.

'No. Not just yet.'

'But you might . . . ?' John Paul looked pleased for his friend. 'So miracles do happen.'

'Wait until I tell you about what *your* father really wants, and then you'll think twice about miracles,' said Anders.

Anders was most apologetic when he slipped in at Chicky's big dining table. 'I'm sorry I'm a bit late,' he said as he sat down next to the doctor and his wife.

'No problem. It's duck tonight. I kept it hot for you. Everything all right with John Paul?'

'Fine, fine. What's St Joseph's like as a place to stay?'

'As good as they come. If they could only persuade Matty to go in there, he'd love it. I have an aunt in there, and she barely has time to talk to you when you visit.'

'No, he *wants* to go in. It's John Paul who has the doubts.'

'We can sort him out on that. And you tell John Paul he should go away and travel a bit, let some of the other brothers and sisters come back and pull their weight here. Visit Matty from time to time, instead of leaving it all to John Paul.'

'I do have an idea at the back of my mind.'

'If it means giving John Paul a bit of a chance in life, I'm all for it.'

'I was thinking of opening an Irish bar in Sweden. Asking him to come and set up the music side of it for me. I can deal with the business side.'

'So *that* is what you were doing here. I did wonder.' Chicky seemed pleased to have found out without interrogating.

'No, it wasn't what I intended. It just sort of evolved.'

'Things *do* evolve around here. I've seen it over and over. There's something in the sea air, I think.'

'I haven't spoken to my father about it yet.'

'And if he is against the idea?' Chicky was gentle.

'I will explain it to him. I will be clear and courteous, as he has always been. I will not pour any scorn on *his* dreams; just

250

point out that they are not mine.' His voice sounded very much more confident.

Chicky nodded several times. It was as if she could see it happening. 'And when you're hiring, you might ask my niece Orla out there, for a season anyway, to do the food for you. It would be the making of your pub, and prevent her from growing old and mad with me.'

'There are worse places to grow old and mad,' Anders laughed. He hoped he could explain all this to his father, and that he would not be too disappointed. Klara would take over Almkvist's. The company was in her blood just as much as it was in his. She knew and loved the business in a way he never would. Now all he had to do was persuade his father that a woman could head up a prestigious company like Almkvist's. He sighed and settled back in his seat. And who could he get to help him persuade his father? He pulled out a pencil and pad and started to make lists of things that he had to do. Calling Erika was top of the list.

The Walls

They never introduced themselves as Ann and Charlie, they always said, 'We are The Walls'.

They signed their Christmas cards *from The Walls* also, and when they answered the phone they would say, 'Walls here'.

Possibly it was an act of solidarity. You rarely saw one without the other, and they always stood very close to each other. They apparently never tired of each other's company, which was just as well as they worked together in their Dublin home correcting and marking papers as postal tuition for a correspondence college. They had both been teachers, but this was much more companionable and less stressful. They had a little study in their house where they went in at nine a.m. and came out at two. The Walls said it was very important to have total self-discipline when you worked from home. Otherwise the day ran away from you.

Then, in the afternoons, they would walk or garden or shop, and at five o'clock settle down to what was the high spot of the day – entering competitions.

They had won many, many prizes. Anything from choosing

a name for a chocolate Easter bunny to writing a limerick in praise of garden sheds. They had won a holiday in the South of France because they wrote a slogan for a new perfume; they got a set of heavy cast-iron cookware for guessing the weight of a turkey. They had won the latest television, a top-of-the-range microwave oven, his-and-hers sports bikes, velvet curtains and a whole range of smaller items like trendy electric kettles and leather-bound photo albums. It was a poor week when they didn't win *something*. And they so enjoyed the fun of the chase as well as the extra comforts that came from the prizes.

They had two sons who seemed to play very little part in their lives. This had always been the way. When the boys were at school they always went to play in other boys' houses: The Walls weren't into entertaining groups of children. Then one son, Andy, was taken on by a major English football club and became a professional soccer player; the other boy, Rory, had become a long-distance lorry driver and drove for hours on end all over Europe.

Both of these careers bewildered The Walls, who could not fathom why their sons didn't want to go to university, and the boys, on their part, could not begin to understand a mother and father who raked the newspapers and magazines in search of winning something like an electric toaster.

But the years went on peacefully for The Walls. They were very satisfied with the life they lived. They chose their competitions carefully and only entered for something where they felt they had a reasonable chance of winning. They scorned the kind of competitions they saw on television: a multiple-choice question asking if *Vienna was the capital of a) Andorra b) Austria or c) Australia. Choose option a, b or c.* These were not *real* competitions, they were only schemes to make money from premium-rate call lines. No self-respecting competition entrant would consider them.

They knew also that you must not make your jingles or rhymes too clever. They had seen that the middle of the road was the way to go. They would examine each other's solutions looking for puns or references that might be beyond the ordinary punter. They must beware of stepping outside the mainstream. And so far, it had all worked very well.

As they sat one summer's evening on the garden seat that had been theirs because they had matched twelve garden flowers with the months in which they bloomed, and drank from Waterford Glass tumblers that had come from the competition to write an ode to crystal, The Walls congratulated themselves on their twenty-five years of happy marriage. They were in a great state of excitement this evening: they planned to win something quite splendid to celebrate their silver wedding anniversary in a few months. There was a cruise to Alaska, for one thing. That would be heavily subscribed. Competition entrants from all over the world would be trying for that one, so they should not be too confident of winning. There was a residential cookery course in Italy, which would be nice. There was a week in a Scottish castle. The possibilities were endless. It was not a question of being mean or careful with money; The Walls could well afford a holiday abroad, but the thrill of winning one was much more satisfying, and they filled in forms and made up slogans with great vigour.

Then they found the dream prize. It was a winter break in Paris, a week in a luxury hotel. There would be a chauffeur-driven car at their disposal with an outing planned for each day of the week: Versailles, Chartres, as well as city tours, meals in internationally known restaurants. It was a once-in-a-lifetime experience.

It looked a very good bet. They had seen it in a rather elegant magazine with a small circulation; this was helpful. It meant that it would not have caught the eye of millions of readers. The task was to explain in one paragraph why they *deserved* this holiday.

The Walls knew not to make it jokey. The judges were the editor of the magazine, a travel agent and a couple of hoteliers in Ireland and Britain who were offering second and third prizes. These were people who took their product seriously. No satire or disrespect would win. The question must be addressed with equal seriousness.

And they were pleased with their entry. The Walls explained quite simply that after twenty-five years of contented partnership, they would love to bring back a little romance into their lives. They had never been people with a glittery lifestyle but, like everyone, they would love it if some magic was sprinkled on their lives. They had used words like 'sprinkle' and 'magic' before in captions or slogans, and they had worked well. They would work again.

They were now quite certain that the prize was theirs, and were unprepared for the shock of hearing they had won *second* prize – a holiday in some remote place on the cliffs over the Atlantic at the other side of the country. They looked at each other, dismayed. This was a poor reward for all the effort they had put into composing the burningly sincere essay about the need to have a little stardust shaken over them!

The woman on the telephone expected them to be very excited that they had won a week in this Stone House place, and because The Walls were basically polite people they tried hard to summon up some degree of enthusiasm. But their hearts were heavy as they thought of someone else in what had started to become *their* chauffeur-driven car in Paris, and *their* reservation at a five-star restaurant.

Ann Wall had been laying out the wardrobe she would pack. It included a designer handbag and a Hermès silk square that they had won in previous competitions. Charlie had reluctantly put down the guide book he had bought so that they would appear well informed about the Paris buildings and art treasures when they got there.

They both fumed with rage and annoyance that they had been so wrongly confident about winning the first prize. They were desperate to know what the winning essay had been about, and were determined to find out.

The Walls telephoned Chicky Starr, proprietor of Stone House, to make the arrangements for their visit. She was cheerful and practical as she gave details of train times and arranged to have them collected at the station. She was, they had to admit, perfectly pleasant and welcoming. If they had intended to win this holiday, they would have been delighted with her, but Mrs Starr must never know how very poor a consolation this holiday was going to be for The Walls.

She checked if they were vegetarians and advised them about bringing warm and waterproof clothing. No place here for designer scarves and bags, they realised. She said she would post them brochures and reading matter about the area so that they could decide in advance what they would like to do. There would be bicycles to ride, wild birds to see and a group of like-minded people to have dinner with in the evenings.

Like-minded? The Walls thought not.

Nobody else would be going there with such an aura of second best.

Mrs Starr said she would not mention to anyone that they

were competition winners: it was up to them to discuss it or not. This puzzled The Walls. Normally they were very pleased to tell people they had won a competition and had got there by their wits rather than by handing out money. Still, it was thoughtful of Mrs Starr.

With heavy hearts they agreed on the train and bus times, and said insincerely that they were looking forward to it all greatly.

Their two sons came back to Ireland to celebrate the silver wedding. They took their parents to Quentins, one of the most talked-about restaurants in Dublin.

The Walls marvelled at how sophisticated the boys had become. Andy, who was used to a high life now as a soccer player in a Premier League team, went through the menu as if he were accustomed to eating like this every night; even Rory, who mainly dined in transport cafés and places where long-haul drivers met to eat quickly and get back on the road, was equally at ease.

They asked with baffled interest about their parents' recent successes in the competition stakes. There had been a set of matching luggage, some colourful garden lights and a carved wooden salad bowl with matching servers.

Andy and Rory murmured their approval and support. They spoke about their lives, and The Walls listened without comprehension as Andy spoke of transfers and relegation in the League, and Rory told them about the new regulations which were strangling the whole haulage business, and the money that they were constantly offered to bring illegal immigrants in as part of their cargo. Both boys had love lives to report. Andy was dating a supermodel, and Rory had moved into an apartment with a Spanish girl called Pilar.

The Walls said that they were going to the West of Ireland in a week's time. They described the place and listed all its good points. They said that Mrs Starr, the proprietor, sounded delightful.

To their surprise, the boys seemed genuinely interested.

'Good on you for doing something different.' Andy was admiring.

'And it's something you chose yourselves, not just something you won,' Rory approved.

The Walls did not enlighten them. It wasn't exactly lying, but they just didn't say it – that it had indeed been a competition. Partly because they still felt so raw about the loss of the Paris trip, but mainly because they were flattered by the way their sons unexpectedly seemed so pleased with their decision to go to this godforsaken place.

They wanted to bask for a bit in that enthusiasm rather than diminish it by giving the real reason why they were heading West.

Andy said that his supermodel girlfriend had always wanted to go to the wilds for a healthy walking holiday, so they were to mark his card. Rory said that Pilar had seen the old movie *The Quiet Man* half a dozen times, and was dying to see that part of the world. Possibly this hotel might be the place to go.

For the first time for a long while The Walls felt on the same wavelength as their children. It was very satisfying.

A week later, as they crossed Ireland on the train, the depressed feeling returned. The rain was unremitting. They looked without pleasure at the wet fields and the grey mountains. At this very moment some other people were arriving at Charles de Gaulle airport in Paris. They would meet the chauffeur who should have been meeting The Walls. They would have rugs in the car in case it was cold; he would take them to the superb five-star Hotel Martinique where the welcome champagne would be on ice in the suite. It wasn't just a bedroom, it was an actual *suite*. Tonight those people would eat at the hotel, choosing from a menu that The Walls had already seen on the internet, while they were going to some kind of glorified bed and breakfast. The place would be full of draughts and they would possibly have to keep their coats on indoors. They would eat, every night for a whole week, in Mrs Starr's kitchen.

A kitchen!

They should have been dining under chandeliers in Paris.

The fields seemed to get smaller and wetter as they went West. They didn't need to say all this to each other. The Walls shared everything already; they each knew what the other was thinking. This was going to be one long, disappointing week.

At the railway station they recognised Chicky Starr at once from her picture on the Stone House brochure. She welcomed them warmly and carried their bags to her van, talking easily about the area and its attractions. Chicky explained that while she was in the town, she had a few more things to collect, and The Walls saw their expensive matching suitcases being loaded on to the roof. They looked quite out of place compared to the more basic bags and knapsacks belonging to Chicky Starr.

She seemed to know everyone. She asked the bus driver whether there had been a big crowd at the market, and greeted schoolchildren in uniform with questions about the match they had played that day. She offered a lift to an elderly man but he said that his daughter-in-law would be picking him up, so he'd be fine sitting here watching the world go by until she arrived.

The Walls looked on with interest. It must be extraordinary

to know every single person in the place. Sociable certainly, but claustrophobic. There had been no mention of a Mr Starr. Ann Wall decided to nail this one down immediately.

'And does your husband help you in all this enterprise?' she asked brightly.

'Sadly he died some years ago. But he would have been very pleased to see Stone House up and running,' Chicky spoke simply.

The Walls felt chastened. They had been intrusive.

'It's a lovely part of the world you live in,' Charlie said insincerely.

'It's very special,' Chicky Starr agreed. 'I spent a long time in New York City, and I used to come home for a visit every year. It sort of charged my batteries for the rest of the year. I felt it might do the same for other people.'

The Walls doubted it, but made enthusiastic murmurs of agreement.

They were pleasantly surprised by Stone House when they arrived there. It was warm, for one thing, and very comfortable. Their bedroom had great style and a big bow window looking out to sea. On the little table by the window were two crystal glasses, an ice bucket and a half-bottle of champagne.

'Just our way of congratulating you on twenty-five years of happy marriage. You were very lucky to have it and even luckier to realise it,' Chicky said.

The Walls were, for once, wordless.

'Well we *have* had a very happy marriage,' Ann Wall said, 'but how did you know?'

'I read your entry in the competition. It was very touching, about how you got pleasure out of ordinary things but you wanted a little magic sprinkled on it. I *do* hope that we can provide some of that magic for you here.'

Of course, she had read their essay.

They had forgotten that she was one of the judges. But even though she had been touched and moved, she hadn't voted for them to have the holiday of their dreams.

'So you read all the entries?' Charlie asked.

'They gave us a shortlist. We read the final thirty,' Chicky admitted.

'And the people who won . . . ?

'Well, there were five winners altogether,' Chicky said.

'Yes, but the people who won the first prize. What kind of an essay did they write?' Ann Wall had to know. What kind of words had beaten them to the winning post?

Chicky paused as if wondering whether or not to explain.

'It's odd, really. They wrote a totally different kind of thing. It wasn't at all like your story. It was more a song, like a version of "I Love Paris In The Springtime" but with different words.'

'A song? It didn't *say* a song. It said an essay.' The Walls were outraged.

'Well, you know, people interpret these things in different ways.'

'But words to someone else's song – isn't that a breach of copyright?' Their horror was total.

Chicky shrugged.

'It was clever, catchy. Everyone liked it.'

'The original song may have been catchy and clever but they just wrote a parody of it and they got to go to Paris.' The hurt and bitterness were written all over them.

Chicky looked from one to the other.

'Well, you're here now, so let's hope you enjoy it,' she said hopelessly.

They struggled to get back to their normal selves, but it was too huge an effort.

Chicky thought it wiser to leave them on their own. It was so obvious that for The Walls, this holiday was a very poor second best.

'If it's any consolation to you, everyone, all the judges, thought that even if the Flemmings got the first prize, *your* story was totally heart-warming. We were all envious of your relationship,' she tried.

It was useless. Not only had they been disappointed but The Walls knew now that they had been cheated too. It would rankle for ever.

They made an effort to recover. A big effort, but it wasn't easy. They tried to talk to their fellow guests and appear interested in what they had to say. They were an unlikely group: an earnest boy from Sweden, a librarian called Freda, an English couple who were both doctors, a disapproving woman with a pursed mouth called Nell, an American who had missed a plane and had come here on the spur of the moment and a pair of unlikely friends called Winnie and Lillian. What were they all doing here?

The food was excellent, served by Orla, the attractive niece of the proprietor. Really, there was nothing to object to. Nothing, that is, apart from the fact that the Flemmings, whoever they were, had stolen their holiday in Paris.

The Walls didn't sleep well that night. They were wakeful at three in the morning and made tea in their room. They sat and listened to the wind and rain outside and the sound of the waves receding and crashing again on the shore. It sounded sad and plaintive, as if in sympathy with them.

Next morning, the other guests all seemed ready and

enthusiastic about their planned trips. The Walls chose a direction at random and found themselves on a long, deserted beach.

It was bracing, certainly, and healthy. They would have to admit that. The scenery was spectacular.

But it wasn't Paris.

They went to one of the pubs that Chicky had suggested and had a bowl of soup.

'I don't think I could take six more days of this.' Ann Wall put down her spoon.

'Mine's fine,' Charlie said.

'I don't mean the soup, I mean being here where we don't *want* to be.'

'I know, I feel that too, in a way,' Charlie agreed.

'And it's not as if they won it fair and square. Even Chicky admits that.' Ann Wall was very aggrieved.

'Wouldn't you love to know how they are getting on?' Charlie said.

'Yes. I'd both hate to know and love to know at the same time.' They laughed companionably over it.

The woman behind the bar looked at them with approval.

'Lord, it's grand to see a couple getting on so well,' she said. 'I was only saying to Paddy last night that they just come in here, stare into their drinks and say nothing at all. Paddy hadn't noticed. They probably have it all said, was what he thought.'

The Walls were pleased to be admired for having a good relationship twice in twenty-four hours. They had never before thought that it might be unusual. But then Chicky had said that the judges had been envious of them. Not envious enough, of course, to give them the main prize . . .

They said they were on a holiday from Dublin and staying at Stone House.

'Didn't Chicky do a great job on that place,' the woman said. 'She was a great example to people round here. When her poor husband, the Lord have mercy on him, was killed in that terrible road accident over there in New York, she just set her mind to coming back here and making a whole new life for herself, and bringing a bit of business to this place in the winter. We all wish her well.'

It was sad about Chicky's husband, The Walls agreed, but in their hearts it didn't make them feel any more settled in this remote part of Ireland when their dreams were elsewhere.

They didn't mention that they had won the holiday in a competition until dinner on the fourth night. Everyone was more relaxed around the table in the evenings; by that time they realised that no one had been quite what they looked. The two women, Lillian and Winnie, weren't old friends at all and they had almost drowned and were rescued; the doctors seemed more relaxed and Nicola chatted happily with the American who was revealed to be a film star; the Swedish boy had a passion for music and Freda the librarian seemed to be uncannily right in her pronouncements about people's lives. Nell was still disapproving – at least that hadn't changed. But they did feel like people who knew each other, rather than a group of accidentally gathered strangers.

They were all fascinated by the idea of winning competitions. They had thought that they were all fixed, or that so many people entered you just had no chance.

The Walls listed some of the items they had won and were gratified by the fascination that it seemed to hold for everyone.

'Is there a knack to it?' Orla wanted to know. She'd love to win a motorbike and travel around Europe, she explained.

The Walls were generous with their advice; it wasn't so much a knack, more doggedness and keeping it simple.

They were all fired up and dying to enter a competition. If only they could find one. Chicky and Orla ran to collect some newspapers and magazines, and they raked them to find competitions.

There was one where you had to name an animal in the zoo. The Walls explained that it was in a section aimed at children, and so every school in the country would be sending in entries. The odds were too great against them. They spoke with the authority of poker players who could tell you the chances of filling a straight or a flush. The others looked on in awe.

Then in a local West of Ireland paper they found a competition, 'Invent a Festival'.

The Walls read it out carefully. Contestants were asked to suggest a festival, something that would bring business in winter to a community in the West.

This might be the very thing. What kind of festival could they come up with for Stoneybridge?

The guests looked doubtful. They had been hoping for a slick slogan or a clever limerick. Suggesting a festival was too difficult.

The Walls weren't sure. They said it had possibilities that they must explore. It had to be a winter thing so a beauty pageant made no sense – the poor girls would freeze to death. Galway had done the oyster festival, so they couldn't do that. Other parts of the coast had taken over the surfing and kayaking industry.

Rock climbing was too specialist. There was traditional

265

music, of course, but Stoneybridge wasn't known as a centre for it like Doolin or Miltown Malbay in County Clare, and they didn't have any legendary pipers or fiddlers in their past. There already *was* a walking festival, and Stoneybridge could boast no literary figures that might be used as a basis for a winter school.

There was no history of visual arts in the place. They could produce no Jack Yeats or Paul Henry as a focus.

'What about a storytelling festival?' was the suggestion of Henry and Nicola, the quiet English doctors. Everyone thought that was a good idea, but apparently there was a storytelling event in the next county which was well established.

Anders suggested a Teach Yourself Irish Music seminar but the others said the place was coming down with tourists being taught to play the tin whistle and the spoons, and the Irish drum called the *bodhrán*.

The American, who seemed to be called John or Corry alternately, said that he thought a Find Your Roots festival would do well. You could have genealogists on hand to help people trace their ancestors. The general opinion was that the roots industry in Ireland was well covered already.

Winnie suggested a cookery festival, where local people could teach the visitors how to make the brown bread and potato farls, and particularly how to use the carrageen to make the delicious mousse they had eaten last night. But apparently there were too many cookery schools already, and it would be hard to compete.

They all agreed to sleep on the problem and to bring new ideas to the table the following night. It had been an entertaining evening and The Walls had enjoyed it in spite of themselves.

Once back in their bedroom, their thoughts went again to

Paris. Tonight was when they should have been going to the Opéra. Their limousine would have been gliding through the lights of Paris; then they would have purred back to the Martinique where they would be welcomed by the staff, who would know them by this stage. The maître d' would suggest a little drink in the piano bar before they went to bed. Instead, they were trying to explain the rules of competition-winning to a crowd of strangers who hadn't the first idea where to start.

As always, just thinking about it made them discontented.

'I bet they don't even appreciate it,' Charlie said.

'They probably called off the opera house and went to a pub.' Ann was full of scorn.

Then suddenly the thought came to her.

'Let's telephone them and ask them how they are getting on. At least we'll know.'

'We can't ring them in Paris!' Charlie was shocked.

'Why not? Just a short call. We'll say we called to wish them well.'

'But how would we ever find them?' Charlie was dumb-founded.

'We know the name of the hotel; we know their name – what's hard to find there?' To Ann it was simple.

The Walls had already written all the details of the Paris holiday in their competition notebook, including the tele-phone number of the Hotel Martinique. Before he could think of another objection she had picked up her mobile phone, dialled the number and got through.

'*Monsieur et Madame Flemming d'Irlande, s'il vous plaît,*' she said in a clear, bell-like voice.

'Who are you going to say we are?' Charlie asked fearfully.

'Let's play it by ear.' Ann was in control.

Charlie listened in anxiously as she was put through.

'Oh, Mrs Flemming, just a call to ask how the holiday is going. Is it all to your satisfaction?'

'Oh, well, yes . . . I mean, thank you indeed,' the woman sounded hesitant.

'And you are enjoying your week at the Martinique?' Ann persisted.

'Are you from the hotel?' the woman asked nervously.

'No, indeed, just a call from Ireland to hope there are no problems.'

'Well, it's rather awkward. It's very hard to say this because it *is* a very expensive hotel. We *know* that, but it's not quite what we had hoped.'

'Oh dear, I'm sorry to hear that. In what way, exactly?'

'Well . . . It isn't a suite, for one thing. It's a very small room near the lift, which is going up and down all night. And then we can't eat in the dining room – the vouchers are only for what they call *Le Snack Bar*.'

'Oh dear, that wasn't in the terms of agreement,' Ann said disapprovingly.

'Yes, but you might as well be talking to a blank wall for all the response you get. They shrug and say these arrangements have nothing to do with them.' Mrs Flemming was beginning to sound very aggrieved.

'And the chauffeur?'

'We've only seen him once. He is attached to the hotel, and apparently he's needed by VIP customers all the time. He's never free. They gave us vouchers for a bus tour to Versailles, which was exhausting, and there were miles of cobblestones to walk over. We didn't go to Chartres at all.'

'That's not what was promised,' Ann clucked with disapproval.

'No indeed, and we hate complaining. I mean, it's a very generous prize. It's just . . . it's just . . .'

'The top restaurants? Have they turned out all right?'

'Yes, up to a point, but you see it only covers the *prix fixe*, you know, the set menu, and it's often things like tripe or rabbit that we don't eat. They *did* say we could choose from the fine-dining menus, but when we got there we couldn't.'

'And what are you going to do about it?'

'Well, we didn't know *what* to do, so that's why it's wonderful you called us. Are you from the magazine?'

'Not directly, but sort of connected,' Ann Wall said.

'We don't like to go whingeing and whining to them; it seems so ungrateful. It's just so much less than we expected.'

'I know, I know.' Ann was genuinely sympathetic.

'And individually the people in the hotel are very nice, really nice and pleasant, it's just that in general they seem to think we won much more of a bargain-basement prize than the one that was advertised. What would you suggest we do?'

The Walls looked at each other blankly. What indeed?

'Perhaps you could get in touch with the public relations firm that set it up,' Ann said eventually.

'Could *you* do that for us, do you think?' Mrs Flemming was obviously a person who didn't want to make waves.

'It might be more effective coming from you, what with your being on the spot and everything . . .' Ann was feverishly trying to pass the buck back to the Flemmings.

'But you were kind enough to ring us to ask was everything all right. Who are you representing, exactly?'

'Just a concerned member of the public.' And Ann Wall hung up, trembling.

What were they going to do now?

First they allowed the glorious feeling to seep over them

and through them. The dream holiday in Paris had turned out to be a nightmare. They were oh so well out of it. They were better by far in this mad place on the Atlantic, which they had thought was so disappointing at first.

Everything that had been promised was being delivered here. Perhaps they had won the first prize after all.

They decided that the following morning they would call the public relations firm and report that all was not as it should be at the Hotel Martinique.

For the first time they slept all through the night. There was no resentful waking at three a.m. to have tea and brood about the unfairness of life in general and competitions in particular.

The Walls took a packed lunch and walked along the cliffs and crags until they found an old ruined church, which Chicky said would be a lovely place to stop and have their picnic. It was sheltered from the gales and looked straight across to America.

They laughed happily as they unpacked their wonderful rich slices of chicken pie and opened their flasks of soup. Imagine – the Flemmings would be facing another lunch of tripe and rabbit in Paris.

Ann Wall had left a cryptic message with the PR agency, saying that for everyone's sake they should check on the Flemmings in the Martinique or some very undesirable pub-licity might result. They felt like bold children who had been given time off at school. They would enjoy the rest of their stay.

That night, everyone at Chicky's kitchen table was ready with their festival suggestions; they could barely wait for the meal to finish to come up with their pitch. Lillian, whose face had softened over the last couple of days, said that the essence of a festival nowadays seemed to be, if everyone would excuse the use of that *horrible* phrase, a 'feel-good factor'. Sagely they all nodded and said that was exactly what was needed.

Chicky said that a sense of community was becoming more and more important in the world today. Young people fled small closed societies at first, as well they should, but later they wanted to be part of them again.

Orla wondered about organising a family reunion. They liked the notion but said it would be hard to quantify. Did it mean the gathering of a clan, or the bringing together of people who had been estranged? Lillian thought that an Honorary Granny Festival might be good. Everyone wanted to be a grandmother, she said firmly. Winnie looked at her sharply. This had never been brought up before.

Henry and Nicola wondered if Health in the Community might be a good theme. People were very into diets and lifestyle and exercise these days. Stoneybridge could provide it all. And Anders said suddenly that you could have a festival to celebrate friendship. You know, old friends turning up together, maybe going on a trip there with an old pal, that kind of thing. They thought about it politely for a while. The more they thought about it, the better it sounded.

It didn't exclude family, or anything. Your friend could be your sister or your aunt.

Most people must have felt from time to time that they would love to catch up with someone that they hadn't seen as much as they would have liked.

Suppose there was a festival which offered a variety of entertainments, like the ideas everyone had suggested already but done in the name of friendship? They were teeming with ideas. There could indeed be cookery demos, keep-fit classes, walking tours, birdwatching trips, farmhouse teas, sing-songs, local drama, tap-dancing classes.

The Walls watched with mounting excitement as the table planned and took notes and assembled a programme. They had a winner on their hands.

They checked the newspaper again to see what prize was being offered.

It was a 1,250-euro shopping spree in a big Dublin store.

The Walls worked it out. They would share it equally between them, with extra for Anders as they had chosen his idea. Would that do?

Everyone was delighted.

What would they call themselves? The Stone House Syndicate? Yes, that seemed perfect. Orla would type it out and give everyone a copy. They would watch for the results, which would be published the week before Christmas.

When the festival was up and running, they would all come back and celebrate here again. And best of all, they still had the rest of the week in this lovely house with the waves crashing on the shore. A place that had not only lived up to its promise but had delivered even more.

It wasn't *exactly* romance and stardust sprinkled all over them like magic, but it was something deeper, like a sense of importance and a great feeling of peace.

Miss Nell Howe

The girls at Wood Park School thought that Miss Howe was ninety when she retired. She was actually sixty. Same difference. It was old. They didn't pause to think how she would spend her days, weeks and months afterwards. Old people just continued to boss and grumble and complain. They had no idea how much she had dreaded this day, and how she feared the first September for forty years when she wouldn't set out to begin a new school year full of hope and plans and projects.

Miss Howe had been there as long as anyone could remember. She was tall and thin with hair combed straight back from her forehead and held there with an old-fashioned slide. She wore dark clothes under an academic gown. She had taught the mothers and aunts of these girls in the past but in recent years, as headmistress, she had been rarely in the classroom and mainly in her office.

The girls hated going to Miss Howe's office. For one thing, being there always meant some kind of disapproval, complaint or punishment. But it wasn't just that. It was a place without soul. Miss Howe had a very functional and always empty desk: she was not a person who tolerated chaos or mess.

There was a wall lined with inexpensive shelving holding many books on education. No handcrafted bookcases, as might have seemed suitable for a woman whose life had been involved for decades in teaching. Another wall was covered in timetables and lists of upcoming functions, details of various rosters and plans. Two large steel filing cabinets – presumably holding the records of generations of Wood Park girls – and a big computer dominated the room. There were dull brown curtains at the window, no pictures on the walls, no hint of any life outside these walls. No photographs, ornaments or signs that Miss Howe, Principal, had an interest in anything except Wood Park School. This is where she interviewed prospective pupils and their parents, possible new teachers, inspectors from the Department of Education and the occasional past pupil who had done well and had returned to fund a library or a games pavilion.

Miss Howe had an assistant called Irene O'Connor who had been there for years. Irene was round and jolly and in the staffroom they always called her the 'acceptable face of the Howe office'. She didn't appear to notice that Miss Howe barked at her rather than spoke to her. Miss Howe rarely thanked her for anything she did, and always seemed slightly surprised and almost annoyed when Irene brought tea and biscuits into what was likely to be an awkward or contentious meeting.

There were no plants or flowers in Miss Howe's office, so Irene had introduced a little kalanchoe in a brass pot. It was a plant that needed practically no care, which was just as well as Miss Howe never watered it or apparently even noticed it. Irene wore brightly coloured t-shirts with a dark jacket and skirt. It was almost as if she was trying to bring a stab of colour into the mournful office without annoying Miss Howe. Irene was quite possibly a saint, and might even be canonised in her own lifetime.

She worked in a little outer office which was full of her personality, as indeed was her conversation. There were trailing geraniums and picture postcards from all of Irene's friends pinned to her bulletin board; there were framed photographs of her on the desk. On her shelves were souvenirs of holiday trips to Spain and pictures of herself wearing a frilly skirt and a big sombrero at a fiesta. Here was a record of a busy, happy life, in contrast to the bleak cell that was Miss Howe's pride and joy.

She went home every day at lunchtime because she had an invalid mother and a nephew, Kenny, who was her late sister's child. Irene and her mother had given Kenny a good home and he was growing up to be a fine boy.

In the staffroom they marvelled at Irene's patience and endless good humour. Sometimes they sympathised with her, but Irene would never hear a word against her employer.

'No, no, it's only her manner,' she would say. 'She has a heart of gold, and this is the dream job for me. Please understand that.'

The teachers said to each other that people like Irene would always be victimised by the Miss Howes of this world. What did Irene mean, 'it was only her manner'? People *were* their manner. How else were we to know them?

Miss Howe was rightly named Her Own Worst Enemy. They giggled over the cleverness of this, and somehow it tamed her. She was less frightening when they could call her this behind her back, though they made very sure that the children never got wind of their name for her.

In the year before Miss Howe retired there was much speculation about her successor. None of the current staff appeared to have the seniority or authority to replace her. That was the way Miss Howe had run things, with never a hint of delegation. The new appointment would most probably be someone from outside. The staff didn't like that idea either. They were used to Her Own Worst Enemy. They knew how to cope and they had Irene to soften the edges. Who knew what the new person might want to introduce? Better the devil you know than the entirely new and imposed devil that you didn't know at all.

They also wondered about Irene. Would she stay and serve the new Tsar? Would she find excuses for the next principal and her manner? Suppose the new person didn't want Irene?

It was change. They feared change.

Then there was the matter of the presentation to Miss Howe. None of them had the slightest clue as to where her interests lay. Even desultory conversation at the beginning of term had failed to discover anything. Miss Howe had no holiday story to tell, nothing like that was ever mentioned, or any family gathering, or repainting of a house, or digging of a garden. Eventually they had given up asking.

But what could you give to this woman to celebrate all her years at Wood Park? There was no question of a cruise or a week in a spa or a set of Waterford Crystal or some beautifully crafted piece of furniture. Miss Howe's taste had been seen to be completely utilitarian: if it functioned, it was fine.

The teachers begged Irene to come up with an idea.

'You see her every day. You talk to her all the time. You must have *some* notion of what she would like,' they pleaded.

But Irene said that her mind was a complete blank. Miss Howe was a very private person. She didn't believe in talking about personal things.

The parents' committee was asking Irene the same question. They wanted to mark the occasion and didn't know how. Irene decided that she really must stir herself and find out more about her employer's lifestyle.

She knew Miss Howe's address, so the first thing she did was go and look at her house. It was in a terrace of houses called St Jarlath's Crescent. Small houses once thought of as working-class accommodation, which had later been redefined as townhouses and were now, of course, dropping in value again because of the recession. Most of the small front gardens were well kept, many with window boxes and colourful flower beds.

Miss Howe's garden, however, had no decoration. There were two flowering shrubs and a neatly mowed lawn. The paint on the door, gate and windowsills needed to be refreshed. It didn't look neglected, more ignored. No hints there.

Irene decided she must be brave and get to see the interior. With this in mind, the following morning she slipped Miss Howe's reading glasses into her own handbag and then called round to the house to deliver them, pretending that she had found them on the desk.

Miss Howe met her at the door with no enthusiasm.

'There was no need, Irene,' she said coldly.

'But I was afraid you wouldn't be able to read tonight,' Irene stumbled.

'No, I have plenty of replacements. But thank you all the same. It was kind of you.'

'May I come in for a moment, Miss Howe?' Irene nearly fainted at her own courage in asking this.

There was a pause.

'Of course.' Miss Howe opened the door fully.

The house was clinically bare, like the office back in Wood Park. No pictures on the walls, a rickety bookcase, a small old-fashioned television. A table with a supper tray prepared with a portion of cheese, two tomatoes and two slices of bread. Back in Irene's house they would be having spicy tomato sauce and pasta. Irene had taught Kenny how to cook, and tonight he would make a rhubarb fool. They would all play a game of Scrabble and then Irene and her mother would watch the soaps and Kenny, who was now eighteen, would go out with his friends.

What a happy home compared to this cold, bleak place.

But since Irene had come so far she would not give up now.

'Miss Howe, I have a problem,' she said.

'You have?' Miss Howe's voice was glacial.

'Yes. The teachers *and* the parents have asked me to tell them what would be a suitable gift for you when you retire this summer. Everyone is anxious to give you something that you would like. And because I work with you all day, they wrongly thought I would know. But I don't know. I am at a loss, Miss Howe. I wonder, could you direct me . . . ?'

'I don't want anything, Irene.'

'But Miss Howe, that isn't the issue. *They* want to give you something, something suitable, appropriate.'

'Why?'

'Because they value you.'

'If they really value me then they will leave me alone and not indulge their wish for sentimental ceremonies.'

'Oh, no, that's not how they see it, Miss Howe.'

'And you, Irene. How do *you* see it?'

'I suppose they must think I am a poor friend and colleague if I can't tell them after twenty years' working for you what would be a good farewell present.'

Miss Howe looked at her for a long moment.

'But Irene, you are *not* a friend or colleague,' she said eventually. 'It's a totally different relationship. People have no right to expect you to know such things.'

Irene opened her mouth and closed it several times.

When the teachers in the staffroom had railed against Miss Howe and called her Her Own Worst Enemy, she had stood up for the woman. Now she wondered why. Miss Howe was indeed a person without warmth or soul; without friends or interests. Let them buy her a picnic basket or vacuum cleaner. It didn't matter. Irene didn't care any more.

She picked up her bag and moved to the door.

'Well, I'll be off now, Miss Howe. I won't disturb you and keep you from your supper any longer. I just wanted to return your glasses to you, that's all.'

'I didn't leave my glasses on my desk, Irene. I never leave *anything* on my desk,' Miss Howe said.

Irene managed to walk steadily to the gate. It was only when she was a little way along the road that her legs began to feel weak.

All those years she had worked for Miss Howe, shielded her from irate parents, discontented teachers, rebellious pupils. Tonight Miss Howe had told her face to face that she must not presume to call herself a friend or a colleague. She was merely someone who worked for the Principal.

279

How could she have been so blind and so sure of her own position?

She held on to a gate to steady herself. A young woman came out of her house and looked at her with concern.

'Are you feeling all right? You look as white as a sheet.'

'I think so. I just feel a little dizzy.'

'Come in and sit down. I'm a nurse, by the way.'

'I know you,' Irene gasped, 'you work at St Brigid's heart clinic.'

'Yes; you're not a patient there, are you?'

'I come with my mother, Peggy O'Connor.'

'Oh, of course. I'm Fiona Carroll. Peggy's always talking about you and how good you are to her.'

'I'm glad someone thinks I'm good for something,' Irene said.

'Come in, Miss O'Connor, and I'll get you a cup of tea.' Fiona had her by the arm and Irene sank gratefully into a house that was so different to Miss Howe's that it could have been on another planet. Between them, Fiona and her two little boys provided tea, chocolate cake and a lot of encouragement.

Irene began to feel a lot better.

Always discreet and loyal, she resisted the temptation to unburden herself to this kindly Fiona, who must know her difficult neighbour and might even be able to give her words of consolation.

But old habits die hard.

Irene felt that you could not be someone's assistant and bad-mouth them to others. She said nothing at all about her upsetting encounter with Miss Howe. She assured Fiona that she felt strong enough now to get her bus home, but at that very moment a man called Dingo arrived at the house delivering topsoil and trays of bedding plants. The Carrolls were going to have a gardening weekend, they told Irene. The boys were going to have a flower bed each.

'Dingo will drop you home, Miss O'Connor,' Fiona insisted, 'it's on his way.'

Dingo was perfectly happy with this suggestion.

'They're a delightful family,' Irene said to him as she settled into his van. 'Are you a family man yourself, Dingo?'

'No, I've always been a believer in travelling solo,' he said. 'Believe me, Miss O'Connor, not every marriage is as good as Fiona and Declan's. Some of the couples you meet are like lightning devils. You never married yourself then?'

'No, Dingo, I didn't. I did have a chance once but he was a gambler and I was afraid, and then my mother needed me, so here I am.' She realised she sounded defeated, which was not her normal response. Miss Howe had done this to her today.

Dingo drove on, unconcerned.

'My uncle Nasey is just the same. He says he fancied someone years back but missed his chance. He's always asking me to look out for someone in their forties for him. Are you in your forties, Miss O'Connor?'

'Just about,' Irene said. 'Don't ask me next year. I'd have to say no.'

'Right, I'll tell him about you now before it gets too late,' Dingo promised.

Irene went home and prepared the supper. She never mentioned the events of the day to her mother or to Kenny. They could have no idea that all Irene's work for Miss Howe had been dismissed in one cold, cruel sentence.

Nor did they know that at the very moment they sat down to supper, efforts to find Irene a husband were under way. Dingo had called to see his uncle Nasey with the news that there was a very pleasant woman of forty-nine on the market. And he was so convincing, so persuasive, that Uncle Nasey was very interested in finding out more about Irene . . .

Over the next few weeks, the teachers at Wood Park School noticed that something about Irene had changed. She became shruggy rather than eager when they tried to discuss what kind of leaving ceremony they could arrange for Miss Howe, and what gift should be chosen.

'I don't think it matters, really,' Irene would say, and change the subject. Possibly she was worried about her position there, they thought. Maybe the next Principal would want to choose her own assistant.

Irene continued to do her work as reliably as always but without any warmth and enthusiasm. If Miss Howe noticed, she gave no sign of having seen anything amiss. Irene stopped serving tea and biscuits at awkward meetings. She retrieved the little kalanchoe, fed it plant food and nursed it back to glowing health in her own office. Gone were the days when Irene would tell cheerful tales of the world she lived in.

But now Irene had a social life of which Miss Howe was totally unaware. Nasey had called, and said that his eejit of a nephew had spoken very highly of her, and perhaps she might accompany him to the cinema on the odd occasion. Then they went bowling and to a singing pub. His real name was Ignatius, he explained, and at least it was better than being called Iggy, which another lad at school had been named. He worked in a butcher's shop for a Mr Malone, who was the most decent man ever to wear shoe leather.

He took to calling at Irene's house and bringing best lamb chops, or a lovely pork steak. Irene's mother Peggy loved him and lost no opportunity to tell him what a wonderful woman Irene was.

'I know that, Mrs O'Connor. You don't have to sell her to me. I'm hooked already,' he said, and Peggy was pink with pleasure about it all.

Nasey came from the West of Ireland and had little family of his own in Dublin. He had two nephews: Dingo Irene had met already; he drove a van and did odd jobs for people. There was his sister, Nuala, and there was his sister's boy, Rigger, who had been unfortunate in his life and spent a lot of time at reform school. He'd been sent away to the West of Ireland, and it looked as though he'd fallen on his feet over there. He had found a nice girl, grew vegetables and kept chickens. He had a job as a sort of manager for a place that was just setting up; a kind of small Big House, if you could understand that. It was perched on a cliff and the view would take the sight out of your eyes. Nasey promised that one day he would drive Irene and her mother to see the whole set-up. They'd love it.

Kenny liked having Nasey around too, and was always on hand to keep an eye on his gran if the two lovebirds, as he called them, wanted to go out on the town.

Then, just before the end of term, after six months of courtship, Nasey proposed to Irene. A small wedding was planned, and when she told him, Kenny offered to give his aunt away. But Irene had something else on her mind. She waited until Peggy had gone to bed.

'I have something to tell you, Kenny,' Irene began.

'I've always known,' he said simply. 'I knew you were my mother when I was nine.'

'Why did you never say?' She was astounded.

'It never mattered. I knew you'd always be there.'

'Do you want to ask me anything?' Her voice was small and she started to cry.

'Were you frightened and lonely at the time?' he asked, sitting down next to her and putting his arms around her.

'A bit, but he wasn't free, you see. Your father was already married. It wouldn't have been fair to break up everything he had. Then Maureen died in England and so we pretended you were hers. For Mam's sake. Mam got her grandchild, I got my son – we all did fine.' By now Irene was smiling through her tears.

'Does Nasey know?'

'Yes, I told him early on. He said you had probably guessed, and imagine, he was right.'

'Will Nasey come and live here?'

'If you don't mind,' Irene said. 'He's great with your gran.'

'Don't I know it? I love the way you play three-handed bridge at night like demons. Watching you is better than being in Las Vegas.' He said that he was delighted Nasey would be there, since he had been hoping to travel. There was a chance of a trip to America. Now he felt free to make his plans.

For eighteen years Irene had been dreading the day she must tell Kenny this news, and now it had passed almost without comment. Life was very strange.

Irene wore her engagement ring to work; Miss Howe made no comment and Irene did not bring the subject up. All the teachers noticed it, of course; Irene told them that her mother was going to be her matron of honour, and that Nasey's nephew Rigger was coming over from Stoneybridge and that Dingo was to be his best man, and that they would be having sandwiches and cake in a pub on the last Saturday in August and she would love all the teachers to come to that. They got into a fever of excitement planning a wedding present.

With Irene, it would be easy: she liked everything. It could be a holiday in Spain, a garden shed, a painting of Conne-mara, a weekend in a castle, a set of luggage with wheels, a croquet set, a big, ornate mirror with cherubs on it. Irene would love any one of them and praise the gift to the skies.

They were still no nearer any decision about Miss Howe's retirement gift.

There was a lot of pressure on Irene to make a decision on what it should be; she in turn didn't care one way or the other but she felt that for the teachers and students, she had to come up with some sort of an idea and she didn't want to disap-point them. It was so wonderful to be able to tell Nasey everything when she finished work in the evenings.

Nasey said he'd give the matter some thought. In the meantime, he had news of his own. His nephew Rigger had been on the phone.

'They're in a panic over at Stone House. They don't have any proper bookings for the week that it opens. He and Chicky are afraid it's going to be a flop after all their hard work.'

'Well,' said Irene, 'we should ask Rigger for some bro-chures, and I can hand them around at school. It's the sort of thing some of the teachers would enjoy.'

'Why don't you send Miss Howe there?' Nasey said trium-phantly.

'But if she's so awful, should we inflict her on them?'

'She mightn't be too bad outside the school. I mean, she could go walking; she wouldn't annoy too many people.' Nasey's optimism wouldn't allow him to think too badly of Irene's boss.

'I'll suggest it. It might be the perfect solution,' Irene said.

'Let's keep our fingers crossed that she doesn't close the

place down overnight,' Nasey said with a big smile. Then they put their minds to their wedding.

The teachers noted that Her Own Worst Enemy was even more buttoned up than usual these days, more unforgiving about high spirits at the end of the school year than ever before. More concerned about examination results than the children's future, and if possible even more ungiving of herself on any front.

They reported that her car was seen later and later at night in the school yard, and arrived there earlier in the mornings. Miss Howe must only spend seven or eight hours out of Wood Park every day.

It was not natural.

Finally she spoke to Irene about the wedding.

'One of the parents tells me that you are thinking of getting married, Irene,' Miss Howe said with a little laugh. 'Can she be serious?'

'Yes indeed, Miss Howe, at the end of August,' Irene said.

'And you never thought to tell me?' There was disapproval and sorrow in her voice.

'Well, no. As you said, I am not your colleague or your friend. I merely work for you. And as it will all take place during the holidays, I didn't really see any point in telling you.'

Although it was not exactly discourteous, there was something abrupt in Irene's tone that made Miss Howe look up sharply. This was the time for her to say that she was very pleased and wished Irene happiness. This was even the time when she might say that indeed she *did* consider Irene a friend and a colleague.

But no; years of being her own worst enemy clicked in, and so she laughed again.

'Well, I don't suppose you have any intention of starting a family at this late stage of your life,' she said, amused at the very thought of it.

Irene met her look but without smiling. 'No indeed, Miss Howe. I already have been blessed with a son, who is eighteen now. Nasey and I do not hope to have any more children.'

'Nasey!' Miss Howe could hardly contain herself. 'Is that his name? Goodness!'

'Yes, that's his name, and goodness is a very good way to describe him. He is *very* good. To me, my son Kenny and my mother. He works as a butcher, in case you find that funny too.'

'Please calm yourself, Irene. You are being hysterical. I have just discovered two extraordinary things about you. You were always showing me photographs of Kenny, and said he was your nephew.'

'I thought it more discreet since I was not a married woman.'

'But this Nasey will make you respectable, is that it?'

Irene wondered how she could have worked for this woman for twenty years, not to mention made excuses for her that it was just her manner. Miss Howe had no heart, no warmth.

'I always considered myself respectable, always. And everyone who knows me thinks I am too. But then you don't know me at all, Miss Howe, and never have.'

'You will presumably want to continue working here after I am gone and after this . . . er . . . marriage?' Miss Howe's eyes were full of anger.

'Certainly I do. I love this school, the staff and the pupils.'

'Then you would want to watch your tone, Irene, if I am to

write you a good reference. My successor would not necessarily like the legacy of someone who is secretive and has a bad attitude.'

'Write what you like, Miss Howe. You will anyway.'

'You are being very short-sighted over all this, Irene.'

'Thank you, Miss Howe. I'll get back to my work, while I still have a job.' And Irene walked out without looking back.

She sat at her desk, shaking, and had barely the strength to answer her mobile phone.

It was her mother, with wonderful news. Nasey had been around to the house at lunchtime and had shown her how to go online and look at outfits for Mother of the Bride. She was going to choose a navy and white dress and jacket. Would that suit Irene's plans?

Soon the goodwill and excitement began to seep back. The toxic, cold loneliness of Miss Howe beyond the door in her prison-like office was ebbing away.

The new Principal had already been chosen. She was a Mrs Williams, a widow who had run a large girls' school in England but who now wanted to return to her family in Ireland. Apparently she was bringing her own furniture to the Principal's office, and was happy to keep the present level of administration. Irene would work for July and part of August helping her to get installed. She had been informed that Irene would then be on holiday for three weeks but back in the office for the first day of term.

The school assembled to say goodbye to Miss Howe. She stood on the raised dais of the school hall as she did every morning. Still wearing her black gown, her hair held by the same slide. Her face was still totally impassive.

Various teachers read out their words recognising Miss Howe's achievements; the head girl made her speech and the chairman of the parents' committee expressed gratitude on behalf of all the girls who had succeeded so well at Wood Park, thanks to Miss Howe. There was no mention of a well-deserved rest, or assurance that her real life was just beginning. Finally the envelope was handed over as a token of everyone's appreciation. It was a voucher for a holiday in the opening week of Stone House, a new hotel in the West of Ireland. Miss Howe made no attempt to thank anyone, and her face registered nothing when the gift was announced. But no one really expected any other reaction.

Mrs Williams had been invited to the farewell ceremony for Miss Howe but had refused. She did not want to be a distraction, she said. This was Miss Howe's day.

In fact, people would have been glad of Mrs Williams' presence. She would have helped the torturous ceremony and the endless wine-and-cheese event that followed. People looked at their watches begging for it to be an acceptable time to leave. Had time ever moved so slowly? Was there ever such a joyless speech deploring modern trends in education, stressing the need for discipline in schools and learning by rote, pleas that so-called creativity never take the place of good old-fashioned basics?

The audience of teachers who had done their best to make the curriculum interesting as well as draconian; the parents who were guiltily relieved that their daughters got good points and university places; the pupils who couldn't wait for the school holidays . . . everyone was praying for it to be over.

Irene went back to her office to collect her things. She was dying to get home and tell Nasey about the wedding gift which had been arranged for them by the teaching staff at Wood Park. It was not only one of those fabulous gas-fired barbecues, but also a garden firm were going to lay a little patio for them and build a special wall to enclose the area. All they needed now was a lifetime of good summers to enjoy eating out of doors!

To her surprise, she heard a sound from Miss Howe's office. She knocked on the door. Miss Howe stood there alone behind her desk, which was empty apart from her car keys. Behind her the window, framed with the heavy dark brown curtains, looked out on the empty school yard.

'I just wanted to make sure that it wasn't an intruder.' Irene started to back out again.

'Stay for a moment, Irene. I want to give you a wedding present.'

This was certainly not something she had foreseen.

'That's very kind of you, Miss Howe. Very kind indeed.'

Miss Howe handed her a fancy bag with a lot of glitter on it. Not at all the kind of thing you would have expected from Miss Howe. Irene was at a loss for words.

Her immediate response was guilt. She had paid not one euro towards the going-away voucher for Miss Howe; she had signed no card and given no good wishes. Now she was ashamed.

'Not at all. Just a little something to remind you of me.'

'I won't forget working for you, Miss Howe.'

'And I very much hope that Mrs Williams will see her way to keeping you.'

'Yes, indeed. And thank you again for the gift. Will I open it now?'

'Oh, please, no . . .' Miss Howe withdrew in a sort of

fastidious distaste, as if opening the gift would somehow sully this empty office.

The books had all been removed but the cheap hardboard shelves stood empty, ready to be removed in the next few days, although Miss Howe didn't know this. There was no trace of anyone having worked here for so long.

'Well, I will open it tonight, and let me thank you in advance for going to the trouble of choosing something for us. I do so appreciate it.' There was sincerity radiating from all over Irene.

Miss Howe gave a little shudder at the familiarity of it all.

'Well, I hope it will be suitable. One doesn't know what to get, really. Especially when it's a late marriage.'

'Sorry?'

'I mean, you probably *have* everything already, not like young people excited about setting up a new home.'

Irene would not let the light go out on the good feeling of the gift.

'No, of course not, but to us it's still very new and exciting. Neither of us has ever been married before.'

'Quite.' Miss Howe's lips were pursed in disapproval.

'Anyway, I wish you all the best, Miss Howe. I'm sure you have plenty of things planned for the years ahead.'

Miss Howe could have thanked her for the kind remark. She could have said vaguely that there was indeed a lot to do. But Nell Howe didn't do vague and pleasant. Instead she said, 'What a wonderful fairy-tale world of platitudes you live in, Irene. It must be very restful not to think things through.' Then she took up her car keys and left.

Irene watched from the window as Nell Howe got into her small car and drove out of the only life she had known for years. She stood there for a while after the car had driven through the gates of Wood Park. What *would* Miss Howe do tonight, and during the many other days and nights to follow? Would there always be a tray laid in that cold room? Was there anyone to share it with her?

There had been not one friend or relative at the gathering held in her honour. Who goes through life with *nobody* to invite to her retirement party?

Irene was a very generous person. She could not think all bad of the woman who had insulted her, and who even now at the very last was trying to ridicule her. Miss Howe had bought her a wedding present, after all. And even more important, if Irene had not gone to visit Miss Howe that day she would never have met Dingo, who had found his uncle Nasey for her.

She sighed and caught the bus home, clutching the shiny glittery bag with the wedding present.

They opened it at suppertime. It was a lace-trimmed tray cloth. There were little rosebuds on it. Irene looked at it in wonder. She could hardly believe that Miss Howe had gone to a shop and chosen this. Not at all practical, and rather old-fashioned, but such a kind thought.

Then she saw that at the bottom of the bag there was a card in an envelope. Irene opened it and read: *To Miss Howe, Thank you for getting our girl to study and turning round her life*. It was signed by the parents of a child who had recently won a major scholarship to the university. Miss Howe had passed the gift on unopened. She hadn't even opened the card to read the gratitude it contained.

Irene crumpled up the card quickly.

'What did she say?' Peggy O'Connor loved every detail, every heartbeat.

'Just wishing us well,' Irene said. In her heart she decided that she would never think about Miss Howe again. She would just exclude her from her mind and her life. The woman was a shell. She was not worth another thought.

But a week later, when Mrs Williams was in place, Irene was forced to think about Miss Howe once more. Mrs Williams had changed the Principal's office so much that it did not look remotely like the same place.

A small laptop replaced the huge, bulky computer; the hand-carved desk held attractive raffia trays, brightly coloured files and a photograph of the late Mr Williams. The new bookshelves were filled but with spaces for ornaments and little flower pots. Mrs Williams even kept a tiny watering can at hand to make sure the plants got attention.

The hard chairs had been replaced by less daunting furniture. She had established a routine that seemed more normal and less driven than her predecessor's. She seemed to be delighted with Irene, and constantly thanked her for her efficiency and support. This was a personal first for Irene, who had been used to the grim silence of Miss Howe as the best that could be hoped for.

They were going through the day's agenda when Mrs Williams looked up and said, 'By the way, why didn't you tell me you were getting married?'

'I didn't want to bore you with all my doings. I'm inclined to go on a bit!' Irene said, and smiled apologetically.

'Well, if we can't go on a bit about our wedding day, what *can* we go on about?' Mrs Williams seemed genuinely interested. 'Tell me all about it.'

Irene told her about Nasey, and how he had served his time in a butcher's shop and was going to sell his flat and come and live with her and her mother. They were going to put an extra bathroom in the house . . . she bubbled on full of enthusiasm, hoping that the day itself would be a great one, and not silly or anything.

Mrs Williams looked at the photograph on her desk and said she remembered her wedding day as if it were yesterday. Everything had gone right.

'Was the sun shining?' Irene wondered.

Mrs Williams couldn't remember the weather it was so unimportant. Everyone had been so happy, that was the main thing.

At that point, the direct telephone line rang. Irene was a bit nonplussed. She had never known calls to come in on that line. It was for the Principal's convenience, in case she wanted to make a quick call out rather than going through the whole system. At a nod from Mrs Williams, Irene took the call.

A man asked to speak to Nell Howe.

'Miss Howe has retired as Principal and no longer works here. Do you want to talk to Mrs Williams, the current Principal, and if so, perhaps you can tell me in what connection?'

'Tell me where she lives,' he said.

'I'm afraid we never disclose staff addresses.'

'You just said that she was ex-staff.'

'I'm sorry, but I'm not able to help you. We are not in touch with Miss Howe, so I am not in a position to pass on any message,' Irene said, and the man hung up.

Irene and Mrs Williams looked at each other, bewildered.

A week before the wedding, Irene saw Nell Howe across a street. Irene couldn't help herself. She ran across to her.

'Miss Howe, how good to see you.'

Nell Howe looked at her distantly and then, as if after a great effort, she said flatly, 'Irene.'

'Yes, Miss Howe. How have you been? I have been meaning to contact you.'

'Have you? Then why didn't you?'

'Could we have a cup of coffee somewhere, do you think?' Irene suggested.

'Why?' Miss Howe was surprised at the overfamiliarity of the request.

'I need to tell you something.'

'Well, there is hardly anywhere suitable around here.' Miss Howe sniffed at the area.

'This little café does nice coffee. Please, Miss Howe . . .'

As if giving in to the inevitable, Miss Howe agreed. Over cups of frothy Italian coffee, Irene told her about the wedding plans and the honeymoon they had decided on. She asked Miss Howe if she was looking forward to going away in the winter.

'Why would anyone want to go to such a remote place at any time?' was the only response.

Irene changed the subject. There was the man on the phone and his odd behaviour.

'Have you any idea of who it could be?' she asked. 'He didn't leave any message, and wouldn't give a number.'

'It must have been my brother,' Miss Howe said.

'Your brother?'

'Yes, my brother Martin. I haven't seen him for a long time.'

'But why?' Irene felt her heart racing. It was the casual way Miss Howe spoke that was so disturbing.

'Why? Oh, it all goes back many, many years ago.' Miss Howe's face was non-committal and unmoved. 'And none of your business, anyway. Is that it? Is that all?' And with a chilly nod of her head, Miss Howe left the café.

It was a wonderful day for the wedding. Kenny gave the bride away, and Peggy looked as though she might burst with pride. Dingo, all dressed up in a new suit, was the best man and in his speech said that he was very proud of being the match-maker who had brought the happy couple together.

Carmel and Rigger had managed to get time off for the occasion; Rigger's mother, Nasey's sister Nuala, was there. The sun shone from morning until late evening. Mrs Williams joined them in the pub and mingled with the teachers, the butchers from Malone's shop and all the friends and neigh-bours. In a million years poor Miss Howe would never have been able to mix like this.

There was a honeymoon in Spain and then back to work at Wood Park, where life promised to be much easier and more pleasant than in the previous regime.

Rigger and Carmel kept in touch all the time about Stone House. The voucher they had designed for Miss Howe had given them more ideas, and a week at Stone House was now going to be one of the prizes for a competition in a magazine. The list was filling up nicely; it looked as if Chicky Starr would have a full house for her opening week. There was great excitement all around the place. Rigger said his mother was going to come and visit soon. It would be her first time in Stoneybridge since she was a girl.

She didn't want to stay in the big house but Rigger and Chicky were insisting. It would be such a great return for her.

Irene did try to warn them that Miss Howe might be difficult to please.

'We can handle it,' said Rigger cheerfully. 'It will be great practice for us. We saw off Howard and Barbara; your Miss Howe will be no problem for us, you'll see.'

Miss Howe travelled by a late train, and so Rigger went to meet her. He saw a tall, stern-looking woman with one small case looking around the station impatiently. This must be the one.

He introduced himself and took her suitcase.

'I was told that Mrs Starr would meet me,' the woman said.

'She's at the house, welcoming the other guests. I'm Rigger, her manager. I live in the grounds,' he said.

'Yes, you told me your name already.' From the tone of her voice she seemed highly disapproving of it.

'I hope you will have a wonderful week here, Miss Howe. The house is very comfortable.'

'I would have expected no less,' she said.

Rigger hoped he would have a moment to warn Chicky that it was time to fasten the seatbelts.

Chicky didn't need the warning. The body language alone was enough to alert her that Miss Howe was not going to be a happy camper. She stood stiff and unyielding in the group that had gathered in the big cheerful kitchen. She refused a sherry or glass of wine, asking instead for a glass of plain tonic water with ice and lemon. She nodded wordlessly when introduced to fellow guests.

She said she didn't need to see her room and freshen up; since she was one of the last to arrive, she wouldn't delay the meal by absenting herself. She had a knack of bringing conversations to an end with her pronouncements.

She showed no interest in the itineraries and options that Chicky laid out for them. One by one the guests gave up on her.

The American man asked her what kind of business she was in, and she said that, unlike in the United States, people here didn't judge others on what occupation they had or used to have.

A Swedish boy told her that it was his second visit to Ireland, and he barely managed to reach the end of his first sentence before she made her boredom clear.

A nurse called Winnie wondered if Miss Howe had toured in the West before, and she shrugged, saying not that she could remember. Two polite English doctors told her that they were astounded by the spectacular scenery. Miss Howe said that she had arrived in the dark and hadn't seen anything remarkable so far.

When Orla, who served at the table, asked her if the meal was satisfactory, Miss Howe replied that if it hadn't been she would certainly have mentioned it. It would be doing the establishment no favours not to speak her mind.

As Chicky Starr showed Miss Howe to her room after dinner, she waited for some small expression of pleasure at the beautiful furniture, the fresh new linen on the bed, the tray with the best china tea things . . . everybody else had admired them.

Miss Howe had just nodded briefly.

'I'm sure you're tired after the journey,' Chicky Starr said, biting back her disappointment and trying to forgive the lack of response.

'Hardly. I just sat in a train the whole way from Dublin.' Miss Howe was taking no prisoners.

And for the days that followed, alone among the guests Miss Howe found nothing to praise, no delight in the wild scenery, no appreciation for the food that Orla and Chicky served every night.

Chicky sat beside the strange, uncommunicative woman in order to spare the guests from the ordeal of trying to talk to her. Even for Chicky, with a background of years working in a New York boarding house with a room full of men dulled by work in the construction industry, this was hard going.

Miss Howe never asked a question or made an observation. Whatever had gone wrong in her life had gone very wrong indeed.

On the fourth morning when Miss Howe had yet again shown no interest in exploring the coastline, Chicky begged Rigger to drive her to the market town with him.

'Oh God, Chicky, do I have to? She'll turn the milk sour.'

'Please, Rigger, otherwise she'll just sit staring at me all day and I've a lot of cooking to do.'

Rigger was good-natured about it. Apart from Miss Howe, the week was going so very well. All these people were going to praise the place to the skies. Stone House would take off as they had always believed it would. One day with Miss Howe wouldn't kill him.

Any questions about how she was enjoying the holiday met with a brick wall, so he chatted away cheerfully about his own life. He told Miss Howe about his two children: the twins, Rosie and Macken, and nodded proudly at their photographs stuck up on the dashboard of his van.

'They get their looks from their mother,' he said proudly. 'I hope they get their brains from her too! Not too many brains on their dad's side.'

'And were your parents stupid?' she asked. Her voice was cold, but it was the only time she seemed interested in a conversation.

'My mother wasn't. I never knew my father,' he said.

Most people would have said they were sorry, or that was a pity, but Miss Howe said nothing.

'Were your parents bright, Miss Howe?' Rigger asked.

She paused. It was as if she was deciding whether to answer or not. Eventually she said, 'No, not at all. My mother was a very unfit person to be anywhere near children. She left home when I was eleven and my father couldn't cope. He lost his job and died of drink.'

'Aw God, that was a poor start, Miss Howe. And did you have brothers and sisters to see you through?'

'One younger brother, but he didn't do well, I'm afraid. He made nothing of his life.'

'And there was no one to look out for him?'

Again a pause.

'No, there wasn't, as it happened.'

'Wasn't that very sad. And you were too young to do anything for the lad. I was lucky. I hit a bit of a rough spot but I had my mam always looking out for me, writing to me every week even when I got sent to the reform school. She tried her best for me, even if it took coming here to sort me out properly. I'd fallen behind on the old reading and writing, you see. It took me a while to catch up. I didn't get any exams or anything, but I got my head together and everything.'

'Why didn't she make you do exams?'

'Ah, she knew I was never going to be a professor, Miss Howe. She worked all the time to put food on the table but still, it wasn't easy to see everyone else with money when I didn't have any.'

'Did you get into trouble again?' Miss Howe's lips were pursed as if she had expected him to go to the bad.

'I met all the fellows I used to know. They were all doing

well but not legit, if you know what I mean. They said it was dead easy and you couldn't get caught. But my uncle Nasey put the fear of God into me. He thought I should get a fresh start in the country. I didn't want that at all. I was afraid of cows and sheep, and it was very dull compared to Dublin. But my mam had lived here when she was young, and she said she had loved it.'

'Why did she leave then?' Miss Howe hated grey areas.

'She got into trouble, and the man wouldn't marry her.'

'And did she bring you back here?'

'No, she has never been back herself but she is coming. Soon, as it happens.'

The market was busy. Miss Howe watched as Rigger sold eggs and cheese made from goats' milk. He heaved bags of vegetables out of the back of his van and carried large amounts of meat back into it, ready for the freezer. He bought two little ducks, which he said would be pets for the children rather than food for Chicky's table.

He seemed to know everyone he met. People asked about Chicky Starr, about Rigger's children, about Orla. Then Rigger had to call on his wife's family and drop in some eggs and cheese. Miss Howe said she'd stay in the van.

'They'll offer me tea and apple tart,' he said.

'Well then, eat it and drink it, Rigger. Leave me to my thoughts.' She watched people looking out the window of the farmhouse, but she had no intention of going into a small, stuffy kitchen and making small talk with strangers.

As an outing it was hardly a success, but Chicky was grateful to Rigger.

'Did you learn anything about her?' she asked.

'A bit, but it was like the confessional of the van. She probably regrets having told me.'

'Let it rest, so,' said Chicky.

The following day, Miss Howe called on Carmel in Rigger's house at the end of the garden. Carmel, knowing of the situation, welcomed her more warmly than she might have if left to her own devices. She introduced Miss Howe to the babies, who smiled and burbled good-naturedly; together they went to see the rabbits, the tortoise and the new ducks, who were called Princess and Spud.

Miss Howe drank tea from a mug and refused to be drawn into giving any praise for Stone House or for the holiday in general. Carmel struggled on, even when Miss Howe lectured her on the merits of learning poetry by rote.

Suddenly Miss Howe asked to look through what books Carmel and Rigger had in their library.

'We're not really the kind of people who'd have a library,' Carmel began.

'Well then, what a poor example you will be giving your children,' Miss Howe snapped.

'We will do the best we can.'

'Not if you have no dictionary, no atlas, no poetry books. How are they going to see the point of learning if there is no sign of learning in the home?'

'They'll go to school,' Carmel said defensively.

'Yes, that's it, leave everything to the school, and then blame them when things go wrong.'

Miss Howe's tone was hectoring. It was as if she were speaking to a disobedient child in her school rather than a kindly woman who had tried to help her to enjoy her holiday.

'We wouldn't blame the school; we're not like that.'

'But what have you to offer them? What is the point in anything unless the next generation get a good grounding and a proper start? You don't want them ending up uneducated and in a reform school like your husband.'

Carmel could take it no longer.

'I'm sorry, Miss Howe, but I cannot have you insult my husband like this. If he told you about his past, and he must have because Chicky wouldn't have told you, then he did so in confidence, not to have it hurled back at us in accusation.' Carmel was aware that her voice was sounding shrill, but she couldn't help herself. What was wrong with this woman?

'I'm sorry but I'm going to have to ask you to leave. Now. I'm too upset, and I'll say something I might regret. I know nothing about you or your life and why you are so horrible to everyone, but someone should have shouted stop long, long, long ago.'

Without warning, Miss Howe's face crumpled. Suddenly, she put her head down on the table and cried so hard her whole body shook.

Carmel was astonished. For a moment, she didn't know what to do, but then she tried to put a comforting hand round Miss Howe's shoulder.

Stiffly, Miss Howe brushed it aside. There were two spots of red on her long, pale face.

Carmel made a fresh pot of tea and then sat down in front of her unwanted guest and gazed at her in silence.

Slowly, hesitantly at first, Miss Howe started to talk.

'It was 1963. I was eleven; Martin was eight. There were just the two of us. President Kennedy came to Ireland that year, and we all went out to line the route to see him.'

This was all unreal, Miss Howe talking about her private life fifty years ago.

'I remembered that we hadn't locked the downstairs windows at home. That was my job. The house was empty. Dad

303

was at work, and my mother was going to her sister's and they were very strict about locking up. So even though I didn't want to, I had to leave the grand place I had and run home. In the house I heard noises like someone was being hurt, so I ran upstairs and my mother and a man were on the bed, naked. I thought he was killing her and I tried to drag him away . . . and then my mother went down on her knees to me and begged me not to tell my father. She said she'd be good to me for the rest of my life if I would keep this little secret between us, and the man was getting dressed and she kept saying, "Don't go, Larry. Nell understands. She's a big, grown-up girl of eleven. She knows what to do." And I ran out of the house and I telephoned my dad at work and said to come back quick because a man called Larry was hurting my mother and she wanted me to keep it a secret and he came home and . . .'

'You were only a child,' Carmel said soothingly.

'No, I knew. I knew what she was doing was wrong and that she had to be punished. I wasn't going to be part of any secrets. I *wanted* her to be punished. I didn't know Larry was Dad's great friend. But even if I had known, I'd still have told. It was wrong, you see.'

'And what did your father do?'

'We never knew, but when Martin and I got back from waving at President Kennedy, our mother was gone and never came back again.'

'Where did she go?' Carmel tried to keep the horror out of her voice.

'We never heard, and Dad looked after us but he was no good and then he took to drink. And he kept thanking me for exposing his whore of a wife and he would hit Martin over nothing. And Martin got in with a tough crowd at school and did no study whatsoever. I just put my hands over my ears and studied all the hours God sent. I got scholarships all the way and when my father died of drink, I managed on my own. Martin said I'd ruined his life twice. First I'd sent his mother away and now I'd lost him his father.'

'And he never forgave you?'

'No. He made nothing of himself. I haven't seen him for years. He rang the school not long ago, I don't know why. I don't want to see him again.'

'So he has not been part of your life since then?' Carmel asked sadly. The best she could hope for was to escape from this situation before she heard any more; already she knew that Miss Howe would never forgive herself for the loss of self-control, nor would she forgive Carmel. She must have looked anxious to end the conversation because Miss Howe spotted it.

'All right, so you want me to leave now. I'll leave. I don't care!'

Carmel reached out to shake her hand. 'I will bid you farewell, and wish you well in the future.'

'You will bid me farewell, *bid me farewell*, no less,' Miss Howe sneered. 'What a great line of clichés you will teach those unfortunate children. I weep for them and for their future.'

'Then go and weep over them. We will love them and look after them always and give them a great life,' Carmel said sadly.

'I suppose you and your husband will spread this all over the country before the night is out,' said Miss Howe bitterly.

'No, Miss Howe, that is not how we behave. Rigger and I are people of dignity and decency, not of gossip and accusations. What you have told me is your business and will go no further.'

As Miss Howe left, Carmel sat at the kitchen table shaking. Rigger would be furious; Chicky would be annoyed. *Why* couldn't she have held on to her temper? Miss Howe would never forgive her for knowing about her past.

'I don't want that Miss Howe in our house again,' she told Rigger when he came home. 'She said we were ignorant parents, and that she wept for Rosie and Macken.'

'Well, she's the only one who does,' Rigger said. 'Everyone else is delighted with them. And who the hell cares what Miss Howe says?'

Carmel smiled at him. It was quite true. She would comb her hair and they would go for a walk on the beach; they would walk along the damp sand and gather shells as the salt air stung their faces. They would give their son and daughter the best life they could.

Later that day, Rigger whispered to Chicky that it was only fair to warn her that words had been exchanged between Carmel and Miss Howe.

'Don't worry,' Chicky said. 'She was never likely to get us any business. She's just told me she's going back to Dublin tonight. In a while she will be gone and out of our lives. Tell Carmel not to give it a second thought.'

'You're great, Chicky.'

'No, I'm not. I'm lucky. So are you. Miss Howe was not.'

'We made a bit of our own luck.'

'Perhaps, but we listened when people tried to help us. She didn't.'

Before dinner, Chicky carried Miss Howe's small case to the van.

'I hope *some* of it was to your liking, Miss Howe,' she said. 'Perhaps when the weather is better, you might come back to us again?' Chicky was unfailingly courteous.

'I don't think so,' Miss Howe responded. 'It's not really my kind of holiday. I spent too much of my life talking to people. I find it quite stressful.'

'Well, you'll be glad to get back to the peace and quiet of your own place,' Chicky said.

'Yes, in a way.'

The woman was brutally honest. It was her failing.

'Did you discover anything here? People often say they do.'

'I discovered that life is very unfair and that there's nothing we can do about it. Don't you agree, Mrs Starr?'

'Not entirely, but you do have a point.'

Miss Howe nodded, satisfied. She had spread a little gloom even as she left. She would sit alone on the train back to Dublin and then get the bus back to her lonely house. She looked straight ahead as Rigger drove her to the railway station.

Freda

When Freda O'Donovan was ten, Mrs Scully, one of her mother's friends, read everyone's palms at a tea party. Mrs Scully saw good fortune and many children and long, happy marriages ahead for everyone. She saw foreign travel and small inheritances from unexpected quarters. They were all delighted with her, and it was a very successful party.

'Can you tell my future too?' Freda had asked.

Mrs Scully studied the small hand carefully. She saw a tall, handsome man, marriage and three delightful children. She saw holidays abroad – did Freda think she might like skiing? 'And you will live happily ever after,' she said, smiling down at Freda.

There was a pause. After what seemed a long time, Freda sighed. Although her mother seemed pleased about what she was hearing, Freda was confused. She just knew that none of it was true.

'I want to know what's going to happen,' she insisted, and she started to cry.

'Whatever's the matter? It's a good future,' said her mother, pleading with her daughter not to make a fuss about silly fortune-telling.

But Freda wouldn't listen and just cried harder. She was having no part of this prediction. It just wasn't right. She knew. Sometimes, she thought she knew what was going to happen, though she had already learned to keep quiet about it.

She didn't see a husband and three children. And she certainly didn't see herself living happily ever after. She cried all the more.

Freda's mother just didn't understand why Freda was so upset. Never had she regretted anything as much as persuading Mrs Scully to tell a child's fortune, and she would make sure it never happened again.

Mrs Scully wasn't invited to tell fortunes after that. And Freda never told anyone what she saw about the future.

Life at home was quiet and a bit frugal for Freda and her two older sisters. Her father died young, and there was no money for luxuries like central heating or foreign holidays. Mam worked in a dry cleaner's, and Freda had a very undramatic time at school, where she was bright and worked hard and got scholarships. She had her heart set on becoming a librarian; her best friend, Lane, wanted to work in theatre. The two were inseparable.

Freda couldn't remember when she got the first inkling that she might have some unusual insights. It was hard to describe them. The word 'feelings' didn't quite cover them because they were more vivid than that. Nor did she recall when it had been that she realised not everyone had the same insights; but over the years, she had learned not to talk about them to anyone. It always upset people when she mentioned anything, and so she had kept quiet; she didn't even talk to Lane about it.

There was no passionate love life: as a student, Freda went to clubs and bars and met fellows but there was nothing there that made her heart race. Mam was inclined to be overcurious about Freda's private life, and yet at the same time disappointed to hear that there was no love interest at all.

Freda loved books, and felt she had everything she ever wanted when she got her library certificate and was lucky to find a place as an assistant at the local library. Her sisters, though, were dismissive about her lack of love.

'Well, of course you can't find a fellow. What do you have to talk about except books,' Martha said.

'You could have bettered yourself if you had tried,' Laura had sniffed.

Freda looked very defeated, and her sisters felt remorseful.

'It's not as if you're a *total* failure,' Martha said encouragingly. She had a very stormy relationship with a young man called Wayne, and was not predisposed to believe the best of men.

'You did get taken on as a library assistant, and now you could earn a living anywhere.' Laura was grudging but fair. She was going out with a very pompous banker called Philip, to whom style and reputation meant everything.

Theirs was not neutral advice.

It was during the run-up to Christmas that Freda got another of her 'feelings'. They were having a family lunch to plan the Christmas festivities. Freda was coming for the day for sure, but Laura would be going to Philip's parents' big Christmas Eve do. Martha was very irate because Wayne would make no plans. What kind of person made no plans for Christmas?

Their mother edged the conversation back to the turkey. They would have their Christmas lunch at three p.m. with whoever wanted to join them, and that would be fine.

Laura fidgeted; she had something she wanted to share. She wasn't absolutely certain but she thought that Philip was going to propose to her on Christmas Eve. He had been very vague about his parents' party. Normally he put a lot of store by these events, and would tell her in advance who everyone was. No, there was something much bigger afoot. Laura was pink with excitement.

And totally unexpectedly Freda knew, she didn't just suspect but she *knew* that Philip was going to break off his relationship with Laura before Christmas; he was going to tell her that he was expecting a child with someone else. It was as clear as if she had seen a newspaper headline announcing it, and Freda felt herself go pale.

'Well, say something!' Laura was annoyed that her huge news and confidence was not meeting with any reaction.

'That would be wonderful,' her mother said.

'Lucky you,' Martha said.

'Are you *sure*?' Freda blurted out.

'No, of course I'm not sure. Now I'm sorry I told you. You're just saying that because I dared to say you couldn't get a fellow of your own. It's just spite.'

'Did you and Philip ever talk about getting married?' Freda asked.

'No, but we talked about love. Leave it, Freda. What do you know about anything?'

'But you might have it wrong.'

'Oh, don't be such a sourpuss.'

'Are you going to be talking to him before the party?'

'Yes, I'm meeting him this evening. He's coming round to my flat at seven.'

Freda said nothing. Tonight was when he was going to tell her. It was there in her chest like indigestion all day, as if she had eaten something that she couldn't swallow properly. At nine o'clock she called her sister.

Laura's voice was unrecognisable.

'You knew all the time, didn't you? You *knew*, and you were laughing at me. Well, are you happy now?'

'I didn't know, honestly,' Freda begged.

'I hate you for knowing. I'll never forgive you!' Laura said.

In the weeks and months that followed, Laura was very cold towards Freda. She cried when Philip's engagement was announced on Christmas Eve: his marriage to a girl called Lucy would take place in January.

Martha said that Laura would never believe to her dying day that Freda had not known about Lucy way in advance. There was no other explanation.

'I got a feeling, that's all,' Freda admitted.

'Some feeling!' Martha sniffed. 'If you ever get a *feeling* about me and Wayne just let me know, will you?'

'I don't think I'll ever let anyone know about a feeling ever again,' Freda said fervently.

The Friends of Finn Road Library will hold their first meeting on Thursday September 12th on these premises at 6.30 p.m. All are welcome, and we hope to have ideas and suggestions about what you want from your Library.

Freda knew within minutes of printing out the notice in the library that all was not well. It didn't take a psychic to see it: Miss Duffy's face was stern with disapproval, peering over her shoulder. This Library did not need Friends, the look said. It was not a dating agency. It was a place where people came to borrow books and, even more importantly, to return them. This kind of thing had no place in a library. It was, to use the worst criticism possible, *quite inappropriate.*

Freda fixed a smile very firmly on to her face. In advance, she had tied her long dark curly hair back with a ribbon to make herself look more serious in preparation for this encounter. This was a time to look businesslike. It most definitely was not the time to get into a serious battle. And if she lost, then she would just wait and try again.

She must never let Miss Duffy know how very determined she was to open up the library to the community, to bring in those who had never crossed its threshold. Freda wanted passionately to make those who *did* come in feel welcome and part of it all. Miss Duffy came from a different era, a time that believed people were lucky to have a library in their area, and should want no more than that.

'Miss Duffy, you remember you telling me when I applied to work here that part of our role was to bring more people in . . . ?'

'As library users, yes, but not as *Friends*.' Miss Duffy managed to use the word as a term of abuse.

Freda wondered had Miss Duffy always been like this, or had there ever been a time when she had hopes and dreams for this fusty old building.

'If they sort of thought of themselves as Friends, they might do a lot more to help,' Freda said hopefully. 'They might help with fundraising, or getting authors to donate books . . . Lots of things.'

'I suppose, as you say, that it can't do any harm. But where will we get seating for them all if they *do* come?'

'My friend Lane has lots of fold-up chairs in her theatre. She won't need them that night.'

'Oh, the theatre, yes.' Miss Duffy's interest in the small experimental playhouse down the street was minimal.

Freda waited. She couldn't put the notice on the board until she had Miss Duffy's agreement; she was nearly there, but not quite.

'I'd be happy to sort of run the meeting, I mean, I'd sort of introduce you as the Librarian, and then when you had spoken I could throw it open to them . . . the Friends, you know.' Freda held her breath.

Miss Duffy cleared her throat. 'Well, seeing as you're so keen on it, then why not put up that notice and let's see what happens.'

Freda began to breathe properly again. She fixed the paper to the notice board. She forced herself to move slowly and not to show her excitement at having won. When she was quite sure that Miss Duffy was safely installed at her desk, Freda took out her mobile phone and called her friend Lane.

'Lane, it's me, I have to speak very quietly.'

'And so you should. It *is* a library that you work in,' Lane said sternly.

'I got the Friends idea past Miss Duffy. We're in. It's going to happen!'

Halfway down the street, Lane paused in the middle of writing begging letters for support of her little theatre.

'Fantastic, well done Freda! The killer librarian.'

'No, don't even *say* that, it could be such a disaster. Nobody might turn up!' Freda was delighted that she had got this far, and yet terrified that it would all collapse on her.

'We'll get them in somehow. I'll get all our team here to go, and we can put up a notice about the meeting and pull in our audience as well. Listen, will we go for lunch to celebrate?' Lane was eager to seize the moment.

'No, Lane, I can't, no time. I have work to do on the budget allocations.' Imagine – people thought there was nothing to do in a library except stand around! 'But we're meeting at Aunt Eva's tonight as planned, aren't we?'

Eva O'Donovan was pleased that Freda and Lane were coming to supper. It meant that she had to galvanise herself and get into the day. First she must finish 'Feathers', her weekly birdwatching column in the newspaper. Eva had found that if she was very reliable about getting her copy in early, typing it neatly into her laptop, she could get away with outrageous views.

Then she must find something in the freezer that those girls could eat. They never had a proper lunch and were always hungry. Besides, she didn't want them reeling around after a few Alabama Slammers. She studied the contents of her freezer with interest.

There was a sort of fish and tomato bake. She would put that in the oven when they arrived with some fresh tomato and basil. She defrosted some French bread. Nothing to it; people made such a fuss about cooking when all it took was a bit of forward thinking.

When she had pressed Send on her article about the great flocks of waxwings that had come in from Northern Europe, then she would choose a colourful stole and a hat and would lay out all the drinks ingredients on her little cocktail table. This was the best part of the day.

Chestnut Grove was a house that would have suited nobody except Eva: it was in poor repair with a wild, rambling garden, very shaky plumbing and unreliable electrical works. She really couldn't afford the cost of maintaining it properly, and it might have seemed sensible to sell the place – but when had Eva ever done the sensible thing? Besides, the garden was full of birds that nested there regularly and were great material for her column.

The walls of her study were covered with pictures of birds and reports from various conservancy and birdwatching groups around the country. There were shelves full of magazines and publications. Eva's laptop computer was there, half buried in papers. In this room, as in every room in the house, there was a divan bed ready to be used at a moment's notice if someone wanted to stay overnight. And someone often did.

There were clothes hanging in every room; on almost every wall there were hangers holding colourful, inexpensive dresses, often with a matching stole or hat. Eva would pick them up at markets, car-boot sales or closing-down sales. She had never bought a normal dress in what might be called a normal shop. Eva found the price of designer clothes so impossible to understand that she had refused to think about it any more.

What were women *doing*, allowing themselves to be sucked into a world of labels and trends and the artificial demands of style? Eva couldn't begin to fathom it. She had only two rules of style – easy-care and brightly coloured – and was perfectly well dressed for every occasion.

Eva took out her highball glasses and lined up the Southern Comfort, amaretto liqueur and sloe gin. She had a very well-stocked bar but drank little herself. For Eva, the serving and making of cocktails was all in the preparation, the theatrics and the faint whiff of decadence.

Freda and Lane let themselves in through the back gate of Chestnut Grove and walked through the large sprawling garden. There were no formal flower beds, no lawns, no cultivated patios or terraces; instead it was a mass of bushes and brambles ready to trip the unwary in the dark. Here and there, some late roses peeped through. But mainly it looked like a site which was going to be cleaned up for a makeover on television.

'It's so different to my parents' garden,' Lane said, avoiding some low-hanging branches filled with vicious thorns. 'Their garden looks as if it's auditioning for some prize all the time.'

'Still, they do have it in great shape. You wouldn't put your life at risk like here,' Freda said.

'Yes, but Dad isn't allowed to have his vegetables anywhere that they can be seen. What would the neighbours say if they saw drills of potatoes and broad beans?'

As they reached the house, Eva ran to meet them. She was wearing a dark orange-coloured kaftan and had tied her hair up in a scarf of the same material. She looked like a very exotic bird that you might see in the aviary at the zoo. She could have been heading out for a Moroccan wedding, a fancy-dress party or the opening of an art gallery.

'Isn't the garden just wonderful right now?' she cried.

Wonderful wasn't the first word Freda and Lane would have chosen to describe the great wilderness they had just ploughed their way across, but it was impossible not to get caught up in Eva's enthusiasm.

'It's got lovely bits of colour in it, certainly,' Lane said.

'Just the way the branches look against the sky, that's what I love.' Eva guided them into the front room and began to mix the cocktail.

'Here's to the library, Freda my dear, and to all the many, many Friends waiting to join in its celebration.'

She was so genuinely delighted that Freda felt choked.

Nobody else except Lane and Aunt Eva would understand and care that she had made this great step. How lucky she was to have them. Most people had nobody to share excitements and celebrate with.

The cocktail nearly took the roof off her head. Freda placed it down carefully. Eva didn't expect you to knock the drink back in one go; she liked you to appreciate its different flavours. There must be about five things in this, Freda thought, all of them alcoholic except for the orange juice. She treated it with great respect.

Eva wanted every detail of the new scheme in the library. Was Miss Duffy grudging? Was she hostile? Had she given in with a bad grace? What did Eva want the Friends to do, once she had assembled them?

She was so eager and enthusiastic that Freda and Lane felt dull and slow in comparison. If Eva had been running the library, there might be fairy lights around it, and music blaring from inside. She could have set up a cocktail bar in the foyer. Her life was like her house – a colourful fantasy where anything was possible if you wanted it badly enough.

Miss Duffy was dealing with people who wanted to be Friends of the Library, and she was not dealing with them very well. She handed them the leaflet that Freda had prepared and had said there was a welcome for everyone at the Friends' meeting, but she was vague when people asked what it was going to involve.

Some people with anxious faces asked would there be money involved, like an admission fee, or a collection. No, nothing like that, Miss Duffy said. But then she wondered. Had Freda suggested there might be a fundraising aspect?

A man asked would there be advice about what books they

should read. Miss Duffy didn't know. Two girls asked would there be an entrance test, or could anyone at all come? Miss Duffy said there was no test, but she knew she had frowned at the expression 'anyone at all'.

A nervous young man arrived, saying he had written a lot of poems which had won prizes when he was at school, and wondered would there be a chance that he could give a reading. He was shy and awkward and kept looking as if Miss Duffy was going to order him off the premises for such a suggestion.

Miss Duffy was starting to feel it was all a bad idea.

'Oh, *there* you are, Miss O'Donovan,' she cried, even though Freda was over half an hour early.

Freda looked at her watch anxiously.

'It's just there were so many enquiries about this Friends business, it's beginning to upset our routine.'

Freda's face lit up. 'I am sorry, Miss Duffy, but isn't that great news! It means that people *are* interested.' Freda had hung up her coat and was down to work at once.

Miss Duffy relented. It was hard not to be pleased with this attitude, and even though the silly girl was inviting more enquiries, more trouble and distraction on herself, she seemed perfectly happy to do the work associated with it.

'Did you have a good weekend, Miss O'Donovan?' she asked, to show that her irritation was not serious.

Freda looked up at her, surprised. She smiled and said that it had been very good but she was happy to be back here in Finn Road. It had been the right answer.

Miss Duffy didn't want any details, only a sense of commitment.

Freda went through the list of enquiries: she telephoned the man who wondered would there be advice about what books to read and said yes, there would if people wanted it. She called the girls asking was there an entrance examination, and she said it was going to be a fun evening – they should bring all their friends. She invited the young poet, whose name was Lionel, to come in and see her.

She ignored the nagging feeling that something really important was about to happen.

The next meeting of the Friends of Finn Road Library will be on the history of this area, and admission is free. Please bring photos and stories. All are welcome!

They would be talking about the Friends evening for days. It had been such a success on so many levels despite the rain that night. Even Miss Duffy was enthusiastic.

They had all come: the young poet, Lionel, had read some beautiful poems about mute swans. He was elated at the response, even more so when Freda introduced him to her aunt Eva. The author of 'Feathers', no less!

Miss Duffy had been suspicious when around half a dozen young girls had turned up, but they had turned out to be full of suggestions for reading groups.

'I must say, I was surprised that they held us in such esteem,' she said the very next day. Lane and Freda had cleared the place up perfectly and had returned the chairs to the theatre. There was nothing that Miss Duffy could complain about, so instead she decided to be pleased, gratified even.

Freda had long ago decided that she would accept no credit for it all, even though she would have had to take all the blame if it had turned out badly.

'It's only what you deserve,' Freda said, as if it had all been

Miss Duffy's idea. 'You have been here for years building this place up; it's only right they should honour you and say how much the library means to them.'

Miss Duffy accepted it all graciously as her due.

That was good: it left Freda time to get on with things. There was so much to organise in an ordinary working day. They would have to check the Issue, the list of items currently out on loan. Then there were the notes to borrowers of books that were overdue. They would go through the Issue looking for requested items and report on their status. Then today there was the Stock Selection meeting, where they all sat down with Miss Duffy to choose what new titles they could order. They would examine books sent to them as approval copies, and look at notes from the book magazines as well. There was little enough time to think about this Friends meeting, never mind organise the next one. It was curious that she felt so deflated. Whatever it was she had been so sure was going to happen just hadn't materialised.

Miss Duffy was surprised to see the great bunch of very expensive flowers that had been delivered. The message was simple. *I am already a Friend of the Library . . . Now I want to be a Friend of the Librarian.* The evening had been a success, of course, but who would have sent these as a thank you? The only person that ever sent flowers to Miss Duffy was her sister, and she was more of a potted violet sort of person. So who could have sent her this bouquet? She admired the flowers once more. Miss O'Donovan might arrange them for her if they could find a big enough vase.

Freda, of course, found a vase. She went into the store room and brought out a huge glass jar. Those flowers must have cost a fortune. Who on earth would have sent them?

Miss Duffy was vague, and said they were from a friend. She looked at her reflection in the glass doors and patted her hair several times. There was a thoughtful look in her eye.

Freda gave up.

When she was separating the long roses from the green ferns to arrange them better, she found the card that had come with the flowers.

. . . Now I want to be a Friend of the Librarian. They were for her. She realised it with a shock that was almost physical. But who was it? And what did he mean? And why had he not put Freda's name on them, instead of letting Miss Duffy think they were for her? She felt everything slowing down and becoming slightly unreal. There were far too many questions. She wanted to be alone to think about why she felt so uneasy and slightly shaky.

Lane had been on the phone to Eva to ask her what colour were a puffin's legs.

Eva hadn't hesitated. 'Orange,' she said. 'Why?'

'And the beak? We're painting scenery. Tell me about the beak, I know the shape and everything but what colour is it?'

'Blue, yellow and orange. But you have to get the colours in the right order.'

'I don't mean an exotic puffin like in an aviary, I mean just an Irish puffin.'

'That's it, that's a home-grown puffin. Come into the library – I'm just on my way there myself. I'll point you to the books.'

'I think I'd better. Birds with a blue, yellow and orange beak! You'd have to be on something very attitude-changing to see that in Ireland.'

They met on the steps.

'We're painting these huge backdrops for the next production,' she explained. 'I need to be sure about the puffins' beak and legs. Are they really all colours of the rainbow, or were you having me on?'

'Beaks have three colours, legs are orange – mostly during the breeding season. Much duller in winter,' Eva confirmed.

'Merciful God, in Ireland, birds like that!'

'Well, if you ever came with us over to the Atlantic coast, you'd see them for yourself, whole colonies of them,' Eva said reprovingly. 'There's a place called Stoneybridge. You should come along.'

And as they went in, they saw Freda at the counter talking to someone. She was pointing at a brochure and Freda was laughing and shaking her head. Her eyes were bright and she looked so young, so animated and alive in this old, grey building. Miss Duffy wore her usual navy wool cardigan with a small white lace collar; she was demure and full of gravitas. Freda in contrast wore a red shirt over black trousers. She had her black curly hair tied back with a big red ribbon. She looked like a colourful flower in the middle of it all, Lane thought. No wonder they were all queuing up to talk to her.

Waiting next in line was a man in a cashmere scarf and a very well-cut overcoat. He was looking at Freda intently.

Lane held back suddenly. She didn't know why, but she felt faintly uneasy.

'What is it?' Eva asked.

'That man, waiting to speak to Freda,' Lane whispered.

'I can't see him,' Eva complained.

'Come this way, so. You'll see him then and you won't distract her.'

They both saw the way Freda was looking at the man who

had approached her. It was just too far to hear what she was saying but her face had changed completely.

Whoever he was, he was significant.

Lane disliked him on sight.

'Did you like my flowers?'

'The ones for Miss Duffy, the Librarian? They're lovely. Shall I get her for you?'

He paused to smell one of the roses. 'They were for you, Freda.' He was very good-looking, and there was such warmth in his smile.

She couldn't help smiling back, though if Freda had ever known how to flirt she had forgotten the technique.

'You weren't at the Friends evening,' she said. 'I'm sure I'd have remembered you.'

'Oh but I was here. I didn't know about the meeting, I just came in when the rain came on. I stood at the back, over there.' He pointed to a pillar beside the back door.

'You didn't sit down?'

'No, I only wanted to miss the worst of the downpour, and I thought a talk in the library would be boring.'

'And was it?' She felt as if she were probing a sore tooth.

'No, Freda, it was a great evening, there was warmth and enthusiasm and hope all here in this very room. That's why I stayed.'

This was exactly what she had felt. She thought that people had been given some kind of lifeline that night. They were dying for something new, something to get involved in; they were all so anxious to help. She looked at him wordlessly.

'I came to ask you to have dinner with me.' She saw his neck redden slightly. Suddenly he looked uncertain. 'I mean, it doesn't have to be dinner, it could be a walk, a coffee, a movie, anything you like. Oh – no, wait – my name is Mark. Mark Malone. Will you come out with me?'

'Dinner would be nice . . .' she heard herself say.

'Good. Can I book somewhere tonight?'

Freda didn't trust herself to speak at first. 'Well, yes, tonight is good,' she said eventually.

'Where would you like to go?'

'I don't know . . . anywhere. I like Ennio's down on the quays, I go there with my friends sometimes for a treat.'

'Well, I don't want to muscle in on your special place for you and your friends. What about Quentins, that's good too, isn't it? Is eight OK with you?'

'Eight o'clock it is,' Freda said.

He grinned, and then ostentatiously took her hand and kissed it.

When he had gone, Freda raised her hand to her cheek and held it there. She didn't know it but she was being watched by her aunt Eva, her friend Lane, Miss Duffy, Lionel the poet and a young girl who happened to be looking for a job as a cleaner.

They all saw Freda's face as she moved her hand slowly to her lips. The hand that the man had kissed. Something momentous had just happened in front of their eyes.

The rest of the day passed. Somehow.

Lane said, 'Have you anything to tell me?'

Freda had asked, 'About puffins?'

'No, about men coming in and kissing your hand.'

Tomorrow, Freda had promised.

He was already there when Freda went into Quentins. He wore a dark grey suit and a crisp white shirt. He was very handsome. He grinned and stood up to welcome her as Brenda, the elegant owner and manager, led Freda to the table.

'I thought you might like a glass of champagne, but I didn't order for you,' he began.

'Right on both counts,' Freda said, smiling. 'I would indeed like a glass of champagne, but thank you for not assuming.'

'I wouldn't do that, I hope,' he said. 'I'm so pleased to see you – you look terrific,' he said.

'Thank you,' she said simply.

'Well you do, you are very beautiful, but that's not just why I asked you to dinner.'

'Why did you ask me?' she genuinely wanted to know.

'Because I can't get you out of my mind. I loved what you said about that man's poetry, the elegant sadness of it. Someone else would have taken twice as many words to say it. And then you got all excited about those schoolgirls and their reading groups; you enthused them all and you have so much energy, so much life radiating from you. Since the first moment I saw you in the library I noticed it; I see it here. I wanted to be part of it. That's all.'

'I don't know what to say. I've been lucky; I'm very happy in my job, and life and everything . . .'

'And are you happy to be here? Now?'

'Very,' Freda said.

They talked easily.

He wanted to know everything about her. Her school, her college, the home she lived in with her parents and sisters. How she had got her job at Finn Road Library. Her little flat at the top of a big Victorian house. Her eccentric aunt who wrote the long-running 'Feathers' column in the newspaper, and took Freda on birdwatching outings.

'Sounds like a lark,' he said solemnly.

'I can't top that,' she snorted. 'It's your tern again.' And they both collapsed laughing.

He seemed interested in every single thing she had ever done in her life. The conversation moved towards holidays, and whether it was worth all the hassle of going away to the sun just for one week, or whether you had to be an athlete to go skiing. Wasn't that amazing – he had been to the very same Greek island, wasn't the world a very small place? They liked the same movies, the same songs. He had even read some of Freda's favourite books.

Freda asked him about his life too. After all, it was like a blind date; they knew nothing about each other, yet here they were, sitting having dinner in one of Dublin's best restaurants. He had been brought up in England, in an Irish family. His parents still lived there, and his brother. No, he didn't see much of them, he said sadly. He shrugged it off, but Freda could see that it hurt him.

He had been to university in England, studied marketing and economics but it wasn't nearly as important as all he had learned through his experience in the leisure industry. He had been in car hire, in yachting charter, in mass catering, all the time learning about what made business tick. He had worked in London, New York and now Dublin; even though he had come here as a child on holidays it was still a new city to him. He was now working for a leisure group that was going to invest in Holly's Hotel; they wanted to develop it into a major leisure complex.

'I'm sure it all sounds dull to you but it's really exciting, and it's not all about money,' he said eagerly. 'And I would love to know more about the history of the area. You could be very helpful.'

He hadn't found a proper place for himself yet, so he just had a room in the hotel. It was good to be on the premises, as it meant he could see what kind of business the place was. It was such a personal hideaway, the kind of place people believed they had actually discovered for themselves. The staff remembered your name, they seemed eager for you to enjoy the experience of being there. No wonder they were successful.

On the day of the rainstorm, he'd been in a meeting with the developers which had run late, and he'd been dashing along Finn Road just as the downpour was at its worst. It was only a happy accident, pure chance that he'd seen the library was open and decided to take shelter for a while. That's when he'd spotted her. Suppose he'd just gone on down the street? Suppose the meeting had ended on time and he'd got away before it had started raining?

'You and I might never have met.' He laughed, and gave a mock shiver to think this could have been on the cards.

Freda felt her shoulders relax. She loved Holly's Hotel just as it was; it was a great place for a celebration, and the idea of it being turned into a 'leisure complex' sounded awful. But it didn't matter by what chance she had been introduced to this exciting man, who for some impossible-to-understand reason seemed to fancy her greatly. She gave a sigh of pure pleasure.

He smiled at her and her heart melted.

Freda hoped that he wouldn't want to come home with her. The flat was in a total mess, and there was all the business of it being a first date and being thought a slapper, and if he were going to come to her place she would need a week getting it ready. Suppose he suggested going to Holly's Hotel?

But he wouldn't, would he, he had too much class.

Or maybe he didn't want to all that much?

They were the last people to leave the restaurant. Quentins arranged a taxi for them. Mark said he would see her home. When the cab stopped, he got out and saw her to the door.

'Lovely place, as I would have expected,' he said, and he kissed her on each cheek and got back into the taxi.

Freda climbed the stairs and went into her little flat, which looked as if it had been ransacked by burglars but was actually just the way she'd left it. She sat on the side of her bed, not knowing whether to be relieved or disappointed that he hadn't come in.

When she had been telling him about the library, he had listened to every word as if she was the only person in the room. But what if he was that way with everyone? Did he really like her? Of course not, how could he? She was just a librarian; he was so smart and had travelled everywhere.

She felt suddenly lonely here tonight. She might get a cat to talk to.

Eva had advised her against it; she said that cats were the natural enemy of birds, and anyway, if you became fond of them it stopped you from travelling. Still, if she had a cat it might purr at her, be some kind of presence in this empty place, perched at the top of a big house.

She fell into a troubled sleep and dreamed over and over that she was trying to get on to a ferry but it kept leaving the shore before she could get on board.

'Come on, Freda, we don't *do* vague,' Lane said over coffee in the little theatre the next morning.

'I'm not being vague, I'm telling you every single detail of

the menu down to the chocolate shaped like a Q at the end.'
Freda was indignant.

'But what about *him*? Did you like him? Was he easy to talk to?'

'He was fine, very smooth, very charming. He's in what they call the "leisure industry . . ." '

Lane snorted in derision.

'. . . and he's here to discuss investing in Holly's. They want to do a major expansion.'

'Holly's doesn't need expanding. It's fine as it is. Did you . . . ?'

'No.'

'And did he want to . . . ?'

'Again, no. So now, does that answer every interrogation on the sexual front?' Freda wondered.

Lane looked hurt. 'We always tell, that's why I asked.'

'Well, I *have* told. Nothing, nada, zilch.'

'Ah yes, but will you tell when there *is* something to tell?' Lane speculated.

'We'll never know, will we?' Freda sounded more light-hearted than she felt.

'Suppose I were to warn you off this guy Mark,' Lane looked serious. She couldn't put a finger on what it was, but there was something about him that worried her. 'Suppose I said I didn't trust him. Suppose I said you don't know anything about him, that he's just spinning you a line. If I were to do that, would I lose you as a friend?'

'Nothing to warn me off – one bunch of roses which went to Miss Duffy, one dinner . . . hardly an affair.'

'Early days,' Lane said darkly. 'He'll be back. I feel sure of it.'

*

Joe Duggan, a man Freda had last met in college five years ago, rang to ask her to a party that night. Freda had no intention of going to a group of strangers with a fellow she barely remembered, but polite as always, she asked him what he was doing these days.

'Lecturing in technology, mainly to dummies,' he said. 'You know, people who are afraid of gadgets and who don't want to miss out. I'm not too bad at it, actually; I tell them machines are stupid and that calms them down.'

'Joe, I may have a great job for you. Can you come and see me in the library on Friday,' Freda said. This could be the next Friends meeting settled.

Perfect.

Miss Duffy had a face that would stop a clock.

'When you have quite finished organising your social life, Miss O'Donovan, I wonder can I ask you to help with the Library Fines? And there are several people waiting for your attention at the counter.'

The first in line at the counter was Mark Malone. He said nothing, just looked at her.

'Do you have any work to go to?' she asked him to keep the conversation light and to break his stare.

'I work very hard,' he said. 'Way into the night often, but I made time this morning to come and see you.'

'Thank you so much for dinner,' Freda said. 'I was going to write you a little note, in fact, to say how much I enjoyed it.'

'What would you have said?'

'That it was a very warm and generous evening and to thank you.' She kept an air of finality to the way she spoke, as if she thought it was a one-off and that she was just being grateful without regrets.

'You said you have a day off tomorrow,' he said.

Normally on her day off, Freda would do what she and Lane called the everyday business of living: she would bring her sheets and towels to the launderette, do some shopping at the supermarket, maybe persuade Lane to take a long lunch. Sometimes she went to an art exhibition or did window-shopping in the boutiques. She might tend her window boxes, filling them up with bulbs for the spring, and in the evening she might go to a wine bar with friends.

But not tomorrow. That would be a very different day.

Mark had wondered if Freda would like to go down to County Wicklow with him. He had to go to a meeting with Miss Holly, and maybe they could have lunch there. In the shower, Freda planned the day. They could go for a walk in the afternoon, then they would go home and she could get his supper ready. Maybe they would stay at Holly's. In any case, he would say she looked very beautiful. He would take her in his arms.

'We don't have to wait any longer,' he would say; or maybe, 'I wouldn't have been able to get through tonight without you.' Something. Anything. It didn't really matter.

She wondered what it would be like. She hoped she would be attractive enough for him. Please him properly. She wasn't very experienced, and certainly no one recently.

The last time must have been nearly two years ago when she had had a holiday romance, a lovely guy called Andy from Scotland who had promised to stay in touch and said he would come to Ireland to see her. But he didn't stay in touch and he hadn't come to Ireland. It hadn't been a big deal. Andy already had a life planned for himself: it involved banking, living near his parents and his married brothers, playing a lot of golf.

Freda didn't know why she was even thinking about Andy now, except to worry that she might not have been any good at it, which was possibly why he might not have kept in touch. Perhaps as a lover she had been useless. She had quite enjoyed it all herself, that magical summer holiday, and thought that Andy had too. But then, you never really knew.

It would have been lovely to have had some reassurance about that side of things. Freda smiled to herself wryly at the thought of telephoning Andy at his bank, years after the fling, and asking for reassurance about her performance.

But then Mark wasn't looking for some kind of sexual athlete. Was he? Women must have been throwing themselves at him since he was a teenager. She wished she knew more about him, and what he wanted.

And then, when she least expected it, Freda got one of her feelings. She saw as clearly as if it were an advertisement in an estate agent's catalogue a book-lined apartment with a living room and kitchenette, two big bedrooms and a study with an overflowing desk. There was a view of the sea from the window. At the door was a small woman with short blonde hair, reading glasses around her neck on a chain and a vague, worried smile.

She was saying, '*There* you are, darling. Good to have you home!' to whoever was coming in the door. But who was the woman? And who was she talking to? The breath left her body with a great rush, and she felt light-headed and as if her legs had turned to paper. Was it Mark?

*

It couldn't be. It was wrong, the *feeling* must be wrong. She hadn't seen a man, she hadn't seen who it was arriving at the door. It couldn't be Mark. It couldn't be.

Shaking, she got dressed and, hands still trembling, applied mascara and lipstick. She put up her hair, found her good boots and she was ready. She felt a shiver. She felt very glad she had told nobody about this date.

The shrill bell of the intercom buzzed. He was on the doorstep.

'I'll come straight down,' she said into the receiver.

He looked at her with great admiration as she came down the steps to the hall. 'You look so beautiful,' he said.

Freda still felt shaken. She wanted to make a jokey remark to take the intensity out of it all. She wasn't used to saying thank you and accepting such praise as almost her right. She said the first positive thing that came into her head.

'And you look very handsome, just terrific, actually.'

He threw his head back and laughed. 'Aren't you *so* kind to say that! Now, let's stop admiring each other and get into the car, out of the cold.' He held open the door of a dark green Mercedes.

The drive down to Wicklow passed in a blur. Freda could scarcely remember how they got there, what they talked about. All she could see was Mark's face as he concentrated on driving, as he smiled at her from time to time.

While Mark went to have his meeting with Miss Holly and her senior staff, Freda sat in the lounge by the fire in a big chintz-covered chair, a magazine unread on her lap, a cup of coffee untouched on a little table beside her. Instead, she looked into the flames and thought about what had been happening; and as she did so, from nowhere the pictures started forming in Freda's mind. She fought them back, closed her eyes and opened them but still the pictures were there. Mark was in a room with people who were shouting. Miss Holly was sitting in a corner, weeping. Mark was looking calm and dismissive; he was telling her something very unwelcome and frightening. Whatever it was, it was wrong, it was all wrong.

Shakily, she pushed the vision aside. It was nonsense; it didn't mean anything. She'd just dozed off and had a silly dream. She sighed, and again tried to rid herself of the images. But she felt dizzier and more confused.

Soon he was back.

'How did it go?' she asked.

'Don't ask. I'll tell you when we are well out of range. Let's go. You and I are free agents, nobody waiting for us; we don't have to be anywhere except where we want to be.'

'I have to be back. I open the library tomorrow, and I have to be in before eight.'

He smiled back. 'Right. We'll go for a meal, and no talk about work for either of us – is that a deal?'

'It's a deal,' Freda said.

In the car they were quiet; Freda studied his face but Mark looked relaxed and happy. Freda began to feel that it had just been a mad dream. As he helped her out of the car, he kissed her, and all through dinner she could think of nothing else.

That night, they made love for the first time.

The following night, they went to the cinema. Freda didn't even remember the film afterwards, just the sensation of sitting with her shoulder touching his. Later they went back to her flat.

On Friday he asked her to go to a concert but she had set up the meeting with Joe Duggan, the computer expert, and she hesitated. Mark's face clouded over and he looked so disappointed, she knew she had to do something.

She called Lane.

'I will do anything for you for the rest of my life. *Anything*. Scrub floors in your theatre . . .'

'Who do I have to kill?' Lane asked.

'No, it's this guy, Joe Duggan, who's going to give the talk next week. I can't meet him tonight at the library. Could *you* do it, tell him everything?'

'Freda. No.'

'I'm begging you on my knees.'

'I can't, I run a theatre. You're the librarian.'

'It's only an old talk; you know the kind of thing they want.'

There was a silence.

'Lane?'

'It's not like you, and it's *not* only an old talk. It's something you set up, and a lot of people are depending on you.'

'Never again, just this once! I'll tell Joe that I'll contact him on Monday morning.'

'And if I don't?'

'I don't know what I'll do.' There was a catch in Freda's voice.

'I think this is the shabbiest thing I have ever heard,' Lane said.

'But you'll do it.'

'Yes.'

'Thank you, Lane, from the bottom of my heart . . .' Freda began.

'Goodbye, Freda.'

Freda called Mark.

'Well?' he asked.

'I'm free this evening,' she said.

'I was so hoping you might be,' Mark said.

The concert was heaven and at dinner afterwards, he told her that there was no one like her. He said how much he admired her work, and even gave her some ideas for a Friends night; he wanted to spend all his time with her, and make up for lost time. She couldn't help herself: he was so sweet and caring, and she melted at his touch.

It was too sudden, too quick, she told herself. But then everyone had to meet somewhere and somehow. Would it have been any different if they had met at a dance, a club, in a crowded bar? But still she was nervous about letting herself go with the tide. But whenever he called, or they were together, she forgot all about her misgivings.

The Friends of the Library welcome all those who don't know a thing about computers but want to learn. Joe Duggan will be here on Friday night to help all ages who want to be part of the tech world.

When Mark suggested they go away for a weekend, she hesitated once again. He couldn't go away with her if he was married, it wouldn't be possible. But the dreams kept coming. The face of the woman with the short blonde hair would not go away. She just knew it was Mark the woman was welcoming, and she could see the wedding ring in the dream.

If he were married, what would he be telling his wife as he headed off to the Dublin mountains with Freda? Freda was very confused. But she wasn't about to give up the chance of such happiness.

When she called Lane to cover for her again with Joe, Lane

didn't have much to say. She listened to her friend and then agreed.

'For Joe's sake, not yours,' she added icily.

Freda felt bad for her friend, but then thought about her weekend with Mark. Mark needed Freda on many levels, that was obvious. He wanted her for company, for friendship and for support as well as for sex. He loved her; he told her so. The marriage could only be one of convenience, she was so sure of that.

Eva hoped that this romance would settle down soon so that Freda could concentrate on other things apart from Mark Malone. She did seem besotted with the fellow and in a way, Eva could understand why. He was such a charmer, such an enthusiast. In many ways very suited to Freda. But Eva thought they were also very different. Mark was tougher, and he was going to get there, wherever it was, taking no prisoners. Freda was happy with life the way it was now.

He had got off on the wrong foot with Lane, but that would sort itself out in time. Lane had taken against Mark in a big way; she complained that Freda had lost interest in everything – her work, her friends, her whole life. 'It's as if a sort of mist or fog or something settled on her,' she had said. 'He controls her every move.'

They'd met him a number of times now but Lane still didn't trust Mark.

Silly, foolish Agony Aunt, Eva told herself. Useless trying to work these things out logically, rationally. Still, it was a worry, all right. There was a possible storm gathering. Lane didn't like him and didn't trust him. He was the first man who had threatened such a solid friendship. Usually they encouraged each other about boyfriends and gave enthusiastic, supportive advice.

Freda would say that Lane had an army of brooding young men who fancied her. Lane would laugh, and say that these were all out-of-work actors; all they fancied was two weeks' work in her theatre. Lane said that she knew of at least three people who went in to that library just to talk to Freda rather than to open a book. They were always wanting to ask Freda out, but she never seemed to understand this and kept finding books for them instead . . .

This strong reaction both for and against Mark Malone had been so out of character for both girls.

Due to the success of Joe Duggan's 'Don't Fear Technology' lecture last week, the Friends of Finn Road Library have decided that there should be twice-weekly sessions on this topic.

Freda called to Eva to borrow a black beaded jacket. She had been invited to a drinks party at Holly's Hotel in a couple of weeks' time. Mark had gathered some journalists and tour operators for what he called a social drink. It was really part of his long-term plan to get the press on board over the plans for the hotel.

Eva had hoped Freda would stay for lunch.

'You see, Eva,' said Freda, guiltily, 'I don't really have all that much time . . . I have so many things to do just now.'

Eva looked at her directly.

'What, exactly?'

'Oh, you know, all the stuff at the library; this Friends thing has really taken off due to Joe Duggan, and they can't get enough of him.'

'No thanks to you, though.'

'What do you mean?' Freda was startled.

'Well, you weren't there to show him round the library, Lane and I did that. And then you took off for a weekend with Mark the actual night of his talk.'

'Yes.' Freda looked at the ground.

'So he had an elderly twitcher like myself, and the manager of an experimental theatre to help him set up. Lord knows what he would have been able to achieve if he'd had a real librarian on the case.'

'You were great, you and Lane, I thanked you, you did brilliantly.'

'You weren't there.' Eva was stern.

'Look, you know . . . you know the way things are.'

'No, I don't, actually. Why don't you come looking for woodpeckers with me? And why don't you ask Mark along too?'

'Thank you so much, Eva, but when I said I was busy, I really am. I have a few fences to mend, if you know what I mean.'

'I know what you mean.'

Freda knew Aunt Eva was right. As far as Lane was concerned, it was as if a curtain had fallen over their friendship. She would put on her polite face, which was more unsettling to Freda than her angry face. It was so distancing, so chilly.

Lane had not forgiven Freda for disappearing the night of Joe Duggan's talk.

To Freda, it was really most petty and unfair of Lane to take this attitude. Joe had been a huge success; he was going to have his own series. In all her years at the library, Freda had never taken any time off like this before. And this was not even real regular library hours: this was something she had arranged as a volunteer, for heaven's sake.

And Joe had understood. He had said that she was very kind to have arranged such a pleasant person to greet him. It wasn't as if she had abandoned him or anything.

Such a fuss over nothing.

Mark had to be in London for a few days, so Freda felt easy about inviting Lane and Eva to have dinner at Ennio's. She hoped that they would understand how she felt. It would be all right.

It was a happy evening as Freda, Lane and Eva sat in Ennio's restaurant eating pasta and catching up.

Eva was organising her next birdwatching trip to the West of Ireland. There was a new hotel opening in a couple of weeks' time, up on the cliffs above Stoneybridge. Perfect for birdwatchers. Eva was already planning her visit.

She paused dramatically and then proposed a toast. 'You two are not to have a fight,' she announced, 'I won't allow it. Especially over something as foolish as a man.'

By this stage, both Freda and Lane were laughing.

'You're such a stirrer, Eva, there's no row,' Freda said.

'I'd never fight with Freda,' Lane promised.

'Great, that's sorted, then.'

Lane and Freda looked at each other helplessly.

'My aunt, the drama queen!' Freda said.

'Whatever made her think that we were going to have a row?' Lane asked.

'My saying I love Mark Malone, you saying he is a shit . . . that might have given her food for thought.'

'I'll never say anything like that about him again. I just thought you would have wanted to be there for Joe and his talk. But as it happens, it has worked out – he has asked me out on a date, so I forgive you,' Lane said.

Freda leaned over and patted her on the wrist. And then, right in the middle of the meal, Freda was called to the phone. The waiter led her to a little desk which had the reservations book and handed her the phone.

'Hallo?' Freda had no idea who knew she was here.

'*Ciao, bella,*' the voice on the phone said.

'Mark!'

'Just wanted you to know I miss you, and it is quite ridiculous that I am at one boring dinner and you are at another when we could be together.'

'Mine's not a boring dinner, I told you – it's friends,' she said. 'And anyway, you're back tomorrow, aren't you?'

'No, sadly not. I have to stay on here. More meetings. It won't take much longer; I'll get away as early as I can.'

The smile vanished from her face. 'Oh no, but I've booked to have some time off!'

'Well, I won't make so many arrangements in future. Is that OK? Would you like me to cancel my business meetings?' He sounded angry.

'I'm sorry. I didn't mean anything.' Freda was confused.

There was a pause.

'All right,' he said eventually. 'I'm sorry, I'm under a lot of pressure here. We'll speak tomorrow. I'll know more then.'

'Tomorrow, then,' she agreed, shaken. And then as a thought just struck her, she asked, 'Mark, why didn't you call me on my mobile?'

'I didn't bring mine with me so I don't have the number,' he said smoothly. 'I remember you said Ennio's, so I looked it up in the book.'

'Tomorrow, then,' she said.

Back at the table, Lane asked her, 'Was that him?'

Freda smiled. 'It was, as it happens.'

'Why didn't he ring you on your mobile? Was he checking up to see if you were really where you'd said you'd be?'

Eva looked up sharply.

Lane's tone had been light, but Freda found herself feeling very tense. After all, she had asked Mark the very same question herself. But she would admit none of this to Lane.

'Oh, definitely, that's it, a martyr to jealousy he is,' she said with a very insincere little laugh.

'What's worrying you?' Eva asked.

'Nothing,' Freda said. 'He's just having to stay on in London.'

For the very first time since she had gone to work there, Freda didn't want to go in to the library. There were too many calls on her time. Lane still didn't understand Mark; even Eva had lost patience. They just didn't understand. Miss Duffy was being so demanding about categories. 'A misfiled book is a lost book,' was her great mantra.

There was that bossy woman who had complained that some book was sheer pornography and that she had mistakenly recommended it to her book club up in Chestnut Court. Someone else had thrown a tantrum about the lack of Zane Grey books. She needed to find Joe Duggan, and apologise again for not being at the library for his talks.

And she could deal with it all if she didn't feel so uneasy after their conversation the night before. She had dreamed about the blonde again, and now she was sure Mark was married. But she didn't care. He loved Freda. He told her so many times.

She straightened her shoulders and walked slowly up the steps that normally she took two at a time when she went into work.

A few days later, Eva invited Lane to come for lunch with her.

'There's a report of a great flock of Common Scoters over the other side of Howth, and there might be some rare ones among them.'

'Uncommon Scoters?' Lane suggested.

'Well, Velvet Scoters, they're called actually.'

'Velvet? Sounds good.'

'They're sea ducks, the males are all jet black with yellow bills, the females have white necks and dull grey bills. Winter visitors. Come with me in the car and we'll have a sandwich in a pub out that way,' Eva suggested.

'And what will I wear?'

'Nothing too bright that would alarm them. Don't know what the weather's doing but, you know, lots of waterproof anoraks and scarves and sweaters and maybe a backpack or lots of pockets.'

It was the best offer Lane had had. Freda was like a weasel, with Mark making plans and then cancelling them at the last moment; when he wasn't around, she just sat staring at her phone waiting for him to ring. Lane said she'd love the drive.

As they left the main roads behind and headed towards the sea, Eva pointed out the migrating birds newly arrived: flocks of white-fronted geese as well as the ducks, swans and wading birds that came down from the Arctic. Now they would have plenty of things to see.

Eva concentrated hard on the busy traffic.

'Will we go somewhere there's easy parking?' she suggested, and that was why they chose the dark wine bar near the sea.

Which was where they saw Mark Malone, who was meant to be in England at a conference.

He was sitting at a table over by the window. Opposite him was a blonde woman in jeans and a thick Aran sweater. Between them was a little girl. She looked very young and very happy. They were the perfect happy family, as if there was nobody but the three of them in the place.

Mark and the woman were feeding each other forkfuls of pasta and then laughing after each mouthful. The little girl was laughing at them gleefully. The three of them shared such affection and closeness, there was no doubt that they all belonged together.

Eva and Lane looked at them, stunned.

They were unable to back out of the restaurant before being seen. As Mark looked up and caught sight of them, his face froze into an angry mask.

Eva and Lane looked at each other and at exactly the same moment they both said, 'The bastard!' Then without another word they walked out, got into Eva's car and began to drive back to the city.

As they drove off, Lane asked, 'Do birds do that, you know, cheat all round them?'

'It's complicated.'

'I bet it is.'

'Do we say anything?' Eva wondered aloud.

'Of course we do. The question is, to which of them? To Freda or to Mark?'

'If we hadn't gone in there . . .' Eva began.

'That's no use – we *did* go in. And we saw him. She can't be made a fool of like this.'

'But it would humiliate her if we said—' Eva was protective.

345

'Well, it would humiliate her more if we didn't say,' Lane countered angrily.

'We don't actually know . . .'

'Of course we know. That wasn't his office colleague or his sister. That child was his. Let me tell you that if you saw my lover with his wife and daughter, I'd say you were a poor friend not to tell me.'

'You say that now, but you might think differently if it really *was* the case.'

'Well, I'm glad we cleared *that* up, anyway, because I would most definitely want to be told. That puts the ball back in my court, gives me the right to make a decision.'

'But we can't tell her, Lane. Come on, think about it.'

'It's important enough for him to lie about it, tell her that he's in London, and be holed up in a wine bar where he's not going to meet anyone.'

'Or so he thought,' Eva said. 'Don't tell her, Lane, it would destroy her.'

'She should be told. Let her take him back if she wants to, but she has the right to know.'

'Leave it, just for a bit, anyway.'

In the end, neither of them had to tell Freda. Mark got there first.

It was the night of the reception at Holly's. She hadn't heard from Mark all day but she knew he was busy. She hoped she would be a credit to him tonight. Eva's black jacket looked very well on her; she would wear a scarlet silk skirt and her good black and red shoes. She knew Mark would have to circulate and that she would have to manage on her own, but later they would be together.

The reception was in full swing when Freda arrived at the

hotel. There was a buzz of conversation, and trays of elegant canapés were being passed around.

She slipped in without acknowledging Mark. He was at the centre of a laughing group near the window. Freda moved to the other side of the room and watched him talking. He was animated and able to include everyone around him in whatever it was that they were talking about. His easy smile rested on one person and then the next. And then he moved on seamlessly to another group.

She must not stand here like part of the furniture, looking at him. She was an invited guest.

She recognised a few faces. A man who ran a TV chat show, a woman columnist, a well-known television reporter. He had certainly the kind of people he needed. He would be in good form later on.

She chatted easily to people around her, and drank little from her glass so that it could not be topped up. She met a man who was in charge of IT for a large company. He agreed with Freda that there was an almighty waste with technology being updated every week and systems becoming obsolete in a year or two. Freda wondered what they did with their old equipment, and made a very strong case for him to consider Finn Road Library. She explained about the computer classes, and he seemed very interested. Then she saw Mark looking across at her oddly and hastily changed the subject to the splendours of the hotel. It was such a jewel of a place, and everyone felt that it was their own little secret.

'That's why it would be insanity to change it,' the man said.

'But to make sure it survives, to get a steady flow of visitors . . . ?' she was repeating Mark's words now.

'There are dozens of hotels with big conference facilities,

spas, entertainment for the busloads. Holly's is different; it should stay different,' he said.

'And what if it gets squeezed out, if it just gets crushed by all the others because it was afraid to expand?'

'You've bought the line,' the man said. 'You're well indoctrinated already, you don't even need to stay for the speeches.'

'I'm not sure I know what you mean.'

'Oh, the spiel, disguised as a nice warm welcome, lovely to see you all in this old-fashioned place, now we plan to change it and ruin it.'

'And will they?' Freda could hardly breathe.

'Don't know yet,' he said. 'A few of us on the board want things to stay as they are, the others all see a great glittering future and a franchising of the Holly brand abroad. They're obviously going to tear it down, and this little circus is to get their friends in the press to help them get planning permission. Anyway, don't get me started. What's your library called, in case we can send a few computers your way?'

They exchanged details. At that moment, Mark appeared at their elbows.

'You're never cruising the room looking for help for your library, Miss O'Donovan?' he said.

'My suggestion entirely, Mark. This young lady is doing something worthwhile with her life, and that's a rare treat these days.'

Mark steered her away firmly.

'Who was he?' Freda whispered.

'Never mind who was he, what the hell is going on?' Mark hissed at her. 'What do you think you're doing, trying to sabotage my event? Who put you up to it? No, don't tell me, you and those bitches . . .'

'*Mark?*' Freda was bewildered. The look on his face alarmed her. What on earth had happened?

'What did you think you were going to do?' His eyes raked her face. 'Stand up here and make accusations? Wreck my chances?' His voice sounded clipped and furious, though his face wore a forced smile as he continued to steer her towards the door.

'I don't know what you're talking about,' she said with spirit, trying to free her elbow from his grip. 'I don't know what's gone wrong, but why don't I call you tomorrow, and we'll fix that nice relaxed evening we were going to have for tomorrow night instead? Right?' Her voice sounded doomed and hollow inside her own head. 'Or perhaps you could come round to my place later tonight and tell me what this is all about?' She hoped she didn't sound as if she was begging.

'I don't think so,' he said derisively. 'It's too late for all that. Sending your friends to spy on me! Why couldn't you leave things alone? You fool, you stupid fool . . .' He was hardly able to get the words out. 'How could you have been so stupid? You've wrecked everything. And when I think how much I loved you, and the risks I took for you.'

She was frightened now. 'Tell me, what *is* it? What did I do? Whatever it was, it was a horrible accident. And whatever I did wrong, I'm sorry . . .'

By now, they had reached the front door of the hotel. Freda was distraught, but Mark's face was cold as he half dragged her outside.

'Do not contact me again. Don't call, don't text, don't email. Stay out of my life. And don't you or your friends *ever* come near my wife and child again . . .'

Freda watched him, mute and hopeless, as he turned and walked away from her, back into the hotel. The door closed.

She passed the line of taxis without seeing them. Her eyes were blurred with tears. Then, out of sight of the hotel, she stopped and leaned on a railing to cry properly. She stood there in Eva's black beaded jacket and wept.

Passers-by looked at her, concerned. Some even stopped to ask could they help, but Freda just cried more. Then she felt an arm on her shoulder and realised that it was the IT man she'd been talking to earlier.

'Have you anyone to go to?' he asked kindly.

She was fine; it was only something personal and silly, she would get over it, she reassured him through her sobs.

Did she want him to call someone for her?

And even though she always thought of herself as someone surrounded by friends, tonight there was literally nobody she could ring.

He put her into a taxi; later, she realised, he had paid the driver. In the back of the cab, she sat staring ahead of her for twenty minutes. In her little flat, everything was perfect: candles arranged carefully on tables and in the grate that would barely take minutes to light; the food and wine in the refrigerator, a big bowl of scented lilies on the windowsill.

A warm and welcoming place. It mocked her for all her hopes and confidence.

Then the walls seemed to be closing in on her, and it was as if she couldn't breathe.

Sometimes when she woke suddenly at night, she wondered had she imagined the whole thing. Maybe it was all a dream, a fantasy, everything about that night at Holly's Hotel. She thought she had known him so well. He was gentle, funny and loving. He could not have been with her all this time unless he did love her as he swore he did.

Eventually, the story had emerged from Eva and from Lane. The day out, the lunch, Mark, the blonde woman, the child. *The child*. He had a daughter. She turned over in her mind all the visions she had tried to repress: at no stage during these visions had there been any sight of a daughter. But then she had seen his wife, hadn't she? The blonde woman in her vision really was indeed his wife. Freda had seen her and done nothing.

Over the days that followed, Freda lost weight and her face became drawn and lined.

Eva was seriously worried, and turned from sympathy to bewilderment and then to genuine concern. 'I feel so power-less to help you,' she said sadly.

'I have no idea what to do,' Freda wailed. 'I loved him so much. I thought he loved me. How would I know what to do?'

'You are full of guilt,' Eva said. 'You probably don't need to be, but you are. You are trying to make amends, to make things right somehow, but you can't. You have to look to the future now.'

Eva made a decision. Freda needed to get away; she needed a change of scene. She needed to be somewhere where she wasn't reminded of Mark every day, where she could see clearly once again. She made two phone calls: one to a Mrs Starr at Stone House in the West of Ireland to change her reservation, and the other to Miss Duffy. Freda wasn't feeling very well. She was going to need a few days to recover . . .

As she drew near to the house, Freda wondered had she made a great mistake. This place would do her no good at all. She knew nobody here; all she could do was think about the time

351

she had felt so happy and then so devastated. Why was she here? There weren't any ghosts to lay. Just very real memories of her great love.

Mrs Starr was very welcoming. She showed Freda to a pretty room at the side of the house, and said that Eva had said to be sure to mention all the birdwatching opportunities. Freda stared dully out of the window and watched as the wind caught the branches of the tree outside her window. Holm oak, she thought, sadly. *Holly* oak. The memory of her humiliation came flooding back.

Oddly, the wind seemed to be shaking only one of the branches of the tree. Freda watched transfixed as a small black and white face emerged from the leaves and stared in at her quizzically for a moment, before disappearing into the foliage again. She held her breath as the little cat clambered further and further up the tree, patches of black and white appearing every now and then.

'Don't worry,' said Chicky Starr, following her anxious gaze. 'That's Gloria. She's fine. She's afraid of nothing. Whatever it is she thinks she's chasing will be long gone and she'll make her way down again. I'll introduce you, if you like. Come down to the kitchen and I'll give you the cat treats she loves. Three pieces, mind, no more than that.'

Downstairs in the kitchen, Chicky opened the side door and whistled. Within seconds, Gloria appeared looking hopeful, wound herself around Chicky's legs then sat down abruptly for some urgent leg-washing.

'Three pieces,' reminded Chicky, passing the box of treats to Freda. 'Don't believe her when she tells you she should have more.'

Freda sat down by the fire and immediately Gloria jumped up on to her lap, purring loudly with anticipation. One by one, Freda dispensed the little pieces of dried food; delicately, Gloria accepted them. Then she curled up in a very tight ball and promptly fell asleep.

If only, Freda thought wistfully as she stroked the top of Gloria's head, if only she could stay here by the fire all week with this warm little bundle of fur in her lap. If only she didn't have to move, to meet anyone else, to make small talk. She dreaded meeting her fellow guests.

The feeling intensified when she met the others as they gathered for pre-dinner drinks in Chicky Starr's kitchen. They were all perfectly pleasant: Freda looked from one face to another and felt that each and every one of these fellow travellers had some deep secrets; her heart felt heavy at the thought of having to talk to any of them. Perhaps if she kept herself totally to herself, they would just leave her alone.

Of course, in the end it wasn't like that at all. Chicky Starr's welcome was warm, and they gathered around the roaring log fire; the atmosphere was generous and relaxing and soon the conversation rose to a much higher pitch. Suddenly Freda found no difficulty in talking to these total strangers, and for a while she recovered her old animation.

She talked to a nice young Swedish man who turned out to be interested in Irish music. Before she realised what she'd done, she had agreed to go off to the town with him the next morning and find a music pub. On her other side, she had a spirited debate with a retired schoolteacher about standards of literacy among the young people of today. To her surprise, Freda felt her spirits lift as she told Miss Howe about the Friends of Finn Road Library and the young girls' reading group.

That night as she lay in bed, she thought about the events

of the day. On an impulse, she got up and opened her door quietly. A small lamp on the hall table showed her there was no one around. Softly she whistled. At first there was no response, but after a moment she heard a soft thud and then the purposeful padding of small feet.

Freda slept that night with Gloria curled up beside her. In the morning, she set off with Anders and let herself be carried along with his enthusiasm. She found herself laughing out loud at his stories at lunchtime; and then moved to tears by the plaintive sounds of the music they listened to in the afternoon.

Freda was slowly starting to feel better. Dinner that night was even easier than the night before. She said nothing when she dreamed about storms, but pushed aside any notion of trying to warn anyone. She was relieved when Winnie and Lillian were found safe and sound.

It was on the fourth day that Chicky found Freda and Gloria curled up together by the fire in the Miss Sheedy Room. Gloria was dreaming, her pink little paws were twitching and she was making snuffly noises; Freda was stroking her fur and daydreaming.

Chicky was carrying a tray with a teapot and two cups. As she set it down on the small table, Freda looked up at her, startled. Gloria, affronted, jumped down on to the floor where she lay on her back with her feet in the air and surveyed the room gravely.

'I thought you might like some tea,' Chicky began. 'Gloria knows she's not supposed to be in here, but the two of you have definitely bonded.'

It was true: Freda and Gloria had by now become inseparable. The little black and white cat followed Freda throughout the house and escorted her on her walks through the garden.

The two of them were seen admiring Carmel's twins and being formally introduced to the two new ducks, Spud and Princess. Gloria had considered them from a safe distance; then she had jumped up on to a fence-post and washed her face thoughtfully.

Chicky told Freda about Miss Queenie and how she had rescued Gloria and carried her into the house in her coat pocket. Rigger had thought her quite mad at the time, but like everyone else, he doted on them both. This room, she said, was named after Miss Queenie.

'I don't know if it's true or not,' she said, 'and I never asked her about it, but apparently some woman from the travellers had told all three sisters years back that she saw three unhappy marriages ahead, so they all refused whatever offers they got . . .'

That was when Freda told Chicky Starr about the second-sight experiences, about the times she had spoken out and had regretted it, and how she had tried to suppress her knowledge ever since. Even if she had a feeling, she had learned to keep it to herself. She couldn't change anything by speaking up; she would only have people shun her or be angry about what she saw. Whether she said anything or not, she couldn't win.

Then she told Chicky about Mark Malone, and how she had pushed aside the notion that he might have been married.

Chicky listened carefully. She passed no judgement; she seemed to understand totally that Freda could have loved Mark and put aside her fears.

'Why are you worried about talking about seeing these things?' she asked.

Freda loved her for accepting totally that she *had* seen them; there was no attempt to persuade her that they were imagination, dreams, coincidences.

'Because they've brought nothing but grief.'

'Suppose you had one about me now? Would you tell me?'

'I don't think so, no.'

'You'd let me blunder on? Even if it's something avoidable, you'd be afraid to tell me?'

'But I myself don't want to accept that I have them. If I don't tell anyone, then I don't have to face it. I never know when they're going to come, that's what's so unnerving.'

Chicky listened to Freda and shook her head. She had more to say, but there was a commotion in the kitchen; Rigger had just arrived with the vegetables for tonight's dinner and she had work to do. She patted Freda on the arm and left her with Gloria, who had decided that the fringe on the fireside rug was in need of serious chastisement.

The next night, the entire table gave a cheer when Henry and Nicola announced that they would be staying on as doctors in the town. Freda was happy to be part of such a cheerful group, and she went to bed feeling relaxed and content.

There had been something of a fuss earlier on when Miss Howe had suddenly decided to leave. Rigger had been called to drive her to the station, and she had gone without a word to the other guests. There had been something very sad about the droop of her shoulders as she got into the van. It was all a bit unsettling.

All the same, the holiday was turning out to be a great success, each day bringing something new: wild scenery, the trip into town for music with Anders, good food and conversation at night and always at least eight hours' sleep. Freda felt stronger and better every day.

*

And it was on the last day of her holiday that, just before dinner, Chicky beckoned Freda into the kitchen.

'I wanted to talk to you because I've worked out what you should do about, you know, your problem.'

'You have?'

'I think you should change your tactic,' said Chicky as she laid the table for dinner. 'You say you are afraid that people will know you have this power, so you have been keeping it all a secret.'

'I don't want to admit to anyone, even myself, that what I say might come true.'

'This is the problem, Freda. I think you should tell everyone you meet that you are a psychic, say you can see the future and know what's going to happen. Offer to read their palms, tea leaves, cards. Then it's all out in the open.'

'And how would that help?'

'It would take the magic out of it, the secrecy, the power. People might think you are flaky but it sort of devalues the whole thing. That's what you want, isn't it?'

'Yes, it is, in a way.'

'Then this is the way. This devalues it. This way, nobody will think it's serious, no matter what you see or what you say.'

'You want me to *tell* people that I have second sight?'

'Call it what you like. Tell them any kind of vague, hopeful things about the future to cheer them up – that's all people really want from their horoscope, anyway. It will tame it for you, make it harmless. The way I look at it is that you are full of guilt over these visions. You have to try to make them insignificant. They were just thoughts, like anyone has thoughts, that's all.'

Freda stood there in the kitchen of Stone House and felt

everything shift slightly. There was a huge sense of relief as well as the sense of loss. She always thought that Mark had loved her. But why should she have believed this when there was absolutely no evidence that she had been anything except a pleasant distraction? It was both liberating and sad.

'I'll tell them over dinner,' she said. 'I'll tell them all that this is what I do.'

'Let's see how you get on,' said Chicky. 'That's it, Freda. You go and knock them out.'

As Chicky Starr's guests sat down for the last dinner of their winter week together, Freda heard herself telling this group of strangers that she was a psychic. They murmured their response with varying degrees of interest.

John, the American, said that many of his friends in the States consulted psychics regularly; the two doctors looked less enthusiastic but curious all the same. Winnie said cheerfully that she would love to book a session with her, while Lillian said it was a pity that so many so-called psychics, present company excepted of course, were charlatans. Anders said that they had a client in his father's accountancy firm who wouldn't make a single investment without consulting astrologers.

It proved to be just an easy conversational topic. So much more open to discussion than when she had said she was a librarian. The feeling of dread began to recede.

The evening was becoming very animated. The guests were still busy with the competition to set up a great Irish festival, and then someone asked Freda if she would tell their fortune. She looked around her wildly. This had not been part of the plan. Chicky Starr came to her rescue.

'Perhaps Freda might have come on a holiday to escape from her work. We shouldn't impose on her.'

They all looked disappointed; then Freda remembered Chicky saying that all people wanted from psychics was vague good news and promises about the future. She looked around the group. It would be harmless and even easy to tell them that life ahead looked good.

She held their hands and saw all kinds of good things: success and challenges and peace and long relationships.

For Winnie, she saw a wedding in the near future and great happiness in store. Lillian would meet someone at the wedding, possibly for love but certainly for friendship. Lillian's face was pink with pleasure.

So far, so good.

In Henry's hands she saw a new beginning, a happy life.

In Nicola's there was a child. Really, Nicola wondered. A child? Definitely, Freda was certain. And then, suddenly, Freda found herself saying, 'You're pregnant now. A little girl. I can see her. She's lovely!' She could see the little girl wrapping her arms around Nicola's neck. And when she saw the tension disappear from Nicola's forehead and the huge smile break out over her face, Freda realised for the first time that she could bring real joy to people's lives.

For John, or Corry, as they knew him, she foretold a whole change of direction, different kind of work and a different place to live. A much less complicated lifestyle, and a grandchild who would be part of his life. She was moved when she saw tears spring to his eyes.

Anders had a great love in his life; he must go home and ask her to marry him very soon. Only then would he be successful in his business.

For The Walls, she saw a cruise. Somewhere warm; she could see sunshine on the water.

She turned to Chicky Starr last. Freda took her hand and concentrated. Nothing. She paused, and then said hesitantly that Stone House would be a great success and that there would be a man, perhaps someone she had already met.

And then Freda knew. There had been no accident. There had been no wedding. But it didn't matter; Chicky was going to be fine. She smiled. It was *all* going to be fine.

They were delighted with her. It seemed to end the week well for everyone.

Names, phone numbers and email addresses were exchanged. A toast was proposed to Chicky, to Rigger and his family, to Orla and to Stone House.

They all signed the visitors' book with warm messages. The timetable for the next day was arranged. For those going home by train, Rigger and Chicky would provide a taxi service to the station. Carmel had made a small pot of Stone House marmalade for each guest.

And that night, Freda stroked a gently purring Gloria as she stood at her window looking at the patterns the clouds made going across the moon. She would call Lane and Eva as soon as she got back. Time for dinner at Ennio's. They had a lot of catching-up to do.

It was a scramble in the morning to see everyone off on time. Chicky Starr finally waved goodbye to each of her guests, but she saved a special hug for Freda, who now looked so much happier than when she had arrived.

It was time to get ready for the new guests, who would arrive in just a few hours. Carmel had come in to help clean the rooms, change the bedding and get everything ready for the new intake. Chicky would make a casserole that would cook slowly and be ready whenever they needed it. There would be freshly baked bread, and chocolate mousse for dessert.

Chicky knew she would miss the people who had made her first week at Stone House such a success, but she was looking forward to greeting the newcomers with all their new challenges and demands. She took a deep breath of sea air. She was ready for them.

Gloria wound herself around Chicky's feet. Chicky picked her up and scratched her ears. Then the two of them went back into Stone House.